D1737156

1

LOVE PARTITIONED

a historical novel

Manjula Waldron

DEDICATION

My family and Ken and those committed to loving another

Table of Contents

FOREWORD

About the novel:

Set during the Partition of India and Pakistan, this novel tells the inspiring story of the protagonist Mangla, her sometimes strained relationships with mother Ammaji, her best friend Basanthi, and her husband Anand as they navigate their own conflicts of religion, sexuality, and social privilege. Raised on Gandhi ideals of equality, peace, and unity, Mangla strives to become the social change she wishes to see, and to work for social freedom for all women.

The reader follows Mangla on her personal route to freedom as she learns about the theosophical foundation of Annie Besant that established the university Mangla attended. Evolving historical events and her *Ammaji*'s actions inform us about the domesticity, male dominance, and Gandhian values she holds sacrosanct. These values lead this Hindu family to adopt an abandoned Muslim child and an indigenous child and raise them as their own, learning and teaching them the customs of both religions. The family chooses to love and live by Gandhi ideals through the nation's turbulent history.

Mangla's transformation involves coming to an understanding about the complexities of historical changes and the cost and meaning of love and freedom. Her priorities shift to allow her daughter Mina to overcome the ever-present grim hurdles being faced by a woman in India.

Through Mangla's grit and fortitude we experience how India's diverse social fabric was torn by the carnage of interreligious, intergender strife among otherwise loving and caring people. Life became dispensable.

The colonial divide-and-conquer approach ruptured bonds between friends and neighbors before India gained its freedom and created Indian refugees in their own country. Charismatic political leaders motivated by power, greed and hate exploited common folks especially the disenchanted fickle youth.

Colonial rulers, in the wake of WWII, withdrew from the country, leaving a plundered treasury and a country in chaos without a coordinated plan.

The cherished ideals of nonviolence, and love and acceptance of "the other," were often sacrificed in the conflict-ridden road to freedom. This steep price was exhibited for the world with the assassination of Mahatma Gandhi, who worked tirelessly for a free India but did not survive beyond the promise of its dawn.

----Manjula Waldron, 2022

1 Road to Independence

Mangla boards the train and finds herself an empty first-class compartment. She waves goodbye to her in laws to begin her epic journey of freedom to the Northwest Frontier Province popularly called NWFP, to meet her husband of two weeks, Anand.

She looks through the steel bars of the train window at the blue sky dotted with cotton candy white clouds. She hears the sharp two-tone whistle accompanying the whoosh as the engine belches out its steam and smoke to gather speed. From her cushioned berth in a NWFP Railways compartment, she watches the soot rise, lightly veiling the trees and the changing Indian village scenes. Clothes change with geographic regions, giving away their ethnic identities from Desis to Sikhs, but the theme remains the same farmers tending their fields and walking their water buffaloes, oxen, sheep, and goats to pasture, all with twigs wrapped in bundles balanced on their heads, the fuel to cook their evening meal. There were few odd camels and elephants carrying loads for their masters, and along the way these beasts trimmed the tops of the trees for their own fodder.

Mangla taps her fingers to the clickety-clack of the steel wheels as they grind and rock on the iron rail joints. The words of the soulful song of an imprisoned woman wishing to be free spill from her lips. *Mai man ki baat bataun*, l will tell you my mind-talk; *Babul mora Naihar Chhooto Hi Jaye*, father, I am leaving your home for my lover, the lyrics from Saigal's Street Singer movie.

***

Often at University, Mangla used to sing, and she conjures up her best college friend, Basanthi, when they met in the first couple of weeks at BHU. Together, they saw all of Saigal's movies. That first year at BHU was full of heady days. The girls sang in the dining room every night, making do with table utensils as accompanying instruments. There were many accomplished singers--including herself. She smiles as more songs find their way to her lips.

She sings *Jab dil hi toot gaya—har sathi choot gaya*; when my heart is broken ---my beloved friends leaves me. She sings this with heartfelt emotions. The more frequent Anand's letters, the more distant her friend Basanthi became. It was Mangla's decision to leave her studies to marry Anand that gave the friendship its

1

final blow. Basanthi tried to dissuade her from it, close as she was to earning her Master's degree. But Mangla's friend could not understand there were family pressures, not to mention the love letters from Anand that Mangla could not resist. Basanthi did not understand the power of family loyalty. She could not imagine having to oppose the demands of her mother and her fiancé, who insisted on astrologer's bid for Mangla leave her master's program. "Does our work together to liberate women through education mean nothing to you?" Basanthi had cried. "Were they just idling words?"

But by that time, Mangla had been corresponding with Anand for more than two years. She loved the way he supported her values of freedom, education, and independence. She had fallen in love with his character. The more Basanthi challenged his values regarding dowry, child marriages, and Hindu orthodoxy, the more his replies warmed Mangla's heart and negated Basanthi's reservations. Basanthi had viewed these letters, herself. She knew well his commitment to women's education—but she was still angry and didn't trust his words.

Anand had asked her parents for their blessings. They found an auspicious date, for Mangla's mother feared they would upset the Gods if she questioned the ancient horoscopes. Her mother, *Ammaji* forbade her to negotiate marriage dates with Anand, even though it meant leaving university before finishing her degree. As progressive as she was, she still believed Mangla's sacred duty as a Hindu woman was to serve her husband and make him happy. As for Mangla, she felt unable to reason with her mother. It was like an irrational puppeteer operated deep within her. But, now married, she has faith that she will be able to influence Anand to support women's progress through education and action; she knows in her heart that he'll want her to finish her degree. It's a detour, that's all—and one that seems easier to take than to challenge *Ammaji*.

Basanthi had come to the wedding after all with Shamla, though she'd remained distant and disdainful. Mangla felt like a grain caught and crushed between two grinding stones—Basanthi, with her mission of change, and her mother, with her devotion to the Hindu traditions she grew up with. As for Anand, he was the most eligible catch in *Ammaji*'s eyes. *Pitaji* couldn't believe that he refused his offer of dowry. It was against his principles, Anand wrote. Given the greed for dowry in the Hindu community, Mangla's family soon thought Anand walked on water. But Basanthi remained skeptical of his motives. She didn't know his culture. She didn't believe a man could be so unworldly. Mangla's marriage broke open a wide chasm in her friendship with Basanthi, and Mangla hopes to repair it when they meet again. ***

An egret takes off from a nearby pond and flies through the sooty mist, passing by her window, unfettered and free.

Mangla looks forward to being an independent married woman—the wife of a railway officer. She will be able to live her life as she chooses, a life befitting a college-educated woman far away from the social shackles of in-law obligations.

2

Love Partitioned

Sweet anticipation fills her as she thinks of reuniting with Anand, her beloved husband.

The cool air of a late October day feels good on her soot-covered cheeks. Each time she washes her face in the small bathroom and wipes it, the towel has black streaks. Now she hurls the filthy towel across the berth. No one is there to see her in this empty compartment so why bother cleaning?

It's been a comfortable journey despite the soot, dust, and grime. She has the solitary company of her own thoughts. Two days are over and two more to go. She opens the novel she brought with her to pass time. But her mind wanders. She thinks of reigniting her husband's passion. Her pulse races as she throws the book down. Goose bumps rise all over her body as she puts the red *sindoor* powder in the parting of her hair. Her hands are covered with dark orange henna, arms have gold bangles—interspersed with red and green glass ones—they clink when she moves, announcing to the world her newlywed status.

To cool her face, she walks to the window, opens it further and looks out.

Her back is to the door of the compartment. Over the sounds of the brakes, she doesn't hear the click of its latch as it opens. The sudden appearance of an Englishman in her periphery alarms her. He's tall, white, red-faced with red hair, a color of hair she has never seen. She has never been in the presence of a white man. Flustered, she recoils and covers her head with the edge of her sari.

He asks, "Madam what are you doing in this compartment?" "Mr. Conductor, my husband sent this pass for me." She brings out the railway pass.

The red-haired man scrutinizes it, returns it to her, and leaves the compartment. She breathes a sigh of relief and sits down with a thud.

But soon the Englishman returns with another Englishman in an official black uniform with a black cap and a badge on his chest that reads *conductor*. Mangla feels her cheeks warm as she realizes her mistake. The first one was not a conductor.

The conductor asks her, "Miss your ticket please."

She hands her pass to him.

"There's an error. This English gentleman 'ere, 'as 'igher priority over you to be in this compartment. You can't be 'ere with him."

"But my husband, who's a railway officer in NWFP railways, sent me this pass."

"'ere, I don't bloody care who your 'usband is. 'e maybe Gandhi 'isself, I know the bloody rules. Englishmen and English ladies 'ave priority over any native darkies like you and you can't be in the same space as them."

"But-- "

His lips curl as he says. "But- nothing. Maybe 'e doesn't know that the quit India movement fizzled out. You'll bloody well follow the rules and show white people deference."

The other Englishman leans against the doorway and drums his fingers on his chest with an amused smile on his face.

Mangla continues to sit, unsure of what to do. Why hadn't Anand warned her? "C'mon we don't 'ave all day to wait. The train's about to push off." "But where will I go?" Her fear-laced voice rises an octave.

"I don't much care." With that he picks up her things.

"What're you doing? They're mine."

He throws her bags out onto the platform.

"But you can't. How dare you? You're here to help passengers."

"Not the likes of you."

She gasps, and then he's back, grasping her arm and dragging her light frame to the door. He pushes her out onto the platform. Then he blows on his whistle and waves his green flag, signaling for the engineer to move the train.

As the train picks up speed, she feels the warm hissing steam blow past her humiliated fiery face.

The lock on her steel trunk has broken, spilling some of the contents. She picks up her gold band leather slippers and tightens her hand into a fist around them. She throws her slippers after the receding train, aiming at the conductor, and screams, "My husband will get you, you lout of a man. He's an officer in the railways and not a low scum English dog like you."

***

She repacks her things and manages to fix the latch with the knife in her bag. In the engine's steamy wake brings the memory from her wedding, her departure in a palanquin on shoulders of four men to the words of the traditional song sung at *Vida*, "I am going to my in-laws never to return, for now I am a foreigner in my father's home and must embrace my husband's----"

She can see *Ammaji* wiping tears. Her mother is happy for Mangla's future but sad to give away her daughter to another house. So different from promises of Gandhiji's progressive agenda for educated women to be independent. Mangla shakes her head and looks around. She assesses the situation. No one else got off the train. She is alone on the platform and doesn't know her surroundings. It's a small station, with mountains in the distance. It's a pretty setting but, doesn't give her a clue as to its whereabouts. She can see a village in the distance. Too far for her to carry her things. There are no rickshaws. Besides, she needs to know when the next train to Abbottabad leaves. She looks for a timetable but finds none on the wall.

The last time she traveled through this area was over four years ago when she went to Jammu and Kashmir with Basanthi. Its milieu looks vaguely familiar. Basanthi. How she misses her. Their disagreement was more harrowing than the tears of her mother. Stranded at this Godforsaken station, Mangla rubs her chest as if to apply a salve on that unhealed wound.

***

She'd not slept with Anand before the wedding. Even after marriage, their intimacies had to be stolen during the day in between her new bridal obligations of serving his family. Only at night could she be with him alone, undisturbed. It had been a new ecstasy and she wanted it to go on forever. That night, in his bags, she found pamphlets for the continuation of the Quit India movement. She asked him, "What are these for?"

"I'm going to take them with me to NWFP to distribute. You know the Quit India movement fizzled, but the Pathan's are resurrecting it." "How?" Mangla said feeling all warm and fuzzy as he stroked her breasts. "Well, the British, along with other congress leaders, jailed their *Khudai Khidmatgar (KK)* leader Abdul Gaffar Khan. The *Pathan*s are seeking revenge. They're a violent lot when they get emotional. Mind you, Gaffar Khan follows Gandhi's nonviolent movement. Anyway, enough of that, we have more important things to do." He coaxed her to lie down as he embraced her in his arms.

Khan sahib is her father's friend. Her father, *Pitaji* told her many times why he avoided activist support of freedom movement because it would be considered as a seditionist act. To this Anand had replied, "Maybe, but the freedom of India is more important than my life or my job."

Mangla stayed quiet, convinced that there were others better suited to distribute these pamphlets. Before she went to bed, she removed the pamphlets and hid them under their bed.

After only two days, Anand received a telegram, and swore under his breath.

"'Unrest in NWFP. Stop. Return immediately by next train. Stop.' Can't a man even have his honeymoon in peace? I'm not their indentured servant." He threw the telegram on the nearby table.

"You are junior and new to the job," she offered, putting her hands on his shoulders as she stood and picked up the telegram and read it for herself. Sure enough, there it was in black and white, a missive to return. "Well you'll come with me," Anand said. "It's a four-day journey to the North West Frontier Province NWFP. We can get a coupe and lock the doors and make love all the way there. Won't that be wonderful?" He wrapped his arms around her.

Mangla blushed. She looked beyond the draped open doorway to be sure that no one could hear or see.

"I've only been there less than a month. The house isn't set up for a woman. I'm afraid it's a bachelor pad right now. I expect you'll set it up the way you want."

When they told his father, he protested. "She can't go with you. She must stay here for some more time, so she gets to know us, and we get to know her."

"Shouldn't I know her before her in-laws?"

"What'll people say if she goes off with you instead of showing respect for your family?"

"I thought you didn't want me to marry her."

Mangla's eyebrows rise. She hadn't realized that he defied his parents to marry her. She had new respect for his courage.

"But you're married, now, aren't you? We must follow the proper protocols owed to our status, to keep our social *izzat*."

"*Izzat* be damned."

No one asked Mangla. She wanted to go with Anand but swallowed her words. In her father-in-law's patriarchal world women just followed what their elders dictated. She would bide her time. As the altercation grew, Mangla felt both important to be wanted by her in-laws and husband and terrified at the loudness of their voices. So different from the quiet voice of her father.

The upshot of it was that Anand stormed out of the door and went to the station to arrange for his travel. His *chaprasi* packed his bags. Mangla would have liked to do that herself, to smell his clothes and feel them in her hands. But this was not the way a new bride was expected to behave. She held on to her empty hennaed hands as she swallowed her tears. Then he was gone, still angry, and without even saying goodbye embrace.

***

Within a week Anand had arranged for a railway travel pass to be sent to her, with a letter to his father that said he needed Mangla by his side. If no one could be found to accompany her, then she should be allowed to travel by herself. He felt that to live in NWFP she would need to learn to be alone and independent, that word was music to her ears. The journey would prepare her and provide her that sense of confidence. He wanted his wife with him and SOON. His capitals had brought a smile to her face and warmth to her heart. Of course, she could make the trip by herself.

"Who does he think he is ordering me around like this?" her father-in-law said. "As if she isn't our *Bahu* with obligations to us. Just because he is a railway officer now, he thinks he is above everyone." Her father-in law had a devil's temper. Enraged, he stomped his feet and threw pots and pans about before his wife calmed him down. In the end he could find no one who would accompany Mangla that far at such a short notice. "If something happens, she is his wife," her father in-law said. "I wash my hands of this whole affair."

"I'll be fine. My father let me travel alone in college," Mangla said quietly, without qualifying that it had been just a few hours journey and not to a politically troubled remote area. She had been so confident. Thinking only of how much she wanted to be with Anand, to let him ravish her.

***

Now, at the platform of the desolate station, she's angry.

At her in-laws for letting her go alone even though she had insisted that she would be fine; with her husband for allowing her to be in this difficulty. What was he thinking? And she has no way to contact Anand that she won't be on the train. Maybe the stationmaster could send a telegram or advise her what to do. She drags her trunk and bedding roll towards the office door marked Hari Chand, Stationmaster. She notes from his name that he is a Hindu.

The office is next to the room marked *ladies*. Good; at least she has some place she can find shelter until the next train. She takes her stuff to the ladies' room, and leaves everything but her handbag. Then she makes her way to the stationmaster's office and knocks.

"Come in."

She opens the door. Instead of a Hindu, she faces a muscular, tall man with a red turban on his head and a Bryllcream moistened mustache. Many men wear turbans, but she's not seen this kind before.

"Excuse me. I want to report the rude behavior of the English conductor on that train."

As she tells her story, the man scrutinizes her slender, comely body. By now, she is old enough to know this lecherous look. Her stomach churns as she realizes she is alone with this man, and he wants to take advantage of her vulnerability.

"Can you please send a telegram to my husband. Mr. Anand Rai. He's an officer of the Railways."

"Only the stationmaster can do that. I am in training. He left for the day and won't be back until ten in the morning, my loved one. My *Soniye*."

The familiarity with which he addresses her makes her skin crawl.

"When will the next train leave for Abbottabad?"

"Not until tomorrow at the same time. There is only one daily train that stops here." The man closes the distance between them and reaches for her. She anticipates his move and turns to run, but trips. His arms grasp her waist.

She must think fast. She looks at the clock on the wall. It is one in the afternoon. This means that it will be almost twenty-one hours before the station master arrives, and she can get him to send a telegram to Anand. Too long.

She screams, "Please, someone help me."

'Who's going to hear you, my beautiful?" His face is only a few inches away from hers. He twists her arm behind her, and she winces in pain.

She can't believe this is happening to her. How could an official treat her like this? If only she can get to the ladies' room, she can lock herself in. How to escape? She tries to buy time with reason. "Sir, you're an official man of Railways. Aren't you here to help someone like me?"

"Ah! I'm helping you, my beauty, aren't I?" He twirls his moustache. His grip tightens. "Have you had a handsome man make love to you?" He wipes his lips

7

with his tongue. "I don't get this opportunity very often. A gourmet dish served to me on a platter in my office."

She shuts her eyes. She must think. And think fast.

Maybe she can keep massaging his ego. She won't win against his brawn. At least they are both dressed. Perhaps it will buy her time.

In her handbag is a knife she brought to cut fruit. If only she could free herself to get it. The glass bangles tinkle on her arm. The image of women breaking their bangles, when they learn that they are widowed, comes to her mind. They bang their arms on the table to shatter them.

She wrings her one arm free and strikes it on the end of the table. With a crash her glass bangles break. She breaks free, reaches for the biggest and sharpest shards, and brings them to his eyes and face, gouging him again and again until blood flows. His yell fills the room, the sound of a wounded animal. His grip loosens. She wrests free and runs.

***

Inside the ladies' room she double bolts the door. She unbolts and bolts again to hear the reassuring clicks of the latches, then slumps against the door, sliding to the floor. She'll stay here all night until the stationmaster arrives tomorrow. He'll help her contact, Anand.

But how to be safe until then. She looks around her for any possible sources of entry. There is a window high above that provides light to the rest area. The solid vertical thick steel bars on it reassure her and she lets out her breath.

She feels dirty. She gets up slowly and crawls to the sink, turning on the tap to wash herself. She hadn't even realized she was bleeding, and now she keeps washing and scrubbing with her nails until blood flows freely from the bangle gashes on her arm. She washes herself as if she could be rid of the feeling of his paws on her body.

The reality dawns on her. How is she going to tell Anand? Will he believe her? Or will he say she must have done something to provoke the man?

Suddenly she worries she doesn't know her husband well enough. Can she trust him? Will he support her story?

Best is for her to stay silent. Like all others, it will be her secret shame. She again slumps to the floor. Her wail subsides into sobs so relentless and thorough that they seem to come from every pore of her body.

XXXXXXX

2 Mangla's Road to BHU 1922+

They are outside the kitchen, and nine-year-old Mangla is running fast to avoid Badri's paddle. She runs to the opposite side of the little brick structure surrounding the hand crank of the water pump and sticks out her tongue. "Na--nanna--na--na--Ding dong your mother's dead. You are adopted—not born to my mother. You aren't my brother, not my *Bhayya*." Mangla follows Badri's gaze and turns to face her mother, *Ammaji,* who has her index finger on her lips to ward off evil spirits as she emerges from the kitchen and says, "Sh-h thu-thu—Mangla *beti* it's hurtful—we don't say that even in jest. Where would he go without us?"

"He tried to hurt me."

"You must have done something to provoke him."

"No, I didn't. He picks on me all the time. He's a mean boy. You don't see it."

"How about you learn to be a good girl."

Mangla looks at Badri. He's hidden the paddle behind him and is smiling at *Ammaji* as she tousles his hair. Oooh he's sneaky. *Ammaji* is blind to his faults. All boys are angels in her books. It's not fair. Badri is twelve. Her cousin. He came to them when his mother died, and his father couldn't

cope. That should have alerted her parents to his failings.

But no—her parents are committed to reducing children's suffering. They follow Gandhi's ideals of human love and kindness towards everybody. Her father has a habit of bringing destitute children home.

In a huff she stomps out. *Ammaji* is oblivious to her anguish. Mangla complains that the children in school poke their tongues out at her and chant, "People who go to sweeper colony na--nana--na-na and interact with Muslims na-na-na and are brown like shit are *Bhangi, Bhangi.* You are i--t- t- t-- "

But *Ammaji* just lectures Mangla. Mangla can't let kids intimidate her. She should be strong. Like Gandhi, she has a duty to tear down the evils of caste boundaries.

***

9

Mangla has always had to share *Ammaji* with others. From the very beginning with Shabbu, her older brother, the same age as Badri.

In 1922, even before Mangla's birth, Sabiha*jiji* came into their family from Chauri Chaura. *Ammaji* is fond of telling this family lore to anyone who will listen as an illustration of her deeply held Gandhian beliefs. Mangla has heard it so many times she can recite it and just rolls her eyes. It happened back when the riots between Hindu and Muslims erupted the result of an incident in which a poor Muslim boy asked his mother for water. Their water pot was empty, so she asked him to go to the local well. This was during a severe drought, and the wells in the Muslim neighborhood were dry, so he went to a neighboring well and drew water. It was a Hindu well, and the boy didn't know about the Hindu caste system. A Hindu witnessed his transgression, and they all came in force to beat the boy up. They left him bruised and bleeding in the hot sun begging for water. When he died, the Muslims retaliated, and soon the Hindus, who outnumbered the Muslims, burned Muslim dwellings, and killed them all. No help, of course, from the divide-and-rule policies of Brit colonialists. Local police were divided as well.

Sabiha's story began when *Pitaji,* Mangla's father, was traveling to Gorakhpur. While riding with his assistant, he saw a pretty, tiny girl in a clean red muslin shirt with a scarf over her head. She wandered into the street, holding her little rag doll and calling for her *Ammijan.* A Hindu mob had gathered, but no one reached out to help her.

Pitaji got off his horse, looked around at the mob, and said, "She looks thirsty and hungry. Why is no one helping her?"

The mob leader said, "Sahib, she's Muslim. How can we look after her? Our family will become untouchable *harijans.*"

" Do you know where she lives? I'll take her."

They shook their heads. " Somewhere in the Muslim colony. You're a Hindu. You understand, don't you? Maybe some *harijan* will help her." As the story goes, the mob dispersed. One man threw her a piece of bread as he would to a rabid dog. He shooed her, "Eat. Don't come back for more." She picked it from the ground and devoured it.

Pitaji was appalled. He lifted the girl in his arms and soothed her. He brought out food and water from his bag and gave it to her. As she ate, he asked her name. "Sabiha."

"*Beti* where do you live? Let me take you."

She pointed to a neighborhood still smoldering from the recent riots. Everything was charred. People. Houses. The child's mother probably tried to save her, *Pitaji* reasoned, but there was no one left to ask. Finally, they came to a narrow alley where everything was in flames. Again, the child pointed, to a smoking door, partially open.

He could see charred bodies. He could see that she was too young to understand the tragedy that had befallen her. He brought her home.

Ammaji was at first very angry and upset. She knew how much was at stake if they went against the caste rules. But Pitaji drew her attention to Gandhiji's message that one has to be the change one wishes to see. For Hindus, Sikhs, and Muslims to be "*bhai-bhai*" and live as brothers in harmony, each had to understand the other's religion at a deep level. *Ammaji* was moved. She brought home a Quran and went to the local mullah to learn how to say the *Namaz* and *Kalma* prayers and to recite them with Sabiha as her *Ammijan* would have done. From then on, Sabiha followed *Ammaji* everywhere. The family was subjected to a lot of condemnation from the Hindu community—even *Ammaji's* mother disowned her and would not allow her to come into her home and kitchen. But *Ammaji* soldiered on. Sabiha was in the habit of hugging her knees and sari, not letting go until she was picked up and held close.

***

Ever since, the family melded the Hindu and Muslim religions in their home—traditions Mangla has come to know well. Daily, the family recites the *Namaz* and *Kalma* provided by the local mullah. They kneel on the floor and rock back and forth with hands on their foreheads, reciting praises to Allah.

Daily, they also rendition the Hindu *havan. Havan* consists of a small, square, iron pot holding shaved wood pieces. Around the pot are placed brass bowls of ghee and dried herbs. The family recited mantras from a book, throw ghee and *samagri* herbs into the fire, and said, "*Aum Bhur Bhuva Swaha.*" After each ritual, Mangla waits for her *prasad*, the spoonful of brown sugar she received at the end as a reward.

Every morning, *Pitaji* and *Ammaji* spin yarn on their own *charkahs*. Since she was three, *Ammaji* or *Pitaji* allows Mangla to pull and spin. With practice and steadier hands, she is pretty good. Like Sabiha, she has her own *charkah*.

Badri and Shabbu, the boys, are not made to join the family rituals of spinning and prayers. One day Mangla decides to skip the *havan*, too. When her father calls, "children it's *havan* time," she yells back, "I already said my prayers when I said my *Namaz* with Sabiha*jiji*. I'm going out to play." With that she runs to the door only to find it blocked by *Ammaji*.

"Mangla go and join Sabiha in *havan*. In our family we do both Muslim and Hindu prayers."

"But Badri and Shabbu *Bhayya* often don't come. They are allowed to play outside. Why can't I?"

"Because you're a girl. Just like Sabiha you need to learn all the traditions to carry them into your husband's home."

"What if I don't marry? And I want to study. I want to go to BHU like cousin Yashi."

"It's the duty of every Hindu girl to marry the man her parents choose and give birth to a son. I did. You will too. Both *Sharia* law and *Manusmiriti* have this message for women and not for men."

"But I want to study and then educate girls. You only studied until the fourth grade and Nani, your mother, can't even read or write."

"What use is education if you can't take care of a house and children to make it a home?

"Swami Vivekanand said that in India we need to educate women if we want to uplift the country. Besides, Nani sits there and smokes *hukkah* all day. Is that what you want me to do?"

"Mangla. What's got into you? If you talk like this no one will marry you."

Wishing she was a boy, Mangla turns around and joins Sabiha for *havan*. It seems that her quest for education has no value to *Ammaji,* whose radar doesn't scan beyond marriage and motherhood. Still, Mangla sits with Sabiha reads with her. She dreams of going to BHU.

***

It isn't just Sabiha who Mangla shares her family with. Her father inspects soil conditions for various construction projects, a job that often requires him to stay out at night. One cold winter night several years after Sabiha was adopted he walked in with a young girl bundled in his arms.

"What's in the quilt?" *Ammaji* asked with a suspicious frown. *Pitaji,* with a guilty grin, unwrapped a little bit and exposed the face of a very dark girl with slanted eyes. "Her name is Surjjo."

He then told them her story.

When he was riding, he heard faint pitiful cries, "Rama ho, Rama ho..." Then he saw a dark, shivering, emaciated girl wrapped in a thin, tattered cloth. Her hair was matted and crawling with lice. A deep wound on her foot oozed pus. Maggots fed there, and she had been trying to extricate them with a piece of straw. *Pitaji's* assistant translated that Surjjo's father and brother had been murdered by the indigenous *adivasis* and her mother had also disappeared. Surjjo searched for her in vain, developing the infection in her foot. The girl was of an untouchable caste with no relatives and no one to help her. She had been living like a stray dog, eating whatever she found in the trash and sleeping by the dying embers of the shop hearth to stay warm.

"What kind of man would I be if I left her to die?" *Pitaji* said. "We took care of Sabiha and she's been a blessing to us. We can take care of Surjjo too."

"You're not the one who has to put up with the taunts of the community." *Ammaji* shook her head.

"Well if you feel you can't take care of her—I'll take her to the orphanage and pay for her upkeep. Gandhiji says we are to do *seva* service for those less fortunate than us. If we don't have the courage to stand up to the unfairness in our society, how can we expect to win our freedom from the British? Surjjo is showing us a way."

Mangla looked at her mother and her father and thought, you don't have to go to school and face the children as they make fun of you and your family.

Ammaji hit her forehead with her hands and said, "*Hai*, my kismet first Sabiha, now Surjjo—what sins did I commit in my last life to be married to this man and walk through these fires?"

A patient smile lit *Pitaji*'s face as he listened and waited. Mangla watched her mother and father with the hope that Surjjo would go to the orphanage. She didn't want to share her mother with yet another child.

Ammaji extended her arms in surrender. "OK. I was brought up to think of my husband as God. Let me have a look at her."

Pitaji unwrapped Surjjo, and the room filled with the putrid smell of rotting flesh. Maggots crawled out of Surjjo's skin. *Ammaji* put her sari pallu around her face and nose.

Mangla came closer to Surjjo. Her nose crinkled at the smell.

"Go and boil some water Mangla," said *Ammaji*.

Clearly her mother had caved into her father yet again. Mangla vowed that when she grew she would not be ordered about by any man. "I picked up an ointment from a *vaid*, country doctor on my way," *Pitaji* said. "He told me to clean her wounds and apply this twice a day, and in a few days she'll improve."

"And I have to survive until then," *Ammaji* said looking down. "Mangla, stop staring and go and bring boiled water."

***

Surjjo got better with *Ammaji's* compassionate and loving care. Like Sabiha before her, she followed Ammaji around like a pet dog and learned domestic tasks of fetching water, lighting a fire, making bread, sewing, and spinning *charkah*. Mangla and Sabiha undertook to teach her to read and write.

Like them, with practice, Surjjo got better at spinning and got her own *charkah*. She grew very excited and couldn't wait until it was time to spin each morning. Soon it was all she wanted to do, to spin yarn into thread that could be taken to the shop for trade into cloth. Then she also learned to sew.

Mangla couldn't understand it. She tried shame. "Surjjo you'll never make it to school if all you want to do is spin and sew."

"I enjoy spinning better. Like *Ammaji*, I'll work and win swaraj." "How will you do that?"

Pan-faced, she replied, "by making our own clothes. *Ammaji* doesn't read."

Mangla laughed, "You are hopeless."

Ammaji overheard her. "Leave Surjjo be. Each one has different abilities, Mangla. Never forget that. Surjjo won't change the world, but she'll be able to take care of family and herself."

13

It was clear to Mangla that repetitive use of hands was easier for Surjjo, and she dropped trying to teach her to read.

***

For Mangla, spinning has always taken a back seat to learning science, languages and mathematics. Her hero is her uncle Ramesh *tauji*, her father's older brother, and his wife aunt *Taiji*.

Ramesh is the headmaster of a school in Aligarh, and insisted on marrying a girl who was educated. *Taiji* was home schooled and well-versed in Hindu literature and sacred texts as well as math. She is thin, light skinned and pretty. She can also sew, cook and keep a house. At fourteen she was already old, according to Hindu child marriage practices, but a union was proposed, and they were married soon after. Unfortunately, they have no children. Over the years, the family have pressured Ramesh to get himself a second wife, but with his progressive views he always refuses. Instead, he and *Taiji* have dedicated their lives to improving the education of other children, especially girls.

He runs a local boy's high school, while *Taiji* helps in the girl's school; in their home, she coaches local untouchable girls who workday jobs, girls who, because of their caste, can't study with the girls at the school. In this way, Mangla's aunt and uncle fearlessly defy Hindu caste rules.

***

"*Tauji*, do you know there's no future for my education?" Mangla complains when her aunt and uncle come to visit for a family wedding.

"Why do you say this *beti*?" her uncle says. He looks at her through his bifocals over his *paan* stained red mouth. His gold teeth show as he talks. "I've finished fourth grade, and there are no more classes for girls here. *Ammaji* won't let me go to the boys' school. She says I've studied enough. I think it's not fair that my brothers can study further but I can't. And they don't even like to study. I do."

"I agree. *Beti*, let me talk to them."

He goes to find *Pitaji* and *Ammaji* in the other room. Mangla follows. "Daya Prasad, is it true that you won't allow Mangla to study further? "*Pitaji* points *to Ammaji* and says, "It's not me. Ask your sister-in-law."

Cocking his head, Uncle Ramesh turns to her.

Ammaji sits up and adjusts her sari *pallu* to cover a bit of her forehead to show respect for her brother-in-law. "Ramesh *Bhayyaji*, you know how it is. How will we get her married if she studies with boys? No one will look at her in this community."

"You can't hold a girl's life in ransom, Sheelvati. You're all for India's freedom and for everyone to follow Gandhiji. He advocates women's education too."

"But *Bhayyaji*, we've got to live in our society. What future does a girl have if she's not married and has no children? You know that with your brother's

14

government job, we aren't wealthy. Even if we can find a dowry, no one will look at her if she studies with boys."

"I hear you." He takes his scarf and flips it around his neck. He takes the nutcracker out of his pocket and crushes his betel nut before putting it in his mouth. He then walks to the window and looks out at the children playing in the street.

"Besides, adopting Sabiha and Surjjo has already put her marriage in jeopardy," *Ammaji* says pointing her hands in Mangla's direction. "What will studying with boys do—I'm afraid to even imagine."

"Will you let her come and stay with me?"

Ammaji sighs. "How will that help? You're the principal of a boy's school."

"I haven't told you as yet, but I've got our patrons to add high school classes to our girls' school. Her *taiji* will help."

Mangla comes forward. "Really, *tauji*?" She looks at *Ammaji* and says, "Can I go and live with them?"

"Sheelvati, I know Mangla's *taiji* will be happy to have a girl to spoil," says Ramesh. "We'll personally coach Mangla and make sure she learns all our Hindu ways, same as you do."

"Please, *Ammaji*. I want to go to BHU and study further." Mangla dances around her mother and gives her uncle a hug. She takes *Ammaji*'s silent smile as a sign of victory.

"So that's settled. I'll enroll her. She can always move back with you if there is an opportunity here. Maybe Sabiha can come, too. It's not good for her to sit at home and not study further. That way Mangla will have her sister."

"But we've raised Sabiha as Muslim."

"We can do the same. I'll make sure that the *Maulavi* from the madrasa comes and augments her school with teachings from the Quran. That's not a problem. Besides you will still have Surjjo, Badri, and Shabbu here to help you."

"Sheelo, what's the harm?" *Pitaji* says, "They have no children. It'll give them joy. We're blessed with many."

"You know we, too, support Gandhiji's message of communal harmony. Where did Daya Prasad get those values?" He proudly points to his own chest.

Ammaji looks down and stays quiet. Mangla notices tears in the corner of her eyes. She goes and hugs *Ammaji*.

"We will come home for vacations, and you can visit us, too. We will write to you often."

Ammaji holds her close. Then releases her as she gets up. "I smell our lunch, Surjjo, Oh Surjjo is the dal boiling?" She makes a hasty exit towards kitchen.

Mangla claps her hands and runs out to tell Sabiha. She finds her reading a novel. "What are you reading?" she asks, as she holds both her hands out and pulls the girl off the chair. "It doesn't matter! We can go with *tauji* to Aligarh and study further in his school! *Ammaji* agreed."

***

In Uncle Ramesh's house, Mangla and Sabiha share the same room. Mangla loves the attention she gets from her aunt. It is nice to be not tormented by Badri and Shabbu. It's nice not to hear *Ammaji's* taking the boys' side, her constant harping on the virtues of being a 'good Hindu wife.' Sabiha doesn't get the same pressure—maybe because *Ammaji* hasn't grown up with how to be a 'good Muslim wife'.

Once a week, *Maulavi* from the Madrasa teaches Sabiha and Mangla Urdu. Mangla loves Rumi's poems, and during the week they talk about love and how they will marry for love. *Taiji* ensures that they continue their daily spinning and prayers.

At the girls' school, Mangla excels in all her subjects. Hindi literature, English, Indian history, Science, and Mathematics are her favorites. Sabiha loves home economics and history. *Taiji* teaches them cooking and sewing after they finish their homework. Years hum along and Mangla is excelling in all her classes as is Sabiha, under taiji's tutelage. *Taiji* loves the girls to death. They can do no wrong in her eyes. She spoils them and showers every luxury on them as if they were her own. Both girls respect and adore her in return.

***

In summers, they return home and continue to learn domestic skills from *Ammaji*. By the time Sabiha is sixteen, *Ammaji* is keen to get her married. Muslim sharia law demands that a cousin has a first right for her hand, and *Pitaji* never gives up on his search for any living member of Sabiha's family.

One day in his travels to Aligarh, he meets Mahmood Ali, who studies at the Aligarh Muslim University and is training to become part of the Indian Civil Service. He talks to *Pitaji* about losing his family in Chauri Chaura, and they soon discover that Mahmood Ali's father is Sabiha's mother's brother. After the riots, Mahmood's father searched for his sister but was told that the whole family perished in the ethnic violence. Mahmood Ali's family lives in Peshawar n North West.

Mahmood is surprised to learn that Sabiha is still alive. *Pitaji* arranges for a meeting between them and gives him Sabiha's recent photo. Mangla dances around Sabiha when it is decided that Sabiha will meet Mahmood. At six-feet-three, he is a well-built Muslim, a dream man for the fourteen-year-old Mangla. To her imagination it is a storybook romance. *Maulavi*, her Urdu teacher from the mosque insists that Sabiha is only allowed to talk to Mahmood with a veil covering her face. *Taiji* makes sure that the veil is of thin and near transparent muslin. She says that it is only fair that after a lifetime of separation they deserve to see each other. Sabiha and Mahmood like each other. There will be a wedding, the first one in the family. *Pitaji* and *Ammaji* bless their union, as do Mahmood's parents. Mangla and Surjjo are in stiff but playful competition all that summer as to who will spin more cotton to exchange it for woven cloth to stitch it into a scarf with a gold border for Sabiha's wedding, *nikka*.

Mahmood soon passes his civil service exam with flying colors. Sabiha can continue her high school studies until the end of Mahmood's civil service training, when he will get his first posting and can get longer leave for the wedding.

It turns out that his first post is in Peshawar, in the Northwest near his family. From her readings, Mangla knows it is distant and that she has never been there. Maybe one day she will visit Sabiha. The marriage is set for the Diwali holiday season of 1938. By then, Mangla hopes to be in college, and to help *Ammaji* with the wedding preparations over the school break.

Sabiha wants to get married, which is just as well for Mangla. It's taken *Ammaji*'s attention away from her hopes that Mangla will get married after high school. Mangla wants to make difference in the world through her own achievements. She wants to work to free women of so many expectations. She marvels that she and her sister are so different in what they want.

Mangla also continues to study hard. Her goal of going to Benaras Hindu University has not waivered. Everyone calls it BHU. It is the most acclaimed and competitive university for women. She knows the stakes are high, but so is her determination.

Despite the excitement and drama about the wedding, Mangla concentrates on her studies. *Taiji* continues to support her ambition to go to BHU. She makes nutritious brain food for her, like blanched almonds and fresh fruits and vegetables—a high-protein vegetarian diet. She gets Mangla special tutoring. No expense is spared.

Mangla's hard work pays off and she graduates cum laude. She is young not yet sixteen. Still, most girls enter university around that age. She applies to BHU. She gets a letter that she is admitted. Finally, she gets her reward. She skips out of the room to tell Sabiha. The sisters dance together in happiness for each other, each one about to get exactly what they've dreamed of. They both say special prayers for their future success. When *Taiji* hears she plans and throws Mangla a big graduation party.

At the party, Mangla overhears *Taiji* telling *Ammaji*, "Sheelvati, I know you are concerned about Mangla going to BHU. You want her married. But let me tell you, Mangla's marriage prospects will only be enhanced by her college degree. Young men these days prefer educated women."

Unconvinced, *Ammaji* looks at her sister-in- law.

"Mangla will do very well at BHU. Mark my words, she will marry well also. "*Ammaji* lowers her head in deference to her sister-in-law. Mangla knows this means she will be able to go to BHU unimpeded by any objections.

XXXXXXX

Manjula Waldron

3 Basanthi's Road to BHU 1922+

Basanthi taps Ayah's chest and asks, "Ayah how much longer before Papa's home?"

"Be patient, baby. Soon."

"You said he'd be home by the time I see the cows returning."

"Maybe his train got delayed." Ayah pushes Basanthi off her lap and says, "Why don't you run to the back and see if the cook has dinner ready for him?"

Basanthi hears the hum of a car and heads to the front porch instead. It's her father, Bhumi, and she runs to him with outstretched arms. "Papa, Papa you're home."

"Of course, I am. I told you, didn't I?"

"But you're late."

"I know. Don't *Ayah* and the cook take good care of you?"

Basanthi nods. Sure enough, *Ayah* takes good care of her. She takes her to school and to the park and tells her stories. She tells her folk tales. Her favorites are Snow White and Cinderella. She loves animal stories, too, like the fox when it can't get grapes and calls them sour grapes. *Ayah*, like Bhumi, is Anglo-Indian. Like all Anglo-Indian women, she wears dresses and has short hair that she puts in curlers at night. She reads the bible and tells her bible stories. When Bhumi is away, she takes Basanthi to church.

Her father, Bhumi, is different. He reads to her scriptures from different religious traditions, including Hindu, Christian, Buddhism, and Islam. He tells her stories from Science, Theosophy and English literature. He reads to her from Shakespeare and Kipling. When she doesn't understand words, he patiently explains them. He connects these stories to her grandfather and to the Maharajas, and to her ancestors from England and India. The stories fill her with wonder and make her feel a part of a larger world.

Bhumi picks her up in his arms as she puts the cross dangling on her chest in her mouth.

"How old are you?" he asks.

She puts up both her hands to show eight fingers and one bent.

He smiles and pats her shoulder. "Really? Eight soon to be nine. I won't be able to lift you up anymore."

"Yes, you are a big girl now," *Ayah* says as she brings a glass of water on a tray. "Let Papa take a bath and rest."

"Oh, she's OK." He ruffles Basanthi's hair. He puts her down and takes the glass of water, then heads to his room to wash up.

"We'll wait," Basanthi calls after him as she goes inside with Ayah.

Ayah shakes her head and mutters, "Life hasn't been easy for him since Marge memsahib left."

"When was that?" Basanthi asks. She climbs up into Ayah's lap for her own life story. By now she knows it by heart, but Ayah recites it again while they wait for her father to emerge.

"Let me see, must have been three or four years ago. It was soon after Bhumi sahib's father died," Ayah says. "Those were dark days when Marge memsahib went back to England without even saying goodbye. She just disappeared one day. You must have been around four. You cried all day and ran from room to room calling for your Mama. What could I do but just hold and love you during the day? Bhumi sahib took over in the evenings. He told you many stories. Bringing up a young girl alone is no job for a man. Sue memsahib came from Gorakhpur to help when she could. But I could see that he was lonely for a woman."

"But you are a woman," Basanthi says.

"It's not the same. And now we have Jill memsahib, of course, and Alice and Sally those two daughters of hers." Ayah's grip tightens around Basanthi's shoulders. "That woman is rich in money but stingy of love."

"You don't like her much, do you?"

"That's not my place to utter," Ayah says.

***

After her dinner, Basanthi runs to the front porch of their bungalow where Bhumi sits in the easy armchair with his feet up reading a book and half dozing. She jumps on him.

"Oomph!" he says as he straightens himself and holds her.

Fingering her cross, she says, "Tell me the story of how I got this."

"I've told you so often. Aren't you tired of it?"

She shakes her head as she snuggles up to him. She loves to hear it. Ayah doesn't know it as well. And Bhumi's voice becomes magical when he talks about meeting her mother. This is all Basanthi has left of her mother. Bhumi's memories. As he talks, she fondles her cross.

He tells her that her grandfather, Bhuminder Singh Raina, who died when Basanthi was a wee girl, came from a long line of Kashmiri Brahmins. His ancestors were scholars in the Maharajah of Jammu and Kashmir's court. Bhuminder Singh, too, was groomed for this role. He was a liberal thinker and followed Theosophy.

20

"What is Theosophy?" Basanthi asks, even though she has heard the answer before.

"It is to be free to think for ourselves; to believe with reason, and experience—not superstition."

They sing together her grandfather's favorite poem from Tagore, "*Faith is the bird that feels the light when the dawn is still dark.*"

He tells Basanthi that the Maharajah introduced Bhuminder Singh to Jane Macdonald, the woman who became Bhumi's mother. She wanted Bhuminder Singh to become a Christian before she married him. No one approved of the marriage. The Maharajah didn't approve because it violated the Hindu caste, and the English didn't approve because of the English Law, the diktats, that separated English and Indians. However, the Anglo-Indian Christian community accepted them when Bhumi was born. His face saddens as he tells her of his mother's death when he was only two. Bhuminder Singh never remarried and educated Bhumi himself about theosophy and sacred scriptures in addition to English literature, math, and science. He told Bhumi, "My son, life will call upon you to turn the other cheek, both figuratively and literally. I live that way no matter what the other does. Love in your heart sustains, and the cross is its symbol."

Bhumi missed the daily light his mother brought to him. Over time, he connected to her through his father's memories, just like Basanthi, Bhumi had the light skin inherited from both a Kashmiri father and an English mother. He was often mistaken for an Englishman until the English found out that he was of mixed race. He was then banished from their social circles. He succeeds in school and cuts a very dashing figure. At twenty-one, he passed the exam to become an assistant stationmaster and was posted in Gorakhpur. Everyone expected that he would rise far in his career.

Basanthi loves the next part of the story as it is about her own mother. She snuggles closer and begins to jiggle the chain around her neck, so the pendant hits her skin in a slow rhythmic beat.

One day, when Bhumi was on duty at the Gorakhpur station, he saw a young English woman disembark from the noon train. She wore a simple white starched muslin dress, and her brunette hair was bobbed and fell around her shoulders. She reminded him of his own mother. Something touched him deep within. He felt that he was witnessing a princess from his dreams.

He saw her full lips, fair skin, and small, upturned nose. He fell in love with her face.

He couldn't stop looking at her as he blew the whistle and took out his green flag to signal the train to move on. Something in his body's subterranean physiology stirred as he put the flag back in its container and watched her.

She stood there. Her posture was straight, but she looked lost and confused as she searched for the exit gate. He loved the strangeness in her expression. To him she looked like a *farishta*, someone from another world another time.

The rest of the passengers soon left the station. Clearly there was no one to meet her. He asked her, "Miss, may I help you?"

She looked at his name badge and official uniform. "My uncle was supposed to meet me here, Mr. Raina," she replied.

He fell in love with the melody of her voice as she spoke.

It began to rain, and as she looked up, the raindrops glistened in her hair like diamonds.

He fell in love with her hair.

Basanthi, like she always does, takes his hands, and puts them in her own hair. "You forgot to tell me that my hair is so much like hers."

He fondles her hair and in a dreamy voice continues his story. "Would you like to sit in my office and wait until your uncle arrives Miss--?"

"Marge Smith. Thank you." Her whole manner conveyed that, like his mother, she was educated.

He escorted her to his office, and on the way, as they passed the little canteen, he ordered a fresh cold lemonade and a packet of Britannia bourbon biscuits.

Marge tarried at the door of his office, taking in the cool air and clean scent emanating from the *khuskhus punkah* suspended from the rafters in the ceilings.

He pulled out the chair for her and seated himself behind his desk as the waiter brought their lemonade and biscuits.

Bhumi told the waiter to look for an English sahib who might come looking for a Memsahib. Then he turned to Marge. "It's hot. You must be thirsty, Miss. Please do have a drink and some biscuits as we wait for your uncle."

"Thank you. I'm rather hungry and thirsty. I didn't get to eat this morning before I boarded the train."

Marge told him that she was visiting from London to take a job as a teacher in a local school chosen by her uncle who lived in Gorakhpur. She had always wanted to come to India to teach, and her mother had located her long-lost cousin and arranged for her to stay with him while she tried out living in India. They sat and exchanged more pleasantries, but still no one came to receive her.

"Maybe there's some mistake. They were supposed to meet me at the station."
"Where do they live? Maybe I can take you there. I'll be off duty soon,"

She reached into her purse and handed him the address on a piece of paper. He looked at it and realized that her uncle didn't live far from his own home.

"It's on my way. I can easily take you there."

She gave him a thank-you nod.

"I've got to go out to meet the 3:20 train, but I'll be back soon. Please make yourself comfortable. It's cooler in here than outside."

She took a book out of her bag and began to read. He fell in love with her ability to concentrate.

"You remind me so much of her when you read," Bhumi says to Basanthi. "Maybe you will be a teacher one day."

Basanthi hugs him harder and says, "When I grow up, I will be a teacher, just like my mother."

"Yes." Bhumi continues. When they got to her uncle's house, they found that he had left for a month on vacation. The caretakers didn't know how to reach him. Bhumi told her that letters to and from England were slow and at times delayed because of port problems. He would help her find accommodation until her uncle returned.

He took her to his adopted aunt Sue, who lived next door to him.

After that, Bhumi met Marge almost every day. His work times were similar to hers. He escorted her to and from school. Sue encouraged their romance and encouraged them to spend time together. They took after dinner walks under the magical Indian sky. They went to church together. Some evenings Marge went over to his house and explored his extensive library. They sat in his living room and discussed, Austen, Shakespeare, and Marlowe as well as contemporary fiction. When Bhuminder Singh visited Gorakhpur that May, he blessed their union. Soon a beautiful baby was born. They called her Basanthi -- Basanthi because it was Springtime, and everything was blooming. Now Bhumi kisses her forehead and whispers, "You will always be my blossom."

Basanthi holds his hands to her forehead.

When Basanthi was christened, Sue was Basanthi's Godmother. She gave Basanthi a gold necklace with a cross pendant at its center. It was specially blessed by the local priest, and Marge placed it around her daughter's neck every day, through good times and bad. They were a very happy family. When they moved back to Jammu, they hired her Ayah. But something in Marge continued to miss England. She still called it "home." After Bhuminder Singh's death, when Basanthi was around four—

Basanthi interrupts Bhumi. "Stop. I don't want to hear any more," and he stops. Then she falls asleep in his arms and he takes her to her bed, where Ayah sleeps on the cot in her room.

***

After Marge left, there were long, sad days for Bhumi. Especially when Basanthi looked for her mother wandering around the house, asking over and over when she will be back. As she grew older, she wrote daily letters with the same theme: Mother, when are you coming back?

After five long years, with no word, no-contest divorce papers arrived from England. Bhumi was to sign and release Marge from all connections to him and Basanthi. The return address is a solicitor's office with a brief note from Marge. She is starting a new life with an Englishman. Tears fill his despondent eyes.

"What's wrong, Papa?" Basanthi asks.

He shakes his head. "I'm afraid Mama isn't coming back to us."

"You are lying. I'll ask Ayah." She hits him and, crying, she runs to find Ayah. "Ayah, tell me Papa is mistaken. Mama would not abandon me, her only daughter. It's not right. She beats on Ayah and cries. Bhumi comes and holds her, but her arms flail as she screams and wails, which brings the cook in.

"Basanthi, baby, I have made your favorite dinner."

Basanthi wrestles herself free and runs out of the house. Cook follows her.

Ayah calls after Basanthi. "Remember we're going to church for the feast of the saints. I'll pray for us. Maybe God will help us. Christ loves us all. The lord will help us."

Bhumi follows them.

Just then, Jill walks in with Alice and Sally. Jill is an old friend of Bhumi's from high school. She recently moved into the area after her wealthy husband passed away.

Quite oblivious to the turmoil, Jill says, "Are you all ready to go to church? Basanthi, you aren't going in those rags are you? Ayah, please get her ready. We're getting late."

At church, all Basanthi hears is everyone extolling Jill's virtues as she struts in her finery. What an eligible catch she is for Bhumi, they say. Why doesn't he ask her?

Sure enough, Bhumi comes home from work one day and says, "Basanthi, I've asked Jill to marry me. Now you will have a loving mother and sisters to play with."

Basanthi's hand goes to her cross. She thinks, Jill will never be my mother if I have this, but she stays quiet. Her father hadn't asked for her permission. Besides, it's his life. She has Ayah.

***

After the marriage, Jill moves into their bungalow. Basanthi sits for dinner with them, often playing with food. Ayah notices and afterwards brings dinner to her room. In the morning, she is the first to get to school while Alice and Sally, her stepsisters, laze around and are often late.

When he's home, Bhumi provides academic coaching to all three girls. Basanthi is a natural learner and soaks in academic knowledge. Under Bhumi's tutelage she excels at school and wins high accolades. She can't wait for high school. In contrast, Alice and Sally are only interested in material things. Jill encourages her daughters to look for suitable matches in the boys at community and church events. But the boys prefer the prettier Basanthi, even though she pays them no mind. Jill scowls when she sees this. She finds any excuse to make Basanthi help her in the kitchen.

***

Love Partitioned

Then one day, when Bhumi is traveling, Basanthi comes home from school and as usual, calls, "Ayah, I'm home."

There is no response.

Basanthi runs around the house to Ayah's quarters, calling her name. There is no Ayah, and her meager possessions are gone.

She asks the cook, who has tears in his eyes. Basanthi beats on his back, "Where's Ayah? Why won't you tell me?" It is the first time in her memory that Ayah isn't there to greet her when she comes home from school. It's like losing her mother all over again. She sobs.

"Ask Jill, memsahib," the cook says. She's never heard him so desolate. Alarmed, Basanthi runs to find Jill. "Where's Ayah?"

"She stole money from Alice and Sally's purse. I dismissed her."

"Ayah Would never do that."

"I've caught her lying and stealing. Beating her hasn't stopped her bad habits." "You beat her?" Basanthi's chest heaves like she got a beating herself. She punches her fist on the table. "How dare you do that?" She runs out of the house calling for Ayah.

Jill's gleeful voice follows her. "You won't find her. The police took her to jail." Basanthi crumples to the ground and shakes as sobs wrack her body. As night falls, the cook comes and carries her inside. He gives her a drink of milk and coaxes her to eat something and puts her to bed. "I want my Ayah," she whimpers. He just pats her in empathy.

Basanthi cries for days, but then, as she did after Marge left, she stoically buries herself in her studies, knowing her father will be pleased with her academic success. He never discusses with her Ayah's leaving, and she doesn't ask him about it.

***

Jill is not only mean to servants. She's also mean to Basanthi. The more boys favor her over her own daughters, the meaner she becomes. Basanthi tries to avoid all community events under the pretext that she has to study. If she can't, then she dresses in drab, ill-fitting clothes. It is then, in front of the boys, that Jill taunts her. "Look at you, you look like a maid in those hideous clothes."

Basanthi fights tears. She retaliates, not caring who hears their row. "What do you expect? You buy me inferior and unbecoming clothes that are a size too big, but for your own daughters you spare no expense and care. It's not my fault that boys ignore your daughters."

After these dust-ups, Jill is even meaner. Especially if Bhumi isn't present. Jill calls her *Haramzadi,* a bastard and daughter of a whore. She blames Basanthi for misdemeanors committed by her own daughters and accuses her of leading them astray. Basanthi often finds herself grounded and not allowed to participate in community activities when boys are there.

25

If Basanthi ever makes the mistake of asking Jill for something, it's always refused. Jill tells her that the twin's father left them a lot of money, but that Bhumi's salary barely covers their living expenses. If Basanthi asks Bhumi for what she wants, there is hell to pay after he leaves. It is easier not to ask. When she feels sorry for herself, the story of Cinderella that Ayah often told her comes to her mind. Was Ayah prescient? Basanthi will wait for her fairy Godmother. How she misses having Ayah to console her.

When she complains to Bhumi about Jill's unfair treatment, he tells her to live a Christian life. Turn the other cheek, like her grandfather. She learns that Bhumi has no patience with her domestic disputes. He looks tired, and there is a new distance between them. He doesn't have the will to confront Jill.

"One doesn't have to live in the trough with the pigs," he tells Basanthi. "We have the freedom to think and choose and rise above things. Focus on your academics, Basanthi. That's your strength and the ticket to a better life. Everything will fall into place."

Based on her performance, Basanthi is admitted to the prestigious Convent of Jesus and Mary High School. Jill's daughters aren't.

Jill argues with Bhumi against separating the three girls. "Pay more for Basanthi's education at the convent? How will we afford it on your salary?" "But Jill---"

"No. This is only fair. Alice and Sally aren't accepted. We treat the three girls equally." With that, Jill stomps out of the room.

"Jill, we can look for a scholarship for Basanthi, "Bhumi calls after her. In the other room, her tirade continues. He rolls his eyes, but for the sake of domestic peace he gives in to her in the end. His unwillingness to stand up to Jill appalls Basanthi Where is her old Papa, who treated her like a princess? She must take matters in her own hands. She walks out and goes to the convent school to meet with the principal. She explains her whole sad situation. The principal, impressed by Basanthi's resourcefulness and academic achievements, offers her a full tuition, room, and board scholarship on the spot, so that Jill can't impede her education.

That night, Basanthi announces her good fortune to the family. Jill thumps the table. "You didn't understand the argument, Basanthi. It's about three of you going to the same high school."

"Basanthi has already accepted her financial support, Jill," says Bhumi. "The deed is done. Argument over. Girls, go to your rooms and finish your homework for tomorrow and study for your exams."

"Thank you, Papa," Basanthi says. She understands the courage he has shown. From then on, things with Jill are even worse. Sometimes she slaps Basanthi. Sometimes she takes a switch to her backside. When Bhumi is around, Jill appears angelic. Basanthi thinks of running away or jumping in the river. But then she fingers the cross around her neck and thinks of Christ's suffering. She remembers Ayah's words that God will never forsake her.

Love Partitioned

Basanthi can't wait for the day when she can leave home and begin her high school education away from Jill and her daughters. She resolves to have very little to do with Jill. She vows that she will live by her brains as her father has urged her to do. The principal of the convent school has shown her the way.

***

At the high school, Basanthi is an excellent student and wins all the academic awards. Her father is proud of her and visits her often in the convent away from Jill's prying eyes. On one of these poignant visits he says, "Basanthi sometimes I have been weak in my dealings with Jill and her daughters. However, in my heart you have always been special. You are my blossom."

She takes his hand in hers. "I know Papa. You've always wanted best for me. Even when you were marrying Jill. I love you for your ways." "Thank you. I know sometimes I don't live up to my ideals. At times I failed you."

She looks at his moist eyes and squeezes his hand.

"With faith in yourself, you'll go far," Bhumi says. "Remember, we all have freedom of thought. You chose wisely to stand up for your education. I am proud of you. I'll support you to the best of my ability."

Basanthi avoids going home and stays in school through summer to help the nuns and earn money, so she has extra funds during the school year. She tells the nuns that one day she plans to be a nun, herself, so she can help those less fortunate than her and wipe out evil from this world. In her final year of high school, the nuns encourage her to apply to Benaras Hindu University. She is apprehensive. As an Anglo-Indian in a University with Hindu in its name? The memories of rejection by her grandfather's Hindu family are still raw in her psyche. However, her research leads her to the stories of its founders Pandit Malviya, a Hindu man, and Annie Besant, an atheist English woman. They were both political activists and committed to India achieving its independence.

The more she reads about Annie Besant, the more she becomes fascinated by her independent, adventurous "can-do" philosophy and lifestyle. She was an educator, a women's rights activist, a writer, an orator and a scientist. In 1915, she helped to pass a bill for the foundation of BHU. BHU opened its doors in 1918. In addition to humanities and comparative religion, the study of science and educating Indian women became one of its core missions. Basanthi has never met a woman like that. Now she wants to, and she thinks she knows where to find them. Basanthi feels that Annie Besant's theosophy links her to her father and grandfather. The idea of freedom of thought brought her closer to Bhumi. Basanthi now has a female role model, someone who promotes women's education to set them free which is exactly what her father told her education could do. Basanthi. Besant. She is proud to have five letters in common with the founder of BHU.

Sitting on a park bench, away from prying eyes, she reads her letter of acceptance from BHU. They have offered her a full scholarship. BHU are first

27

three letters in her grandfather and father's names. This thought connects her to all the people she has loved and lost: her Ayah, with her love and kindness, her grandfather and his love of learning, and her father's message to believe in her own academic abilities--her road to freedom.

Her hand tightens around the cross on her chest as she rereads her BHU scholarship letter. She is actually going. No one can stop her now.

XXXXXXX

4 Anand: The Revolutionary

It is early morning. The sun is barely up, but the city is abuzz with activity. Twelve-year-old Anand, soon to be thirteen, points to his hair that has grown long and says, "I want some money to get my hair cut at Mr Nai's. He is the best, and he cuts the hair of my friends."

His father, Vishnu Lal, with a vigorous shake of his head side to side shouts, "He is expensive. Don't be an idiot. You think money grows on trees? Spend that time on your studies and make something of yourself." Anand's mother, Parvati, doesn't look up. She will never contradict his father. Anand has been through this routine before. He will need to use his charm with Mr Nai, yet again.

He stomps out of the house and walks over to the barber shop, where he finds the man sitting reading a magazine. Anand breathes a sigh of relief. "*Nai sahib*," he says.

The barber looks up and recognizes Anand. "You are Vishnu Lal's son, aren't you?"

Vishnu Lal is well known and respected as an altruistic community leader, though one of limited means. Vishnu Lal has learned how to use his reputation in a charming way, and Anand has learned from watching his father.

Anand says, "I have looks and hair but no money. My rich friends have money, but they don't have good looks."

Nai smiles. He pulls out the chair. "You want a free haircut, is that it?" "Oh no! Not free! I am offering my hair for you to experiment with the latest new teenage hairstyles my wealthy friends want. It will make them popular with girls and happy with you."

Nai puts his hands on his smiling mouth and gives a cough. "OK. I am not busy, so come sit down and tell me what you want."

Anand pulls out a photo he cut out from the latest magazine. Nai looks at it and says, "It's doable, and I like it. You are right, I need practice. Tell your friends to come to me before the style changes. The plateau of hair on top of your head will highlight your beautiful smile and charismatic face. Let's get to it."

***

Anand storms into the house, banging the front door to announce his arrival. He walks across the verandah and peeks in the door of the small windowless living room where his mother, Parvati, is seated cross-legged on the *charpoi* mending clothes. She looks up and her jaw drops; she holds the sewing needle high in the air over the garment, as if frozen. "What happened to your hair? Where did you get the money? What will your father say?"

"None of your business," Anand mutters.

"What did you just say?"

He ignores her.

"How come you're here and not at school?"

"I'm going to be a Congress revolutionary, like you and Pitaji. I quit school and joined the youth brigade of the Indian Congress."

Frowning she says, "How can you do this? That isn't right. You should talk to your elders first."

His eyes glaze over at "elders first." She means his father. It is always her pat answer when she knows she has no control over him or the situation. Like they can change his mind. When will they ever learn? Anand's mother is a strong and active woman and has been involved in the freedom movement right alongside her husband and other prominent freedom fighters like the Nehrus. She goes to marches with them. But is she independent? Not in his opinion. His father is the one who commands her on everything. What he says, she follows. She treats him like God. He treats her like a child. Of course, he is thirteen-years her elder. And she was only thirteen when Anand was born. Technically she is his mother.

But practically? She babies him like he has nothing between his ears. His father is always angry with him. Nothing he can say or do is right. They treat him like he can't think. But Anand knows better. He makes his own decisions based on logic and reason.

"You don't use logic," he says now to his mother. "You just worry about what will others say."

"Without working in society together where will we be?"

"You don't have to always follow what your husband says."

"You don't understand women's constraints."

"You have a good mind. Use it."

"Are you my father instead of my son? Stop treating me like a child." Anand can see he is having an impact on his mother.

"Then stop acting like a child," he tells her. "You both treat me like I'm an imbecile. I am intelligent human being. Indu's mother treats me very well. She has my respect. If you want me to respect you --YOU have to earn it." He points his finger at her.

"Well, you—" she points back at him, "act more responsible.

Anand knows how to win and control his mother. But his father, Vishnu Lal, he hasn't figured him out.

Love Partitioned

"Dr. Ghosh, the principal of Modern School, he deserves respect. I heard him today at school. He made a fiery speech to appeal to the youth to join the youth brigade because the country needs their participation to win its freedom. We are its promise, he said. Not children to be controlled." The man had treated Anand with dignity when he asked to sign up for the youth brigade. He asked how old he was, and when he said seventeen, and in college, he trusted him and signed him up right then and there, without putting him through an inquisition his parents would have done. Just then, his father walks in for his meal before going to the high court where he practices criminal law. His hair and mustache are combed, and he's dressed in his usual long black *achkan*, buttoned in front with a high collar, with a comfortable pair of *churidar* pants that crease up around his ankles and calves. He wears a Gandhi cap on his head and two starched vertical white bands around his neck like a tie. They are the symbols of justice signifying the two tablets of Moses on which the 10 commandments were written. This attire for barristers is sacrosanct in Indian courts.

Anand represses the giggle that always arises from his core when he sees these bands around his father's neck like two chains to be pulled. He did that as a child. Now he smiles.

Vishnu Lal says, "What did I just hear?"

"I told Ma that I've quit school and decided to join the independence movement."

"You'll do no such thing. You are just a child." The anger in his voice is unmistakable. Vishnu Lal picks up a spoon and bangs it on the table as he sits down. He eats, uncivilized, with his hands and not with knives and forks as Anand has seen the Nehrus do.

"Gandhiji's coming to Allahabad and staying at the Nehru house. They'll have a big rally for the youth. Besides, what good is school if we continue to be ruled by the British and act like their patsies?"

"Without education, what will youth do when we get independence? I joined the revolution *after* I got my Law degree. We will need technology in a free India. You will be an Engineer."

"Well, Dr. Ghosh said we need to free India first. *Then* we can educate youth. We have to mobilize youth to free India. I believe as the principal of Modern school he knows more than you do."

"Humbug. Hogwash. What rot. Who do you think you are? What do you know? Like your uncles, you will go to engineering school. That's your father's edict."

Parvati, forever a peacemaker, puts her hand out. "Anand. Show some respect. Don't talk to your father that way."

She turns to her husband and says, "We don't need to do anything this minute. Let it go. Please eat your meal or you'll be late for High Court."

"I'll be who I want to be and when I want to be it," says Anand. "We, the youth, will change the world." He raises his fist as a salute to power. "Bunkam! Brash talk by one who knows nothing." Vishnu Lal raises his hands as if to strike.

"Go ahead hit me. See if I care. Your generation is so caught up in your *sanskar* and set ways that nothing's accomplished. You went to jail over a decade ago. But are we independent? No." Anand sneers.

"How will your march be any different? And you won't even have education to eke out a living. How stupid can you get?"

"But we won't be working or going to school. We'll actually get something done. That's what Dr. Ghosh said."

Vishnu Lal pounds the table. "Don't you see that man's evil? He incites the young and vulnerable. He follows Bose and supports violence. He'll lead you astray. I know the likes of him."

"That's why we, the youth brigade, will make salt and impede transportation, bring the English to their knees. We can't do this if we are sitting in some school learning useless things from ignorant teachers. We will be about action. Unlike our parents."

Outside, a car horn sounds. Vishnu Lal's ride to the courts is here.

Parvati heaves a sigh of relief and says, "Here's your bag."

"Parvati, make sure he goes to school. You've spoiled him. You give in to everything he wants. He rules this house and that is not good."

She looks down and nods.

"If you aren't successful, try Indu's mother. Why not get her to talk sense into him? We can't let the boy win on this." With that he picks up his bag and marches out.

"See what you've done? Your father didn't get to finish his food." Parvati picks up the half-eaten plate from the table.

"I'm not going to school, and that's that," Anand says shaking his fist at his father's disappearing back.

"You remember Shravan's story? He was a dutiful son. You should follow his example." Parvati begins to recite that poem. Once a blind couple who could have no heir, visited the Child God, Krishna, to get a boon. He was granted and soon they had a beautiful son, compassionate and loving, to care for his parents, blind or not---

Anand has heard it a thousand times. He loved it as a child. But now it sounds like drivel.

"And what did it get him?" says Anand. "Dashrath's poison arrow, and he died." "What's wrong with you. Why are you so stubborn?"

"I'm stubborn? What about you? Why can't you do as I say?" "Because I am older and your mother."

"Aren't I your first-born son? You've always said that I have privilege because of that."

"But not to disobey us."

"Aren't you disobeying the British?"

Parvati closes her eyes, as if in prayer, listening carefully to a voice deep inside. Then she opens them. "Well, if you won't go back to school, you can't live in this house."

Ah! Her usual ultimate weapon is now unsheathed. After this, she has nothing left.

"Then I won't," Anand says. His words are sharp, clear. He doesn't care about his mother's threats. "Who wants to live with tyrants anyway? After all, you lost one son. Now sacrifice your other to starve to death on the streets." An arrow aimed at her heart, he walks out of the house and around the neighborhood. His anger gives him new energy. He will to do menial jobs in homes. But it is a small community, and every house he looks at, he knows the people on the other side. They will surely force him to go home. It is getting dark, and he's tired and hungry. Smells of dinner waft from every window. He can imagine his mother's delicious meal. His mouth drools. His stomach growls. But he would rather starve than go back to his unreasonable and uncaring parents. Let them live without him. Still, he begins to miss his bed and his mother's night ditties sung in her melodious voice. He lies down on the round parapet around the banyan tree and shuts his eyes, praying that God will end his misery. A snake bite or scorpion sting will be better than shame of admitting defeat. As tears well his eyes, he pounds his chest and says aloud to no one. "See if I care."

***

He feels someone shake him. He opens his eyes. It is Ahmad *chacha*, the local policeman who often comes to their house to see his father about his clients' cases. Ahmad is a Sufi Muslim who sympathizes with the freedom fighters. He went to jail with Anand's father as a young man before he joined the police force. Anand calls him *chacha*, a term for father's younger brother even though he is a Muslim and not related.

"Anand, your mother and father are very worried. They looked everywhere for you and finally they sent me. You are a sensible boy. Tell me what's bothering you."

Anand says nothing. He makes no effort to get up, just lies there with tears filling his eyes, his new haircut tousled.

Ahmad says, "There's something I've never told you before, but now is the time to do so."

He tells him, in his singsong sonorous voice, how he met Anand's father. An English policeman falsely accused Ahmad, a Muslim, of murdering a Hindu, thereby inciting communal disharmony. Ahmad was poor with no money to fight for his innocence and nothing to pay a lawyer for his defense. He was jailed with no hearing. At the time, Vishnu Lal was working by day to support his family, and by night studying for his law degree. Despite his own financial needs, he took Ahmad's case *pro bono*. He believed in Ahmad's innocence.

Vishnu Lal's community disowned him for befriending a Muslim, for spending so much time with him while Ahmad was jailed. Even Vishnu Lal's mother, wouldn't let them near her. But Vishnu had joined the Gandhi movement and believed Allah and *Parmatma* and God were the same, and that they loved all humans. Around this time, Vishnu Lal married young Parvati young and she too joined Gandhi's *swaraj* movement. She accepted Ahmad as her brother and learned *namaz*. Vishnu Lal did his best for Ahmad and finally he won his case. Ahmad was acquitted.

Anand sits up and listens attentively. He's never heard this.

After that, both men decided to promote Hindu-Muslim unity. They participated in Gandhi's noncooperation movement, for which they were arrested in 1921. "I know you get frustrated with your parents," Ahmad says. "At thirteen that is understandable. But your father is a man of great principles and lives by them. He has a golden heart. Your mother is a devout and dutiful Hindu woman who pays attention to what your father says."

He pulls Anand to his feet, holds his hand and begins to walk slowly. "When we went to jail, your mother was left alone with no money, and you and your younger brother to look after. Your uncles supported her. The length of our incarceration was uncertain. Your mother was young and had very little education before she married your father. When your younger brother died, she was only fifteen and heartbroken. She felt she had failed your father. But your father guided her from jail to deal with her grief through education. She took care of the home and her in-laws while educating herself. The respect she earned in the community comes because she is self-educated now. Vishnu *Bhai* always told me that India would need engineers, and that when he got out of jail he would go to America to learn engineering. From jail, he encouraged your mother to learn English for that reason. But after reading Uncle Tom's Cabin, Parvati was convinced of the heartless cruelty of Americans, and they dropped that idea of going to America."

"I didn't know that." Anand says. In the trees, crickets chirp and he can hear frogs and bats flying to get *gooler* berries.

"He doesn't talk about it. But in his heart, he believes that education opens the doors for young people. He educated himself and your uncles in engineering, and now they have good jobs. He paid for me to go to night school so I could pass the exams and become a policeman. I help maintain order and harmony within communities so innocent people aren't punished. It is my way to pay back your father's generosity. He still believes that technical education holds the key to India's future, and that America has the best engineering schools. Now it's your turn to talk. What brings you here?" Anand tells him about the signing up for the youth independence movement.

34

"I know you want freedom for India. So did we. But Allah has his ways. We can't always bid Him to our timetable. We must do our duty and Allah will do his. That is the Sufi way." With an affectionate hand he ruffles Anand's hair. "I know your Dr. Ghosh well. He's charismatic and wants what is best for himself, to become powerful, and not necessarily what is best for you. When they find out that you lied to them about your age, what then? Think hard, my son. You are fortunate that your parents have given your education top priority, the same as the Nehrus for their daughter, Indu. They all want the best for their children."

They walk in silence, drawing closer to home. Anand can hear her mother's humming and prayers for his safe return. He feels regret for the way he spoke to her.

Outside the door, Anand looks at his feet. He kicks at a big rock in the dirt. "I'm ashamed to go in and face them. And I don't want my father to give me a thrashing for making my mother suffer. I know he will. He always does."

"How about if I go in and talk to them first. If they come out to meet you, then you can go in. If they don't, then you come home with me. How's that?"

"OK."

***

Two years pass, and Parvati becomes president of the local chapter of the All India Congress. Anand helps her at every turn. At fifteen, he is tall, handsome, and still well-groomed by Mr. Nai, the barber. When he walks by with his chiseled, clean-shaven face and agile physique, he makes many a head turn. He is conscious of his own appeal. He knows that as a first-born male he can do no wrong in Parvati's eyes. When she calls on him to help her organize things at the Congress, he gladly does so, as it helps him to meet a lot of young women. Like Amila Ganguli.

Amila's father is wealthy. Mrs. Ganguli often marches with Parvati, and the two teenagers are thrown together while their mothers are busy. He knows Amila is beyond his social class; she is from a prominent wealthy Brahmin family, and he is from a poor family of a lower caste. But according to Gandhiji, these things are not important. Anand, therefore, takes every excuse he can to frequent their big mansion nearby. He is ashamed of his own very modest and humble abode, especially as he and his father still get into awful fights. Amila's family is more civilized and respectful towards each other. They have been to England. Her father is Oxford educated and suave, not like his own father whose uncouth language in public embarrasses him.

***

One day Parvati asks Anand to help organize a "jailpool." She explains that women with children shun marches as they fear getting arrested—who would take care of their families? If they were guaranteed their children would be safe, taken care of, they would join the marches. It makes Anand proud that his mother has confidence in him. He gets a big blackboard from the trash heap, cleans it, and installs it in the living room. On it he draws a chart. In one column he writes all the local congress members' family names along with the number of children they have. On top he puts the dates of the organized marches. In each cell he writes down the names of all who will not be marching, ensuring that at least one of the parents from each family will be home and that there will be at least two women who will not march.

"Son, it is brilliant," Parvati says. "Wait till others hear about it."

He doesn't tell her that in his assignments he has ensured that he and Amila are in the same "jailpool." So as to not arouse his mother's suspicions, he has made sure that there is at least one other girl around his age who is also included.

Soon Parvati gets a buy-in for her "Jailpool" idea from all the other organizers, including the Gangulis. Women's participation in marches increases. They gladly go, reassured that their children and family will be taken care of should they be arrested.

Everyone who meets Anand congratulates him on his "jailpool." He now takes greater care of his looks every morning and struts like a peacock. One day, when they are walking home from a Congress meeting, Parvati tells him about her cousin who was very beautiful. She had met a Kashmiri Brahmin on one of the freedom crusades. His father was in the Maharajah's court. When he asked her to marry him, the family opposed the idea as they feared community backlash and that their children would become untouchables, as is dictated in *Manusmriti*, the Hindu holy text. Parvati was eleven, and she remembered the whole societal upheaval. So her cousin and paramour eloped to Jammu. That was the last her family heard from them. One day the news came that his family had disowned her and her mixed caste children. Even though he was a Gandhi follower and felt that when India became free all these caste distinctions would go away, in the end her husband couldn't go against his Brahmin beliefs, and his family married him to another Brahmin girl. Soon after, Parvati's cousin died of a broken heart in Jammu. They never heard what happened to her children. "But that is against Gandhi's view," Anand says. "The caste system is a curse of the Hindu religion and should be eliminated. You yourself say so."

"Son, I am just saying that it is very hard to go against society norms. What I have seen is that marriages succeed only when one marries within the caste."

"That's plain hypocrisy. How can you even say that and still be a Gandhi follower?" In disgust he stomps ahead.

Having warned him, and knowing his temper, Parvati stays quiet and walks steadily. She suspects his affection for Amila, and she has fulfilled her maternal duty.

XXXXXXX

Love Partitioned

5 Revolutionary or Sahib?

One day it happens.

During one of the marches that his mother has organized everyone is arrested, without hearing, including women. However as per his design there are women still free to take care of the children. Both Amila's and his mother are in the women's jail. They assure their children they will be safe. He's seen other women with deep spiritual faith in God come out unscathed. They will too. His exhilarated teenage hormone-driven brain provides him a rosy image of being with Amila in the evenings until his father can pick him up.

Vishnu Lal must work during the day and sometimes late into the night. They cannot afford help at home, whereas the Gangulis have an army of servants and a palatial estate and all the luxury foreign goods, like the hand cranked, His Majesty's Voice record player and the latest 78 rpm records. In Anand's house there is only a very old and cranky radio that works intermittently, if at all, but at the Gangulis, they can play patriotic songs from the latest movies sung by famous artists like Iqbal, Mumtaz, and Sehgal.

Every day, Anand looks forward to the end of school when all his "jailpool" members gather at Amila's house. They eat good food, sing, and dance; best of all, he can be close to Amila and revel in her presence. In class, he is distracted with his own eager mind, and ashamed by the erection his daydreams produce. What if his teachers were to see?

When Vishnu Lal's late, he finds himself huddling with the other boys and girls under blankets, pretending they need the cover to stay warm. As they talk, some of the girls rub against him. It gives him goose bumps and he gets hard. Then he feels overwhelmed with shame. He runs to the bathroom and splashes cold water all over himself. At home, nights, the erotic feelings are really strong. He sleepwalks to where his cousins sleep and lies with them. Then he wakes up in the middle of the night and finds that he's wet the bed. His sense of shame intensifies. He is confused and embarrassed. He doesn't know who to turn to.

***

On Tuesdays they are allowed to visit their mothers at the jail.

Mr. Nehru is in jail and so is Mr. Ganguli. Vishnu Lal makes sure that he takes Amila and Indu to jail with him, so Indu, too, can visit her father and Mrs. Nehru can tend to the jail pool at home. Amila, as a female, can visit Mrs. Ganguli inside. The warden allows male visitors Vishnu Lal and Anand access to talk to Parvati in a small, barred visiting room in the ladies' wing. Through the window, Anand sees Amila and her mother walking and talking in the mud-paved courtyard. The women who must breast feed their infants are walking there, too, consoling their crying babies. He can see the small cells where the women sleep. It is cool outside, and he sees cots with very skimpy bedding on them.

On one of these visits, they discover that Amila's mother is very ill. "She's not used to this rough living, I'm afraid. Our doctors are not able to find out what's wrong. Her fever isn't abating. I'll talk to the authorities and see if she can be discharged on humane grounds," the Warden says. Vishnu Lal talks to Mr. Ganguli senior, Amila's grandfather, who is India's leading lawyer and has many friends in Europe.

"She'll be sent to Switzerland immediately when her mother's released," says Mr. Ganguli. "They have the best medical facilities. My son is in jail, but Amila can accompany her. She'll be a great comfort to her mother at this time."

No, you can't send her away. Anand thinks, what about me? He stays quiet. He's not asked. He has no status to express his sentiments.

Then Mrs. Ganguli is released, and just like that, Amila and her mother are gone.

***

His mother, as the President of Congress, is still in jail. He feels lost in the evenings. The Ganguli's house feels so big and empty. His own feels even emptier. He feels morose, like there is a hole in his heart that gets bigger every evening when he enters Amila's house. He's lost interest in other girls. They can't seem to cheer him up.

Why is God doing this to him? Bringing him all this suffering. Is it because he has these wild dreams and desires that he cannot explain? Was God protecting Amila from the evilness of crossing caste lines, like his mother warned him? He keeps his shame hidden.

He is listless. Abdul offers him a cigarette in school and teaches him to smoke. He goes for it and feels calmer. Then some of the boys invite him to a smoke out. They fill a hukkah, similar to what his grandmother and aunt smoke, and offer it to him. He likes it. He feels light-headed and laughs loudly at their jokes. It is the first time he has laughed since Amila left.

The Ganguli servants don't question his late return from school. He tells his little sister he is late because he is studying for his exams with his friends.

***

One Tuesday morning, Anand walks in the door and sees his father reading his legal briefs before leaving for court.

He says, "So you know, *Pitaji*, I'm going with Abdul to the youth freedom march today and can't come with you to see Ma in jail. I may be late."

Vishnu Lal looks up. He takes his reading glasses off his nose and suspends them in mid-air and yells. "No, you can't. I've told you a thousand times to stay away from that useless good-for-nothing fellow." Anand's body bristles. He looks at his father and realizes that he has lost weight since his mother has been in jail and hasn't been there to cook for him. He looks older from the responsibilities he's carrying—working, being a single dad, and organizing freedom events while his comrades are in jail. But instead of feeling compassion for his father, Anand feels anger. Why can't he allow him to just be, and to learn from his experiences, good or bad? It never fails. When he takes initiative, his father doesn't appreciate him or trust him. He just wants to control him. Anand misses his mother too. He turns around and walks out.

***

He walks to where Abdul said the youth brigade is meeting to march, but no one is there.

He feels a need to smoke hookah. He has money. It is easy to find it in Ganguli house. No one seems to care that he takes a little bit from Mr. Ganguli senior's wallet. He probably doesn't even notice any missing.

Abdul has taken him to the old part of town where the Muslims live. He finds the hookah shop, pays, and sits down to smoke. He understands he stands out as a non-Muslim, and that for the first time, he doesn't have his local friends to protect him. He smokes at a fast and furious pace. Soon he feels lightheaded and gets up to wander the neighborhood, swaying and giggling.

He hears instruments and women dancing to the music and sounds of *ghungrus*, their ankle bells. He follows the sounds, and they get louder. He is curious. It leads him to a *kotha* with a balcony overlooking the street. When he looks up the sun is in his eyes. He sees three beautiful women looking down at him, beckoning him with their fingers and full, red, glossy lips. They jingle their bells in rhythm. They are in tight fitting bodices and full dance skirts that show off their large bosoms and hips. They wear jewelry befitting *nauch* dancers, at least as Abdul has described them to him. Anand's never been to a *nauch,* but Abdul has many times. "Are you lost?" a couple of women call out.

"You could say that." it is his unsteady reply.

"You look like you are from a good home. Why are you doing here?" He doesn't know.

"Then come in and let us look after you."

They guide him up the stairs and sit him down on a red satin-covered mattress with red and green throw pillows and give him a hookah and a drink as the music and *nauch* dance commences. The sound of dancing bells on their ankles and their rhythmic gyrating bodies, entice him. They move their hips and uncover part of their breasts. He's never seen women's breasts before. The dancers rub their bodies together in their dance, exciting each other, and then come close to him, suggestively licking their lips. They sidle up to him and take a sip of his drink, a puff on his hookah. Then they put it to his own lips, inviting him to smoke and drink and even play with their bodies with vivacious smiles that he finds unable to resist.

"You are a virgin, aren't you, my handsome?"

He gulps the drink and takes a puff. They refill it. The more he smokes and sips the less he's able to refuse their advances. He feels the same arousal in his groin as in his daydreams, but now he doesn't feel shame, just longing as they expertly undress him and guide him into delicious lovemaking. He feels he has entered heaven, and he doesn't want it to end as he explodes into one of them. But strangely he feels no embarrassment, just relief and heavenly delight.

Then they ease him back on the bed and say, "Sleep my loved one. Sleep."

When he wakes up, he is alone. They are gone. The musicians are gone. Was this just some kind of a dream? Hallucination? How did he get here? He has no recollection, only a sense of dread.

He looks out and sees the afternoon sun outside. He picks up his bag. He finds his money missing, but everything else is there. Money comes easy and goes easy, but shame stays around a long time; he hopes that no one from the family and their friends saw him.

***

Parvati has been released from jail and is home. She takes over the kitchen again. The whole family including Anand is glad to have her cooked food. They fight over to be the first in the kitchen to enjoy new dishes she prepares for them.

Vishnu Lal's younger brother, *chacha*, is visiting them. Parvati serves savory biscuits and tea. They sit in the verandah drinking tea.

He asks Anand, "So what are your plans after high school? Have you thought of a college to attend before going to the University?"

"Not sure as yet *Chacha*." Anand replies.

"You know I went to Ewing Christian College. Everyone calls it ECC. You should apply there. It's a great college and was founded by Arthur Ewing, a Presbyterian American missionary in 1902."

"Did you like it?"

"Oh yes. Their values are very close to ours. To narrow the disparity between the rich and the poor; the privileged and non-privileged; the hungry and well fed; and the literate and illiterate. They treat all students with kindness and respect and focus on justice and freedom. I felt at home."

"I haven't a clue what I need to do to get in," Anand says.

"Oh, that's easy," says his father. "Go to the college and get an application. I can help you fill it out and pay the fee."

"You want me to go there?" Anand asks him.

"Your father is the one who encouraged me to go, and he was generous enough to pay part of the tuition until I won a scholarship," *Chacha* says.

" You worked hard if I recall. Besides it opened the doors for you to go into engineering and to your first-rate job in the railways," Vishnu Lal says. "Don't get me wrong, Anand. It's not automatic. At every step you need to take initiative, work hard, and perform. In summers you can visit me, and I'll help you. It's the least I can do to pay back my brother."

"Anand it's up to you," Vishnu Lal says.

Chacha has always been Anand's role model. Because of his excellent standing in the railways, he has visited England and America. Now Anand can see a path to that future for himself. He stays quiet. He still feels conflicted between becoming a freedom fighter or a professional. One day he sways one way and another his father's ambition for him wins. He doesn't have anyone to confide in who won't side with his father. Then there are still memories of Amila. From what he hears, she will be in Europe studying and living with her mother. Mr. Ganguli flies over and brings back her news that he gets from his father. Parvati is happy with this arrangement. She knows his obsession with her will wear off when they marry her off to a good brahmin boy.

About college, Anand can't decide. He wants to keep his options open if possible. They don't push him.

***

Anand rides his bike to ECC. He likes what he sees. The buildings are deep red and contrast well with the majestic greenery of the great Banyan tree that sits in the center of the quadrangle. It's a picturesque setting. The 42-acre campus on the northern bank of the river Yamuna is about three kilometers away from the sacred Sangam. Here the river Ganges and Yamuna meet. It is a lore that there is a third river below them that gives their waters their sacred medicinal property. He loves the tranquility he feels sitting under the shade of the old Banyan tree.

He fills out his application. Vishnu Lal, true to his words, pays his admission fee.

Soon he learns that he is accepted. He is jubilant as he writes and thanks *chacha* for the coaching he received from him.

He studies mathematics, science, and English from American missionaries. He loves their "can-do" self-empowering attitude towards learning, which is so different from the rote and authoritarian instruction in his high school.

The teachers demand punctuality and academic discipline, but Anand doesn't mind. They are Christian, but they treat with kindness, those, like Anand, who are not. They are big on prayers, and the day begins with a Christian service in the chapel. These are not required of Hindu and Muslim students, but Anand leaves home early to not miss them. Their message of God's love and mercy is not that different from his mother's as received from Mahatma Gandhi. Every freedom meeting in his home ends with the sermon-on-the-mount from the New Testament. After all, that is where Mahatma Gandhi got his idea for nonviolence. It is in the air; it is throughout the freedom movement. The missionary attitudes are a switch from the aristocratic and autocratic attitudes of British colonialists. The long bicycle commute gives him little time to devote to his studies, but the cost of living in the dormitory is beyond Vishnu Lal's budget. Anand is torn between the two demands. Daily after lunch he sits alone under the banyan tree and prays.

One day the principal comes by and sits down beside him and says, "Mr. Anand Rai, right?"

"Yes sir."

"I see you are an earnest student. You come early to the chapel even though you don't need to and work late in the library. You have done well in your exams. The workload must be a lot for you."

"Yes sir. I'm finding it very difficult. But my father can't afford the fees to pay for my living in the dormitory."

"I know. In the staff meeting today we discussed your case. We believe that you're a deserving student who exemplifies our college values. We decided to give you a scholarship that will pay for your room and board and part of your tuition. In return, you have to maintain your grades in the two years before you graduate and go to the University."

Anand breathes in. His prayers seem to be answered. He takes a moment before expressing his gratitude and feeling proud for his father's faith in him.

"Thank you, Sir. My father will be very pleased."

"Good luck young man. We want more students like you in our college." With that, the principal shakes Anand's hand, and leaves.

***

One morning, Anand sits in the chapel listening to the fire and brimstone sermon from a visiting American minister. The topic is the moral behavior God expects of young men. What filters into his psyche is that it is sinful to fornicate and waste one's manly energy by masturbating. God punishes those who commit these sins. And God watches and knows all. Godly men shouldn't be like the heathens that live all around them.

Anand finds himself turning hot. No one ever said this to him before. Is he one of the heathens the minister is alluding to? Consumed with shame and soiled by disgrace, he shrinks in his chair as if cringing from God. He has engaged in both these activities. Even now at night his mind wanders to Amila, and he is unable to control himself. He has also stolen, told lies, smoked hookah, and drank. He feels unclean all over.

What sort of punishment he can expect from God for his misbehaviors? Was that why He took Amila away? Was that why she never returned to India after her mother died recently? She now studies in England. He hears that she is doing well and will be going to Oxford University to study political science. She'll make a great political leader, he thinks. He is filled with longing for her. The hole in his heart suddenly reopens.

He feels his soul tarnished. It is hard to concentrate in his classes. He feels God is pointing an accusing finger at him that everyone can see. After such a long time without them, he is suddenly filled with an uncontrollable urge to find Abdul for the drugs he provided.

He wanders through the Muslim neighborhood but doesn't find him. The hookah shop isn't there either.

"Allah be praised," says a familiar voice. "Is that you, Anand? What are you doing in this neighborhood?"

"Oh, Ahmad *chacha*! I hadn't been here in so many years, I was just curious how it has changed since we had the youth march."

"How's college? Your father's so proud of you getting a scholarship. Congratulations. How do you like it there?"

"Most days it's OK. Some days, like today, I miss the safety of being home. Ma's food and old friends just having a good time without care," Anand says.

"When I went to the police academy, it was very hard, and sometimes I lost faith that Allah still loved me. I got discouraged and my mind played tricks. Then I remembered my mother teaching me to recite *layhe layhe ilaha--*, there is no God but God, fifty times and it calmed me. Ahmad lowers himself to a nearby bench and leans back, looking at Anand and pointing in the direction of his home. "I'm sure your mother did the same for you."

Anand gazes mindfully at an ant crawling nearby. He heaves a sigh of thoughtful release of breath. "She did actually through reciting her daily prayer. 'Oh God guide my boat to the other shore as you have done so far with your grace." Ahmad seems to have a knack to always to be able to go to the root of Anand's problems. Just as well he didn't find the hookah shop. If Allah loves you no matter what you do, did Allah just rescue him? But the American minister said he wouldn't be forgiven for his manly sins. How many Gods are there? Are there two Gods, a punishing God and a loving God? Then there are the Hindu Gods. Anand is confused.

Anand tells Ahmad about the fiery orator that morning in the chapel. Ahmed nods. "I know it's difficult to grow up to be a man. But you do everyone proud. Allah tries us all in His own way but never to hurt us or punish us, just to teach us through his mercy. That's the Sufi way."

"But he-- "

"You remember Dr. Ghosh? You learned that day that many people are misguided in getting you to do their bidding—not out of love but control. What if this American man was wrong? He isn't God, is he?"

"But he said that it's God's word."

"God talks to everyone, including you and me—not a few selected people. What is the song your mother sings every morning in her prayers? God keep me safe and help me to reach my destination with your blessings. Only trust *Paramatma* to direct you. He is Allah. *One God layhe layhe ilaha.* You have that power, Anand. Discover it and trust it. Don't fear falling. Allah is compassionate and merciful. He will lift you up when you help yourself."

Anand looks at him sideways.

"Come, let us go and sit down, and let me buy you some chai and samosa. I know the best tea shop here." He pats Anand on the back. "I'm so happy to see you."

***

There are days when Anand is despondent and full of guilt and grief, and then he remembers to recite Sufi chants and his mother's prayers. They calm him and give him strength.

He graduates and is admitted to the University. Wherever he goes in the community, people greet him with respect.

Mothers ask him to speak to their sons, to influence them to do well in school, and he is happy to oblige. He understands, though, that his own power is limited. The glory lies in what he can only explain as God's grace. At the Allahabad University, he continues to study Math and Science.

After living away from home for two years, it's hard to go back. The house is small, his siblings noisy, the workload heavy, and commute time consuming. He's done well on his exams, but it is taking its toll on him. He is exhausted most days. He doesn't know how long he can sustain this academic pressure. He must do well if he is to get into the engineering school.

He tries to get an appointment with the warden to see if there is a way he can get a dormitory room but has no luck getting on the man's calendar. He prays for a way out.

One day he decides to camp in front of the warden's home.

When the warden comes out next morning he asks, with raised eyebrows, "Explain the meaning of this."

"Well, sir, I need a room I cannot afford. I want to do well at the University but cannot do it living at home. I've tried to get an appointment with you to resolve my situation but without success. This is the best I can do to solve my problem."

The warden raises his eyebrows. He looks up and down at his confident posture. "Well, come to my office at 9AM, and we'll see."

Anand does. He shows the warden his excellent grades and tells him that he tutors children in the neighborhood; he can pay part of his room if the University will match it. "Sir, I believe I will get a scholarship in the next round."

"My father says that an independent India will need civil engineers. I need to do well at the University and pass my entrance examination to Roorkee University where I can study civil engineering like my uncle. I want to be of value to my country after I graduate."

The warden closes his book and says, "Let me see what I can do. Come back in the afternoon."

"Life teaches us that we need to help ourselves. God does the rest."

The warden not only finds him a room but gives him a small single room for a very nominal rate.

True to his word, that summer his uncle coaches him for the national entrance examination for Roorkee engineering school. Only thirty students are selected from more than six hundred applicants. Anand not only passes the examination, but his second position guarantees him a scholarship.

***

Now he is twenty, and ready to become a *pucca* sahib to be groomed by this prestigious professional school in Roorkee University. His social standing has just increased—he is now the most eligible bachelor in the community. But marriage is far from Anand's mind. He wants to be the best civil engineer he can be, and then, like his uncle, a successful railway officer. Thomson civil engineering in Roorkee University requires an English dress code: each day he must wear a tie, a sola hat, khaki pants and ironed and starched shirts. Anand must have his own orderly to coach him.

Fashioned after Oxford, there are regattas on the Solani River canal, as well as swimming, squash, tennis, billiards, and bridge. The four meals a day are sumptuous. Alcohol is served, and they are taught the proper etiquette befitting officers of his majesty. It is luxury like he hasn't seen since he was at Amila's. Revolutionary life is left at his parent's doorstep as he now fits into this elite club of following English traditions. He is glad and thankful to his family that he pursued a profession.

There are no women students at the University, but plenty are available for the student's pleasure if they so desire. This is against the University rules, but the orderlies are well trained in discretion. Even though some of Anand's classmates indulge, he can't afford it. He still has urges, but University life is distracting and fulfilling in and of itself. Occasionally peer pressure is high to join in and he does. Even though he's been away from the missionaries for a time, he finds his mind is still confused about his sexuality. That summer when he goes home, there is a marriage proposal for his older cousin Arvind. The family looks at the girl's black and white professional studio photograph and critiques it. They like what they see and read of her age, physique, education, and accomplishments. Some members have reservations about her looks and limited financial means. They feel these young men can do better. Others go for family prestige. His cousin says, "Anand, want to come with me to see Mangla?"

"Sure, who wants to refuse a free feast?"

XXXXXXX

6 Mangla: University Life Begins at BHU

Mangla feels the breeze on her face as brief clouds gather overhead. She is glad she dressed in her pink *khadi* muslin, Lucknow-embroidered *chikkan* sari. Its light weight allows the air to circulate on this hot and humid July day. Her black braids hang behind her ears, framing her face. She's glad for the drink of water the University *piaow* offered as she entered the gates. Her dry throat feels quenched.

The *tongawallah* was an hour late to pick her up, despite reassuring her that he would be on time. He probably sat at some *pan* shop to smoke with his buddies while his horse rested in the shade. She's caught him in this act before. But it is hard to get any transportation from her home to BHU. It takes almost an hour, and there is no return ride back for him to make money. She is glad she persuaded her parents to let her stay in the dorm. Now she taps her feet as she waits in the long line to register at BHU's Vasanta women's college founded in 1913 by Annie Besant. Again, she wipes the sweat off her brow. Nearby, Mangla spies a light-colored brunette in a simple blue printed poplin dress and white sandals. The girl stands tall. Around her neck, a silver cross pendant reflects the sun, giving her a regal bearing.

At the registration window, Mangla gets her room number, room key, and a packet with relevant BHU information. The University busboy follows her to her room. She unlatches the door and enters a small dark space. The busboy sets the bags on the cracked dull gray cement floor. Next time she's home she will have to remember to pick up a colorful throw rug. The chipped walls are freshly whitewashed to provide a clean look.

She hangs her bag on the hook by the door and flicks the switch, but the bulb dangling on a wire is feeble. The plug and the bedside table by the jute-woven charpoys beg for a bedside lamp. Mangla picks the one near the window. At least she will get some daylight and cool air. She unrolls her thin mattress, pillow, and sheet, and covers them with the beige handwoven *khes*—a bedcover during the day, and a top sheet at night.

The room has a small window with green shutters on the outside and a screen on the inside to keep insects out. She runs her fingers over the dust-covered open-paned casement. The paint on it is peeling, and the grout between the windowpanes is tan with dirt.

She hums a song as she unpacks her box of books and puts them on the desk by the bed. She stacks her clothes in the wooden cupboard, her *charkah* by the bed and her *havan* tray on one of the shelves. Her growling stomach and the lunch the schedule, tells her it's time for lunch. She locks the door and makes her way to the dining hall.

Mangla is one of the last ones there. She washes her hands in the sink by the entrance and sits cross legged on one of the little wooden *piddhas*, about six inches off the ground, in front of low tables. By this time, most of the tables have emptied. The Hindu Brahmin waiter, with his sacred thread around his chest and over his shoulders, serves her a *thali* of dal, vegetable *sabzi*, rice, *chapati*, pickle and yogurt. It smells good. She eats with her hands as is the custom. She smiles at the girl sitting next to her whose *thali* is almost empty.

"I guess I'm a bit late for lunch."

"Yes! Forgive me, I must go and unpack." With that the girl gets up, washes her hands, and rinses her mouth at the basin.

Despite her cousin's warning about dorm food and weight gain, Mangla savors her food. Clearly, she needs to come earlier if she wants to meet other girls.

Outside, she walks under the shade of the *peepal* tree. She looks up at the twittering sparrows foraging. One day, she too will fly, she thinks as she looks for the classroom building.

***

By the entrance Mangla finds a big earthenware pot full of drinking water. She dips the ladle then cups her left hand by her mouth. She pours water carefully into it with her right while sipping. "Ah---- hhh!" an audible sigh of relief escapes her. When she looks up, the pretty girl with the cross is waiting for a drink. "Here, let me pour water," Mangla says.

"Oh, no! I'm fine. Thank you." The girl frowns and turns her face away, puts out her hand and swiftly takes the ladle to help herself.

Mangla feels rejected. What is up with this girl? She tries again. "Hello, I'm Mangla. Isn't it hot?"

"Yes." The girl juts her chin out as if someone is dragging the word out of her. Finally, with a haughty tone the girl says, "I'm Basanthi." Basanthi gulps down water and wipes her satiated face with her scarf.

Her name surprises Mangla. It is a Hindu name, but she wears a dress and a cross like an Anglo Indian. From the corner of her eye, she sees a couple of older girls approach them. One of them has a pitted face from smallpox and the other has long flowing hair to her waist.

The humid air could be cut with a knife. Mangla mops her brow with the end of her sari *pallu* as she says, "I love the spring season."

Basanthi smiles. "I was born in Spring. Despite my name, I can't wish away this beastly heat."

At least she has a sense of humor. Mangla says, "What's your major?" Before Basanthi can answer, the pockmarked girl yanks the ladle from her hand, and the longhaired girl tugs at her cross. "You are now at a Hindu University. Take that off."

Basanthi tries to put the cross under her dress. "No! Annie Besant the founder said all religions are welcome at BHU."

Mangla notices her defiant moist eyes. The cross must be sacred to her. The pock-face girl tosses her hair, frowns, and jerks at the cross chain. "You're insubordinate to a senior. Say, "I hate Christ, fifty times."

Mangla's cousins had warned her of self-anointed hazers. Before Basanthi can say anything, Mangla says, "Who gave you the right? Leave her alone."

The two girls turn to her. "Who are you?"

"I'm Mangla. You should be ashamed of yourselves. We're fighting for freedom of our country and Gandhi--" Mangla waves at Basanthi to scram and is relieved to see the girl retreat.

"Ah! So, we have a freedom fighter amongst us, do we?" The two girls grab hold of Mangla's arm and pull at her sari so that it unravels, and she is left standing there in her petticoat and blouse.

Her face reddens as she sees the gardener look up at them. He waves his hoe at the girls and yells, "Have you no shame? Humiliating a young girl in public? I'll report you to the warden if you don't leave her alone right now."

The older girls bolt, as Mangla wraps her sari around her. Full of anger and shame, she slowly makes her way back to her room.

***

Still no roommate, and it is almost time for dinner. The whole incident with the hazers unnerves Mangla. She has experienced bullying from boys but never from mean girls. How could they be so?

Mangla doesn't feel like facing the girls, but she's hungry. She walks back to the dining hall and sees that dinner looks a bit more formal than lunch, although the servers are still attired in *dhoti*. The dishes are served in bronze brass copper amalgam *kansi* metal *thalis* and *katoris* to hold gravy and yogurt dishes. The professors and administrators are dressed in robes and seated at the head table on a raised platform.

She looks around for Basanthi. She imagines they will sit together and commiserate about the behavior of the older girls—clearly out of line with BHU stated doctrine of interfaith tolerance. It would be like being called a *bhangi*. But Basanthi is already at a table that is full.

Love Partitioned

After dinner, the faculty and administrators take off their gowns hang them up on the stand and leave from the door behind their dais. At the student tables, the girls begin to chat with each other.

Mangla's *chauki* is agog with the latest Kundan Lal Saigal movie. A girl who has seen the "Street Singer" tells them that it is a tear-jerker. Kanan Devi is phenomenal in the movie. Saigal's rendition of Nawab Wajid Ali's *Thumari* is loaded with metaphors of cruelty and incarceration by the British, like a bride who is being abused by cruel in-laws. She begins to sing it in a soulful melodious voice. Girls from other tables turn to hear her.

But before she gets to the end of her song, there is a commotion at the door. Mangla sees the senior girls enter, including the ones from the water pot. As the group move towards their dinner tables, Mangla spies Basanthi slipping out the faculty door behind the dais.

She tries to follow Basanthi, but finds her exit blocked by the two girls. "Where do you think you're going?" they ask.

All the girls at her *chauki* turn to Mangla as if to say, do you know them? She doesn't say anything but looks down.

The older girls drag Mangla up the steps to the now empty dais, prod her chest and push her. "Girls, we have a Gandhi follower amongst us. She will bow and touch our feet in extreme humility."

The pock-marked girl pushes Mangla down to the ground and says, "Repeat after me. I'm a whore. I'm a brother fucker."

Mangla stays quiet.

The girl with long hair chews on the cigarette in her mouth as she wallops a fist on Mangla's back. Mangla winces but stays stoically quiet. "Practicing non-violence, are we?"

"Looks like you need reinforcement here." A couple of other senior girls come to the stage and kick and punch Mangla in the chest and face. It hurts. She feels taste of blood in her mouth. But she's not going to let these evil girls win. She looks up as if asking for divine help.

There is general cry from the girls sitting on *piddhas*. "Leave her. What has she done?"

More girls tower over the protesters and drag them up to the stage where they begin to taunt and kick them. Mayhem ensues and water glasses spill.

One of the senior girls comes running in and says, "The warden."

The room clears fast in fear of the menace as the freshmen girls look around in a daze and yell after them, "cowards." Mangla wonders if Basanthi alerted the warden.

***

Mangla finds her first class in a beautiful colonial central administrative building. The broad verandah makes the rooms dark but cool, and she takes a seat by the window.

She counts ten girls in her Hindi Literature class. Ram Mohan Rai, a brilliant author, is their professor. One of the girls in the class is Basanthi. Their first assignment is to tell their personal family story and what they hope to do in the future. The professor points to a girl to start.

She stands up in a white sari and, rubbing her hands together, tells her story. She was engaged to be married at age nine to a man twenty-five years her senior. Fortunately, he died before the marriage date, so she doesn't have to live a widow's life. But her family now cannot find a suitable marriage partner for her because everyone is afraid that she will bring their son bad luck. She has decided to not marry but to study and dedicate her life to teaching widows how to respect their lives.

The next student who stands up wears a white khadi sari, like Mangla. Holding her head high, she tells them that she gave birth to four children every nine months. The first three were girls. Her husband's family wanted a grandson, of course. That was why he raped her every night until she fell pregnant. Her youngest, a boy, was born without fingers or toes. Her in-laws threw her out. Fortunately, her own family were forward-thinking and believed that women deserved better. They took her back to their home and are raising her children while she studies. She joined BHU to study politics. She wants to free India from the curse of spousal rape and to write poetry to uplift the lives of women.

The next girl sheds tears as she tells her story. She was to be married at 10. But because her family couldn't pay the dowry, the groom's family got up and walked out right after the exchange of garlands. So technically she was married, but practically she wasn't. Her mother felt she couldn't face the community ever again and set herself on fire. This girl was studying Hindi and sociology to bring about change in child marriage.

Then Basanthi tells her story. Her journey to BHU is full of courage and fortitude. Mangla can't believe the hardships that came her way. Her family lives in Jammu and Kashmir. Her Brahmin grandfather married an Englishwoman and was rejected by his Hindu family. Basanthi says that Hindus are a bigoted lot, hidebound to their archaic caste system. Her grandfather converted to Christianity because it was important to her grandmother. In doing so, he lost his caste. Only the Anglo-Indian community accepted them. Then Basanthi's own English mother left her to return to England. Then her beloved, trusted Ayah left when she was about eight, thrown out of the home unfairly by her stepmother. The cross she wears around her neck is the only remaining connection to her mother. She admits she has problem trusting people and wants to educate women to be free thinkers like Annie Besant.

Mangla is filled with compassion. How awful it must be to lose your mother. She wonders if it would have been easier to have your mother die. She can't imagine *Ammaji* leaving them. And to lose her Ayah—how awful. She wants to tell Basanthi that not all Hindus are bad. She thinks of Sabiha and Surjjo, and how lucky they all are to have *Ammaji*'s love. She silently applauds Basanthi's moxie that took her to the convent and then to BHU.

Mangla's sheltered life pales in comparison to the courageous stories of these women. She fiddles with papers on which she has scribbled some notes about her own story. Should she even bother to read? It is about her parents and their love for all. She has no plans, no real suffering or ambition—just a quest for learning and making a difference in lives of women in a free India. Her cousin didn't warn her of this requirement. As she is called to tell her story, she stands up, trembling, and tells it in a small voice.

After class, Mangla walks towards Basanthi with arms held out, and calls, "Basanthi, I really—" But Basanthi hurries on without a backward glance. Mangla drops her hands and mutters under her breath, "Who does she think she is?" Then, as she turns around to go to her next class, a charitable thought occurs to her that maybe Basanthi needed go to the toilet.

***

The religion class is larger than the literature class. Professor Ramdas is their teacher, and when he enters, a hush falls. All the girls make their eyes big. Mangla sucks in her breath and thinks that even a Greek God would be envious of him.

In this class, every girl has to explain their religion and what it means to them. Most of the girls are Hindus. Some wear an "Om" pendent. Mangla doesn't. There are three Muslim girls with star and crescent moon pendants around their necks. Mangla tells the class about her *Arya Samaji* Hindu daily practice of *havan* and *Namaz.*

Basanthi is the only one wearing a cross, so Mangla is surprised when Basanthi tells the class that her father and grandfather both taught her about theosophy, which promotes freedom of thought, truth above all religion, and the universal brotherhood of humanity without distinction of race, creed, sex, caste, or color. Basanthi chose BHU because Annie Besant helped it develop from a college to a university. Annie Besant was not only the president of the theosophy society, but also a personal friend of her grandfather. Mangla has never heard of theosophy and resolves to learn more about it.

Professor Ramdas then recites mantras and sacred verses in his sonorous voice. Mangla can feel the pitter-patter of her heart. Embarrassing. Then he recites verses from the Quran and psalms from the Bible. When he lucidly explains the meanings behind the sacred texts, Mangla feels that heaven has come to earth and all doubts leave her. She's ready to embrace whichever faith he is talking about. She can't take her eyes off him.

Professor Ramdas takes the roll call, and after that he calls every girl by name. By the time he says Mangla's name, she is in a trance, ready to do whatever he will ask of her.

At the dining room *chauki,* every girl talks of Professor Ramdas as if he is God himself descended on to earth. Mangla wants to ask Basanthi more about theosophy, but Basanthi sits at a different *chauki,* where the Muslim girls sit. Mangla waves to her but Basanthi ignores her overture. Is she avoiding her? Mangla wonders.

That Thursday, Professor Ramdas, his lovely young wife, and infant son are the guests of honor at the headmaster's table. Girls at Mangla's *chauki* look at each other, as their teenage romantic dream balloons pop. "He's already married," they whisper. After dinner he recites the Golden rule from every religion. The girls whisper atwitter to each other. I know he is married. But his class is enchanting. He is so learned in all religions. Just the way he recites everything from memory, so impressive. I hope I can learn that skill. And so on.

***

Before bed, Mangla wants to finish reading, "*Dharti Mata*" on which Sehgal's movie is based. With no roommate, the time gets away from her and she reads late into the night. She wakes up and to her dismay sees the sun already high in the sky. By the time she finishes her *havan,* the clock is striking the hour. Out the window, the bulbul sings from the treetop as it flies towards the classroom building, beckoning her to hurry up or she'll be late. She has only ten minutes to make it to her class. She picks up her books and runs, locking the door behind her.

She enters the classroom as Professor Rai calls her name.

"Here," she responds and slips into her seat. Everyone turns towards her as if to say, why late? What happened? Even after just a few days, they are used to Basanthi coming in after her; today the girl is already seated.

Professor Rai tells them to open the book, and as usual he selects a girl to read aloud. Mangla sees with dismay that in her haste she has brought the wrong book with her. She slinks under the desk hoping she won't be called upon.

"Mangla will now read from where Neela left off," the Professor says. Neela is sitting a few tables down. Why was he picking on her?

Mangla gets up and her stomach rumbles. She has skipped her breakfast. "Sir," she says, "I'm sorry, I got up late, missed my breakfast and picked up the wrong book." Hoping that her confession will win his forgiveness, she points to her dog-eared copy of the errant "*Dharti mata.*" Her heart sinks with every deliberate step he takes towards her desk. He holds up the book for all to see. He says, so everyone in the class can hear, "I expect you girls to have better taste in Hindi literature than this movie trash. That's why I gave you an extensive book list to choose from. I'm disappointed in your choice, Mangla."

She colors as everyone's eyes turn to her. Why did she even bother to come to class? She wants to run but feels her feet glued to the ground.

"Did you read any of the Premchand novels I assigned?" says the professor.

"Yes sir, I read *Shatranj ke Khilari*."

"Tell the class about that book and compare its literary style to this." He crinkles his nose in disgust as he waves her book in her face.

Mangla's mouth is dry. Why is he so mean? Other girls all look down. The professor's eyes are steadfast on her. She is hungry, thirsty, and feels downright miserable. "Come on, Miss Mangla. Tell us the story of what you read."

Mangla nods her head and begins. "The story is about chess players who are engaged in game of life--" fortunately she hears the bell ring and heaves a sigh of relief. At least the game of life just delivered her a checkmate.

Professor Rai walks back to the podium and says, "Girls, next time we will talk about term paper and debating society. Come prepared—especially you, Miss Mangla. I gave out that information on the first day of class. I want you all to be responsible students and not behave like Miss Mangla there. Please read carefully what is expected of you for every class. Do you understand?"

All heads nod as he leaves the room.

"A crowing rooster would have paled in comparison," Mangla whispers. But as soon as he's gone, girls cluster around and offer her sympathy.

"You're so responsible—"

"He wasn't fair—"

"So mean—"

Hey, can I borrow *Dharti mata* to read? I've heard it is great—"

"The movie is wonderful—great songs."

"Cheer up Mangla—"

"Maybe he fought with his wife before leaving home—"

Everyone tries to comfort Mangla except Basanthi, who left right behind Professor Rai.

Mangla leaves and goes to her room and lies down on her bed and cries. She misses her home, her siblings, her parents, and now the professor picked on her! Life isn't fair.

She's done everything perfectly, and one slip and she's dragged on the carpet. She's filled with remorse as she realizes she's missed the rest of her morning classes. How careless and irresponsible she is. In her head she hears *Ammaji*'s reprimand. She's starving and thirsty. She gets up to wash her face, drinks water and makes her way to the dining hall. For once she's glad that she doesn't have a roommate who could witness her misery. Maybe she is lucky to have a single room.

Tomorrow will be better. She shakes herself, holds her head high, opens the door and walks out, locking the door behind her.

XXXXXXX

Manjula Waldron

7 Basanthi: Life Begins at BHU

Basanthi's father arranged a work trip to take her to BHU. He offered to show her Gorakhpur, her birthplace, and Benaras, a holy Hindu place they had visited with her mother when Basanthi was a baby. Basanthi was excited to have time alone with her father before starting BHU.

But then, at the last minute, Jill jumps in to say that she and her daughters have never been to this area. They also want to see the Hindu holy places. Bhumi, as usual, acquiesces, and Basanthi's personal trip with him is turned into another battle for his attention. Basanthi has tried hard to patch up her problems with Jill, but the more she tries the worse it seems to get. Just this morning, she wanted to take a *tonga* to BHU to be early to register. But Jill insisted that they go together; she said her daughters needed to see BHU in case they also want to study there. Then they all diddled around and made Basanthi late.

On campus, a long line of girls snake beyond the gate to register. Anger fills Basanthi's body as she twiddles the cross around her neck. When they reach the college gates the uniformed policeman with his long baton stops them. "Only the students can go beyond this point. May I see your admission form please?" He looks at the three girls. Basanthi reaches into her bag and hands it to him.

"Which of you is Basanthi?"

Basanthi comes forward. He opens the door to let her in and closes the door behind her.

Jill says, "But you have to let us in."

The policeman waves his baton at her. "No madam. Please move aside and let other girls enter." He goes past Jill and inspects other girls' admission letters.

"But we've come all the way from Jammu," Jill says.

He ignores her and only lets admitted girls in.

She hears Bhumi say, "Come let's go." He walks towards the waiting *tonga*.

"I'll report you to the principal. Do you know who I am?"

Basanthi hears her father say in a commanding voice, "Jill, please, let's go. The *tonga* is waiting for us."

She waves him aside and continues to disparage the security guard. Bhumi, with sagging shoulders, turns around and shaking his head walks towards the *tonga*. Color creeps up Basanthi's cheeks as she looks around to see if anyone witnessed this scene. She turns back to see her father wave from the *tonga*. Her eyes well up as she waves back and whispers, "I love you Papa. Be strong whatever life brings. I will too. I promise." Then she joins the long line of girls waiting to register.

In the plains, the muggy heat of the monsoon is uncomfortable after the Jammu coolness. Sweat pours down Basanthi's face and her dress clings to her body. She pulls the scarf from her neck and wipes her brow. She flaps the registration envelope in front of her face like a fan. It must be around noon now. Her throat is parched. Her stomach rumbles. She feels sick. The sun plays hide and seek above the treetops and reflects off her cross as she creeps up to the registration desk. After she registers, she collects her bags and sets off to look for her room.

Her room is empty, and to calm her nerves, she sits down cross-legged on the beige jute weave of her charpoy. Her hands automatically go to the cross on her chest, and she says the Lord's prayer her Ayah taught her all those years ago. Her breathing becomes quieter. When she feels quite calm, she goes out to find food and water.

***

Then, of course, on the same day, comes the degrading water pot incident with the Hindu senior girls and that Hindu girl named Mangla. It splits open a long, festering wound of being just a half, never a whole like others. As an Anglo-Indian, will Basanthi ever escape the social stigma and the condemning eyes of Hindus? Will she meet the same fate as she did in Jammu when her grandfather took her to meet his Hindu relatives? His family wouldn't even open their doors. She and her grandfather waited outside for a long time before he said, "Prejudice closes hearts. It is the biggest travesty of humans. We must forgive them, for they are afraid to bend their views."

"What's travesty?" She had asked.

"It's pretending. Like they are doing now. Hiding behind their closed doors when they are afraid to open their hearts."

After her grandfather's death, and after her mother left, Ayah tried again to take her to her granduncle's house, but again, no one opened the door. They stood there until a young boy Basanthi's age ran out of the gate with a cricket bat in his hand. She heard someone call, "Jay don't forget to return by five."

Basanthi moved forward and called, "Jay. I'm--" but Ayah pulled her back and said, "Let's go home. God will punish them."

"Why, what have they done?"

Ayah sings, "Love your kin. Do not sin. Jesus taught us to Love one another."

***

On the charpoy in her dorm room, Basanthi ponders Ayah's simple beliefs. You follow the bible; you go to heaven you don't then you go to hell. But what about Hindus? They have so many Gods. Would they all go to hell? Ayah would have surely condemned those girls at the water pot.

Damn Hindus. Who do they think they are? Rigid, intolerant, and virtuous; reincarnated; blessed by thousands of Gods. Basanthi's teeth clench, and her jaws tighten. She rocks herself and jiggles her cross harder and lies down on the bare jute charpoy. Its roughness feels smooth compared to her jagged nerves.

There isn't much to unpack, just a small bag of clothes. She undoes her thin bedroll and brings out her pillow and sheet. But her mind hasn't let go of the anger she feels towards Mangla, the privileged Hindu girl and whispers, "I don't need Hindu charity. I can cope on my own."

She brings out her notebook and rereads her assigned pre-work for the first literature class; she adds a few more stinging comments about her estranged Hindu family. Especially the way Jay ignored her whenever she saw him around town in Jammu. She gives her pent-up hurt feelings towards all Hindus a free reign on the paper.

**

At the dinner hall, she finds a *chauki* close to the head table where the professors and the warden will sit. Good, no sign of that Hindu girl. An older woman enters, wearing an austere loose gray and black *chappals*, open sandals with leather straps around her big toes and feet. She is short and stocky, with thinning henna colored hair cut to just below her ears. Her eyes are small and beady. Her nose is like a parrot's beak. Her lips are painted red like actresses from a cheap theater. As she dons her robes, the girls whisper, "That's Mrs Karachurian, the warden."

"A name like that would make her Syrian Christian from Kerala," says another girl.

How do they know? Basanthi wonders.

A couple of girls wear the Islamic pendant of a star and sickle moon. Another two girls have crosses like hers. Good, there are a few more non-Hindus around. She will eat with them. She breathes a sigh of relief as the meal is served and introduces herself to other girls around the *chauki*.

Soon other professors in robes take their places at the head table. Curious, Basanthi asks who they are and why they have chosen to eat with them. Do they live on campus? No one seems to know. After dinner, the professors and warden leave. That's when the senior girls from the water pot enter. Basanthi gets up and dashes out of the faculty exit door. She hides behind the door and watches them drag Mangla onto the dais. Up to no good again. She runs, following the signs that lead her to the Warden's home.

Shaking, she knocks on the door.

"Come in."

59

The warden is taking down her hair. She seems to be getting ready for bed. Basanthi's anger gives her courage to steady herself on the door frame and speak, "Sorry to bother you miss---" and then she explains what happened by the water pot and how the same girls were now picking on the girls in the dining hall. "I am worried especially for the girl who came to my rescue by the waterpot. She sits at another *chauki*." The Warden puts on her shoes and shakes her head. "Hazing is against the rules, but they do it anyway," she says as she hurries towards the dining hall.

Suddenly, Basanthi feels exhausted from the day's events. She is repelled by the thought of confronting the mean Hindu girls.

"I'm very tired, miss, from my journey. May I go to my room now and rest? Unless you need me."

The warden waves a goodnight, and Basanthi drags herself to her room, where she falls into a restless sleep.

***

During their first week, Basanthi is surprised to find that she and Mangla are in the same classes. That girl seems to be following her between class meetings, too. Why is she stalking her? When Mangla gives her life story, Basanthi finds it sickeningly perfect. Two parents, two daily prayer practices, spinning *charkah*, following Gandhi principles—everything has perfect for Mangla. No adversity. How is that possible? What is she hiding? Other girls were child brides or lost their families, but not Mangla. And her family are do-gooders, too, earning their karma points.

Basanthi stops by the library and gets Prem Chand's book "Nirmala" from the assigned reading list. She means to use it for her term paper. The first reading deals with Hindu child marriage. Her ex-Hindu roommate in Jammu, who was the Maharajah's granddaughter, told her many stories of child marriages in the royal court. She, herself, was a child widow and had no future other than to sit around and be excluded from life. Instead, she ran away from home and found shelter in the convent, converted to Christianity, and decided to become a nun to serve others. Basanthi feels superior that Anglo-Indians have never believed in the evil child marriage practice.

In the library, Basanthi feels safe. She can immerse herself in the worlds of her mother and grandmother in England and pretend to have a perfect life there one day. In the convent, she found borrowing books early guaranteed her access to the books without having to spend her scant scholarship money to buy them. The library is her haven, the librarians her friends.

Following week, she finds Mangla in the library studying away. She retracts. What is the Hindu girl doing encroaching on her sacred territory? What is she doing in Basanthi's library?

Love Partitioned

But why is Basanthi even wasting her thoughts onMangla? Is she prejudiced? She must admit feeling a sympathetic pang when Professor Rai picked on Mangla in class, but also, she felt the Hindu girl had it coming for doing everything by the rules: coming to class on time, sitting in front, always prepared to answer his questions. In the back of her mind, she hears her grandfather say, "Prejudice closes hearts." Is her heart closed?

She walks to the religion section of the library, far away from the literature section, where Mangla sits engrossed in a book. Basanthi picks up Annie Besant's book on Theosophy. She's sad that the BHU co-founder died in 1933. She would have liked to have met her. She opens the book and thinks fondly of her father telling her how important the views of theosophy were to his own father. As she got older, he kept trying to engage her in discussions, whenever he could get away from Jill's prying eyes. Her heart warms, as she checks out the book and returns to her room.

Basanthi's deeply engrossed in interplay of faith and reason when she hears a loud knock on the door.

"Who is it?" She asks.

"Miss Raina. This is Mrs Karachurian, the warden."

"Just a minute." Apprehension fills her; at the convent, visits from nuns bode ill. Reluctantly she opens the door and looks at the warden. For some absurd reason this woman reminds her of Jill. It makes her want to giggle, but she stifles it and assumes a somber posture.

The warden looks around the room waves her hands and says, "I'm afraid the roommate I assigned you won't be coming. There's been a death in her family, and she has withdrawn her application for this year."

Basanthi waits.

"Since you're a first-year student I can't give you a single room. You understand that don't you?"

Basanthi nods. What's there to say? The Warden holds all the cards.

"Our policy is to give single rooms to seniors and graduate students, and there are many on the waiting list."

Basanthi waits, twisting the end of her sleeve. She prepares herself for more to come.

"There's another girl in the same boat as you. That will be your new roommate." Basanthi nods. At the convent, she's been on this switcheroo road.

"Come, then. Let's walk over to the room and you can look at it."

As they walk to the next building. The warden opens the door to the new room; no one is there, but clearly someone has unpacked and claimed a side—the side with the window.

"I hope this is OK," says the Warden. "I'll have the busboy move your bags later."

"Oh, that's OK, I can do it. I carried them myself when I moved in."

The Warden looks at Basanthi closely. "I hope you are drinking a lot of water. Your body needs to adjust to the heat here after cooler and dryer air in Jammu."

She has been hesitant to drink water from the waterpot. She only drinks it during meals. "I have been ill prepared for this, Mrs Karachurian. Is there any way I can get a jug to bring water to my room?"

"Of course, I will tell the dining hall waiter to give you one. By the way, since your family lives so far away, in the future, if you ever need anything, or feel sick, come to my office and ring the bell and I'll be sure to get you help. Your health and wellbeing are important to us. Now, are you sure you'll be OK in this room?" "Yes, miss."

"Well, I'm looking forward to knowing you better. I've read only good things about you. Your roommate comes from a good family, and like you is cum laude from her high school. Here's your key. As I stressed in orientation, for your own safety and your roommate's, please be sure to always lock the door when you leave the room. When inside, please bolt the door from inside."

"What dangers I should be aware of, Miss?"

"Sometimes strangers get past the night security and try to visit our girls. At other times there are thieves prowling, or hazers looking for easy targets."

She takes the key from the warden and returns to her first room and quickly repacks. Back in the new room, she wonders about her still-absent roommate. She feels grateful to the warden for reminding her to stay hydrated. She ventures out to the water pot, looks anxiously around her, gulps quickly, then retreats to a cool spot under a mango tree, where she spreads out her scarf to lie down. Soon her tiredness takes over. She falls asleep under the tree, grasping her cross.

***

Sometime later she awakens to Mangla gently touching her. '

"Basanthi. Wake up, you sleepy head. Ding! Ding! It's dinnertime."

"Oh, I must've fallen asleep. I was so tired."

"I see that," Mangla says.

"I had to move from my room."

"I don't have a roommate yet, either. Let's go to dinner, "Mangla says "Why don't you go on without me?" Basanthi waves.

"Are you trying to avoid me?"

"Why would you think that?"

"Don't know. Just a feeling I get when I'm around you." Mangla puts out her hand with an invitation to grip.

Basanthi hesitates, but reluctantly grabs Mangla's hand and heaves herself up. "I guess I'm hungry."

"Then let's go," Mangla says. When they reach the dining hall, Mangla opens the screen door and says, "The royalty goes in first."

Love Partitioned

Basanthi laughs and rejoins, "Go on. Is the violet calling the morning glory blue?"

"I have a feeling we're cut from the same cloth," Mangla says as they wash their hands at the sink.

They walk past the head *chauki* and Basanthi waves and says, "Hello Mrs. Karachurian."

"Hello, Basanthi. Are you feeling better and settled in?"

"Yes Miss. Thank you. I moved in."

"How do you like your new roommate?"

Basanthi begins with "I---" but then follows the warden's gaze, which rests on Mangla. The books on the desk should have alerted her. "Mrs. Karachurian, indeed we are in classes together and now we will be rooming together as well, won't we?" Basanthi turns to Mangla and forces herself to smile.

The warden says, "Well, go along and enjoy your dinner. I expect great things from you both." She waves them along.

Mangla looks at Basanthi and bursts out laughing. You--?

Basanthi can't help but join her. God has a strange sense of humor.

They point at each other. "You're my--".

"Okay, laughing feels good," Basanthi says, as she slips onto her *piddha*. As dinner is served, Basanthi contemplates the fate that has given her a Hindu roommate, and not just any Hindu, but miss perfect Mangla. Couldn't she at least have had another Anglo-Indian? She remembers Ayah telling her that God never fails and looks after everyone.

Towards the end of dinner, Basanthi hears the catchy tune of *Duniya rang Rangili baba*—the world is colorful—from Mangla's *chauki*. Everyone joins in. A girl uses the *chauki* as a *tabla*, drum, and another joins with a spoon on the metal *thali*. One of the girls gets up and dances. It's Basanthi's favorite song, from Sehgal's movie *Dharti Mata*. She feels like joining in, but instead she leaves the dining hall for the library to avoid Mangla. She'll sit in the library until closing. Hopefully it will be late enough to find Mangla asleep. Indeed, when she returns to the room, Mangla is sleeping. Basanthi tiptoes in, changes, and slips into bed. But sleep eludes her for a long time. In the next cot, the Hindu girl breathes rhythmically, untroubled in sleep as she is in waking life.

XXXXXXX

8 First year at BHU: Mangla- Basanthi

Few days pass until the Hindu hazers, also called raggers, strike again with their predator paws. This morning, when they got out of class and no professor was around, two of the girls follow Basanthi. Then two more seniors join, and the four of them take turns pushing her. The girls, all Hindus, yank at her cross. Mangla rushes to aid, but the four fight back. Basanthi and Mangla fall in a heap on each other.

"Love birds, love birds," taunt the hazers, and soon there is a crowd of girls pointing at them and laughing.

Mangla is mortified as she sees Basanthi's red perspiring face and feels her panting breath. No wonder Basanthi is so anti-Hindu.

After dinner, they return to their room. To calm herself, Mangla brings out her *charkah* and begins spinning.

"I'll get ready for bed. I feel exhausted. It's been quite a day," Basanthi says as she gets out her towel and change of clothes and heads to the bathroom.

Basanthi returns from the bathroom with a jug of water and sets it on the bedside table as Mangla continues spinning. She connects the cotton to the thread on the spool and begins to move the wheel while pulling out the cotton into a fine thread.

"My that looks complicated," Basanthi says, and turns to get into bed. "Not really. It calms me. Want to try?" She brings the *charkah* to Basanthi's bed, sits, and guides the girl's hand gently to show her the motion. She feels Basanthi's irregular breath and tense hands.

"It helps if you relax. Just breathe in and breathe out. Try it," she says. Basanthi breathes and her hands relax.

"See, it makes it easy. It's not that hard, is it? Next time I go home I'll have *Pitaji* get you one so we can spin together and support Gandhiji to free India. Its wheel is even part of the congress flag."

Mangla explains that Gandhi was promoting *khadi gramudyog* As the villagers spin their own cloth they become part of their local economy, gain pride in Indian goods, and bring Brits to their knees by boycotting British mill cloth on which high taxes are levied for Indians. "My parents joined the movement, and we only wear khadi. Feel my sari." She puts her pallu in Basanthi's hand.

Her eyes widen, "It's a fine and soft cloth."

"It depends on how fine a thread you spin to exchange in community coop shops."

"I like learning new things," Basanthi says. She spins for a moment, but her hands still move stiffly, and she keeps breaking the thread.

"*Pitaji* says to any learning remember the 3 Ps—Patience, Practice, and Perseverance. Give the thread some slack." She has Basanthi hold her hand as she guides her.

"It's relaxing. You're generous. Thank you."

" Let's spin a little longer," Mangla says. "Not all Hindus are the same, you know. I want to be your friend."

Soon Basanthi is spinning quite well. "It is calming." She says.

Mangla closes the *charkah* and stacks it neatly beside her bed. "I'm collecting my spun threads to exchange for a fine red silk *dupatta* for my sister Sabiha's wedding present."

Hindu and Islamic prayers I know. I'd love to learn about Ayah's Christian prayers," Mangla says. "We heard the hymns from the church next door on Sundays, but never stepped inside one. Is it true that only baptized Christians can go in?"

"Mangla, I don't know I find church a bore. But, I too, have a confession to make."

Mangla waits.

"You're right. I've been avoiding you. I feared Hindus. The hazers didn't help. You know my story. Please be patient with me."

"Oh, I know you are a beautiful kindred spirit, Basanthi. My parents say we need courage to stand up to the closed-minded orthodox Hindus if we want a free India from oppression for all people." Basanthi yawns. "I'm tired. Let's talk this over another time."

Mangla watches the girl shut her eyes. She's glad for the crack in their icy relationship. Yes, she will be patient with her roommate. Soon Basanthi's cross rises and falls in steady rhythm across her chest as she sleeps.

***

The next morning Mangla, as usual, gets up early and completes her rituals. She prods Basanthi as requested, but Basanthi only turns over and goes back to sleep. In class, Mangla saves the seat beside hers, so Basanthi can slide in without much notice when she arrives.

After dinner, unlike other girls who walk in clusters of friendly chatter, Basanthi heads to the library and Mangla follows her. That weekend as the library closes, she walks up to Basanthi and looks at what she is reading. It is a reserved book of Annie Besant's personal diaries, donated to BHU by Annie Besant herself. "I know so little about her. I want to learn more," Mangla says, as they walk back to their room.

Basanthi, her face lights up like Diwali lamps, declares: "I want to be like Annie Besant, an educator, maybe a principal of a school. I want to empower women to make a difference in their own lives, and in the lives of their children, family and community."

"Oh, Basanthi, I, too, want to lift women from oppression and provide them freedom. But unlike you, I have no clear way for my ideas. I feel unprepared and inadequate at times." Mangla reaches out for Basanthi's hand. "Let's research BHU founder Annie Besant's life together. Maybe her life will inspire me and guide me how to put my passion into practice."

Mangla has been afraid Basanthi would resist her overture, but the girl just grips her hand harder. "I just got a couple of books on this very topic from the library. Let's make a pact to spend at least 30 minutes every evening to help each other clarify our vision."

"It's a deal," Mangla says.

That night, Basanthi brings out the book on Annie Besant's life, and they take turns reading each paragraph as the other interprets what it means to her. Sometimes, they debate.

Mangla says, "She articulates that both faith and reason have to work together through freedom of thought. Would you agree to create a Faith versus Reason debate society at BHU?"

"What a great idea. It will honor Annie Besant. Maybe we can persuade the Vice Chancellor's office to fund our effort."

"As we both turn sixteen this year, it could be a birthday gift to each other."

"You already know so much about Theosophy from your father," says Mangla. "Would you teach me about it? I know *Pitaji* would be interested as well."

Basanthi nods. She brings out another book she borrowed. "Reading this brings me closer to my father and warms my heart. Perhaps we can find some passages that underscore our own thinking and debate where they differ."

"Yes, that will prepare us for the debating society. But hopefully, we will be on the same team," Mangla says.

"Actually, it might be more fun if we are on opposing teams. It will make our reading hour more entertaining. Don't you think?"

"I like your confidence, Basanthi. I wish I felt that way about my debating skills."

"The nuns encouraged our talent to debate."

"I would love to better mine. Maybe you can coach me?"

"Let's go to bed now. Tomorrow will be soon enough," Basanthi says. Mangla yawns and says, "I'm tired too. But I look forward to learning."

Love Partitioned

***

For their term paper in Hindi Literature, they are each assigned one novel by celebrated writer Munshi Prem Chand to present to the class. They are to research the author's life and surmise the social leanings of the author and hold two debates—one on child marriage and the other on the dowry system. The third debate topic is left for the students to pick on their own, but it should be related to the current issues. The last debate will take them to the end of the year, at which time they'll enter a debate competition with other Universities.

The debate practice is set up for once a month and the teams have to make sure that every member gets a chance to debate. At the end of the term, they will vote for the best debater from each team to send to the inter-university competition.

Mangla chooses *Godaan*, which is Munshi Prem Chand's latest novel about economic deprivation and the exploitation of the poor. She suggests that if Basanthi selects *Nirmala*, one of his early writings on child marriage, they can collaborate in research on the author's life and then practice their opposing points of view.

As the term progresses, the girls discover that he is dead. Munshi Prem Chand was his pen name. His real name was Nawab Rai, and his early work was in Urdu. "Why would he change his name, I wonder," Mangla says.

"The nuns told me that women could not publish so they needed to give themselves a man's name," says Basanthi. "Not that Prem Chand was a woman." "Maybe he did it because he was born in the Northwest province. He was bilingual. Interesting what authors do for their audience "

"Perhaps we can ask Professor Rai about it."

"My cousin, Yashi, told me that Professor Rai, was a student of Munshi Prem Chand," Mangla says. "He was his Hindi literature professor. If you come to my sister Sabiha's wedding, then you will meet Yashi."

"Wow. Quite a connection."

"She will have a Muslim *Nikah* wedding ceremony, " Mangla says. "I've never been to a Muslim wedding," says Basanthi. "Come to think of it, I haven't been to too many weddings, Christian or otherwise."

"Neither have I to a Muslim wedding that is. My family and I are learning about it. We had to find a *wakil*, who can give her away. My father can't do it unless he converts to Islam." She tells Basanthi how Sabiha's wedding was arranged.

"Maybe I'll come," Basanthi says, and smiles shyly.

Mangla tries to give Basanthi a big warm hug, but the girl pulls away as if struck with a jolt of electricity.

***

The grass around Mangla is green and lush after the recent monsoon rains. The trees that line the courtyard are washed of their summer dirt and grime. Mango fruits have been plucked off their trees. Bitter smelling ripe yellow *nimboli* fruits hang off *neem* trees, and temporary swings made of thick jute rope and flat boards hang off their sturdy branches.

The courtyard is full of girls laughing, singing songs, and swinging—pushing each other to go higher and higher. "*Neem ki nimboli.* Bring my lover home soon." Mangla feels the breeze blowing on her face.

Basanthi walks past.

"Basanthi come and join us. It's *Teej*, you know."

Basanthi stops and raises her eyebrows.

"It's a festival to celebrate the monsoon. Young men look for future brides. Not here of course. But swinging is so much fun. I love it."

She gets off her swing and holds it out to Basanthi.

Basanthi hesitates but then comes over and sits down. Mangla begins to push her and sings a *teej* song *Sawan ki bahar.* Bring me my husband.

"Why do they keep singing about love and husbands?"

"Well, it's a festival to celebrate the life-giving monsoon. It's dedicated to the Goddess *Parvati* and signifies the fecundity that will follow the rains." "You don't believe in that kind of stuff, do you?"

"No, but it makes me feel carefree. Like that mynah that just took off." "It's true. I haven't felt so good in a while." Basanthi laughs, and a smile lights up her face.

Mangla continues to push her from behind. "I hope the mess will serve us *ghewar* tonight. It's a special sweet for this festival. You'll like it. At home, I'll have *Ammaji* make some for you. Hers is the best. Actually, my birthday is coming up in a few days. Since there are many festivals near this time of year, *Ammaji* always makes special feast food for me."

Basanthi looks like her heart is twisted. "Oh, that must be nice."

"In fact, I got a letter from her today, and she has invited you to come to my party. I've told her so many great things about you in my letters. She wants to meet you."

"That's nice of her," Basanthi says, and pumps her legs to swing herself higher. The next morning, on the way to class, Mangla sees a beautiful peacock, his feathers like a king's train splayed in a semicircle behind his arched back. A shiny halo pulses. His golden neck with its bejeweled crown is arched to woo the peahen that stands some distance away. He bows his head and shows off his satiny blue plumage. He wants to delight her, dance for her. He demands nothing of the peahen. He just swoons and flutters and preens to honor the monsoon's selfless gift of mating so nature can procreate.

Mangla hums the monsoon song "*Sawan ki bahar*" and approaches the dancing peacock. In fright, he runs away. The peahen follows, disapproving of Mangla's intrusion. She sings to them, "Don't run away from me my beloveds. I've only come to applaud you, to fly with you, to delight in your love. Don't be afraid come to me, my treasured ones. I bring you love. Dance for me with joy."

Mangla picks up the two long beautiful shiny shimmering aquamarine bejeweled feathers. A bequest to her from the peacock. She puts them in her notebook, planning to give one to Basanthi. She thinks how distorted civilized human society has become to oppress the female. How much humans could learn from their animal friends.

***

A few nights later, there is a banging on their door.

"Open up, girls."

"Who is it?" They had both been sleeping deeply and are rattled.

"We're seniors from down the hall. We have special gifts for you."

"For God's sake. Can't it wait till the morning?" Basanthi yells.

"No!" The banging gets louder.

Mangla feels scared. They'll wake the whole dorm. She goes to the door and opens it.

There are ten or more older girls outside. Half of them circle Mangla and half Basanthi. They drag them out separately. Mangla looks at Basanthi, who stares back her eyes wide. The senior girls tie a rope around their wrists and drag them out.

"What have we done?" Basanthi demands.

"You don't crawl in front of us and show deference."

"You aren't General Dyer, are you? What rule or law says that we need to crawl for you?" Basanthi says.

"Our hazing crawl law."

They are taken to an empty room down the hall where more girls wait, smoking. They offer them a cigarette.

"I don't smoke," Mangla says.

"Well, you will tonight," a big girl says and shoves a cigarette in her mouth.

Mangla chokes. The smoke fills her mouth, nostrils, and lungs. She coughs violently and tries to spit the offending thing out, but the girls keep shoving it back in. Nauseous, she feels like she'll die. Then they take a cup with a brown liquid and hold her mouth open and force it down her throat. As the fiery liquid burns her throat and gullet, she feels that she's collapsing. They hold her up and pour more in. She's never seen or tasted anything this foul.

Mangla yells, "Mrs. Karachurian. Mrs Karachurian, help me please."

They gang up on her. "She's not here tonight. It's her night out. You can yell all you want. Louder. Or has the cigarette burned your tongue?"

"Oh, leave her be. Can't you see she's really frightened?" another senior says.

"Oh shut up. It's our night. We need to toughen these lily-livered freshmen."

A couple of seniors begin dancing and disrobing until they are stark naked in front of Mangla. Their young, firm breasts dangle in front of her mouth.

"Now, repeat after us. You are a Goddess, and I am but a child. As I suck thy breasts, I drink your milk of kindness and worship thee." With that, two of them shove a nipple on each side of her mouth and command, "Suck me and say I drink thy heavenly juice. "

"I can't breathe," Mangla mutters as they take her tied hands to massage their groin and they do the same to hers.

She feels tingly and aroused.

"You better show respect. We bring this hazing tradition all the way from Oxford," says one of the girls.

Mangla wants to yell, "I don't know where Oxford is, and I don't care, and I live in this world and am a woman of the world. Our religion and culture demands we don't smoke or drink. What's wrong with that?" But they pour more of the liquid down her throat, and she gags.

Across the hall, in another room, they are doing the same to Basanthi. The last thing Mangla sees as she loses consciousness is Basanthi's stoic expression. She's one tough cookie.

When she wakes up, she is in her own bed. Her naked body is bundled to Basanthi's. Mangla's sari is wrapped around them like an Egyptian mummy. As she tries to untie it, she is forced to rub and wiggle against Basanthi, who stays still, as if asleep. Mangla doesn't understand her body's response—the taut nipples, tingling groin. Is she having a bad dream? Her mouth feels vile, yet she responds to Basanthi's closeness as her muscles go into an involuntary spasm that she has only experienced in her sleep. Maybe she's dreaming, she thinks, as she sinks into a deep, exhausted sleep.

The sun is quite high when she wakes up. Her head feels like a ton of bricks. She closes her eyes and trembles, vexed by the visceral shame she feels. Just as well Basanthi is gone. How can she face her? Today Basanthi will be first to class.

XXXXXXX

9 Healing the Rift

That evening as they walk around the college garden, Basanthi is distant and preoccupied. Mangla, too, maintains a physical distance as if there is an ice block stuck between them. They keep their conversation on the safe topic of movie actors they like.

"Did you see *President?*" Mangla says, knowing how much Basanthi likes its director, Sehgal. "About a woman being the president of the cloth mill?"

"It gave me hope for future of women in our country," Basanthi says. "Although the movie was a tragic love drama."

"Maybe we can go and see *Street Singer* and *Dharti Mata* when they come to the theaters around here. Did you know that Sehgal's related to us?"

"Truly? Maybe we can meet him."

"Maybe we could start a letter writing campaign, and as his fans, we all can invite him. If he's shooting a film around here, maybe he'll drop by."

"Perhaps your influence will help," Basanthi says in neutral tone.

Mangla begins to hum, and they sing "*Ek Bangla Banai Nyara*, --Build a wonderful house-- in which we all live together free and in loving harmony." They sing out of key, but it helps to regain their connection, strained as it feels.

There is something Mangla has been worrying about since this morning. She is supposed to leave the next day to go home for her birthday celebration. Basanthi hasn't said whether or not she wants to come, and after the night before, Mangla is shy to ask her.

"I've been thinking about your party," Basanthi says, now. "I'm sorry, but I don't think I can come. I've so much to study to prepare for our debate. You know it's harder and takes longer for me to read Hindi than you."

"But it's only for the weekend," Mangla says.

"That's when I can catch up."

"But *Ammaji* will be disappointed. Besides, you can meet Sabiha. She's getting ready for her wedding next month." Mangla's hands drop, and she bends to pick up a twig from the ground and snaps it.

"Please apologize for me. Tell her I'll come for the wedding for sure."

"If you come with me, we can go and see a movie. No Sehgal movie is playing but we have a theater nearby. It'll be my birthday treat." Mangla fights tears. She will miss Basanthi.

Mangla watches the other girl's face. Her expression is stony, as if Basanthi has a steel casing around her—a guard, her spikey protection. Mangla has made inroads, but the awful events of last night were a set-back.

"No, I can't," Basanthi says.

It's true that after the hazing, part of Mangla is glad that Basanthi isn't coming. She's not sure she can escape *Ammaji*'s canny eyes.

Mangla suddenly turns to her to hug her friend, but Basanthi pulls away.

The next morning, as Mangla prods Basanthi to wake up, Basanthi groans and clutches at her throat. "Oh, it hurts so bad. I think I'll stay in bed and rest today." Mangla puts her hand on Basanthi's forehead. "Good idea. Rest is best. At least you don't seem to have fever."

After breakfast, she brings dry toast and warm ginger and lemon tea in her flask from the dining hall. As she leaves for class, Mangla says, "Please drink tea to soothe your throat."

Basanthi just lies there quietly, clutching her stomach and neck.

***

Basanthi opens her eyes in a strange place, with Mrs. Karachurian and Mangla looking over her in concern. "How are you feeling Miss Raina?"

Basanthi asks, "Where am I?"

"In the infirmary." The warden tells her that she fainted in the bathroom. "Luckily after lunch Mangla came to check on you and found you. That was a few days ago."

"Oh no," says Basanthi. Her voice is weak. "I missed my classes."

"I took notes and will help you catch up. Now just get better." She orders orders. Mangla says to the listless girl lying on bed.

Basanthi scowls and she pokes her tongue out. Then in a faint voice she says, "Thank you Mangla."

At home, Mangla tells the people at her birthday party that Basanthi was ill and they are studying theosophy together.

One of her friends says, "That's perfect! Tonight, we should listen to Anis Kidwai's program on All India Radio."

"I haven't heard of it," Mangla says.

"Mrs. Kidwai's an eloquent speaker, and the show is broadcast from Lucknow as a part of their series: *Kya se Kya*. Her segment examines women's advances in social, cultural and educational conditions since the time of Indian Mutiny in 1857."

"I heard that they allow some people to be present in the audience. Maybe we can organize a trip there," another friend suggests.

"Lucknow isn't that far. Maybe I can invite my friends from Mr. Rai's class to come along. We're debating these topics. Do you know how to contact her?" Mangla asks.

Her neighborhood friends shake their heads.

"Maybe I will ask the Vice Chancellor's office at BHU, surely someone there will know."

That night, Mangla listens to the interactive talk show over the radio. It is a brief presentation from an invited orator who talks about Gandhiji's vision of women in free India. Then Mrs. Kidwai engages the audience to elaborate on their involvement with the topic.

Ideas begin to swirl in Mangla's creative entrepreneurial mind. If she can recruit more women from Mr. Rai's class to join her, she can persuade the warden to let them listen to this program in the common room. As an added incentive, she can begin a yoga class in the common room after the program. She can hardly wait to tell Basanthi as part of her plan to advance women's issues post-independence.

***

The month leading up to Sabiha's wedding is hectic.

Basanthi and Mangla work together on term papers, extra reading, and debate preparations along with planning for starting the faith and reason society. They still haven't talked about the hazing ritual, but Mangla feels its awkwardness starting to fade into the past.

Now, every week, they listen to Anis Kidwai's program in the common room. Mangla starts a yoga class during that hour and invites Professor Rai's class to join. Soon it is time for *Diwali*, the festival of lights, the Hindu New Year. It's Mangla's favorite holiday. Around the BHU neighborhood, stray firecrackers have begun to sound and shoot in the night sky. Mangla again invites Basanthi home, and this time she agrees.

On their long, slow *tonga* ride, Basanthi explains that in her Christian high school, *Diwali* wasn't a holiday, so Hindu girls couldn't go home for it. But the school did have a special feast and fireworks, "they told us stories from the *Ramayan*. The Hindu girls created *Ramleela*, skits of Ram and Sita's life. It was a lot of fun."

"My school closed for ten days for *Diwali*," says Mangla.

"One of my friend's parents used to send me gifts." Basanthi puts her cross in her mouth. "My stepmother never sent me anything—not even for Christmas."

Mangla puts her arm around Basanthi's shoulder and changes the subject. She tells her that Sabiha's fiancé, Mahmood Ali and his family lives around Peshawar. "They're all coming by train," Mangla says. "We haven't met them, but Sabiha has—though she had to wear a *burqa* and observe strict *purdah* supervised by the *mullah*." Mangla laughs. "Romantic, isn't it? Mahmood *Bhai*'s a progressive

Muslim and is so impressed by the openness to Islam of our family that he helped us to understand Islamic wedding customs.

"Mahmood *Bhai* told *Pitaji* that in Islam the bridegroom pays for the wedding and for the bride. *Pitaji* refused anything from his daughter's in-laws, as it's forbidden in Hindu religion. They agreed that Manhmood *Bhai* won't pay for Sabiha's hand but will pay for a simple *dawat-e-walima,* the wedding reception. That way they both uphold their religious values."

Basanthi says, "A Hindu *Diwali* and a Muslim wedding all in the same weekend. Splendid."

"On my birthday weekend we celebrated the engagement ceremony. The ladies dancing was so much fun. You'd have loved it. Mahmood *Bhai* sent over dinner and dessert for it. So different from a Hindu ceremony. We were so impressed by his generosity.

"They also sent Sabiha the beautiful satin and *salma* embroidered pink *garara.* She looked so elegant.

"Can you believe *Ammaji*'s mother refused to come because it is a Muslim wedding? Some of my relatives too. How small minded."

Basanthi looks ahead at the horse's bobbing head as he canters. "Look even the horse is agreeing with you."

"I'm so glad you're here, Basanthi. I can hardly wait for you to meet my family. I know you'll love them," says Mangla.

They arrive and Mangla introduces Basanthi to her family. Right away, the women start decorating each other's hands with henna.

"I've never had henna on my hands. As it is drying it itches." Basanthi goes to take it off. "The lime juice in the paste expedites its transfer and deepens the color," Mangla says.

"Don't take it off! Just be patient. Look how dark orange your henna is, Basanthi.

"Well, how long it lasts will tell how faithful we are." Mangla laughs.

Surjjo runs to the other room and brings back a beautiful scarf to show them. *Ammaji* puts her hands on Surjjo's head. "Surjjo got this from her own spinning. We're so proud of her."

Surjjo smiles with pleasure as she looks at *Ammaj*i. "I'm spinning more to get clothes for Sabiha*jiji*'s first baby."

Everyone laughs and Sabiha, with a coy smile, lowers her head.

Mangla helps Basanthi select a fancy green silk and gold thread sari from her own wardrobe. She selects a serpentine stone necklace and matching eardrops that reflect the green in her eyes.

"You look beautiful, Basanthi. I bet young men's heads will spin tonight."

"Thanks. I hope I can keep this sari on me through the evening. I'll probably feel more comfortable in a *ghagra*. I feel strange in this finery."

"Let's give it a try. If it doesn't work, we can always change later for the dancing."

Mangla dresses in a pink and gold sari and ruby jewelry. She then helps Sabiha get dressed in a red and gold *Ghagra*, a long pleated shirt, and puts on the heavy gold jewelry that Mahmood's family and *Ammaji* have given her. Then she helps her adorn her head with a red and gold *khadi* silk scarf that Mangla earned from her spinning.

Sabiha's eyes fill with tears as she gives her a hug. "This is so beautiful Mangla."

"You will make Mahmood *Bhai* fall in love all over again tonight with your exquisite beauty and charm, Sabiha*jiji*," says Mangla.

"*Dhutt*-- Go on." She blushes. She looks at Basanthi's hands and says, "how beautiful you and your hands look. How are you enjoying yourself?"

Basanthi looks at her hands as *Ammaji* calls, "*Baraat's* here. Come, everyone. We must stand in line to receive them. Sabiha you stay here."

With that, everyone leaves.

The musicians sing *quawali* songs accompanied by harmonium and drums. Mahmood *Bhai* stands dressed in a cream and gold *Sherwani* with *Shalwar*, a head turban, and rose and marigold garlands around his face.

Mangla and the girls escort Sabiha to the *Nikah* ceremony. Where the *wakil*, a lawyer, is sitting. Sabiha has Mangla's red scarf covering her face and a yellow canopy over her head, to sit some distance away from the groom. She cannot see Mahmood *Bhai* except through a large mirror placed under her veil. The *wakil* asks the groom and the bride if they accept each other, and they say, "*Kabbul hai*," I accept, three times. Then he certifies them married by signing the papers. That's it. They are married.

The melodious reedy *shehnai* music begins as people make their way to the wedding *Shamiana*, open on all four sides to accommodate the large number of guests and their families. The whole tent is decorated with jasmine and marigold garlands. It smells divine. Every so often the turbaned waiters come and spray *kewra* water that has a cool, soothing scent.

The *kathak* dancers perform as they escort the guests to the *Dawat-e-walima* tent, where everyone gathers for the wedding feast. Jasmine and red rose garlands hang all around the tent, giving it a heavenly fragrance. The bride and the groom sit at the podium and are served their dinner first.

There is no alcohol served since both traditions reject it. Mangla's Hindu family is vegetarian, but Mahmood's Muslim family eats chicken and mutton, but no pork, so the rich chicken and vegetarian curries are kept distinctly separate from each other. They announce to the guests that only *halal* meat is served. The traditional Muslim dessert of *sevaiin*—thin vermicelli cooked in sweet milk with raisins, saffron, and grated almonds—is served in silver bowls. Turbaned waiters serve mango and savory drinks in glasses.

Basanthi closes her eyes in pleasure and says, "I've never tasted food so good. Mahmood's family has taken care of every detail."

"I know. I'm still shaking my head," Mangla says, as she drags Basanthi to meet her cousin Yashi. "She's the cousin who went to BHU. I want to ask her about Professor Ram Mohan Rai and Munshi Prem Chand for my term paper." As they are talking, they see a very beautiful girl a little younger than them standing alone. She looks lost in her heavily embroidered yellow *kurta* and *salwar*, traditional Northwest dress. Mangla reaches out and says, "I'm Mangla. Sabiha *jiji*'s my sister."

"I'm Farida. Mahmood Bhai is my cousin. His father is standing there with my father, his brother." She points in the distance.

"This is my friend Basanthi. We're at BHU together."

Farida looks at Basanthi's cross. "Are you Christian?"

"Yes."

"I live near Murree, a hill station Northwest of Jammu. There are many Christians in Murree. I've many Christian friends in my college too," Farida says. "I'm studying education. I want women to get education when India becomes free."

"That's what we want to do too," Mangla says.

"Really? Murree's a long way away, as you know, and it was difficult to get time off in the middle of the year. But Mahmood *Bhai* is so dear to me. I had to come to his wedding," she says. "While I'm here, I thought he could take me to Lucknow to meet Mrs. Kidwai. We love her broadcast *Kya se Kya* in Murree."

Mangla looks at Basanthi and says, "Yes, we do, too! We've been talking about visiting her show and even bringing our class."

"I've never been to Murree, and I grew up in Jammu," Basanthi says.

"It's a beautiful Himalayan hill station. There's no train. One has to come by car or bus."

"My father works for the railways," says Basanthi. "We get free travel on trains. Maybe that's why we go to places like Simla where the British have built train lines, but not anywhere the train doesn't go."

Mangla has never seen Basanthi open to a stranger so quickly.

"Mangla," *Ammaji* calls her and waves. "Come here. Ramesh uncle's looking for you."

"You two talk," Mangla says to Farida and Basanthi. "This is the beauty of wedding parties. We meet so many new, interesting, and lovely people. I'll be back soon."

With that, she leaves them deeply engrossed in conversation and laughing together heartily. Mangla had worried that Basanthi would get bored. She is relieved that it turned out otherwise.

XXXXXXX

Love Partitioned

10 First year BHU

The morning after the wedding, the guests are finishing their breakfast when Mangla and Basanthi walk up, still bleary from the late night of partying with people their age.

"It smells so nice," Basanthi says. "I'm hungry after all that dancing!"

Mangla introduces Basanthi to the whole extended family.

Mamaji, *Ammaji*'s older brother, says. "Wasn't it a wonderful marriage ceremony? Simple and quick."

"*Nani* didn't come. I missed her," Mangla says.

"She's uneducated and an orthodox. What do you expect?"

"She's never forgiven *Ammaji* for adopting Sabiha *jiji* and mixing with Muslims, has she?'

Mamaji shakes his head. "Hindus should follow the Muslims. The groom pays for the bride because he's buying the workhorse not disposing of trash like the Hindus."

Mangla says, "Did you know that father took out dowry insurance for me? Because of my color and looks. He thought he'd have to pay someone a large sum to marry me."

"Really?" Basanthi says. "You are joking. You're so beautiful and charming." "Most fathers take out dowry insurance to meet their obligations," *Mamaji* explains. "I know I have for Vani. Banks have insurance plans to help fathers save money towards paying for their daughter's wedding."

Hearing this her worried look eases. Mangla says, "Really? *Mamaji* do you think that's right? " She smiles, gives a modest wave and looks around, "Where's Vani?"

"Must be somewhere around. Perhaps with her mother." *Mamaji* says. "She had to stop her studies, though. There are no schools for girls."

"But she's such a bright girl. You can't let that happen."

"I know, I know, *beti*, but what can I do? Your aunty won't let her study with boys because then no one will marry her. It's so hard to change the anachronistic rules of society." *Mamaji* wrings his hands.

Just then *Ammaji* walks in with Vani.

"*Mamaji* just told me that you've stopped your studies, Vani."

"Yes, *Amma* says I've learned enough of useless stuff. She says that "I can learn useful things like taking care of a family. She'll supervise it herself. She didn't need studies and neither do I. What do you think Mangla*jiji*"

Mangla looks at *Ammaji* and says, "Your family views showing up again. Maybe it's our turn to pay back for my education."

"What do you mean *beti*?" *Mamaji* says.

"There are so many schools for girls here. Maybe Vani can come and stay with us to finish her high school. Can't she *Ammaji*? Like Sabiha*jiji* and I stayed with Uncle Ramesh?"

"Can I *Bua*? I really want to study further like your daughter." Vani's pleading look rests on *Ammaji*.

"Well, I don't see why not? Both Sabiha and Mangla are out of the house now. It'll be nice for Surjjo to have a sister around and have me to spoil you."

"Maybe I can visit the school tomorrow and enroll right away." Vani looks at her father.

'We'll have to ask your *Amma*."

"I'll talk to her and assure her that in addition to her studies Vani will learn domestic skills from me," *Ammaji* says.

"Then it's settled." Mangla gives Vani a big hug. "Happy *Diwali*, Vani. You'll be such an asset to a free India."

"Yes, I want to be a teacher to educate girls." Vani hugs Mangla back and runs to give Basanthi a hug too. "I loved what you told Farida about Annie Besant and Theosophy. I want to go to BHU too."

That night when the firecrackers light up the sky, Vani, Basanthi and Mangla yell: "To the Future! To women's education!" and clap their hands. "Here's to a free India. May women soar high and sparkle like the *Anarkali* crackers." All three of them jump together and fall down laughing.

"Girls, behave. Act like girls." With a frown Vani's mother says, "you are not in school as yet Vani."

Ammaji rests her hands on her sister-in-law's arm. "Let them be. Their voice is our country's future."

***

On the long ride back to BHU, Basanthi asks if Mangla attended the information session from the Vice Chancellor's office during orientation. "They had a girl tell us about VC's freshman award that we could apply for if we do significant things in the first year to demonstrate our leadership abilities. I could apply with our faith and reason project, or we could start the theosophy society student chapter and apply with that."

"Yes, I was thinking about it too when I heard Mrs. Kidwai's radio program. Instead of us competing with each other, why don't we team up with our ideas.

We can get the warden's support now and apply for the VC award." Mangla watches the greenery they pass by. She drums on the wooden side of the tonga.

"Changing the subject," Basanthi says, "I can't get over how accommodating and caring your family is about differences. They all seem to feel free to have different beliefs and thoughts. Like how your uncle accepts Muslims, but his mother doesn't. He wants women to be educated, but his wife doesn't. Your mother changed her beliefs about women's education. Even Surjjo's mental limitation is overcome by finding her strengths. They really do live theosophy. I'm impressed." "Yes, openness in expression has its advantages," Mangla says. "But it can also bring alienation. Like that between *Ammaji* and her mother, who isn't open to change."

"There are more Muslims in Jammu and Kashmir than Hindus or Christians. But I don't know much about Muslim culture. Everyone is so ethnically and religiously segregated. Each thinks they are superior to the other."

"Well as you know, I grew up practicing *namaz* and I still do after my *havan*. But I don't do it five times a day or fast for thirty days for *Ramzan* like Sabiha*jiji*, a practicing Muslim."

"Will you teach me these practices? I'd like to learn so I can relate to the Muslim and Hindu girls I'll teach when I return to Jammu."

"Of course," Mangla says. "And maybe we should take an Urdu class together. I've never learned to read and write, and the language has a very rich literature that will help us with our paper. And I've also been thinking of starting a healthy food and nutrition pod so we can all learn to shop and cook healthy meals." Mangla's fingers drum faster.

"I don't know much about food and have no experience with cooking. The nuns did everything—we just ate. But I'd love to learn."

"Let's brainstorm about it. We have a great resource in my family. My parents are very keen on naturopathy and nutrition," Mangla says.

"We complement each other so well. We have a real shot at the VC's freshman award," Basanthi says.

"Here's to our first year." Mangla raises an imaginary glass to toast.

Basanthi joins her with an Amen.

Back on campus, Mangla and Basanthi begin working far into the night, brainstorming ideas that they may realize in the coming year. On one of their nightly brainstorming strolls, they see a theosophy section board outside a building. Both clap their hands.

***

They return during office hours and the office director welcomes them. "My grandfather knew Annie Besant and was a scholar in theosophy," Basanthi says. "We are interested in starting a faith and reason society based on her freedom of thought ideas."

"How creative," the director says. "I'm sure if Annie Besant were alive, would applaud and support your youthful efforts." She takes them to big hall with paintings on the walls that depict the various freedom struggles of common people. There are a lot of chairs and a head table.

"This is where you can hold your meetings. We can provide you help to get started with brochures and advertising materials, and we can promise to include your members when dignitaries visit. In return, we'd appreciate it if you'd open your membership to the youth in the community. At the end of the year, we will evaluate your efforts and see where to go from there," the director says.

To kick start it, the director will speak at a date two weeks later; she'll present Annie Besant's ideas, read passages from her writings, and debate pros and cons of faith and reason. "How does that sound, girls?"

Humbled, Mangla and Basanthi nod with a smile.

On the way back Mangla says," I like her! She has charisma and verve. She's a great role model for Indian women."

"She made a dream come true for me. I'm sure my grandfather is smiling from heaven," Basanthi says.

"Isn't it amazing that we're the first to think of doing this?"

Basanthi and Mangla write, illustrate, and post the announcements for the talk on campus bulletin boards. They continue to research Annie Besant's life and print membership forms for their first open house. They design certificates that members will receive if they attend four monthly meetings by the end of the year. At the first meeting, only fifteen people show. But soon word gets out, and lectures given by popular leaders draw more and more interested people. Every session there is a lively discussion among the attendees who want to talk more about the issues. Basanthi and Mangla moderate the discussions. To prevent them getting out of hand.

Soon there is standing room only at each meeting.

***

Mangla convinces their Sanskrit professor to let her read traditional Ayurvedic and yoga texts in Sanskrit for her class credit. She goes to the library and checks out books. Her plan for a healthy living club, to include both food and yoga, will be part of this project.

"I'm not sure I should be involved," Basanthi says. "I'm interested, but It's a Hindu thing beyond me.

" Maybe. But I didn't get it in my home, and you already do it naturally. We can learn together from these library books. Up to you."

Basanthi flips through the books and says, "You're already so active and do most of what they suggest. You go ahead and start. I will join and support you."

"Yoga is just a fancy name for meditative exercise, that's what I found. You do it already through your prayers. But the novelty of the name may attract students," Mangla says.

Together they design a half hour routine including *hath yoga*, the body movement, and *pranayama*, the breathing exercises. They post a notice in the dining hall inviting students to yoga sessions in the morning. They are surprised when twenty-five girls show up on the first day and continue to participate. It is easy for Mangla, as she is an early riser. But Basanthi sleeps in often and comes late or not at all. On those mornings Mangla leads the group alone. Soon more girls express interest. They decide to have morning yoga session that Mangla leads, and add another session, in tandem with Anis Kidwai's program in the evening that Basanthi co-leads.

***

For healthy eating, they design a pod system where each pod has a leader in charge of providing nutritious food for the girls. They form a committee to recruit girls to head pods and train them in nutrition. They obtain Mrs. Karachurian's permission for the pod leaders to accompany the servants to the local market to shop for fresh vegetables, milk, and other groceries. They teach the leaders about staying within their allocated food budget, and the leaders in turn teach the servants. Through discussion, they develop more ideas on how to save fuel, use less fat and salt in *daal*, steam the vegetables, and add the flavor of fresh herbs and spices. Once a week the pod girls work with the cook on how to implement their ideas. They chop vegetables into smaller pieces so less fuel is used. At first cook waves them off. "Go on and study. This is my job. I've been cooking in this kitchen for over twenty years. No one has complained about the taste of my food. You are babes in the woods."

This is part of their study, they tell him. The culinary teacher, Mangla, wants them to discover ancient Ayurvedic wisdom by writing a paper on better nutrition. This is their practice. The warden is to be the judge of each group. The cook accedes. Over time he appreciates their help and looks forward to learning new recipes every week.

One evening as they stroll, Basanthi gives Mangla a spontaneous hug. "Mangla, thank you for this wonderful ancient wisdom of shared food experiences that your family practices."

Mangla, moved, returns the embrace warmly.

***

Professor Rai assigns Mangla and Basanthi to different debating teams and there is no changing his mind.

"Maybe it's not all bad," Basanthi says.

"How can you say that? Now we can't study together," Mangla says.

82

"Yes, but can't you see? We can practice our debates in our room and sharpen our skills."

"I hadn't thought of it that way. And I guess this way, at least one of us will win. Brilliant, Basanthi."

Basanthi is the debate skills coach. Her chosen novel, *Nirmala* is about child marriage, whereas Mangla's *Godaan* is about poverty and the dowry system. They both augment it with additional library materials, giving their term papers more meat and making their debates more relevant. In their nightly practice, they sharpen their views for both pro and con, so it won't matter which side of the issue they have to debate.

Their team strategy pays off, and Basanthi wins the debate on child marriage. She was assigned to defend it. Mangla is to oppose dowry system. She nails it and wins her dowry debate against Kala.

For the third debate, the students pick the topic of Independent India--whether Gandhi's non-violence is good or not. Mangla feels she's won a lottery. Her family has given her a great deal of personal experience on the topic, and Basanthi tells her that she herself debated the same topic in her high school. They have to debate each other.

"Basanthi, with our experience debating, no matter which of us is selected we'll win in the state debate competition."

"I feel confident, too."

The class votes for Mangla to go to the state finals. She walks over to Basanthi and lifts her bowed head, takes her hands and says, "Basanthi, you're equally capable. We'll still work as a team so we win for BHU. You'll be our back up. What do you say?"

Basanthi lowers her head and stays quiet.

"I know you are disappointed. But without your coaching, I won't be able to win," Mangla pleads. "If BHU wins, we'll share the trophy. Let's hold our hands and make a pact, shall we?"

"Of course," Basanthi holds her hand in a limp grasp.

Mangla backs off, knowing that Basanthi needs time to recover for now

***

Their Urdu class is taught by *Ustad* Ali Hussain. It is great fun once they master the different script and learn the subtle differences with Hindi. In class, the *Ustad* extols the virtues of Mrs. Kidwai as an Urdu scholar and friend of Annie Besant. "Maybe *Ustad* Hussain can arrange for BHU to take us to Lucknow to participate in Mrs. Kidwai's radio talk show," Mangla says.

"Then we can ask her to be a keynote speaker for our faith and reason society fundraiser," adds Basanthi.

The *Ustad* indeed arranges for the class to go to Lucknow for a field trip. They each must memorize and recite one of their Urdu poems *shairi* they wrote supporting freedom. They will even be special guests on Mrs. Kidwai's next *Kya se Kya* radio show.

At the radio station they are taken straight to the studio and introduced to Mrs. Kidwai. Mangla whispers to Basanthi, "Pinch me, tell me it's real." Basanthi smiles and holds her hand.

Soon all the girls are seated, and the show begins. Mrs. Kidwai walks to the microphone and says, "We are honored to have a special group of girls from *Ustad* Ali Hussain's Urdu class at BHU."

"Each one is interested in making a difference in the lives of women of an independent India. They will tell their story and recite their f poems for us. I invite each one to introduce themselves briefly tell us about them and read their poem." As girls tell their stories, Mrs. Kidwai responds by emphasizing the aspects that she thinks will make a difference in India. Everyone claps.

After the show, as the on-air light turns off, Mrs. Kidwai comes out to meet them personally. They stand outside the studio on the balcony.

"Hello, girls. Ustadji called and told me about your work. I've been eager to meet you. Women like you are essential to light the torch for free India. Keep up your good work and education."

"We so admire your role in the freedom movement, especially on women's issues. My father admires you greatly," Mangla says.

"It must have taken tremendous courage to come out of *purdah* and defy your culture. We are reading and imbibing Annie Besant's life," Basanthi says.

"Allah's mercy, may her soul be at peace. She was a tremendous force not only in theosophy but on India's freedom movement too," Mrs. Kidwai says.

"We plan to make sure that she continues to be remembered at BHU through our faith and reason society," Basanthi says.

Mangla says, "Our annual gala is the end of March."

"We wondered if you could be our keynote speaker and tell us about Annie Besant's life and how young women might engage in the freedom movement," Basanthi says.

"Please honor us by accepting our invitation," Mangla says.

"That'll be lovely," says Mrs. Kidwai. She looks at her assistant. "Make arrangements so I can do that."

The trip back to BHU is all victory smiles for them. "What a coup! What a team we make! I wish my father was here to witness this," Basanthi says, fingering her cross.

Basanthi continues to regularly go home with Mangla. The elections are over. Colorful slogans and faces of the candidates are painted on the sides of shops as their tonga passes through little hamlets.

Mangla and Basanthi love telling Vani about their activities at BHU like their visit to Lucknow and sharing their Urdu *shairi* on Mrs. Kidwais radio show. Their *shairi* was to help mobilize voters as they canvassed door to door for the Congress party. They helped to organize gatherings of students at the theosophy society to talk about candidates they supported and their hopes of the freedom they will achieve when Congress wins. On election night, they had a special meal planned. Each pod focused on the provincial food from one of the states. Its members dressed in clothes from that state. Then they all sang freedom songs in that language that united them all.

On one of the visit home Basanthi shares with Vani the wonders of growing up in Jammu and Kashmir—the natural beauty of the hills and mountains, its weather, the shimmering *Chinar* trees, its people in colorful dresses and silver headdresses who spin lambswool as they tend sheep. She mentions her father, grandfather, and the stories of the maharajah's court through her grandfather's eyes.

"Didn't you have any women growing up?" Vani asks.

Basanthi stays quiet for a long time, but a frown creases her brow, and she fiddles with her cross. Finally, as if from a distance, she says in a soft voice, "You might say so."

***

After their visit home, Mangla and Basanthi take a *tonga* back to BHU, fanning themselves in the sultry Benaras heat along the way.

"Oh, the weather's getting so hot, and it's only March," Basanthi says. "I miss Jammu. It's so much cooler and drier in the foothills."

"I wish I could see Jammu," Mangla says with a sigh. "I love hearing you talk about it. I feel like there's part of your life I can only imagine, and I'd like to know it better by experiencing it."

"Well maybe you can come with me this summer. My father can get you a railway pass to travel as my companion."

"That would be lovely. But would that be OK with your family?"

Shrugging her shoulders "I'm sure my father would love it, and I don't much care what Jill thinks. In fact, your being there may make things easier for me over the vacation," Basanthi says. "And maybe we can travel with my father to visit Farida and Sabiha*jiji*."

"Can we? I never thought I'd be able to see her home."

"Well, don't pin your hopes yet. I'd better check with my father. I never know what will happen with Jill's mercurial unpredictability." Basanthi shakes her fist at her mental rival.

Just then they hear the *tongawalla* swear under his breath, "*Sala ullu ka pattha*" Mangla looks around as she hears his swear words but sees nothing.

"What's the matter?" she asks.

Basanthi braces against the edge of the tonga.

"Oh! Memsahib, I see the *goondas* coming in the distance. These wastrels are up to no good."

"How do you know? I see no one," Mangla says, peering out the window at the vegetation, lush trees, village huts, and the road behind the tonga.

XXXXXXX

11 End of First Year

I heard that they were going to march to protest the election results," the *tongawallah* says as he whips the horse into a gallop.

"But the elections are long over. Why agitate now?" Mangla says.

"I don't know. But they set fire to my village last week. The villagers had to run for their lives and had nowhere to go now. *Haramzadeh.* Those sister-fucker Muslim *goondas* don't like the Congress winning and the Muslim league losing." He clicks his horse to pick up pace.

Suddenly Mangla sees fire torches coming towards them from all directions. Basanthi grabs hold of her hand as the *tongawallah* continues to whip the horse into a gallop. But one of the men throws his torch right at them, and it lands on its canvas roof. Mangla springs into action, climbs the seat, and holds onto the canvas frame with her right hand. It's still damp from last night's rain, so she has a little time. She reaches up with her left hand and grabs the torch and throws it back. The *tongawallah* turns sharply and rides along an alley until he comes to a hut and asks them to hide in there. "Memsahib, you're Hindu and wear *khadi* without head cover. They'll defile you."

"They can't be that unreasonable. *Pitaji* says--"

"Mangla, this is no time for heroics," Basanthi says. "I live among these types. There's no reasoning with brainwashed prejudice." She grabs Mangla by her arm and drags her off the *tonga* and into the smelly hut where they join cows, goats and chickens roaming around. "Oh, look at my shoes--covered in crap," Basanthi says.

Mangla covers her nose with her sari. She hears the *tonga* leave and wonders what to do next.

"How far are we from BHU?" Basanthi asks.

"Maybe three miles or so. If we sprint, we can make it back by dinner time," Mangla says.

They start a brisk walk when they see vultures hovering above. The rank smell becomes stronger, and they cover their noses and walk faster. The faster they walk, the stronger the stink. Until they come to its source. A body of a woman, young like them, naked, lying on the roadside. Her stomach has been slashed. Her clothes lying nearby are khadi and the red powder *bindi* on her forehead gives her away as a Hindu. Her innards have been spewed across the road. Jackals crouch, feeding, while the vultures wait their turn.

They look at each other in the dim dusk light They need no words. Their eyes speak volumes for their fear, disgust, pain, and horror.

"How cruel can humans be Basanthi," whispers Mangla.

"I don't know, but the murderers will surely burn in hell." Basanthi spits on the road as she makes a cross over her heart.

They increase their pace. Basanthi says, "The *tongawalla* should have waited for us. We paid him."

"With the foul swear words he spewed; he probably wanted the offending *goondas'* blood. We would have gotten in his way. To be charitable, he probably saved our lives."

"It would seem so. I don't want to meet the fate of that poor woman we saw." Basanthi shivers and picks up speed.

Mangla matches her pace, hoping that the fast walk will clear her mind of what she's seen.

***

The intervarsity debate is only a week away, and Mangla can't seem to get the image of the mutilated Hindu woman from her mind. She feels ill and listless. The doctor suspects depression. But then high fever brings her to the infirmary, and the doctor suspects typhoid. How could she have got it? Was it when she was pushed down into the dirt when they marched in the freedom rally during elections? A Muslim league member offended those women were involved in the march, pushed Mangla into a pile of crap. Oh, she knew she shouldn't have gone. She didn't listen to her inner voice.

"But doctor, my debate is next week. I must get better. Can't you do something?" Mangla says through tears. She and Basanthi have worked hard to prepare for all possible topics.

"I'm sorry, Miss, this disease is very infectious, and you are too weak. You'll need at least two weeks of bed rest and quarantine, so it won't spread across campus. Those are doctor's orders."

"I can't. But--"

The doctor has already left, and her protest only reverberates on the silent walls. She tries to get up, but her weakness only helps her fall flat on her face. She picks herself up. Tears of self-pity flow freely down her cheeks as she picks up her pillow and hurls it at the door.

What's wrong with her? What bad karma brought this on? She's been only good. Perhaps that girl she trounced at the last debate cast a tantric spell on her! Her disappointment feeds her mind, bringing back the trauma of her last *tonga* ride. She finds herself aware in a new way of just how vulnerable she is as a woman.

At night, Basanthi sneaks a visit—defying the clinic's isolation rule.

"Maybe God spoke through me when I said we will share this debate," Mangla tells her. "Isn't it good we prepared together?" She can't help the tears streaming down her fever flushed face. Soon sobs rack her body.

Basanthi takes her hands and promises to keep visiting; they can practice as they always have. "Maybe the doctor is wrong," Basanthi says. "Maybe you will get better and go to the debate." She says the Lord's Prayer with Mangla.

But Mangla is not getting better. When the time comes, the doctor won't even let her accompany the debate team. When he learns about Basanthi's clandestine visits, he moves Mangla to a locked room. She hates her prison they've put her in. Mangla tries to escape again, but she's too weak, and she collapses. Her body is emaciated, and the nurses pick her and put her back in bed.

She wants to go home. She dreams of *Ammaji's* care and Basanthi's visits. But no one has informed her family because of the nature of the illness.

"Miss, you're contagious," says the doctor. "We don't know much about the cure, but we know it spreads and it is best to isolate the person who has it. Rest is essential for recovery."

"But you come to see me every day. How come you don't get sick?"

Ignoring her the doctor says, "Rest alone is best."

One night lying there she hears Basanthi's voice at the window. "Mangla—I can't come in, but I will read you your favorite poem." She does so in a loud voice. Mangla hears her, confused in a twilight of fever, but somewhere deep inside she feels comforted and sleeps.

Mangla continues to get worse. The doctor is worried and talks to the warden, who asks the doctor to let Mangla know that Basanthi went to the debate finals and indeed won it hands down. The warden gets the trophy to Mangla through the doctor with a note from Basanthi that reads, I won this for you, Mangla. Now you win your health for me. I miss you. May *Allah* be merciful, and God bless. Your dear friend. B.

The note is covered with hearts and lotuses and crosses and *Om*'s and stars and the moon. But Mangla is confused and too sick to read it properly. The doctor reads it to her, hoping that her friend's blessings will influence her recovery. His own medicines seem to be ineffective.

Three more weeks pass. Finally, Mangla takes a turn for the better. Her fever comes down for the first time. Still weak, she's put on a special recovery diet in the infirmary, and Basanthi is allowed to visit her.

Basanthi brings the notes she has taken for her. She holds Mangla's hand as she holds the notebook and reads it to her. She asks Mangla reflective questions to ensure that Mangla is cogent enough to be able to take her final exams in a few weeks.

Their first year at BHU nears its end. In addition to the debate trophy, Mangla and Basanthi share the University freshman leadership award and the Sanskrit award for the best paper on ancient Indian medicine. They announce that next year they will advance the Faith versus Reason effort into a college-wide Theosophy group to study Annie Besant's life. The Vice-Chancellor gives them a special recognition and awards a substantial prize to fund this activity.

"Mangla you are the best thing that has happened to me," Basanthi says. "And guess what? I got a letter from my father. He wants to thank you by taking you to see Sabiha*jiji*—and to show you around Kashmir."

Mangla's face lights up. "Oh Wow! Really?" She reaches out and gives Basanthi a big embrace, whirling them both around.

***

The trip to Jammu takes them almost three days by train. Finally, they stand outside the modest home of Basanthi's family. Jill doesn't come out to greet them. The servant says that memsahib has a headache. Basanthi's stepsisters are away visiting their grandmother. Basanthi just curls her lips and shrugs her shoulders as if to say, so what else is new? She claps her hands and says, "That means we can enjoy ourselves without worrying about pleasing her. "

"Oh! The sunrise behind the mountains is so beautiful. That must be the East." Mangla points as she soaks in the sunrays and breathes in the fresh, cool Jammu air. It is so much cooler than Benaras. She looks at the distant snow on the Himalayan Mountain peaks with her mouth open in awe. "Basanthi, how stunning. I've never seen anything like this."

Basanthi points. "That way there in the distance is Kashmir. There is so much to show you before we go to Murree."

The next day they set out walking on Basanthi's promised adventure. They stop outside an off-white concrete building. On the side is a small church with its steeple on top.

"That's my high school," Basanthi says. "It's closed for summer now.

"What was it like?"

"Well, the nuns were strict, of course. But I was a good student. I've never told this to anyone before. I had a very close Hindu friend Mira in my dorm, and we shared a room together. She was smart and pretty and came from a Brahmin family in the plains." Basanthi told her about the close relationship she had with her.

They read together lying-in bed under a quilt to conserve heat especially in winters. Neither had a home to go to on weekends. Telling each other personal stories alleviated their loneliness. Mira taught her about the hundreds of Hindu Gods and their role in living a life. It made Basanthi understand her deceased beloved grandfather. But the way they were treated by their families because they followed their hearts had turned her off Hindus.

90

Love Partitioned

"I don't think the nuns liked us in the same bed or talking about many Gods. The nuns would talk about sin in the assemblies. Since Mira didn't attend them, she wasn't aware." Basanthi ignored those nuns. She and Mira weren't stealing, killing, lying, or cheating. Where was the sin? They hung out and did their projects and fitted together like gloves.

Then one day Basanthi was called to the mother superior's office and told that there had been complaints about Mira's behavior, and she had been expelled from school.

Basanthi protested that there was some mistake, but they wouldn't tell her anything and didn't even allow Mira to say goodbye to her. Like she was a pariah. "I was devastated. I never found out what happened. The nun's hypocrisy turned me off. This was against what Ayah had told her about Christ's teaching of love." Mangla reaches out and embraces her friend. "Oh, Basanthi, what a heartbreak. The nuns are supposed to be compassionate."

There were tears in Basanthi's eyes. "The loss was profound for me. My grades suffered. But then I just moved on. My father's words of self-reliance guided me." She lets Mangla hold her for a moment and confesses, "I just want you to understand why it took me so long to warm up to you."

Mangla holds her tighter and feels Basanthi relax. "I'm so sorry Basanthi. I sensed something like that. Especially with the senior girl's cruel behavior. But luckily there are no prudish nuns at BHU. "

Basanthi smiles. "Maybe. But when I lost Mira, I stopped trusting authorities. I find girls like you so much more authentic and fun."

"Let others not disrupt our relationship," Basanthi says.

"Yes, let's support each other to empower women in free India."

Squeezing her hands, Basanthi says, "Mangla, I'm grateful to you and your family for giving me so much love."

They arrive in front of a big bungalow. A young man steps out of the gate. He's the most handsome young man Mangla has ever set eyes on. He's tall with dark hair and dressed in western clothes. He's a little darker than Basanthi but not much. He doesn't see them, but Basanthi stops in her tracks and looks away.

"He's my cousin Jay. My grandfather's grandnephew."

"He's gorgeous. I would love to meet him."

Basanthi looks at her. "He won't, he's a chauvinist. One day my grandfather took me to their house. He thought that as Jay's my age we could play together. But they turned us away. We never had a chance to try again before my grandfather died."

"That anyone could be that way is hard to believe."

"I've seen Jay around town, but he never recognizes me. I learnt early about the Kashmiri Brahmin bigotry." Basanthi jiggles her cross as Jay looks in their direction and hurries on without acknowledgement or recognition. Despite Basanthi's sentiments, something about him draws Mangla like a magnet. She says nothing about it. She doesn't understand her conflict within strong feelings for both Basanthi and Jay.

They continue their jaunt and come to the movie theater. "Look *Dharti Mata* is playing here. Perhaps we can see it here," Mangla says.

They run into Jay again at A H Wheeler's bookshop. Basanthi ignores him and walks in the opposite direction. But Mangla stands next to him, trying to find a pretext to connect. She reaches across him for a book, and her hands brush his. He doesn't look up but moves away. Basanthi is right, Mangla thinks. He's retarded. "I told you not to bother," says Basanthi with a smirk. "He's a man without a soul. In fact, the whole family is like that. Orthodox, and backward my grandfather used to say."

***

They take a train to Rawalpindi and then a bus to Murree that drives over windy roads to 7500 feet. Rawalpindi is much hotter than Jammu, but as they get closer to Murree the weather gets more pleasant. While the distance from Jammu is only 40 miles, it takes them over 4 hours. Mangla needs to suck on salted limes to avoid motion sickness, but not Basanthi. She seems used to it.

Farida greets them at the bus station in Murree with an embrace. She hires coolies to carry their baggage and explains that the house isn't far.

Murree is rightly called Queen of Hills. The view is spectacular. The snow-capped peaks of the distant Himalayan mountains are breathtaking. They see waterfalls and different kinds of soft, green ferns growing on the hillside. Gorgeous flowers dot the sides of the narrow road. Sunlight glistens through the fir tree branches creating its own twinkle of wonderment.

A sign in the road reads, "Whites only. No coloreds allowed beyond this point." "I guess the house isn't that way," Basanthi laughs.

Farida says, "Ignore it. When we get independence, the whites will be gone anyway. Then this paradise will be all ours."

"*Inshallah*, God willing," Mangla says.

The next morning, the three women say their *namaz* prayers together and set out.

"Since you are Christian, I thought you would want to see the tomb of Mother Mary," Farida says. "We must take our shawls. It's quite a hike there." Farida tells them that Mother Mary is called *Hazrat* Miriam in Islam. The legend has it that both Jesus Christ, *Hazrat* Isa, and *Hazrat* Miriam are buried here. The tale goes that Isa survived crucifixion and came to Kashmir on the silk road, and his mother followed soon after. The two figures have a big following in the Himalayas.

Every day is a new day and a new adventure for Mangla. They go on horseback to visit Farida's school, closed for summer of course. But the building is colonial nested in the hills, with a striking view of Nanga Parbat—almost 27,000 feet high, Farida tells them. On the other side they see the snow peaks of K2, which is

28,000 plus feet. Farida says, "Those mountain peaks never lose their snow. What's more, no one has climbed to the top of that mountain as yet. Many have tried and perished. It is a formidable climb."

Sucking in her breath at the raw beauty of what surrounds her, Mangla observes, "Look, there are no trees above a certain height."

Farida says, "Trees can't grow above that height. But there are meadows and beautiful wildflowers there. Maybe we can hike up there and see them. "I'll love that," both Mangla and Basanthi say in unison, and like little girls laugh at their synchronicity. Mangla's mouth opens but she's without words as she takes in the spectacular scenery. Basanthi takes her hand and says, "Our minds read each other's."

The next day, Farida arranges for them to take the hiking trail towards Broad Peak, which is about 28,000 feet. On the way, they meet big gray Langurs with their long white tails and black faces. Macaque monkeys, with their brown bodies and red faces, are not that different from the monkeys in Benaras, just much bigger.Mangla breathes in the smell of the fresh firs kept moist with the patchy fog that descends sporadically on them, giving the place an ethereal feel.

"We come here with children in my class for school trips. They love their exercise, and we sing freedom songs and recite our tables and the alphabet," Farida says.

They climb to around 10,000 feet until they are above the birch and fir tree line and see the stunning snow-covered Broad peak in the distance. The beautiful green alpine meadow is abloom with wildflowers that Mangla has never seen.

Farida has brought a basket of sandwiches and fruits. She spreads a cloth for them to sit on, and they feast on crunchy apples, pears, strawberries, dates, almonds, and pistachio nuts.

However, Mangla notices that Basanthi's face has clouded over.

"What's the matter Basanthi? Are you OK?"

Basanthi looks away in the distance.

Farida says, "Tell us why this foreboding look?"

Basanthi shakes her head. When she speaks, there is a tremor in her voice. "You all have families that love and support you, and you all have been so kind to me. Still, my heart feels heavy and falters. I worry that something awful is going to happen and take away all I hold dear. I feel so lost."

Mangla tries to find reassuring words. None come. She puts her arms around Basanthi.

Farida says, "Basanthi, I've only known you a short time. However, I sense Allah has given you a beautiful spirit to make a difference in the world. I don't live far from you. Should you need a home my family and I are close by."

Mangla shivers and pulls her shawl closer to her body. She looks up and sees a dark cloud covering the sun. She gets up, extends her hand and says, "Come, let's get back before it gets too cold."

Basanthi takes her hand and says, "I'm sorry. I don't know what evil shadow is crossing my heart." Tears well in her eyes. "I still miss Ayah. She took me for walks into the mountains when I was young. Sometimes I feel abandoned by God." Farida says, "*Bismillah ar Rehman ar Rahim.* Allah's compassion and mercy is always with us even though at times we can't feel it—especially through the worst of times."

Mangla looks up and sees a golden eagle hovering in the distance. It soars high and swoops low until it catches its prey and then flies away. Mangla closes her eyes and says, "I'd like to be like that bird—careless, self-sufficient, and flying free."

Then she stretches and embraces the other girls. "Maybe soon we will fly free!" They rejoin and cup their hands to their mouth and yell. "Fl-----y Free-eeeee------" The mountains echo back their words.

When they return, the night *chawkidar* is waiting for them with a telegram in his hand that he hands to Basanthi. She reads it and blood drains from her face.

"What is it?" Mangla says.

Basanthi hands her the telegram as her body slumps on a nearby chair. Mangla reads aloud. "Bhumi in hospital. Stop. Heart attack. Stop. Come home."

Farida, practical and caring, takes charge. She says, "Take deep breaths, Basanthi. *Chawkidar*, please bring some cold water for Basanthi *bibi* and then some tea and biscuits. Let me go and find out about getting back to Jammu. I'll come with you. Luckily I'm on summer vacation." With that, Farida leaves the room as Mangla holds Basanthi in a supportive embrace.

XXXXXXX

12 Mangla Meets Anand

Farida returns. "The last bus left several hours ago. I've booked us on the first bus to Jammu. I'm afraid it leaves at 6 AM. We'll have to get up at dawn and leave early."

"I'm not sure how Jill will receive me," Basanthi says with a frown.

Mangla holds Basanthi's hand. "Try not to worry about Jill. She's just mean and jealous of you."

"I'm on summer vacation—I'll come with you. I have an aunt who lives there. She is Mahmood *bhai*'s younger sister, *Khalajan*. Very lively. You met her at their wedding. I know she will welcome you and Mangla."

They both look blankly at Farida.

Mangla says, "I can't place her."

Farida goes out and brings back Sabiha's wedding pictures and points to a beautiful woman standing in the background.

"Now I remember her. She was such a good singer." Mangla shows the picture to Basanthi, who gives a weak nod.

"*Khalajan* has a large house with lots of room. And no children. Her house is not far from the hospital. We are relatives, and it will be fine if we arrive unannounced. Especially under the circumstances."

***

They arrive in Jammu around 11 AM and take a *tonga* to *Khalajan*'s house.

"*Salam Khalajan*. Surprise," Farida says.

"Come in, come in. You are Mangla, Sabiha's sister, and this is your friend, Basanthi. I remember from the wedding. Mahboob, bring *chai* and cook lunch for three extra people."

She turns to the trio and says, "Go freshen yourselves up, and after lunch Basanthi can visit the hospital."

After they've eaten, Basanthi leaves for the hospital and Mangla tells *Khalajan* what a shock the telegram was. She relates the way Basanthi grew up with him as a single loving father, and with a loving Ayah after her mother left suddenly for England. All was well until Jill married him and moved in with her two daughters. Since then, Jill has driven Basanthi from home and continues to put a wedge between her and her father. She even got rid of Ayah viciously. If it wasn't for her Aunt Sue's generous heart, Mangla says, she can't think what Basanthi might have done.

"We haven't thought how or when we will get back to Benaras," Mangla says. "I guess it depends on what happens with Jill—whether or not Basanthi can stay with Bhumi."

"She will be most welcome to stay here with Farida," says *Khalajan*. And you, too, Mangla. You are now part of our family."

"Thank you. *Khalajan*. That helps. My parents also just love Basanthi and would be happy to have her stay with us should she decide to return to BHU. This buys us time to let her decide."

"Then it is settled. She is lucky to have you two as friends. Now run on and have a look at the city. I will ask the driver to give you a tour."

That evening, when Basanthi returns, she is frowning.

"What happened at the hospital?" Farida says.

Near tears Basanthi says, "Don't ask." She drums her fingers on her thighs.

Mangla puts her hand on her shoulders, waiting for her to speak.

"Aunt Sue was there with him. It was good for the three of us to be together. Papa was resting when the doctor came in. He said that papa was stable and could go home early. Luckily, Papa is young and healthy otherwise. He got to the hospital just in time and they were able to help him with rest, diet, cardiac massage, and aspirin. They plan to release him soon to homecare as they need hospital bed for more serious patients."

"*Allah O Akbar*. He is merciful," *Khalajan* says.

After the doctor's visit, Aunt Sue said that if Basanthi could continue to stay with Bhumi she might go home have dinner, bathe, and return to the hospital to stay overnight. Their house is a long way away, so it takes time for this transition. Basanthi agreed as she was sure Bhumi will like that.

But then Jill enters. When she saw Basanthi, she became belligerent and gave her the fifth degree. Who told her about Bhumi? Who gave her permission to be in the hospital? Basanthi was too young and irresponsible to take care of her father; Jill can't rely on her, etc. She said there was no room in her house for Basanthi, especially if Bhumi is to return shortly. He would need another room for special rehabilitation care. With her daughters and Sue in the house there is no extra space. That is why she didn't inform Basanthi. As though he wasn't even her beloved father. The whole time Jill was talking, Basanthi was afraid that Papa would wake up. But he seemed to be sedated and fast asleep.

Now, back at *Khalajan*'s house, Basanthi is sobbing loudly. Both Mangla and Farida hold her in a consoling embrace. Through her anguish she says, "This exile from my own home is too much for me."

"How cruel and heartless," *Khalajan* says.

"We'll stay here as long as you need us to," Farida and Mangla say.

"Stay, Basanthi, and visit your papa. The driver can take you to their home." *Khalajan*'s compassionate voice soothes the girl's raw nerves.

"Thank you. I don't want to sound ungrateful. But maybe when Papa goes home it's time for me to return to BHU. I don't want to add stress on his heart."

"Nothing needs to be decided tonight," *Khalajan*'s wise voice commands. "It's been a long day. Sleep will clear your heads. Your beds are ready."

Basanthi says, "I'm so tired. I've never felt so tired."

Mangla helps her to bed.

***

The next day, *Khalajan* tells Farida and Mangla that they must visit Srinagar. "We have a holiday home there. A chowkidar takes care of it." *Khalajan* has sent word, and the *chowkidar* will cook them food and prepare for their arrival. Farida's been there, and she can show Mangla around. Who knows when Mangla will have the chance to come back? "Sabiha *bhabi* will never forgive me if I don't take good care of you while you are here," *Khalajan* says with a smile.

Mangla is pleased at the prospect. With her hands together in gratitude, she says, "I could pinch myself. This is an unreal gift from heaven."

"Srinagar is much cooler. It has the big Dal Lake floating many houseboats made of intricately carved walnut wood. They are like hotels on water and many visitors stay there," Farida says.

Basanthi will stay with *Khalajan* and continue to visit the hospital. "Give her time to get used to being with her father. Sue can help shield her from Jill until he's ready to go home and Basanthi decides what to do next," *Khalajan* says.

That evening Basanthi is excited about Mangla's trip. She thanks Farida and *Khalajan*. "I've been to Srinagar often. I am so happy. I can visit Papa daily unencumbered by guilt from not taking you places myself. Don't forget to take a *shikara* ride in the lake and visit the shops on water."

The next morning, Mangla and Farida set out on an early bus to Srinagar. They walk the distance from the bus depot to *Khalajan*'s holiday home. Mangla stops outside an alpine chalet house nestled in an alcove amongst the shelter of deodar trees. The scent from these trees fills her nostrils. She inhales deeply. She can see the snow-capped mountains in the distance.

Farida points in the other direction and says, "Dal Lake is that way. Our stay is short, so let's go in and put our bags down. We can freshen up, eat lunch, then take a romp and let you experience it."

"Seeing is believing. I couldn't imagine it from Basanthi's stories."

Farida calls, "*Chowkidar*, we are here. Is lunch ready?"

"Yes, memsahib. There is water in the bathroom if you want to freshen up."

"Thanks. Tomorrow we plan to take an early bus to Gulmarg to show Mangla around. Please prepare us sack lunches and thermoses full of *chai* to take for the day. We'll eat dinner here."

That afternoon, they take a stroll around Dal Lake, a short distance from the holiday home. It is as Basanthi said, humming with people entering and exiting the houseboats. There are *shikara*s selling their wares--everything from gorgeously embroidered pashmina shawls, to intricately carved walnut wood craft wares, to beautifully painted local scenes. There are *papier mache* birds, and flower bouquets. There is delicious smelling barbecue served on large lotus leaves. The two young women hire a *shikara* to take a spin around the lake. Mangla gapes at all she sees.

The early morning bus ride to Gulmarg is glorious. Roads lined by deodar trees wind through the mountains. It has a beauty of its own. Mangla soaks in the fresh scent of firs while listening to monkey's chatter as they groom each other. She hears the songs of ravens, hawks, robins, mynahs, and green and gold kingfishers as they fly through the trees. A sense of longing sweeps through her spirit and in an awed whisper, Mangla says, "*Inshallah* one day I will fly far, like them.

Farida says, "I love this ride, and Gulmarg. We'll go on a horseback to see more of the back country. One can learn to ski also."

"Really? I have never done that. These hills are so different from Murree."

"Yes. Skiing and ice skating are winter sports," Farida says. "In the summer, people boat and walk. I wish we had more time before the last bus."

"Me too. But we shouldn't leave Basanthi in Jill's clutches too long," Mangla says.

"Yes, I agree. I wish Basanthi could be with us."

When they arrive in Gulmarg, they are hungry. They find a secluded spot on the dried leaf-cushioned ground and sit to eat their picnic lunch.

Soon horse *wallah*s offer them their horses to rent. They select two that will also carry them to the bus stop for the last bus that will get them to Jammu in time for dinner.

On the return bus ride to Srinagar, Mangla says, "Your hospitality is so gracious. Wait until I tell *Ammaji* about *Khalajan*'s generosity. I hope she can come and see Sabiha*jiji* one of these days."

"Sabiha*jiji*'s house is too far to go to in a short time stay, but I'm sure there will be a next time. Maybe I can bring *Ammaji*, too."

On return to Jammu, they learn that Bhumi will be discharged in four days. However, after a couple of days there is a telegram from Sue receives a telegram that her mother is gravely ill. She will leave next day and will return to support Bhumi as soon as she is able. Until then, his Railway servants can take care of him at home. Basanthi can either decide to stay in Jammu or return to Benaras.

"It's only a week left before BHU starts. I would rather not add to Papa's stress if he has to face Jill and me together—our relationship is worse than ever."

"My school starts soon too," Farida says.

"Besides, we need to begin preparing for the activities of the new year. Especially with the theosophy society. Don't we, Mangla?"

"We are here to help you with whatever decision works for you, Basanthi. Should you decide you want to be closer to your Papa you can always stay with me," *Khalajan* says.

"I may take you up on that should it be necessary. Aunt Sue promised that in the future she will stay with Papa and write more frequent letters to me at BHU informing me of how he is doing. I am kind of torn between being with Papa and finishing my studies. If I finish, I can be more independent when I return." Basanthi bows her head in prayer. When she looks up, she says, "*Khalajan*, I can't thank you enough for providing me another home. I feel so supported by you. I will stay in touch if I may."

"Of course, you are like Farida—a daughter to us," *Khalajan* says.

It is decided that they will leave for Benaras the day after Bhumi returns home. Until then, Basanthi will continue to visit the hospital. "This way I can travel with Mangla and Papa doesn't need to worry about me traveling alone. He can't travel as yet."

Mangla says, "Until our dorm reopens, you can stay with us. Like you, *Khalajan*, *Ammaji* loves Basanthi like a daughter. Perhaps you can give our address to Aunt Sue so she can connect with you in case she needs to before the dorm reopens."

"Your *Ammaji* is so kind to me. She makes me feel at home. A home I don't have here with Jill, " Basanthi tears up.

Three days later, they say goodbye to Farida who takes a bus on her own back to Murree. "This will give me time to prepare for my classes. Thank you, *Khalajan.* As always, I so enjoyed my stay with you."

The next day, Basanthi says goodbye to her father as he leaves for his home with Jill. "I'll miss you, Papa. I must return to Benaras so I can get prepared for next year's theosophy society. When you are rested and recovered, you can come to Benaras and we can talk about theosophy. Mangla, too. Won't you love that, Papa?"

Still weak, he nods, and she gives him a big hug.

Mangla says, "Namaste, Bhumi uncle. I hope you continue to feel stronger so you can visit our home soon. Thank you for arranging the Jammu and Murree trip for me. I am so humbled by all the love and attention I have received."

Then the driver takes Basanthi and Mangla to the train station for their return trip to Benaras. He made all the reservations himself, to not bother Bhumi.

***

Back in Benaras, Basanthi stays at Mangla's home until the dorm reopens. *Ammaji* spoils them both by making them special dishes.

"These *pakoras,* fritters smell so delicious. Hot off the frying pan, so to say. The mint chutney is to die for," Basanthi says as she savors a hot one on her plate. "These are Mangla's favorite," says *Ammaji.* "You will return to your dorm food soon enough. I will so miss you both. Luckily for me I won't be alone for long. Vani will return to go to school in couple of weeks."

Their life hums along as they dream about the activities for the coming year. They visit the local student chapter of the theosophy society to find out about the planned activities, and when Basanthi can pencil in Bhumi towards the end of the year. "We can always cancel it if he isn't well enough to travel. But this goal may also give him an incentive to get well. He and Aunt Sue can visit BHU, too. I don't believe she's been here." Basanthi rattles on with an uncharacteristic, dreamy look into the distance.

"You want to be with your Papa, don't you?" *Ammaji* says as she overhears their conversation.

Basanthi bows her head and holds her hands in prayer position to honor her question.

"Yes. But I made a good decision to return. The tension between Jill and me would have torn him apart. Besides, this way I will graduate and return to Jammu sooner."

Soon Basanthi gets a letter from Aunt Sue. It contains news about Bhumi—he is weak but recovering well at home. When he's not resting, they take walks together and play rummy and other card games that he enjoys. It is like older and happier times in Gorakhpur. Basanthi wiggles her cross dangling from her mouth. "*Ammaji,* I wish I could be there, but it's better this way. Sometimes a personal sacrifice is God's will, as Ayah told me. Aunt Sue's detailed and caring letters connects me to him."

***

A few days later, when they return singing from an old movie--*Toofan Mail, Zindigi,* life is like a fast train—they find *Ammaji* awaiting them.

"Girls behave. Anyway, come in and get dressed. We are expecting guests shortly.

"But we went to the movie and are already dressed," Mangla says.

"I want you to dress extra special. Here, I've selected these clothes and jewelry for you and Basanthi." *Ammaj*i is bustling with excitement. "They're coming for tea. The servant's gone to bring sweets from the best *halwai* in town."

"Who's coming?" Mangla asks.

"They're friends of *Pitaji's* -- friends' children, and are in town from Roorkee. We didn't get much notice. You know how it is. Someone sends a word, and we have to oblige."

"We don't have to," Mangla says.

Ammaji frowns. "Stop being childish. Just because you go to college doesn't mean you have to be rude and hoity-toity about friends who visit. Can't you be a little more civil?" With that she leaves the room.

Mangla rolls her eyes and goes to dress. Basanthi follows.

"I'm used to these mystery guests popping up without much notice. That's the way of life in my house," Mangla says. "If I didn't know better, I'd say that the guests are coming for my '*dekhao.*' To examine me and decide if I'm suitable as an eligible mate."

She's been the butt of Badri's putdowns on this and can barely look in the mirror without feeling undesirable all over.

"What do you mean?" Basanthi says.

How could she explain what it's like to a pretty, fair, Christian girl whom she has envied for her light skin, her grace, and charming ways? She will never understand the social stigma that Mangla carries on her shoulders, an albatross around her neck since she was a child. Taunted by neighborhood kids. *Kali Kali*, black, black. *Moti, Moti,* Fatso, Fatso. These names, and what they mean about her social standing, are etched it in her brain.

"We Hindu girls aren't allowed to go out and develop relationships with men like Christians," Mangla says. "You know this. It's all arranged by the family. We need to be born wealthy, pretty, light skinned, not wear glasses etc. etc., to make a good match. And I'm lacking in all those dimensions."

"You've got to be joking. I've told you so often how beautiful and talented you are. I envy your grace."

"You are so sweet, Basanthi," Mangla says, but her face turns pale. "I wish I was as you say. I feel so humiliated and rejected every time we go through this ritual. And there have been many. To be rejected doesn't help one's ego." She gives a wry smile. I feel like a commodity to be given away to whoever will agree to the dowry price my father can offer."

"What happens if the girl doesn't want to marry?"

"We don't have that choice. As we read in Prem Chand's novel, death is considered better. At least my family doesn't believe in child marriages, like those that happen in the villages. Oh, Basanthi, there is still so much work to do. Annie Besant and Buddha are both right to tell us not to believe in anything that doesn't agree with our reason and commonsense, but it's easier to say that than to defy social customs through actions and change them, isn't it!" As she puts on the earrings a sharp wire scrapes her ear lobe and a drop of blood appears. "Damn!"

They hear Surjjo's *charkah* whirring in the other room, and the arrival of strangers at the door as *Pitaji* opens it. They hear him say, "Come in, Come in." He calls out, "Mangla and Basanthi, come meet our guests."

They enter and see two young men sitting with *Pitaji*.

Ammaji says, "Mangla offer the sweets to the guests."

Mangla gives her a peeved look but, passes the sweets around.

The men look up and try to rise when she approaches. *Pitaji* asks them to sit down. Mangla looks at them. One of the guests appears to be younger than the other. *Pitaji* points to the older one who is a bit shorter than the other. "Mangla, *beti*. This is Arvind." Both men are handsomely dressed in white pants with beige blazers sporting Roorkee college insignia on the breast pockets. They wear green striped ties, brown polished shoes, and light-colored socks. They have big eyes and bushy eyebrows. Arvind wears glasses. Their skin is dark but their features attractive with firm jawlines. Clearly, they are related.

Mangla puts her hands together and says, "*Namaste.*"

"This is my cousin, Anand. He came for the feast." Arvind laughs.

In looks, Mangla likes Anand better.

"This is my friend, Basanthi. She is from Jammu. Her grandfather was in the Maharajah's court."

Basanthi also says *namaste.*

"They both attend BHU and study together," *Pitaji* says.

Arvind gazes at Basanthi's bare light-skinned face and arms.

Mangla looks away. However, she notices Anand watching both with curiosity. "Arvind and Anand study Engineering at Roorkee."

"You have much in common, then? Like Basanthi and I." Mangla says.

Ammaji enters with her head covered and says, "What? Mangla *beti*. The guests have no tea. Please pour some tea in their cups. Did you serve them sweets?"

"She did offer," Anand says.

Basanthi looks at Mangla's vexed gaze and moves to serve the sweets herself. *Ammaji* says, "Basanthi *beti* you are our guest. It's Mangla's duty."

Basanthi sits down.

Mangla takes the sweets around again and refills their teacups.

Anand moves to stand next to Mangla and Basanthi and says, "My mother's cousin married a scholar in the Maharajah's court. They were modern thinkers and met in theosophy meetings. Their community advised them against an inter-caste marriage. But as progressives, they believed in change to orthodoxy through action. When they returned to Jammu, he lost his job as a court scholar by the Maharaja's orders."

Knowing Basanthi's background, Mangla glances at her. She has her cross in her mouth and is looking away with a painful frown on her face. Neither man notices.

"Yes, they were shabbily treated—especially their children," says Anand. "We lost touch, and last we heard, she died of grief. If your grandfather was into theosophy, I wonder if you knew them, Basanthi."

Basanthi looks away as if a ghost has crawled over her. She chews on the chain of her cross. Unaware of her anguish, he says, "Perhaps your family can put us in touch with her children. It is sad to lose kin," Anand goes on. "It would be nice to include them in our Gandhian progressive secularist family someday. My mother is always talking about them."

Mangla intervenes and asks Anand about his college life.

He tells her about his regatta on the Solani river, tennis, squash, and studies. "Civil engineering is about construction, and we have to go on many field trips." "Mangla and Basanthi both shared the freshman Vice Chancellor's leadership award," *Pitaji* says as he takes a deep breath from his chest. "Tell them about all the activities you were involved in to win it. So impressive."

To Mangla, Anand seems young and interesting but not that different from Badri and Shabbu and her other male cousins. The girls talk about their admiration of Annie Besant and what inspired them to begin a faith and reason society with the theosophy lodge. They talk of their plans to advance women's education and rights in a free India, and they talk about how they support Gandhi's freedom movement and yoga they've studied and taught at BHU.

In their animated exchanges with the young men, Mangla's quick wit comes through. They laugh and talk freely about the dreams and aspirations they have, and they share interesting tidbits from BHU, including critiquing the literary writing on India's social ills and the movie *Dharti Mata*.

"I'm afraid we don't get much time for movies in Roorkee," Anand rejoins.

"Oh, how the time's gone by," Arvind taps his fingers. "Anand, we'd better get back. We have an early morning train to catch back to the University." With that he gets up to go.

"You have a long journey ahead. Shall I pack some food for you to take on the train tomorrow?" says *Ammaji*.

"Oh, no. Please don't worry. It's a short train ride for us," says Arvind.

Anand takes his time getting up. "Mangla and Basanthi, it's been such a pleasure to meet you. I hope we continue this conversation. I really enjoyed myself. Maybe I'll write to you."

Arvind doesn't say anything to Mangla except goodbye.

Mangla gets up to clear things from the living room.

Basanthi says, "I'll be back in a moment."

When she returns, she says, "I need to confess. I followed them to hear what they said to each other as they waited for the *tonga*."

Mangla picks up the teapot and stands there holding it awkwardly with a worried frown.

"They couldn't see me, silly. I stayed in the shadows. I heard them say that Arvind was here to look at you. He thought you were ugly, and your family were too ordinary. He liked the girl they saw the night before. Anand, though, thinks you are charming and full of sparkle. He plans to write to you and call you 'sparkles.'

Arvind taunted Anand, "Why don't you marry Mangla, then. She is too forward and ambitious for my family." Then he advised Anand to be practical and not to mess with us. Especially me, who as an Anglo-Indian wouldn't be approved of by their family."

"That one stung," Basanthi says. "If I hadn't been in hiding, I would have punched the bigot. I'm sorry you have to go through this kind of thing."

"Well, we had better finish cleaning," Mangla says. "Maybe he'll write to me, maybe he won't. There is no harm in having a pen pal."

"Anand has a strong opinion on every subject," Basanthi says. "And he thinks a lot of himself."

"Well, someone has to cut him down. At times he is just wrong."

"Just as well he isn't the one they're thinking of marrying you to. He will be high maintenance for some poor woman."

"Who said I'd even consider marrying either one of them? Like my brothers, they are full of themselves." Mangla picks up the tray with used cups and plates.

"In free India we will have so much to do," Basanthi says. "Who will have time to marry?"

XXXXXXX

13 Mangla 1941-42 Courtship

Some time passes since Anand and Arvind's visit to Mangla's home for *dekhao*. There is total silence from their family. As she predicted to Basanthi, it translates into no marriage proposal. Always the same story since she was in high school and considered of marriageable age. Her father invited eligible bachelors suggested by *Ammaji* for countless *dekhao* teas. It never translated to a marriage proposal but made her feel socially unwanted. She feels the rejection in her sinews but, shrugs it off. Not that she's interested in marriage. But still it would feel good to be wanted. It would be nice, for once, to be the one doing the rejecting. But she knows she doesn't have that social power.

No promised letters from Anand either. Not that she wants them. He had the swagger of someone from a prestigious University. Obviously, it was a rash promise made in the moment to impress Basanthi, to whom he seemed attracted. A deep twinge of envy sears through Mangla's body. But he didn't write to Basanthi, either. It shakes her faith in men's words. She believes she gave him undue credit. She shrugs and disengages from this useless pukka sahib.

Damn him.

Mangla focuses on her important academic goals to graduate. The projects for which they've received financial support from the vice-chancellor's office. Hopefully, when they graduate, other students will take over its leadership. Plus, her coursework, which is harder and harder. It requires her working long into the night. The next couple of years gallop along at a fast pace. The professors pile them up with lots of papers and books to read. Mangla and Basanthi still support each other but are given different paper topics and work independently of each other. Soon she needs to put a proposal together for next year's senior thesis to be presented to the entire University. They must develop the topic they committed to in their freshman year. It is a requirement for them to get their BA degree.

Basanthi's topic is the dowry system. They both debated these topics in the first year, but now they must do more extensive research and interview people who are affected by these social afflictions. They need to determine the reasons these practices are so entrenched, how they create undue hardships, and the nature of these difficulties.

Basanthi plans to go to Jammu for her research so she can visit Bhumi, who is improving. Aunt Sue has moved to Jammu to support Bhumi after her husband and mother's deaths. True to her word, Sue has kept Basanthi informed of happenings in Jammu. Basanthi has shared these letters with Mangla. They agree that should things get too stressful with Jill, Basanthi can return to Benaras to continue her research and stay with Mangla.

"Thank you, *Ammaji* and Mangla," Basanthi says with her cross in her mouth. "This takes a lot of weight off my shoulders. God willing, I can now go and be with Papa without fearing Jill."

"I wish I could go with you to Jammu," says Mangla. "I so enjoyed it. Maybe next summer after our graduation and before joining the Master's program, *Ammaji* and I can come with you and visit Sabiha*jiji*. Right, *Ammaji?*"

"That would be so wonderful. I've never been there and never thought I could go."

"I'll love to show you around. *Inshallah*, this year I'll go and visit Murree and do some research for my thesis topic. I can stay with Farida for another point of view."

"Now you are making me envious," says Mangla.

"Stop being dramatic. However, it'll be nice to stay with Aunt Sue and visit Papa with her. I'm so excited. Hopefully he will be fully recovered and back at work and take us to Murree. I'm sure a change of scenery and healthy mountain air will do them both good."

"These college years are wonderful," Mangla says. "Thank you, Basanthi, for your hard work to keep our dynamic duo energized." She gives Basanthi a hug.

Their six weeks of summer go by fast. In letters, Basanthi and Mangla share some of the stories that they discover for their thesis topics. They end their letters with a renewed commitment to uplifting women in free India after graduation, and discuss the quit India movement, which is supposed to accelerate the country's independence.

***

By the time their senior year begins, they have succeeded in making the traditional ragging of freshmen a thing of the past. They engage the new freshmen to join their projects and to plan out what they will do towards supporting the freedom struggle.

Then the letters begin arriving. They come fortnightly, and are addressed in Anand's neat handwriting, with a return address to Anand Rai in the left top corner. Her heart skips a beat when the first one comes. Trembling, she puts it atop the dresser, unopened like it's a ticking time bomb. What could he want after all this time? She doesn't want to know.

She does the same with the next one, and soon there are four unopened letters atop the dresser.

Basanthi comes in. "He wrote again, hunh? Is it puppy love?" Sarcasm drips from her voice. "He is persistent. At least open them and then decide what to do." Mangla shrugs and waves her off.

Basanthi says, "OK, I'll count till three and if you don't open a letter, I will. One-- two----"

Mangla makes a quick move to grab the letters but doesn't open them. Basanthi watches her for a moment, then pounces on the letters and runs away with them.

Mangla chases Basanthi around a tree in the yard. "OK, OK you win. Give me my letters and I'll open them."

"Promise? If I lie, I hope to die? Now cross your fingers."

Mangla complies. "You drive a hard bargain."

Basanthi hands her the letters. The two girls sit under the tree while Mangla reads them. "I don't know what he wants. All he talks about is himself and the work. How boring." She yawns and hands them to Basanthi.

"What do you think?"

"Sounds like he really wants to know you. He addresses you as Sparkles. At least he remembers. Aren't you going to reply?"

"Should I?" But she doesn't. More letters arrive.

"He seems determined," Basanthi says. "All this without any encouragement from you. I don't think he'll give up. Is he trying to woo you?"

"Woo," Mangla says with a rueful smile. "I don't think this term exists in our culture."

That's how Mangla's relationship with Anand develops. Part of her wants to respond and part resists. She feels confused.

More letters arrive and Mangla shares them with Basanthi.

"Is he real? He seems to be an idealist and his letters seem one-sided. Maybe you should reply and find out," Basanthi says.

"Perhaps we can get a man's point of view for our thesis topic and let him do some work for us obtaining views of his fellow students. After all, they would be brothers or uncles to women and family members, don't you think?"

"What a brilliant idea. We could educate them to not be so cavalier towards young women. Help change their lenses. We can keep it to specific non-personal topics."

"This way, if he truly wants to get to know me, he can show his gumption. It'll make our theses strong and unique," Mangla says in an upbeat voice.

When Anand begins to reply to the social questions Mangla poses, she responds in kind, and finds similarity their thinking.

A marriage between them would be between two adults of like mind, not one arranged by family.

She learns that Anand's family, too, wears Khadi. They are freedom fighters. His father went to jail with Nehru and his mother is a congress organizer.

"You know, Anand says that his friends feel that any man taking a dowry is evil," Mangla says.

"Ask him if he'll forego dowry for himself."

"I did, and look here in this letter, he says that he definitely will," Mangla says.

"Well, we'll see when the time comes," says Basanthi. "All men promise things and then never deliver."

"You're so disparaging. What's he done?" Mangla says.

"Look, Europe is at the brink of a world war. Prompted by power hungry men who want to possess."

"But Anand is a pacifist and is for nonviolence. You've read his letters. His family, like ours, are Gandhi followers."

"We'll see," Basanthi says. "Like many men, if he's crossed, I suspect he'll resort to violence."

"Why take it out on men? Without them we wouldn't be here."

Basanthi says, "Men are so gullible like my dear Papa and fall for the vices of women doing them more harm than not. That's what turns me off – in many ways they are so weak and yet society gives them so much power over women's lives.

Basanthi's prompts, "Did you ask him about his views on child marriage and widowhood in this society?"

"You read it. He believes that the new Indian constitution should eliminate this practice and give women the power to be productive citizens equal to men."

"How would he plan to do that?" Basanthi rejoins.

"Is it to do with Anand, or because of your prejudice against men in general?"

"Look who's talking! You were against him and now you can't extol enough of his virtues."

They go on and on in this adversarial fashion. Basanthi is often uncharitable towards men generally, but Mangla notices that their conflict accelerates whenever she receives a letter from Anand and talks about his good qualities. Basanthi still prompts her to ask him questions, but when she reads the answers, she's only angrier. If he says something she agrees with, she insists he can't be trusted. Mangla feels compelled to defend the absentee's viewpoint.

"You always take his side," Basanthi says. "He can do no wrong in your eyes. I am the baddie now."

Their friendship seems to be splintering by a moving pen. A relationship between the three of them threatens Basanthi. She distances herself more and more from Mangla and spends more time walking around with Shamla now. Sometimes she ignores Mangla altogether, even when they're in their room.

For Mangla, it's like an arrow has pierced her heart. It's driven deeper every time she sees Basanthi and Shamla walking and laughing together. She misses the intimacy she once shared with Basanthi. When she follows them, they ignore her. It feels like a deep dagger tearing at her heart. She wonders at Basanthi's coldness. How could Mangla have been so mistaken to be so sure of Basanthi's affection? The last straw is when Basanthi goes to a movie with Shamla.

"I would've liked to go with you. Like old times," Mangla says.

"I just thought you'd be too busy writing letters," says Basanthi with a sneer.

"You could've asked," Mangla says quietly.

"I have before, and you tell me you don't have time, as you need to write a letter. Shamla doesn't have that distraction."

The more Basanthi withdraws, the more Mangla pours her heart out to Anand. Her heart warms to him, and she can begin to imagine a new life as his wife. He hasn't proposed to her as such, but the letters indicate he has strong feelings towards her. They give her heart a glow, and she looks forward to receiving them. Even so, she's confused and holds off telling her family of their communication.

Anand keeps answering Mangla's questions freely and openly with an educated man's viewpoint. Hers and Basanthi's thesis presentations bring standing ovations because of their comprehensive, courageous coverage of the dowry system and child marriages. Both their theses are published as bound BHU volumes and noted as the most influential social issue theses ever written at BHU. Mangla and Basanthi both dedicate their work to Annie Besant. They receive congratulatory letters from the theosophy society director and from Anis Kidwai. They share the University gold medal, and each receives a full scholarship to the graduate program.

***

Mangla gets a note to see Mrs. Karachurian. The warden tells her that Basanthi has said she wants to room with Shamla in another house the following year when they start their Master's program.

"But why?" Mangla asks.

"I don't know. I'm afraid that was her request. She seems upset about her aunt's illness. You didn't know? Have you fought?"

"No," says Mangla in a small voice. "I thought we were getting along well."

"She wanted to leave and go back to Jammu to be with her father, but we hated to lose her and were able to increase her allowance. Now Basanthi's planning to stay and earn her PhD. But she wants a change."

Mangla takes it all in. Basanthi hasn't told her about the increase in her scholarship, or of her aunt's illness. But then Mangla has been too busy with her obsession with Anand and final exams to have given her time.

"Anyway, you are planning to return for your master's program aren't you?

"I'm not sure of my plans as yet," Mangla says.

"Is your family marrying you after graduation?

Mangla blushes and says that she's not aware.

"Well, good. Since accommodation is hard at the last minute, I want to know if you have any preference for a roommate yourself next year."

"No, miss." This is a surprise. The master's program is short. "You can choose anyone you want. I'll adapt."

"You've been such a good and diligent student, Mangla. Why don't I give you a single room? I have a small one. Would you like that?"

"That'll be wonderful."

The next time she writes to Anand, she tells him of this possibility for the following year. "I'll get to write my letters in peace without worrying about snoopers."

He responds with a supportive philosophical take. She could enjoy her peace and quiet and take the time to home in on her hobbies and talents. That night, in their room, Mangla confronts Basanthi when she returns from her walk with Shamla.

"What's got into you, Basanthi? What have I done?"

"Nothing." They are now standing and facing each other.

"The warden said you don't want me as a roommate next year. Why're you punishing me like this?" Mangla says.

"Don't I have freedom to choose who I wish to live with?" Basanthi says as she walks to the window and looks out.

"We've shared so many experiences together over these years. How can you move away so easily from your affection?"

"It's time for both of us to move on," Basanthi says in an audible whisper. "To have the experience of living with someone different."

"I don't understand you." Mangla is in tears. "And I'm so sorry to hear about your Aunt Sue's health concerns. Why didn't you tell me about it? I learned it from the warden. It hurt. And you wanted to not room with me next year."

"Like you care."

"But I do," Mangla says. She moves closer to Basanthi, but the girl shrinks away like Mangla is some vicious animal.

Mangla takes a deep sigh, with tears pouring down her face, and watches Basanthi turn around and walk out --a final exit.

Mangla stands there holding her rejection. Her shoulders sag. She has never experienced such profound loss, has never shed the tears of heartbreak. She wonders if this is the kind of grief Basanthi felt as a girl, losing her grandfather, her mother, and then, to Jill, her father. No wonder she has been unable to fully recover. Mangla wonders if she ever will.

***

Love Partitioned

That summer at home, Mangla intercepts Anand's letters from the postman, and walks to the post office to mail her own so no one will know about them.

One day, Vani and Surjjo catch her and tattle to her parents.

"Mangla*jiji* goes to post office to get her letters and mail them to a man, Anand. He lives in Allahabad."

"It's true, I met him at our house," Mangla says. "We've been writing to each other for a few years."

Vani dances around her and Surjjo copies her. "How romantic, just like in Austen novels."

"Mangla, Anand comes from a good family," says *Ammaji*. "He is now working and is a very eligible bachelor. Shall your father take a marriage proposal between you two to his father?"

She nods her bowed head in affirmation. That's the last she hears about it. After encouraging her for so long, maybe he won't be able to stand up to his father. Perhaps his father found him another more beautiful rich woman who could offer them a big dowry. That wouldn't say much for Anand's high sounding but empty words. Already, Mangla feels defeated. Her internal *Bhangi* chant gets louder and starts berating her At least she has the option of joining the Master's program. She lets the warden know that she will be returning.

Mangla is so sure of the outcome, she ignores Anand's letters and burns them unopened. In the final months of her MA program, a letter arrives from her mother. She opens it and can hardly contain herself.

Mangla sets out for the dining room wearing a plain green cotton sari with a black cutwork border. Her long, waist-length hair falls freely down her back to dry. She is hungry and hopes that the dining room is still open for breakfast.

In the distance she sees Basanthi coming from the opposite direction. Basanthi turns her head, as if looking for a phantom friend.

Mangla hurries towards her, letter in hand. The grass around her is green, tall, and lush after the recent monsoon rains. *Teej* is over and soon her college life will be too. The green parrot flies from the tree, and soon she, too, will fly.

"Did you get another letter from Anand *bhai*?" Basanthi asks and points to the letter.

"No. It's from my mother. My wedding date is set. The pundits found an auspicious date and time through matching our horoscopes. It's in couple of months. You'll come, won't you?"

"Of course. You'll finish your Master's degree right? My coming will depend on how much work I have to do," Basanthi says.

"I can't. *Ammaji* wants me married. She can't believe that the most eligible bachelor is asking for my hand without dowry. She doesn't want to upset the apple cart by making my education a higher priority. OK. I know. What about our pact? But *Ammaji* thinks maybe I will be able to persuade Anand to let me finish my MA thesis after marriage."

"I hope she's right. Isn't it your birthday tomorrow?" Basanthi says.

"You remember. The way you've been avoiding me, I thought you'd forgotten," Mangla says.

"Of course, I remember, silly. How can I forget after four plus years? You turn twenty and will be the first of our friends to get married, and to a most gorgeous looking guy.

She seems so upbeat and friendly. Maybe, like Mangla, the summer with her father gave her time to reflect and calm down. Maybe living apart that summer has been good for both girls.

"For my birthday shall we go and see the movie *Basant*? Its title glorifies your name to bring spring home." Mangla begins to hum her favorite song from that movie. "*Hua kya qusoor, jo tum ho dur, jane jigar,* what have I done that you distance yourself, my love?*

Basanthi joins her.

"Mangla, be serious, though. Why are you abandoning your studies? Leaving in the final year of your master's program after investing years of your life.? You fought so hard to get to the University. I don't understand you."

"Even after meeting *Ammaji*?" She laughs.

"Why are you leaving the University now, though? So close to your degree?"
"Well, you know I won't get my degree. What will a few more months do? *Ammaji* wants me to help her with wedding preparation. It's the last time she will spend any time with me," Mangla says her voice sad at the impending separation. It's a rite of passage and a heart break every Hindu woman goes through.

"You're rationalizing—you know you are. Where are all the dreams we weaved of changing the world for women? What would happen if you defied your family customs?" Mangla doesn't know. She's never done it. She stays quiet.

"Anyway, do you even know where you'll be living after your marriage?" Basanthi asks.

"No, because Anand doesn't know yet where he'll be posted. I guess all the recent Quit India political turmoil has delayed his appointment letter."

"So how much dowry is he asking?" Basanthi asks with curled lips.

"None. He declined. My father can't believe that such an eligible bachelor would refuse. He thinks that Anand walks on water!"

She wants Basanthi to know that Anand has integrity.

"Well, he should decline the wedding date, too, so you can finish your degree," Basanthi says.

" *Ammaji and* astrologers say that it's heavenly ordained."

Mangla takes Basanthi's hand. "Aren't you hungry? I'm starving. I hope the dining hall is still open. Let's hurry."

Luckily it is open. They go in and the screen door shuts behind them with a big bang. It startles Mangla, and she puts her hands on her ears to ward off the unwanted sound and to make room for the bulbul song. The bird has just flown from the Neem tree.

"Basanthi, see that bulbul? in a free India I too will fly unfettered."

XXXXXXX

14 1942 Wedding and Move to NWFP

Mangla sits in her room waiting for the daily *tonga Ammaji* hires for their wedding shopping. Her own incompatible conflicting emotions are caught between two stones of a grinding wheel. Part of her regrets leaving her studies before finishing her MA. Part of her wants to be independent and free of her parent's decision making. They didn't allow her to negotiate her educational future with Anand. Their worry is that if they don't comply with the astrologers and his family's demands about the wedding date and time, then Mangla will lose this prized catch. *Ammaji'* feels that education can be negotiated after the marriage. For all Mangla knows, she may be right. She doesn't know Anand's family and *Ammaji*'s fear is contagious. Mangla caves in like a child.

Now she is busy pleasing *Ammaji* and dreaming of her future. But life feels empty. She misses her hostel life and the university.

When Mangla's been home a few weeks-- she asks *Ammaji*, "Why do I need so many clothes? I didn't need them in college."

"Well, my daughter doesn't get married every day. Besides, I want you to look pretty when you go to parties. Men have urges. Even the best ones go astray and find another woman if not pleased. Women don't have that choice."

"Times have changed," Mangla says. She feels lucky. Anand is different. Through his letters he conveys that he believes in women's education and freedom to follow their own pursuits.

"As a new bride, I'm sure you'll be invited to many parties. I don't want your husband to tire of the same old clothes."

Anand is still in training, and they don't know where he will be posted. Mangla comforts herself that after her marriage she'll be free to lead her life as she wants. She writes to Basanthi to tell her about *Ammaji* and their activities. She invites her to come early and be part of the celebration. Basanthi replies that she has a big paper due the day before the wedding. To have company for the long *tonga* ride to the wedding and back she'll come with Shamla.

The closer it gets to the wedding day, the more anxious Mangla feels, and she seems to lose her cool easily. *Ammaji,* instead of getting upset, is patient. "All

114

brides go through these difficult emotions." She brings Mangla's favorite drinks and lets her sleep late and eat when and what she wants to. Mangla sees a new empathic side of her mother. *Ammaji's* sister, Seema *Mausi*, arrives to help plan and execute the wedding celebration. She's a whiz at embroidery, and her magic hands spruce up the numerous saris they've bought. She talks to the cooks to plan the meals and sweets that will be prepared for the hundred-plus family and friends that will live in their house for up to a week.

The excitement is building. So is Mangla's nervousness.

***

In one of his letters, Anand tells her that he loves to play bridge. She knows Hari *Bhai* is a whiz at bridge and asks him if he will teach her the game. She is a quick study and very soon she's proficient.

Hari *Bhai* shakes his head. "I can't believe you beat me at this game. You are a natural for playing bridge. Boy, will Anand be surprised when you beat the pants off him and his friends. Their surprised faces will be quite a sight. A woman beating them." He throws his head back and laughs.

Finally, a week before the wedding, she gets a letter telling her that Anand is going to be posted to a remote place in the Northwest Frontier Province NWFP region of India where they are building a new rail line. He will start as an assistant engineer. It is about 80 miles northwest of Abbottabad toward Mansehra in the foothills of the Indian Himalayas.

Mangla gets out an atlas to look up where it is. Compared to here, it's not too far from where Sabiha and Mahmood live. Mangla hopes that she will be able to meet her sister more often. The place Anand is posted is about a couple of days' by train to Sabiha's place, and it gets much colder there than in the plains.

"We better find you some warm clothes," says *Ammaji*. "We should go to Delhi and buy them for you. But we don't have enough time."

In the end, they take the easy way out and go to the next town's Kashmiri shop. Mercifully the weather is cooler, now, and shopping is quite pleasant.

They finally select a fine Kashmiri embroidered gray pashmina sari. It has a red and gold border and a matching warm blouse with long sleeves and a high collar, which opens part way in the front. Mangla tries it on in the fitting room. She likes the way it reveals her attractive bosom.

The shopkeeper says, "*Bibiji*, feel the pashmina. It's so soft. It's the inner coating of the youngest lamb. You won't find anything softer than this anywhere. It's from my brother-in-law's own herd. We guarantee our quality."

"You look so lovely. Anand will be enthralled." They buy gray woolen socks and red walking leather Jodhpur *jutti*, shoes to complete this winter party outfit.

"Please show us some pashmina shawls for both men and women," *Ammaji* says. "The warmer the better. And also winter coats."

In the mild tropical winters of the Indian plains where they live, a thin shawl is the accepted winter wear for both genders. The differences between men and women's shawls are the size, color, embroidery, and the cost. Women's shawls are finer, more colorful, and with more elaborate embroidery, which jacks up their cost. These shawls are ubiquitous in the shops.

"That intricately embroidered fine pashmina shawl will look lovely and keep you warm.

Mangla looks at the prices in dismay. "These are so expensive."

"Oh, your dowry insurance money helps," *Ammaji* says. She turns to the shopkeeper. "Now show us your coats?"

"No, bibiji. We don't sell readymade coats here. People usually buy cloth and get them stitched to their own design. We have a lot of woolen cloth. Here, I'll show you."

With that he walks over and brings down bolts of fine woolen cloth. They all look thin and not suitable for cold winters in the mountains.

"How long will it take to get a coat stitched?"

"Three weeks or so."

"That won't do. Besides, your cloth is too thin." *Ammaji* turns to Mangla and says, "Perhaps you'll have more time and better luck when you get to Abbottabad because of its proximity to the mountains. I'll give you money to buy one. Maybe they'll sell readymade warm ones there. Until then, the pashmina sari should help.

"That night, Mangla's family take each sari and the matching blouse and petticoat and tie them up in gold ribbon and set them out on a charpoy for the visitors to see. Some are Mangla's personal trousseau, and others are to be given as gifts to Anand's family.

***

Two days before the wedding, everyone is gathered for the *Bhaat* ceremony. At the time judged to be auspicious by the pundits, *Mamaji*, *Ammaji's* brother, arrives dressed in a traditional gold embroidered jacket. He brings trays full of sweets and presents for *Ammaji* and her family. The women sing appropriate songs accompanied by the *dholak* drum and cymbals.

"Hello, Mangla. Where's my *beti*, bride to be? Look what I have for you." He directs the servants to put the trays down on the bed. He brings out the red and gold wedding sari, and jewelry, shoes, and makeup, everything that she will need for her wedding ceremony. Mangla shyly comes forward and sits cross-legged next to him on the bed. He spins a wad of bills over her head and then puts it on the wedding trousseau he brought. He sets it all in Mangla's lap and gives the rest of the family their gifts.

The day before the wedding the *churi* vendor brings colorful glass bangles that are fitted onto the wrists above the henna hands of all the women. On Mangla's wrist, she adds red and green bangles between the gold ones her uncle brought her.

Mangla watches as *Ammaji* supervises the packing of a box that contains gifts for Anand's extended family. Other boxes contain her personal clothes, pots and pans, eating and cooking utensils, a sewing machine, knitting and sewing things. One box contains her *Charkah* and *havan* with *samagri* to go with it, carpets for the house, curtains, bed linen, towels. Anything *Ammaji* can think of, she buys.

It will all accompany Anand to NWFP, if her in-laws see fit or don't have a need for these things themselves. That is the custom, Mangla is told.

The day of the wedding arrives. So does Basanthi, with Shamla. Mangla hugs her and laments about her missing all the fun. The masseuse puts oil and herbal flour paste, *upton* all over Mangla's body and then gives her a bath and leaves.

"What is all that for?" Basanthi says.

Color creeps up Mangla's face, and she says, "Well it is supposed to make the skin and body supple and also lighten the complexion."

"Really? I don't see any change. Anyway, I'd better go and say hello to your family." Basanthi laughs and goes out of the room.

Seema *mausi* dresses Mangla in her finery and decorates her face to look like the most beautiful bride. She covers Mangla's head and face with the red and gold bordered Jaipuri tie and dye *chundri* veil. "There you are, ready as a *suhagan* meet your life partner and bring him good fortune."

Basanthi and Shamla walk in. "My don't you look like a royal bride. Gorgeous. Wait till Anand sees you. Are you ready for this new venture?"

Suddenly Mangla feels reticent and looks down as she shakes her head and whispers, "I feel afraid. Basanthi. I don't know what lies ahead. I really don't know the person I'm marrying other than that first meeting all those years ago and from his letters. In NWFP I will be so far away from everyone I know and am familiar with."

"You are tough and full of dynamism, Mangla. You're a born leader. I have full confidence in you. Besides, you will be closer to Sabiha*jiji.*"

"Take me back to BHU, please. I still have my place there." Tears well Mangla's eyes as she pleads.

Basanthi puts her arms around Mangla and rubs her back to lift her sagging spirit. "Now -now, no tears. You can't mess up Seema auntie's makeup artwork." That brings smile to Mangla's face. "I'm glad you came, my friend," Mangla says. Basanthi holds her hand and sits with her.

They hear the faint sounds of the band playing in the distance, heralding the departure of groom from the *janvasa,* the house where the *baraat,* the groom's entourage, is staying. They can hear the *shehna*i and band getting louder.

Ammaji comes in and sets down the *aarta* she has prepared. She says, "Can someone bring Mangla a glass of water? She's fasted all day. I hope she doesn't faint. Why must I think of everything?"

Shamla replies, "I'll do it, *Ammaji.* Your *aarta* looks so wonderful. I've never seen one."

Ammaji proudly looks at the silver tray with seven oil lamps made from fresh flour dough. She explains, as she lights the lamps, "One lamp is in the center and the other six are evenly placed in a circle on the perimeter. The lamps relate to colorfully decorated flour dough braids. In each sector I have put turmeric, vermillion *sindoor* powder, rice, onion seeds, salt, and a little container with sandalwood paste—all symbols of fertility and wellbeing.

"Could you and Basanthi also help her walk to the front door for the exchange of garland ceremony? Make sure she doesn't faint. She can't eat until after the wedding vows." With that, she takes the *aarta* and goes out to welcome the groom. The girls run in with an excited twitter to say: "He's so handsome in a traditional *achkan* and on his head instead of a traditional turban and *sehra* he has the Gandhi cap of a freedom fighter with jasmine bud strands dangling over his face and a thin pink muslin scarf on his shoulder."

Mangla looks at Basanthi who says, "Why does his incongruency not surprise me?"

"What do you mean?" Mangla says.

"You're blindly in love with him. You've always been that since the first time you met him. That's the way it should be tonight. He's a sahib and a freedom fighter at the same time."

***

Ammaji steps on a silver stool in the mandala decorated doorway. She waves her shimmering *aarta* tray in a circle in front of Anand seven times while chanting Vedic blessings. She puts a welcome red *tikka* on his forehead and gives him a wad of money. Supported by Basanthi, Mangla waits behind *Ammaji* and she steps up onto the silver stool. She is handed a marigold, jasmine, and rose garland. Anand is given a matching garland. He puts this around her neck and then she puts the other around his neck. Mangla steals a look at his face. The girls are right. He is handsome and a contradiction with his Gandhi cap and traditional fancy garb. She suppresses her laugh with hand on her mouth.

Mangla feels Basanthi withdraw in a hurry, as she hands her over to Vani. Mangla looks up and finds Jay standing next to Anand. What's he doing here?

Mangla's friends lead her to the *mandap*, the jasmine and marigold flower-decorated canopy. Anand is already there. On the four corners sit earthenware pots that contain water and grains of different kinds. Smaller copper vessels contain ghee, *tulsi* mint water, fruit, and rice for different rituals. On four sides there are ornate silver and gold *pidhas* set up with red velvet cushions. In the center is the *alpana*, an intricate mandala made with colorful natural powders like white flour, yellow turmeric, red *sindur*, and green henna. The square *havan kund* sits there, and inside are sandalwood twigs to be lit later as the vows are chanted by the priest. It is like Mangla's own *havan*, but bigger and more ornate, with an incense potpourri to be thrown in the fire with the appropriate chants and vows. On one side, Mangla and Anand sit. Opposite them sits the priest. On either side, her parents and her brother sit. Everyone, including the bride and the groom, have bare feet. All the shoes are left outside the wedding hall.

The ceremony is long. It takes more than an hour. Mangla's attention wavers to Basanthi, who is busy chatting to Sabiha. She's curious what are they talking about. Annie Besant? She finds that Anand like her, investigates the crowd for his buddies and waves to them, including Jay.

When her father and brother give her away to Anand, a knot is tied from her sari to Anand's scarf, binding them together. They take their vows by walking seven times around the fire. For the first set of three rounds, he is in front, and the priest tells her to learn to obey, follow and adapt to his and his family's ways. For the second set of three rounds, she is in front signifying that only when she is proficient in their ways can she bring hers to their collective living. In the last round they both walk together in shared leadership of old age.

Anand then puts rings on Mangla's toes. She's bound to him and puts red *sindur* powder in the part in her hair to signify she's not free. Then the wedding ceremony is over.

They walk and touch the feet of the priest and their elders as a mark of respect and honor and in return are blessed by them.

Food is brought to them on one plate to eat together. With her empty stomach she eats slowly.

Jay approaches Anand to congratulate them. just then and, with a scowling look at Jay, says that Shamla and she'll be leaving soon as they have classes in the morning. Their *tonga* is waiting.

"Did you eat?" Mangla asks.

Basanthi points to her bag and says, "Yes, *Ammaji* made sure that we were well fed and has packed us a part of the delicious dinner and sweets to take back to BHU."

Mangla holds her hand and says, "I'm glad you and Shamla came, and thanks for all your support. It meant a lot to me. I'll write to you. And you do, too. Write to me." They wave as other guests are waiting to congratulate them and a line is forming behind them.

Anand looks for his shoes. Everyone's shoes are there but his. Mangla hears the children's sniggering call, "Give us money or no shoes,"

When he tries to playfully grab his shoes, they pass them to the one farthest away of their gang like a football.

"Money first, then shoes," they cry in unison.

The elders chide their mercenary behavior. After some light-hearted banter, laughing Anand gives them tons of money to divide amongst them and retrieves his shoes.

Now it is time for *vida*—Mangla's departure from her home. Anand rides his horse ahead of the red and gold palanquin she sits in as *Ammaji* and the others tearfully wave her goodbye. She no longer belongs to her family. She's a *parai*, a stranger to them, and now belongs to Anand's family, whom she doesn't know. She looks back and sees *Ammaji* wiping her tears with her *pallu*. That vision breaks a dam within Mangla as tears flow and smudge her make up as she wipes them.

***

The next day she arrives at Anand's home and his women folk welcome her with an *aarta*; then they are taken to a room to play newlyweds' games. First, the bride and groom feed each other sweet saffron rice. Next, they untie miniature knickknacks knotted to the red and yellow sacred threads on their wrists. Mangla's family tied a lot of little knots that Anand finds difficult to undo. Frustrated, he yells, "Who tied these bloody knots?"

She wishes her family had not made it so hard for him. She doesn't want to witness this angry side of Anand, but she also feels protective of him. It's a new and strange feeling. The next game has a bunch of things thrown onto a metal plate and she and Anand have to compete with each other to find the ring. The one who finds it, rules the roost. Anand gets aggressive and won't let her win. Finally, she hovers her hand over the things that have been thrown onto the plate, and as she rummages around for the ring, he grabs her hand and holds it in a brutal grip. This first physical contact between them feels like an electric jolt. She's learned that he's strong, and with a temper. She wants to go to bed. It's been a long day.

His sisters help her wash and change. Anand enters the room, and they leave. Mangla feels shy.

He says, "Come here, Sparkles. I finally have you to myself."

Yet she's afraid to be in the same bed with him, not knowing what to expect. He seems experienced and makes love to her. She feels his force. It hurts. But she silently bears it. The next time it is easier and pleasurable. he doesn't seem to be in so much of a hurry.

In the morning, Anand's *chaprasi*, Rehman, comes in and puts Anand's clothes out and ensures that his personal needs are met. Then Anand gets his order to return. He leaves in a hurry, and she makes sure that the potentially incriminating literature is still under the bed. At least in NWFP he can't be implicated for inciting unrest and end up in jail as a seditionist.

A week later she receives her travel pass and edict from Anand to join her, even if she must travel alone to meet him. That's how she ends up in a sleazy evil turbaned man's paws on the strange railway station.

***

The train slows down as it approaches the Abbottabad station. A beautiful sunrise from the train window bathes Mangla in golden rays. She loves this time of the morning. She cleans herself as best as she can in the small bathroom sink.

Now that she is a day late, she wonders if she can still shop for a coat. The train comes to a stop. She doesn't see Anand on the platform.

She alights the train and pulls the shawl closer to her. The platform is open, and the air is cool. The coolies surround her. They are *pathans* with bearded faces. They are big, tall, light skinned, with dirty muscular bodies. They wear grubby turbans and scarfs. They have a distinct odor. Maybe she smells to them, too. Until now, Rehman is the only Pathan she's ever met, but he looks different. He wears a railway uniform. She taps her foot, feeling unsafe and wondering what to do, when she spots Rehman with the stationmaster.

"Salaam Memsahib." He salutes.

"Mrs. Rai?" The stationmaster says.

"Yes."

"We were expecting you yesterday."

Blood creeps up Mangla's face. She wonders if he has found out what happened. But he says nothing.

"Mr. Rai was here yesterday when we received a telegram that due to some problem you would be on the next train."

She relates what the English conductor did and how she spent the night in the ladies' room but omits the sordid behavior of the evil assistant.

"I'm so sorry. Some people don't have human decency." He tells her that at present the times are difficult. There is unrest in the community because of the arrest of Khan Sahib by the British—not to mention the arrest of other congress leaders after the Quit India movement ended. The train line was sabotaged just a few miles away. That's why Mr. Rai had to leave to inspect it, to ensure that it is safe for passenger travel.

"He is delayed. Rehman, please bring Mrs. Rai's bags to my office. Also have the bearer bring some breakfast for memsahib. You must be hungry," he says, turning to Mangla.

She nods. "Yes, I am."

She's peeved that Anand didn't forewarn her of the dangers of NWFP, but then letters take so long to arrive. There is a crease of worry on her forehead. It gives away her concern about Anand's and her safety. She holds on to her purse.

***

It is late in the afternoon when Anand arrives. His face looks harried and haggard. She barely recognizes him. He seems so distant, so very unlike the loving Anand who last held her.

He says, "We waited for you yesterday. The station master told me what happened."

"Yes, the change in plan was an awfully unpleasant interruption."

His disappointment expressed his face softens. "It's been lonely without you. I've missed you. I'll make sure that a charge sheet is filed against the conductor.

That's the only way to discipline their uncouth behavior and arrogance. The sooner we get independence the better."

"Rehman, take the bags to sahib's jeep," the stationmaster says.

Anand says, "Let's leave. We still have far to go, but if we hurry, we may get there before it gets dark. The roads are not that safe at night."

She wants to say, what about my coat? But in the expressed concerns for their safety, she can't find enough courage to utter those words aloud. It seems trivial to worry about a coat just now. Maybe she will find a resourceful way in the future.

"I have to leave early in the morning again," Anand says, steering her to a waiting jeep.

The driver of the jeep is turbaned, and Mangla gives a start as he helps her up to the seat. She sighs in relief when she realizes that Anand hasn't noticed her distress. She remembers her mother's warning: keep the unpleasant stuff from men. Find women to confide in.

XXXXXXX

15 Social Power and Unrest

They leave Abbottabad behind in the direction of Mansehra in the Himalayan foothills. It's only eighty miles, but the roads are very narrow and slow-going.

Anand takes her hand. "When we get home, let Rehman do the shopping until things calm down a bit. The times are quite dangerous here right now. It's not safe for you as a Hindu woman to go out."

Soon the jeep stops at a food *dhaba*. The aroma of freshly baked *naan* tickles Mangla's nostrils, and they stop to eat an early dinner. Anand says he regrets that he'll be working long hours, and so his time at home will be limited, but he'll love having her there. He lives and works amidst the area of Pathan communal unrest. He lowers his voice to tell her that now the emotions are high, and the literacy of the Pathans low, that it is difficult to know which Pathan one can trust. "Rehman is vetted but you never know what forces play outside. I'd hoped that things would have calmed down by the time you arrived, but if anything, they've gotten worse." In the car, she sees a gun on the seat by the driver. Still fresh from her trauma his turban sends tremors down her spine. Can they trust this driver her eyes ask Anand. He follows her gaze and lowers his voice. "We have to protect ourselves. The driver is on loan from the Railway safety police. Sikhs are educated and trustworthy. But even so, we have to be on our constant guard in this part of the country."

"Oh!" Mangla says. Anand's hands creep to her thighs. A shiver of anticipation runs through her.

"I'm sorry that as a woman it'll be lonely for you here. But for me, you're a heavenly gift sent by God. Thank you for making this trip alone, difficult as it has been for you."

She thinks: "If only you knew what happened." She avoids his gaze and looks outside the window.

The sun lowers itself behind the distant skyline of the Himalayan mountains. Mangla shivers and wraps her shawl tighter. The elevation is only about a thousand feet above sea level, but proximity to the high mountains and the dry desert climate of the Indian Northwest Frontier gives the wind a bit of a bite as it gusts through the open jeep. Anand notices that she's cold and lowers the plastic to prevent the wind. She misses her nonexistent coat and snuggles closer to him. He puts his arms around her in a loving embrace.

It's dark when they stop in front of a small cabin. Rehman opens the door as they step inside. There's a living room, bathroom, bedroom and a kitchen, the bed is turned down and ready. Mangla is tired. Rehman brings hot water from the kitchen and puts it in the bathroom for them to wash.

"It's late," Anand tells Rehman. "You can go home now. I have to leave really early in the morning."

As Mangla washes, Anand says, "I forgot to tell you that two days from now I've asked my assistants to come and have dinner and play bridge. Maybe you can tell Rehman what to cook? Please do not go out shopping yourself. It is not a time for heroics. I want my wife safe."

"I understand. I'll be mindful. I'm sure I have a lot to do to get this house organized. Hopefully our things will arrive soon," Mangla says.

That night he whispers sweet nothings as he caresses her body. Hungrily, they make love. Their intimacy restored, Mangla finally feels at home. Exhausted, she falls into deep sleep.

When she wakes up in the morning the pillow next to hers is empty. She vaguely remembers holding onto Anand before rolling over to get another bout of sleep.

She gazes at the distant snow-capped mountains through the paned window. The sun gilds them, filling her with a sense of longing to climb freely like she did in Murree with Basanthi.

She looks around her. The place is sparsely furnished but clean. She wishes she had her *charkah* and *havan*, if she can't go out. but that wasn't practical to bring in her suitcase full of clothes.

She realizes that she hasn't eaten for a long time. She follows her nose to the kitchen and sees Rehman preparing food. She takes stock. There are essential kitchen cooking utensils, enough for the dinner party in a few days.

"Good morning, memsahib," says Rehman. "I hope you slept well. Do you want hot water for your bath?"

"Oh, I already washed with cold water. Maybe tomorrow." She colors. She didn't realize that she could ask for hot water.

"I have your breakfast ready."

Rehman brings hot milk porridge, followed by buttered toast and baked beans, fried eggs and tomato. How *pukka sahibish* she thinks

"Sahib has this every morning. But if you want something different, please tell me and I will bring it from the market.".

"Can you make potato stuffed *paratha*?" Mangla asks.

"Memsahib, if you show me, I can learn even if I don't know."

"Do you have *atta* flour, ghee, ginger, potatoes, and vegetables? Let me look at the spices you have," Mangla says.

Rehman opens a cupboard. It has most of the things she would use in cooking: cumin, turmeric, coriander, mango powder, and hot spices. Not that different from what *Ammaji* has in her kitchen.

"Ok, tomorrow I'll show you how to make it. What does sahib do for lunch?"

She learns that he orders food from the local *dhaba* shop near wherever he is. She decides she will put his health on top priority by sending a home cooked meal to his work.

"Do you have a tiffin carrier?"

He goes to the cupboard and produces a four tiered one with a charcoal tray in the bottom to keep the food hot.

She tells him to put lentil *daal* in the bottom, with the next layer green vegetables, above it *chappatis*, and on top rice, yogurt and pickles.

"*Gwala* delivers milk early in the morning," Rehman says. "I can make yogurt."

"Rehman, sahib said that he's invited his assistants for dinner two days from now. How many does he have?"

"Three. They usually come and play cards with him."

"OK, we'll need more milk that day for *paneer,* cheese for peas and *paneer* curry and rice *kheer* pudding for dessert. Tell the *gwala* to bring extra milk for us. You have rice and flour and potatoes and enough ghee? What vegetables do they have in the market?"

""They have all the winter fruits and vegetables, peas, cauliflower, cabbage, eggplants, okra, apples and pears, etc."

She writes a list and hands it to him.

He looks at her and says, "Memsahib I don't read Hindi."

"I'll rewrite in Urdu. You do read Urdu, right?" He nods.

The novelty of being the boss is exhilarating to Mangla.

Grabbing the shopping bag, Rehman says, "If memsahib has everything on the list, I'll go to the market." He says, Things aren't always safe. We're in difficult times. I'm a member of KK party and follow nonviolence. Many others don't and we fight like children. "Please do lock the door."

She takes her time unpacking and putting things in the wardrobe. She touches each thing and fondly remembers the associations they bring to her. She's excited to begin her new life, even though, reluctantly, she must accept some of its present restrictions.

Rehman returns and sets her lunch on the table. She eats and afterwards brings her writing material and begins a letter to *Ammaji* and another to Basanthi. She's not used to being treated as royalty. Its novelty is intriguing, and she writes about it.

When she grows tired, she lies down and soon falls asleep. She wakes up feeling cold. She finds her shawl and wraps it around her. The sun has set, but there is no Anand.

Anand looks very tired when he comes home quite late. He changes, and Rehman serves them dinner. Over dinner he tells her that they found a fishplate missing on the train line. It looked like a case of vandalism. A fast train over it would have surely derailed. Luckily, they spotted it and fixed it avoiding a disaster. But for how long? This only delays the construction and makes people edgy, including him. He shakes his head. "Why someone does that and increase uncertainty of life?

Mangla has no answer for him.

"Anyway, what did you do?"

She tells him about her plans for the dinner party.

They move to the living room, where Anand sits down in the easy chair with his newspaper and buries himself in it.

Rehman peeks in the door. "Anything else, sahib?"

"No, Rehman, I'll be leaving early again. You can go home now."

"Yes, sahib, I'll be here with hot water for your bath in the morning."

Mangla walks around and says, "Oh look there's a radio. Good-I can listen to news and some music during the day."

Anand peers above the newspaper and says, "I wouldn't hold my breath. Our house must be in a shadow zone for the radio waves. Sometimes late at night it gets better. But it is touch and go." He disappears behind the newspaper again.

She turns on the radio, but there's only static. She jiggles the tuning knob and finally can decipher some voices. She puts her ear closer to it and can make out what sounds like music. She keeps fiddling with it. At least it provides her something to do while waiting for him to finish the newspaper.

He yells, "Turn the bloody thing off."

She does and sits waiting for his next command.

Soon he puts down the paper with a thump and pulls her up onto his lap. "I'm tired. Let's go to bed. I can do with some loving."

***

The next day, as per her plans, she sends Anand's lunch to the construction site. She can hardly wait for him to come home and tell her about this new experience. She waits and waits until his peon brings word that he's delayed and won't make it to dinner.

She asks the peon, "Has the sahib eaten his dinner?"

"Oh no memsahib. There's an accident and everyone is very busy."

"Then wait a moment." She calls out, "Rehman, Sahib can't come to dinner tonight. Let's pack him dinner, as we did his lunch, and send it with the peon."

She sits down to a solitary meal.

"Rehman, tell me about your family."

She learns that he has seven children and the eighth one is on the way. They come from this area and his wife and children work on a small farm near their home. He's worked for many sahibs in the railway over the years. When he's ready to leave that night she asks, "You did ask for extra milk right? Tomorrow night the sahib's friends come to play cards."

"Yes, memsahib. I'll shop early and make sure we have everything ready. Usually, they come late after work."

She goes to bed alone. Anand comes home late and reaches over to make love. In the morning, this is only a pleasant memory as she looks at the empty pillow beside her.

The next day she spends preparing her fancy dinner with Rehman's help. At the last minute, Rehman was unable to find cauliflower. Mangla substitutes rice-potato *tahri* instead. She'll just have to adapt in this part of the world. Their produce doesn't keep the same calendar she's used to.

The fresh roasted and ground spices fill the kitchen with a festive aroma as her dishes cook to perfection one by one.

"Rehman, you know how to fry *puris*, right?"

"Yes, memsahib."

"Then let's fry them fresh just before dinner. That way they will be warm and fluffy."

She goes and wraps herself in a pink pashmina shawl as she waits for the guests to arrive.

They are late. At this rate, the dinner won't taste as good.

The four of them finally arrive together. She says her *namaste,* and the assistants reciprocate. To her shock, she sees that one of them is Jay, Basanthi's cousin.

Anand yells, "OK, Rehman, we're home. Is the dinner ready?"

"Yes, sahib."

Shouldn't he ask her to order dinner? Rehman hurries out with the dishes and sets them on the table. He has already fried the bread. How did he know when to expect Anand? she wonders.

They sit down to dinner. "We better eat fast if we want to get in a couple of rubbers of bridge. I don't know about you, but I could use the relaxation it provides me. Especially today," Anand says.

Mangla wants to know what happened, but they are busy talking shop: about the problems with contractors and labor disputes due to *Pathan* unrest. As she sits there excluded from their conversation, she has plenty of time to observe them and doodle on the tablecloth with her spoon.

After dinner, they bring out decks of cards and a pad of paper. She hears Anand say, "We better hurry. We only have time for one rubber of contract if we want to be functional at work tomorrow."

No one invites her to join. She feels totally dismissed, like a maid. To hide her distress, she goes to kitchen and tells Rehman to go home and take all the leftover food and enjoy it with his family. She will do the dishes.

He protests. "No, memsahib. I'll do them."

"*Jao,* Go! It's getting late. I have time, as sahib's busy with his friends." She shoos him on with her hands. Glad to immerse them in cold water to douse the flames of anger spreading inside her.

***

Mangla has been in her new home almost two weeks. Mail arrives once a week. Nothing comes this morning. She feels abandoned. Anand has his colleagues and work. But she's starved for intellectual interactions. They have very little conversation at the end of the day, and now she doesn't even have the letters to comfort her from family. Soon she's a sobbing mess. She writes to *Ammaji,* who will understand her bereft feelings. She tells her about Pathans, the dangers, the long hours of Anand's work etc. etc. Soon she feels better. She gives it to Rehman to drop it off in the mailbox.

That evening, Anand cheers her up with the news that they have been invited to a party at the officer's club that Saturday. Everyone wants to meet her. It will be her first outing since she arrived.

Mangla looks forward to meeting other women who can orient her to the life of a railway officer's wife. So far, married life hasn't quite provided her the independence Anand promised.

On Saturday she reminds Rehman that they will be out for dinner. He can prepare their bed for the night early and take the rest of the evening off to relax with his family. " God bless you, Memsahib. That'll be nice."

She walks to the closet and selects her warm embroidered Kashmiri pashmina gray sari and long-sleeved woolen blouse. It will hide the scars on her arms. Matching jewelry. She next attends to her make up in front of the dressing table, brushes her waist length black hair, and puts it in a high bun over her head, fastening it with the pearl, jade, and ruby butterfly barrette. Anand said it is not far, but the weather turns chilly when the sun sets.

Finally, she slips her woolen socks, closed shoes, stylish horn-rimmed glasses and examines herself in the mirror. It reflects a satisfied, chic woman. She gets up, hears the front door open and shut as Anand's voice calls, "OK, Sparkles, I'm home. Sorry I'm a bit late. Are you ready?"

Mangla's heart skips a beat as she enters the living room. He looks handsome, with color in his cheeks and the tip of his aquiline nose red from the cold outside. His broad shoulders nest in his warm woolen black coat. "Sorry, I got delayed at work. We'll need to hustle to get to the party."

She says "Tada!" and pirouettes with flair in front of him.

He looks at her, aghast. "You aren't wearing that are you? It's the first time my colleagues will meet you. Are you going to a picnic or a party?"

His voice pierces her, and she is jolted out of her exuberance. Crestfallen, she looks up at him. His bushy eyebrows are knit and raised, and his forehead furrowed. Her heart pounds, and her feet are frozen to the floor as she stands there unable to move.

He charges to the bedroom and opens the cupboard, returning with her red and gold bejeweled wedding reception chiffon sari and matching blouse and *chappals*, with red and gold straps she threw at the receding train. She'll never be able to wear socks with them.

"We're already late. Go change into these. Hurry!" He commands.

"But—" she looks with dismay at her shawl. Now she wishes desperately that she had a coat.

"No buts, you'll do as I say. I want them to see you like I saw you on our wedding day. You looked so beautiful."

Her heart thumps as her disappointment in him registers. She looks down at her hands. Her deflated spirits are reflected in the fading henna. She doesn't know how to tell him that they must walk in the bitter cold outside. He has a coat, she a shawl. He has boots, she the sandals he wants her to wear. Should she retaliate? But her courage leaves her as she looks at his set jaw. Tears sting the back of her eyes. She takes the clothes and goes to the dressing room to change. The cold outside can feel no worse than the icy grip that clasps her inside. She says a silent prayer as she changes into her bridal attire and returns. His face softens as he looks at her. "Wait! That jewelry doesn't go with that sari. How about wearing what you wore at the wedding reception?" He returns to the bedroom and rummages through the drawers. He remembers, and cares. She warms a little towards him They set out. It is dark and cold. He has the torch and walks ahead with his long strides. He seems quite unaware of how she shuffles behind him in her flimsy *chappals*, her toes exposed. It is too dark for her to see much around her. There are no streetlights. She concentrates on her feet as she tries to keep in step with him.

Inwardly she seethes with anger. All the raw emotions from his restrictions erupt inside her. The heat from her resentful internal chatter accompanies her on her walk. She can't go out by herself without him, but he's never there to take her anywhere. She isn't a child. She is a resourceful, educated woman. What happened to his high ideals to help women advance? But she lacks the nerve to openly challenge her new husband whom she feels she hardly knows. She feels entrapped. She can't return home. Her stomach hurts and tenses. She trudges behind him— externally subservient while internally Fuming. Before she knows it, they are climbing the steps of the officer's club. Anand takes off her shawl and folds it as he drapes it on her arms.

He says, "There! They can now see you in your full glory from head to toe when we enter. Those *chappals* show off your toe rings nicely. You look striking and impressive like a new bride should look."

A bit underdressed for the weather, she thinks as the cold wind hits her bare midriff. She feels uncomfortable, self-conscious that she's in her wedding attire. It seems quite out of place. She wraps her sari around her to hold her safe like a cocoon as she braces herself to meet critiquing looks from strangers. She looks at Anand for reassurance, but he only beams at her with a possessive pride.

***

They enter a large, dimly lit hallway. With envy, Mangla looks at the heavy coats hanging on the wall pegs where Anand hangs his own coat.

They move further in to enter a large party hall. One table in the corner holds dirty glasses. Moths circle a feeble bulb hanging from the ceiling as yellow geckos grab them with their long tongues for a satisfying meal.

The festivities are in progress with about fifty people milling around, mostly men clustered in groups with drinks in their hands. Older men in suits are talking to each other. Waiters, dressed in white kaftans and turbans on their heads, take finger foods and drinks around to the assembled guests.

With her assurance deserting her, she wants to hide. However, Anand steers her over to a group of handsome younger men dressed in casual slacks, sweaters, and woolen jackets. With great charm he says, "Here guys, come and meet my wife, Mangla, and your sister-in-law."

They all stop talking and turn. They put their hands together, bow, and greet. The warmth of their voices and the pleasant smiles on their faces signal her that they must have high regards for her husband. She looks at Anand sideways— could she have misjudged him?

Jay breaks away from another group and comes over, "*Bhabhi* do you remember me? I'm Jay. I didn't have an opportunity to thank you for the lovely dinner you made on our bridge night. I guess you were busy when we left."

She wants to tell him that he hadn't included her that night, much like he'd ignored Basanthi years ago, when they were children. Now that she was "the boss's wife" he is more civil. Instead, she smiles. "Oh! I hope you enjoyed your bridge game."

"Yes, very much. Anand *Bhai* is good at it. Do you play also?"

"Yes. I learned from my brothers."

"Next time we should include you," Jay says.

The waiter offers them drinks from a large tray. She asks for fruit juice. Anand asks for a whiskey on the rocks.

She notices a handful of women on the far side of the hall, talking to each other. One of them is wearing a beige burqa with its veil raised from her face. A few are wearing saris with red dots on their foreheads, the same as Mangla. A couple of ladies wear Punjabi *salwar kamiz* and matching *chunnis* arranged in a V shape across their breasts. The Sikh lady also has her telltale iron bracelet. All their shoes are closed, and heavy coats lie on chairs beside them. She suppresses a laugh as she idly wonders what will happen if she pinches one of them. Instead, it emerges as a silent snort through her nose.

XXXXXXX

Love Partitioned

16 Freedom Ventures

Mangla feels her shoulders and arms tighten as her interior protests. Why did she not stand her grounds against Anand and insist on wearing her own warm attire?

Anand's hand on her arm brings her attention back to the group of men around her as the waiter holds a tray in front of them and points, "These are vegetable and those are fish *pakoras*." They each pick one and dip it in the green mint-cilantro chutney and return to their conversation.

A distinguished looking gentleman with gray hair at his temples joins them.

"Hanfi *Bhai*," says Anand. "Did you meet my wife Mangla?"

"Not had that pleasure as yet." He turns to her and says, "*Namaste*." She reciprocates his greetings.

"Waiter some more drinks, please, for everyone." Hanfi *Bhai* waives to a waiter. He seems to be the host of the party.

The waiter brings more drinks. Hanfi *Bhai,* like her, choses juice. Everyone else selects whisky, and they get louder and more irreverent as the political debate gets heated. Topics cover everything from the arrests of leaders of the Quit India movement to whether Gandhi was right in promoting non-violence to the followers of the Indian National Army, SC Bose, who supports Hitler using violence against Brits.

Anand argues for a just and equitable free society. His attitude and the contradiction between what he says and how he acts towards his wife makes Mangla flinch. She doubts his progressive politics he wrote to her about and how he treats her at home. Anand is on his third drink. Did he drink before? Or has he just started this habit in his new job?

The conversation shifts to the *Pathan* unrest around them.

Hanfi *Bhai* says, "The British government and the Muslim league are manipulating Khan sahib's absence."

Anand says in a loud voice and slight drool on the side of his mouth, "*Pathans* are a snuff-using, illiterate lot. Mullahs and Muslim leaders manipulate them."

Mangla wants to put in a kind word for *Pathans*, "But Rehman says—" Anand ignores her and continues in a loud slurry voice, "I heard that the militant *Pathans* are gearing up for revenge on the British." She is hungry and hopes dinner will be served soon. Jay takes over. "Since I'm Kashmiri, I can tell this joke about the poor Kashmiri *Pathan* who was running with a stolen rice bag on his back. When the police arrested him and took him to the police station, he tried to persuade them to release him as he was poor and needed the rice to feed his family. When they wouldn't, he said, 'OK keep the rice, but pay me four *Annas* for my labor.'"

Everyone laughs at his joke.

Another says, "I hear that the *Pathans* kill their prisoners of war very brutally. They put a rod in their mouths and then have their women urinate into the rod until they drown."

They all groan as they look at him in disgust.

Mangla can't imagine Rehman and his family doing this. She wants to protest. Once she would have said freely whatever came to her mind, but that was in the safety of her home with friends and family, or at BHU, where women were encouraged to protest argue and debate. She excuses herself and begins to move towards the women.

The last thing she hears is Jay saying, "That was crude. We shouldn't speak that way in front of Mangla *Bhabi*. I believe we've offended her."

Anand doesn't follow her. That is fine with Mangla. She wants to know the women to help her navigate her social environment. She wonders if they face the same restrictions as her.

"*Namaste*. I'm Mangla. I came less than three weeks ago. " The words, "I'm Anand's wife" elude her.

"*Namaste*. We've been waiting to meet you," is their collective response.

Unaware of the emotional landmine of the evening's dress choices, one of the women says, "You look so beautiful in that sari. It's nice to see a new bride amongst us. I'm Mrs. Desai. My husband thinks a world of Anand." Mrs. Desai wears a printed pink *Tanjore* silk sari and matching closed toe shoes with socks. She continues, "My husband joined the railway 20 years ago when I was a young bride like you. He had just started his work in construction, and it was difficult and lonely for me. How are you coping?" The lady in *burqa* says, "Hello Mangla. I'm Mrs. Hanfi. My husband's very fond of Anand *Bhai*. He always has good things to say about him and his work. How're things for you? Have you seen anything around here yet?"

Mangla shakes her head. "No, Anand has told me not to venture out alone, even to the market with Rehman. He's afraid for my safety, like I'll be abducted." "I know-- to be protective of a new bride is natural. Give him time," Mrs. Desai says. "But really it's not as bad as they fear. You should venture out. Come visit me sometime—I am not that far. Maybe your servant will know the chief engineer's house."

"I, too, am not that far from you," Mrs. Hanfi adds. "Mrs. Desai, why don't you and I visit Mangla during the day and take her out with us to the market? That'll give her confidence. I'll bring a *burqa*. That'll help her blend in and make her feel safe. What do you think, Mangla? Would you like that?"

"Yes! Oh, thank you so much. That'll be so wonderful. I've been dying to see the market. Please come any day. I'm always home." Mangla smiles broadly.

Mrs. Desai glances at her *chappals* and in a concerned voices asks, "Now that the weather's getting cold, do you have comfortable winter shoes?"

"Oh, yes! But I need a coat. There wasn't one available in Lucknow." Mangla avoids the mention of shoes.

"Well, you need to go to Abbottabad for that. Maybe the next time one of us is going, we'll ask you to come with us. What do you say ladies?" Mrs. Hanfi includes the other women in the conversation. The younger ones have been silent thus far.

"Perhaps I'll ask Mr. Desai if he can spare some vehicles one day so we can all go together to Abbottabad and see a movie. My servant says that *Mamaji's* a great movie. It just opened at the movie theater there."

"Mangla. I'm Urmila," says one of the young women in an elegant *salwar kamiz*. I came from Bombay six months ago soon after my marriage too. That's my husband there. He works with your husband." She points to a man standing near Anand.

"Happy to meet you, Urmila." Mangla smiles back at the beautiful, poised woman with a curvaceous figure and an enticing smile. She has noticed many men, including Anand, ogling her.

"I saw *Mamaji* in Bombay. Lalitha Pawar and Nandrekar make such a beautiful pair together. The songs are wonderful. I don't mind seeing it again," Urmila says with a radiant smile. Her radiance is contagious. Mangla smiles at her, mesmerized."Urmila sings really well, too. Please sing a song for us," Mrs. Desai requests.

Urmila hesitates and says, "I'll sing a song from *Mamaji*. *Apna Desh Hai Apna Ghar*, my country is my home." She begins to sing.

Everyone in the room stops talking and listens to her. When she finishes, there is a thunderous applause. Urmila bows her head.

Just then dinner is announced. It's about time, Mangla thinks. She takes her seat with the ladies. She likes them. They are so friendly and nice. The levity of their chitchat warms her heart. Her loneliness evaporates as she is filled with hope.

***

On the way home with the shawl wrapped around her, she says, "You know, the women are so nice. Mrs. Desai and Mrs. Hanfi said they'll come and visit me and maybe even take me to Abbottabad."

"That'll be nice. Their husbands are my bosses. I like them."

She can still hear the alcohol slur in Anand's voice.

"Urmila's husband is my assistant. We should have them over for dinner some time. She's stunning and sings beautifully. The song she sang was so patriotic."

His praise of the beautiful woman makes Mangla feel like a country bumpkin. Urmila seems to have all the Bombay wealth and sophistication that she herself lacks. She wants to be held and loved. But the words that next come out of her mouth are, "I noticed that you all drank a lot of alcohol."

"You know it's expected of us men by our bosses. It would be rude not to drink." "But Hanfi *Bhai* only drank juice."

"What are you driving at?" Anand sounds cross.

"Nothing."

"Are you accusing me of being spineless and without morals?" His voice is a pitch higher and takes on a petulant tone.

"I didn't say that."

"Damn it! Hanfi *Bhai* is a devout Muslim. His religion is his excuse. Everyone respects that and has different expectations of him. I don't have religion as an excuse, woman."

Mangla wants to say, that's a fast one, coming from you. What a story. You seem to like it and don't know when enough is enough. She wants to say, I must watch you and your drink, and to put up with your attitude afterwards. But she keeps quiet, still unsure of her place in his alien world. She looks at him. She chose to marry him, despite Basanthi's reservations. She took sacred vows to stay with him through thick and thin. She has mixed emotions after the tension-filled party. She feels disappointed in her husband, but also anticipates a more hopeful future in her new environment with newfound friends.

She is weary of their long daily separations and suddenly desires to be held, appreciated, and loved. The walk in the cold air releases a profound desire that intensifies in her belly. No matter what tomorrow brings, today is for love, her inner being says.

When they reach home and go to bed, a strange new yearning drives her to entwine her body around him. Aroused, he thrusts himself deep inside her. Her body responds and doesn't care whether his lust is for her or another woman. She feels a strange sense of fulfillment and falls asleep in his arms.

***

A kingfisher, with its bright blue-green shimmery feathers sits on the windowsill high on the wall. It visits daily to peck at the wooden bars on the windows. The bars let the fresh air in, keep the monkeys out, and keep Mangla feeling caged. But she loves talking to the pretty bird, singing it her lonely song of woe.

Basanthi and she talked a lot about how Annie Besant defied authority. But to even think about defying Anand's authority makes her heartbeat faster. It feels uncomfortable, like some internal brakes are stopping her from asserting herself.

Is it fear of his anger or just the social expectations crammed into her growing up? She wonders.

The weather is colder than it was before. Mangla needs a quilt in bed and sweaters and socks during the day.

Even in its daily visits the kingfisher at her window gets more aggressive. She sings --*chee chee*-- pecking on her window as if to say please open and let me in to your warm abode. Mangla sings back, "I hear you, but my hands are tied. Go fly and be free. But please keep coming back until I can fly with you."

She asks Rehman to bring a bird house and hang outside and fills with seeds. The kingfisher continues to visit her window but eschews her hospitality.

***

One day, there is a knock on the door. As Rehman opens it, she hears Sabiha's voice asking for her. Mangla runs and embraces her in a crushing hug.

"Sabiha*jiji*, I didn't know you were coming."

"I didn't either until the last minute. Mahmood has a civil service meeting further down. He asked me if I would drive with him and spend a day or two with you."

"You'll stay with me? We have so much to talk about."

"Yes, fortunately *Khalajan* can take care of the house and children for a few days in my absence."

"Oh, look at me. You must be tired and thirsty after that long drive. Rehman—" she calls and orders him to bring tea and snacks.

"I wrote to you but didn't get a reply," Mangla says.

"You did? I didn't receive anything. The mail is unreliable here. Anyway, we have so much to talk about. Mangla. Are you well? Fortunately, Anand is away traveling and won't be coming home that night. Like two schoolgirls they jabber away under warm quilts until wee hours, sharing the bed like old times. She tells her of the party a week ago where she met other women; the disaster with shoes, alcohol, and lack of a coat. The promised visits by Mrs. Hanfi and Mrs. Desai haven't materialized yet and she still doesn't have a coat.

Sabiha tells her that she can have her warm coat.

"Really, can I?"

"How could I forgive myself knowing my little sister is cold all winter? I have many more at home. In the car, my shawl will keep me warm enough until I get back."

Sabiha's visit is short. Mangla extracts a promise that Sabiha will visit again. After she leaves, Mangla feels more alone and imprisoned. She can't bring herself to tell Anand of Sabiha's visit. A few days later, Mangla stands in front of the polished teak dressing table. A long mirror mounted in the middle reflect sunlight off the distant snow peaks. It gives the room a golden glow.

Her romantic vision of being married to a revolutionary at heart, a man who wooed her, promising the liberation of Hindu women from their domestic bondage, isn't panning out as she imagined. But here she is. She's been here for almost a month and hasn't been allowed to venture out. Not even with Rehman. She remembers endless college arguments with Basanthi about whether Anand was all talk. Her heart won then, but now her head questions its decision.

The next morning when the kingfisher visits her window and pecks at the railing, Mangla says, "Hello, Mrs. Kingfisher. I, too, was free like you not so long ago. Are you telling me to not give up on my quest to be free, to be me?" As if on cue, the bird nods, gives its daily farewell trill of "Chee," and flies away.

A deep sense of longing engulfs Mangla, heightening her feeling of imprisonment. She punches the air in determination and calls after the bird, "OK, my friend. I'm going out today, cold, or hot. If you can do it, so can I. Anand or no Anand." After all, the ladies said she should venture out. Anand was just being overprotective of her.

Her eyes open wide. There, she has unfettered herself from *Ammaji*'s Hindu shackles of only doing her husband's behest. Resolutely she stands up, dons her leather *juttis* over her socks, and puts on Sabiha's coat, which makes her feel warm and supported by her sister. She walks out of the dressing room door to the kitchen. "Rehman. You haven't gone to the bazaar yet, have you?"

"No, memsahib."

"OK. I'm coming with you."

Frowning, he replies. "But sahib said to not let you leave the house without him. He'll be angry."

"Let me worry about sahib. I want to go and see the market and see what else they sell. Mrs. Desai said it is OK, and she's the big boss's wife."

"Whatever you say, memsahib."

Rehman picks up the shopping bag and the list of groceries she has given him earlier, steps out, and padlocks the back door. He leads the way down the back alley. This is her first view of outside in daylight since she arrived. Women sit openly on their thresholds lining the alley sifting grain, singing, and gossiping to each other in a language she doesn't understand. They watch their half-naked children running around freely chasing each other.

Mangla muses that she is not Anand's prisoner but his wife. Her heart thumps with the defiance of a teenager as she enters the street where the market stalls are set up. The tantalizing aroma of baking *naan* and vats full of curry pervade the air. She looks up to avoid the thoroughbred horse that is coming towards her. On it sits a handsome young army officer. Their eyes meet in mutual recognition. She jumps for joy as she folds her hands in *namaste*. "Hari *Bhai*? What're you doing here?"

He dismounts his horse and holds onto the reins. "I'm on patrol. I've been posted here for a couple of weeks before I move on further into the territory. I've been thinking of you, but we've been so busy that I haven't had time to come and see you."

"I'm so happy to see you. I've been missing family. For some reason no letters have arrived from home."

"It's not surprising. The Quit India movement disrupted trains and mail service in this area. It was never the greatest in this area to begin with-- but now---"

"My boxes haven't even arrived yet. They keep promising. I sorely miss my *Charkah* and *havan*. In one of my letters, I asked for one."

"Well, they did get a letter and mailed you a package before I got my assignment. I hope you will get it soon."

"This meeting is divinely ordained. You won't believe it, but today is the first day I've ventured out to the bazaar on my own."

"Really? I'm surprised Anand let you with all his revolutionary savvy." "He didn't. I came."

"Well, it may not be wise for a Hindu woman without *purdah* to be out and about around here."

"That's what Mrs. Hanfi said the other night. Maybe I can buy one today," Mangla says.

"Do you know why they posted me here?"

"Tell me."

"With world war raging in Europe, they don't have enough British soldiers left in India. Brits expect the local *Pathans* to riot over the incarceration of Khan sahib."

"I heard some rumblings about it the other night at the party."

"Well in that case, why don't we buy you a *burqa* first?" He steers her towards a shop where black *burqas* are hanging. Mangla shrinks away from him.

"I know you've spent your college career in the quest to free women of *purdah*. But this isn't that part of the world, and times have changed." Watching her frown, he adds, "As an older cousin I feel it is prudent right now."

She acquiesces and enters the shop. The shopkeeper brings down a few *burqas* and finds one that fits her. She opens her purse to pay for it, but Hari beats her to it and comes forth with the money.

"Oh, no, Hari *Bhai*, I can't let you do this. I have money."

"Well, whose suggestion was it hun-h? Besides I'm your older brother, aren't I? Anyway, how about you feed me a home-cooked meal one of these days?"

With one verbal blow, he essentially destroys her budding independent streak. She is back in the gender specific role of a married woman.

The shopkeeper ignores her attempts and takes the money from Hari. With a scornful look at them, she takes the *burqa* and puts it on, her face now shrouded but arms bare as a faint protest and to keep her cool.

"How's your own family," she asks Hari, steering him to safer topics. "Are they with you?"

"They are of course back home. I saw them before I received my assignment last week. I saw your parents too. They gave me your address." "How are *Ammaji* and *Pitaji* and Surjjo and Vani?" Her voice cracks a little. "I haven't seen them since my wedding. With no letters I feel so cut off."

"They are well," he says. "Mangla, you were such a beautiful bride in your red and gold sari, and Anand looked handsome. How's married life treating you?"

She blushes and lowers her eyes. What's there to say? She keeps quiet. "Last I saw, your *Ammaji* was busy being a *dadi, a grandmother* to Shabbu's little baby. Your *Pitaji*'s busy in his work and of course continues with his daily spinning of *charkah* and his *havan*."

"That's what *Ammaji* was to send me. It hasn't come yet. Now at least I know why. Not because they've forgotten me with Shabbu's baby but because of the political turmoil we're in."

"Well, Mangla, I'd better continue with my patrol before they accuse me of shirking my duty. I'll come and see you when I have time." With that he waves and mounts his horse and trots away.

Mangla waves back and resumes her shopping with Rehman.

Rehman stops at the vegetable stand, while Mangla goes into the shop opposite and asks the man sitting in his Afghani long shirt and *pathani* turban, "*Bhayya dukanwallah* will you know where I can buy a *charkah* and a *havan*?"

He looks at her blankly and shakes his head and hands indicating he doesn't understand her.

"You know, what Gandhiji spins." She gestures spinning one arm around while pulling a thread with the other. He still gives her a blank stare. Frustrated she turns around to look for Rehman when she hears the first Kaboom, a sound like a distant thunder. Instinctively, she looks up expecting to see clouds gathering, but the sky is bright blue and clear. It is followed by another loud, thunderous clang a little closer. She sees Rehman running towards her with his grocery bags, while the fruit and vegetable stall owners trying to cover their shops. That is when she hears the first crack followed by another as chaos descends around her. Everyone is running every way, screaming, and shouting. These are no firecrackers, but gunshots. In her daze, she can't tell where they're coming from. She hears Rehman yell, "Run, memsahib."

She stands there frozen to the ground and asks, "Where? What's happening?" "It's the *goondas*, Memsahib. Here--" Rehman grabs her arm, and as he pulls her into a doorway a bullet ricochets and hits her arm. A second bullet whizzes past her as Rehman pulls her further into the safety of the courtyard. There is a *charpoy* to which he guides her as he helps her sit down. It is then she looks at her arm and sees the blood dripping down it.

"Help, Memsahib's hurt. Please, someone get her some water," Rehman yells as he gets her to sit, and everyone gathers around her.

But Mangla is more worried about how to face Anand when she gets home. This outing is not turning out the way she planned.

Someone says to a boy, "I saw her talking to the officer on patrol. Quick get him. Maybe he can take her to the hospital."

Mangla then pays attention to her wound as she pulls her arm inside her *burqua* and wraps her sari *pallu* around it to slow its bleeding.

"Don't bother him. Please. It's not much. If I rest, I'll be OK," Mangla says, embarrassed by the whole episode and reluctant to acknowledge that indeed she has stepped into a danger zone. She feels mortified at her own folly. Her unsteady hands accept the tumbler full of cool water; she pours a little on her wound; sips, and its coolness calms her jagged nerves.

The clip clop of hooves stops outside, and Hari *Bhai* strides in. In Pashto, he assures people that he is her brother and therefore can violate *purdah*. They all move away, giving them privacy.

He extends his hand to her as he lowers himself down beside her.

"They said you got shot and are hurt. Let me have a look Mangla." His gentle brotherly voice brings stinging tears to her eyes. How she misses her family and the safety of her hometown where she could roam freely. Hari Bhai's touch is her only connection to her past. She holds on to his arm as tears roll down her cheeks and she brings her injured arm out from under her *burqa*.

He wipes her tears and smiles. "I'm so sorry that you got hurt. What are these tears for? Don't cry. Your big brother's here."

He examines her wound. "Luckily it's only a surface wound. But, now let me take you home and you can rest."

"Rehman, you go on home," Mangla says. "Hari Sahib will take me."

Rehman salaams them and leaves.

As they ride home on Hari's horse, he asks her, "How well do you know and trust Rehman?"

"Why?"

"Just wondered. As he's a local tribal *pathan*. Part of my job."

"The railways have vetted him. He's a devoted family man. He's taken Abdul Gaffar Khan's *Khudai Khidmatgar (KK)* pledge of non-violence. I'm at home and I've interacted with him a lot. I feel safe around him."

"That's good to know. Thanks. One can't be too careful in my business." At home he helps her down from the horse. She unlocks the door and asks, "Hari *Bhai*, won't you come in for a cup of tea?"

"Maybe another time soon? I better get back to the bazaar and attend to others and learn more about what happened. After all, I'm the one who will be called on for details, and I'm still on duty."

With that he mounts his horse and gallops away.

***

Inside, Mangla flings the *burqa* across the room as if it is a spitting, venomous cobra. Its poison spreads through her as she tries to salvage her free spirit to face her husband.

What a day.

She goes to the bathroom and brings down the bottle of Dettol. She pours some on a strip of gauze and gingerly cleans her wound, wincing as the antiseptic drips into it. She dusts the Cibazol powder on dry cotton gauze and covers her wound before wrapping a clean bandage over it.

Her body shivers as if experiencing an aftershock as she looks at her bandaged arm. Those were brave words she spoke to Rehman, that she would take care of the sahib. But now the results of her shameful act of defiance hits her like a hammer. At the onslaught of her mind's lashing, she shrivels like a reprimanded child.

How can she pretend that nothing happened? Maybe she will wear her long sleeve blouse. As Anand comes home late, she will go to bed early. Luckily the weather is cool, and she can wear her winter nightclothes. Maybe he will be too tired to notice anything, even if he feels amorous tonight. As long as she doesn't wince in pain if he puts his weight on that arm, and as long as it doesn't bleed, she should be safe. Her wound still stings, but its bite is not as harsh now that she has her defense planned out. She hears the jangle of the tea service on the tray as Rehman walks in with it. "Memsahib will like *chai* h--un--h?"

"Yes, thank you." With shaking hands, she takes the cup that rattles and is glad to see him make a discreet retreat.

She wants quiet time as the warm sweet liquid trickles down her throat.

XXXXXXX

17 1943 - The Life Within

Mangla wakes up nauseous and throws up before she is fully conscious. Even the thought of food makes her puke. She groans, covers herself up, and turns. Did she eat something bad at dinner last night? She remembers the bridge game afterwards was quite loud and almost violent. When one of the players didn't show up, Jay remembered that she played, and she made the fourth to team with Jay. Mangla's hands were consistently good and her play faultless. Anand lost and was mad. Now she knows he doesn't take losing well. Sleeping beside her, it's as though his anger comes through his body to hers, giving her heartburn. She turns over, still queasy. Now she has a headache, too.

Rehman knocks and enters. "Memsahib, wants *parontha* for breakfast, yes?"

The very thought is repugnant. All she can do is to shake her head.

"You don't feel well?" he asks.

She nods her head.

"I'll bring some lime juice with tea and biscuits." He leaves.

He returns and sets the tray down. He asks, "What shall I make for dinner?"

She says, "Just cook whatever sahib likes. You know what he likes better than I do." It is always a struggle to please Anand—and now it seems impossible. And the sicker she feels, the lonelier she becomes. She misses *Ammaji*'s understanding and love. She tries to get up to write her a letter and tell her that she's dying, but her head feels too heavy, and she falls back. Rehman has put a bucket near her bed, and he comes and cleans it every few hours.

"Let me know if you need anything," he says. "Will it be OK for me to go to the market now?"

"Yes, go. I'll be fine."

Mangla feels sorry for her life as it is unfolding. Even Sabiha has not replied to her letter. What is she doing in this hellhole? Her self-pity only makes her feel worse. Mangla wants *Ammaji* to comfort her like she did when she was a child. That night when Anand returns from work and makes his usual call, "Sparkles, I'm home," it is a herculean task for her to force herself to go down to sit at the table with him and face the food Rehman places in front of her. Its smell is repulsive. Still, she sits there.

"Aren't you going to eat?" Anand asks.

She gets up, goes to the bathroom, and heaves.

Rehman says, "Memsahib hasn't eaten anything all day."

When she returns, Anand says, "You were fine last night. Eat something--you'll feel better."

"I can't."

He continues to eat. He raises his voice, "Do as you want, I don't have all night to wait for you. I've work to do." He leaves the table and storms to his office. She tries to force a mouthful but gags and leaves the rest on the plate. She goes to bed frightened. She has never felt like this before.

The nausea stays with her. Anand seems clueless about her suffering, or just doesn't care. Mangla pretend-eats with him. She closes her eyes and stops breathing; she brings the food to her mouth as if to eat it; she returns it to the plate. Fortunately, Anand is too engrossed in his dinner to notice her shenanigans.

After dinner, she sits beside him, listless, with no interest in anything as he works on his files from work or reads his newspaper. She is there but not there. She wants to write to *Ammaji,* but her brain is shut down. No words come. She stares into space.

She's been this way for four days, but her sickness hasn't abated. She's unsure of what's happening. Maybe this is what death feels like. She wants *Ammaji*'s caressing understanding empathy.

To Anand, life seems normal. He comes to bed late after work and leaves early in the morning. It's Rehman who knocks and asks her, with concern, if she needs anything.

"Is there a doctor or a hospital nearby?" Mangla asks. I need a doctor."

"No, memsahib. The nearest railway doctor is in Abbottabad."

What will I do, she thinks, as panic strikes her belly.

Then she remembers Mrs. Desai, who said her door was always open if she needed anything. She hasn't heard from any of the women since the party. However, her need is dire, and she feels that Mrs. Desai's rotund figure and warm personality might provide her the motherly nurturance she so sorely misses. That thought alone gives her courage and hope.

"Rehman, do you know where the big boss Mr. Desai's home is?"

"Yes, Memsahib. It's a big house not too far from here."

"Could you take me? I'll get dressed."

She gets up, dresses, and gathers her energy to walk over to the boss's house and knocks on the door.

The door opens and behind the servant stands Mrs. Desai, dressed as if she is ready to go out.

Mangla feels hesitant. "I'm sorry, it looks like you are going out." She gets ready to turn.

Mrs. Desai says, "Come in. Come in. You are Mangla Rai. Right?"

"Yes. I feel like I'm imposing on you."

"Not at all. Everything can wait. I've been meaning to visit you, but I've been so busy with guests. I'm glad you came instead."

Mangla thinks, I wish I had your problem. Her face feels hot as she says, "Didi. I am so sorry to bother you, but I don't know what's the matter. I wake up nauseous and sick every morning. Like I have some awful bug."

"How long has it been happening?" Mrs. Desai asks.

"For the past week or so. I can't seem to keep anything down. Anand gets upset when I can't eat. But I don't know what to do. Something's wrong with me." Mangla starts to cry.

Mrs. Desai nods in compassion. "Did you have your period?"

"No, that's why I came. I've always been regular. I'm terrified that maybe I'm dying."

"Oh, Mangla, how wonderful! Don't you know? You'll be a mother soon!"

"Oh!" Mangla blushes as relief floods her eyes and she sobs.

She has seen women with babies, of course, but no one told her about the process of being pregnant. Her education at the University didn't cover the birthing of life, and truthfully, she had never been interested enough to ask. She had other things to occupy her time.

Now she feels shy and inadequate, and alone without any family support. More tears flow.

"Don't cry. It's nothing to worry about. I'll help you. Married women go through it all the time. Just take it easy and knock on my door if you need help."

"Will you tell Anand? I feel shy."

"I'll do that. I gave birth to my *Munna* when I was only eighteen years old. Without the help of other women, I couldn't have done that. Just enjoy the life within and know we are all part of the railway family here to help you."

Mangla, in her confusion, only looks down and doesn't say anything. She feels queasy and refuses the snack offered.

"You must force yourself to eat. There's another life you need to feed." The life within is already very frightening to Mangla.

***

She sits down and begins a letter to Basanthi, but she can see her friend's disgusted face at her stupidity of getting pregnant. As if she has had a choice.

Maybe she'll write to *Ammaji* instead. But she doesn't know how. She puts her quill pen down and lies on the bed. Emotionally exhausted she falls asleep.

Finally, a few days later, her parcel arrives. It is like the first rain drop on a parched earth. Mangla takes a deep breath as she opens it and inhales the smell of home.

She now has a *charkah*. She takes it out, caresses the cotton, and spins. Soon its familiar hum calms and comforts her raw nerves.

Among other things there is a *havan* and its essential herbs and a prayer book. She calls Rehman and shows it to him.

"Could you please bring me some small pieces of dry wood for my *havan* and some ghee and water in *katoris*?"

She then does her *havan* and asks for blessings and good health for her son. Everyone tells her she will have a son because of how she carries herself. They should know. Their first born are sons. Maybe that will patch up her strained relations with her husband.

That night when Anand comes home, he sniffs the air. "What's that I smell?" He looks in the corner and notices the *havan*. His eyebrows shoot up. Mangla has yet to recognize these body movements as gathering storm clouds.

Oblivious, she says, "A parcel came from my mother."

He stomps the floor.

"Who gave you permission to do a *havan* in my house?" he says.

Mangla looks at him. His house? Where's my house, she wants to scream. If he turns her out, where will she go? She has no resources to retaliate with. She buries her hurt and anger in her usual way. She stays quiet.

He picks up the *havan* and all the herbs surrounding it and calls out, "Rehman take these out and throw them in the trash. We don't need them here."

What's with him? What has the *havan* done to him? He's totally irrational. She says, "But why, what's the problem?"

That is throwing kerosene on a fire.

He screams, "There will be no *havan* in my house ever. Do you hear? EVER." He flings it on the floor forcefully. It makes a big clang as all the herbs spill on to the floor.

He repeats his scream loudly, "Rehman---"

"Yes, sahib." He comes running into the room and looks at the mess on the floor and then at Mangla with empathetic eyes. He goes out and brings a broom and begins to sweep the floor.

"Do as the sahib says. Throw it all out as far as you can," Mangla says with her teeth clenched. The life within moves. She feels outmaneuvered. She runs to the bathroom and locks the door as sobs torture her bulging frame.

***

It is the end of June when Mangla boards the steam train to travel to Allahabad, the city of Allah. She is in the seventh month of her pregnancy. It's still safe for her to travel. Mangla has no choice but to make this arduous journey to Anand's family home for her delivery. Their culture demands that she deliver her baby in her in-law's home.

Anand was to accompany her. But at the last minute, his leave is denied. It's been like that since their marriage. No predictability on his availability. He seems to owe his soul to the railways.

However, railway wives provide Mangla invaluable support, especially Didi. It's Didi who brings Mangla to the station, as Anand has had to go to the site of the project problem.

"You'll be fine," Didi says. "I travelled this long distance when I was pregnant with my baby *Munna*. Once you have your son, you'll forget all this discomfort." They sit in the first-class ladies' compartment waiting for the train to depart.

Mangla fans the beads of perspiration off her brow with a little rattan grass *pankah*.

"I know it's hot," Didi says. "But Anand has telegrammed the stationmasters where you'll change trains. They'll take good care of you and make the transfers easier. Focus on the baby. These long journeys are a good time to bond."

"*Didi*, I don't know what I would have done without you. You've been so kind to me since the first day you helped me diagnose my malady." Mangla smiles her gratitude.

"That's the least we wives can do for each other. I was helped too. We just pay it forward. That's why we're called piffers, you know."

"You've fed me and spoiled me like *Ammaji* would have. I'm so glad I asked you for help. Thank you."

"Just sip on a lot of water. Get it refilled at stations. I've put an earthenware *surahi* full of cool water with a cup." She points to the corner. "The hot air on it will keep the water cool for you. "

Mangla gets up and pours herself some water and offers it to *Didi* first. "Oh no, you drink," says the older woman. "I can get water at the station. You have a long journey ahead."

Mangla looks up at the pathetic little ceiling fan that is inadequate to relieve her thermal distress.

"Just keep the windows open. I know it brings in copious amounts of black soot, and the deafening clickety clack sound, but it will relieve this heat."

They hear the guard's whistle. *Didi* gets up, and as Mangla bends to touch her feet, the woman pats her on the head. "Be blessed, my child. Try and rest even though it'll be difficult. Bond with your baby."

Didi gets off the train, and as the guard waves his green flag, Mangla's grateful eyes moisten.

The train journey is long, hot, and uncomfortable. She can hardly wait for it to end. The small compartment feels like a coffin. The baby within kicks furiously, protesting its own confined space and giving Mangla dyspepsia, which doesn't help her backache. It's hard for her to sleep.

She wishes Anand was there to hold her—but then he would only get angry at her restlessness. He's been that way since her pregnancy when she needs him most. Last week, he got real angry because she was not feeling well enough to accompany him to his card game at the club. The times when she has gone with him, they serve drinks at the bridge table and he pressures her to drink, too. He came home with a peg too many in him. It was late at night, and he wanted to make love. When she protested that it was too uncomfortable, he lashed into her, comparing her to Urmila with her social graces. Urmila wasn't seven months pregnant, Mangla wanted to retort but stayed quiet not wanting to provoke his ire. Like Basanthi predicted he can be such a brute when displeased. Now on the train, alone in this unbearable June heat, she has trouble bonding to the baby. Her petite five-foot frame feels the baby's constrained existence. She feels unloved. She doesn't know how to develop a loving bond with something that is making her life so difficult and wretched. She tries to imagine the baby boy with all ten toes and fingers. But the image is fuzzy. Mangla feels their bond in tatters already.

The closer Mangla comes to Allahabad, the more petrified she feels of going to Anand's home and meeting his folks all by herself. She remembers when she left almost a year ago, with grand freedom dreams in her mind. It has been anything but that. How can she face them alone? She wants to be with *Ammaji* for her delivery. But their social customs don't allow.

Then Mangla thinks, what if it's a girl? She tries to put this ominous thought out of her mind. But it seems to have taken root. Is she jinxing herself?

***

Finally, the journey is over. She has the same curtained door room with little privacy. She's afraid to be around them without Anand. That other stay was short lived and led to their contentious departure.

Besides this, Anand's parents possess social authority over her and her belongings. Many things she expected to be delivered to NFWP she sees in their house. No wonder they didn't arrive. They were never sent. She wants to be charitable. Perhaps from Anand's letters they knew of the unrest in NWFP, or maybe it was too much effort and cost for them, and they felt that keeping these was their right. At least now she knows. It doesn't ingratiate them to her. She can barely wait for her son be born so she can leave. Little by little she will take some of her things like the swing machine.

Mangla goes to the hospital twice a week in a *tonga* for checkups. It is a new hospital, chosen because of its pristine reputation and good doctors. Anand's job in the railways will pay for the delivery costs.

Two weeks before the due date, she feels her labor pains. It's a long and painful labor for Mangla with only strangers around her in the hospital. She longs for the comfort of her own family and the midwife. But Anand wants her to have a hospital delivery. With the doctors coaching her breathing and pushing, despite excruciating pain and exhaustion, she finally pushes the baby out. She hears a loud infant's wail. She hears, " you have a feisty little girl, Mrs. Rai."

Mangla doesn't move. Her head cries, No! It's a boy. It can't be a girl. The doctor is wrong. Now her in-laws will be even more upset with her. Anand will have even more reason to be angry with her. She has failed them. She has failed her own family for the shame it will bring them because she is not able to bring Anand's family a first-born son.

Anand's grandmother comes into the room. "Where's my great grandson? I can finally climb the golden ladder and reach nirvana."

Someone says, "Come see Mataji, your great granddaughter."

"*Hai! hai*! God forbid. I'm not going to see the face of that *churail*, evil monster. She's already bought bad luck to our family." She then rants and raves and berates Mangla. She knew Anand shouldn't have married her. No looks, no money, no caste. They've all sold out to that no-good Gandhi. She told them nothing good will come of this marriage. Her Anand could have had the girl *Mataji* recommended. In her family every first born is a son. But who listens to an old woman? Now they know. She'll never live long enough to go to heaven. *Hai! Hai*! What bad karma of hers makes her suffer? Why is she being punished this way? She'll go to the Ganges *ghat* to wash her sins. She leaves without even glancing at the baby girl. Mangla hears "tuk, tuk," the sound of her walking stick receding.

The baby wails in a loud and gusty voice. It sounds so strange, so demanding. A demand Mangla feels no desire to meet.

"Mrs. Rai," says a nurse. "I think you should hold the baby and nurse her. She needs comfort."

Mangla lies there without moving. The nurse brings the baby to her. Mangla feels her flailing arms and legs and the loud piercing shrill cry.

The nurse moves the baby closer to Mangla's breasts.

Mangla recoils.

"Mrs. Rai, I understand you expected a son, but the baby needs nursing. Here, let me help you." She puts the baby close to the breast and she latches on eagerly. She sucks vigorously.

Mangla, deep in her loss, feels nothing. It is like something has been detached inside her. She tries to push the baby away. The nurse will not let her. She keeps pushing the baby back to the breast until she feels that the baby has had enough sucking.

"She's a strong, determined little girl, isn't she? She won't take your no for an answer."

Mangla just lies there motionless, frozen by her grief.

"Mrs. Rai, we see this story played out here every day. You aren't alone. We're here to help you to be a good mother to your baby."

With that, she lifts the baby and puts her in the crib next to Mangla's bed. Mangla hears the matron tell the nurse, "We need to make sure that feeding bond is made before she leaves the hospital."

After six days, they come home to Anand's parent's house. No fanfare for the baby girl. The silence of rejection of the girl baby is unbearable to her.

"Mangla, maybe the baby's hungry," her mother-in-law says. "Shouldn't you nurse her?" Mangla listlessly makes a half-hearted effort to nurse the baby. The baby bawls even louder as she rejects the breast.

"Kalyani, come and help Mangla learn to feed her baby," Parvati beckons the midwife. Kalyani pats and cajoles the baby, and finally pangs of hunger overtake the pout and she nurses. Mangla has a limited milk supply, and they must supplement it with boiled cow's milk mixed with water, dripped into the baby's mouth by squeezing a cotton ball dipped in milk. Kalyani gives Mangla and the baby daily massages to soothe them.

"Don't mind Mataji," Parvati reassures Mangla. "She's an old fashioned, orthodox, embittered woman. She's forgotten that her first born was a girl. We are happy that you have a healthy baby. Daughters are as precious as sons. I'm sure in future you'll have a son."

Slowly Mangla begins to bond with her own baby.

In a simple naming ceremony, with just family and a priest chanting the Vedic chants, the baby is given the name Mina. It literally means a fish. Mangla vows to do everything in her power to ensure that in future, Mina will swim far .

XXXXXXX

18 1944 Birth of a Son

Mangla has been away from Anand over two months. She now has a daughter and he's to take leave to travel to his parents' home and bring them back. She rolls her eyes as she reads in the letter from Anand that he has been promoted and transferred to Lahore. He won't be coming to get them after all, but he has moved their stuff into a railway house allotted to him in the railway colony. There is an extra room for the baby. When she returns, she can decorate it the way she wants. He planned for Mangla and Mina to travel back to Northwest Punjab. Mina is less than six weeks old when Mangla makes the long train journey yet again. At least the weather is pleasant and not beastly hot, as it was when she travelled out. She's seen this movie before. Except, now she has a baby to take care of. She's grateful for the expert coaching from Kalyani about what to do for the baby on the train.

Drink plenty of water, the midwife advises as she gets the *surahi* refilled so her milk flows. But on the train, it's a different story.

"Hush little baby." Mangla tries to soothe Mina as she continues to struggle and scream. Mangla rocks, sings songs and lullabies, and in the privacy of her small ladies' compartment lets Mina nurse whether she has enough milk or not. Every time the train whistle blows, Mina screams, matching its loudness. She wonders if Mina was also terrified by these sounds when she was in the womb.

The collective constant noises of the baby and the train gives Mangla's headache. As soon as she lies down, Mina protests with deafening wails. Nothing she does quiets the distressed baby. Mangla hasn't had much sleep since she left Allahabad. It's only the second day of travel. She wonders if she is ready for this maternal responsibility. She wants to throw the baby out of the train. But some instinct within stops her. In despair, she holds her daughter and cries.

Despite her headache, mercifully, the agonizing trip finally ends. She's happy to see Anand at the station ready to receive them. Ignoring wailing Mina in Mangla's arms, he waves the coolies to carry the bags to the waiting *tonga*, as though Mina is someone else's child.

They go through old Lahore into a colony of nice houses. Mangla looks around. Railway colony is in a tidy neighborhood. So different from the construction area they were in before.

When they get home, she wants to feed Mina, who is howling, but Anand will have nothing of it and takes Mangla right to bed. It's as if he wants to get Mangla pregnant again to order God to give him a son—and with complete disregard for her health. Mangla is torn between her two parts and two sets of duties.

Mangla is exhausted and isn't even fully healed from the birth. She misses the friendship of NWFP railway wives, but they are not in Lahore, at least not that she knows of. She will Ask Rehman when opportunity presents herself and she has some time away from this testy baby.

Within the month Mangla is pregnant again. Her milk is totally dry. She lets Mina suckle her breasts to pacify her and gives her cow's milk as Kalyani showed her. She wishes there was someone to help her through these times when Mina seems to be perpetually hungry. When does she give her solids? Perhaps she will walk to the neighbors and ask them how to feed this hungry baby. She misses Kalyani and her mother-in-law's experience. Anand is no help. Maybe Rehman's wife can come and help her. She'll ask him. His family moved to Lahore as well and live in the quarters behind their house. Maybe he knows a wet nurse who can help Mina with additional milk.

Again, the first trimester is difficult for Mangla. She's always tired, and that doesn't please Anand. It doesn't please Mina, either. Like Anand, Mina can't seem to get enough attention.

One morning, as Anand is getting ready for work, he asks Mangla to find his blue tie.

"One moment!" she says. "I'm putting Mina to bed."

"Mina, Mina, Mina— Leave her be. I need you. She'll be fine on her own. It's not like you're abandoning her," Anand's voice rises.

"You know she'll cry if I leave. She's been cranky of late," Mangla says, rocking Mina.

Anand grabs hold of Mangla's arm in a rough grip. "For God's sake, Mangla, she's six months old. Shouldn't she learn to be by herself?" He grabs hold of Mina, shakes her, and flings her on the bed. Mina looks at her mother whimpering with her pupils wide.

Terrified, Mangla says, "Why hurt her? She's only a baby."

"A baby? She's six months old. You've totally spoiled her. You're always at her beck and call. What about me? When I'm home she won't leave you alone!" He drags Mangla out of the room and slams the door shut. Mina bawls louder and harder as the door bangs. Then he takes out a key and locks Mina in the room.

"She's afraid of loud sounds," Mangla says.

Anand walks away.

"Give me the key. She's been crying for so long. It's cruel!" Mangla begs, holding her husband's arm.

"No, she's going to learn once and for all who's the boss around here!" Anand fingers the keys in his pocket.

A half hour later, Mina is still crying. "Please, I beg you!" Mangla says, grabbing Anand's arm again. "That's enough. I can't bear it. She's still yelling— she's an infant."

Anand jerks Mangla so hard she falls to the ground. She holds her belly to protect the unborn. He kicks his feet in the air and stands firm above her. About an hour later, Mina's sobs turn into hiccups, die down to a whimper, and she finally stops.

In the days following, Mina sits. She crawls and walks, eventually, but remains silent.

"I told you," Anand says. "All Mina needs is discipline. She doesn't cry anymore, does she?"

Mangla says nothing. You've broken her spirit like you broke mine, she thinks. "I'll take her for a ride in the car." He takes Mina and puts her on his lap while he drives out.

Mangla has learned to let Anand do what he wants to protect herself and the new life within her. This time she has a deep understanding that it is a boy.

One morning, Rehman brings his 10-year-old sister, Zubaida, to the house to help with Mina. She is light skinned and has long curly dark hair tied in a braid. She's wearing white loose *salwar* pants, and a loose long red, paisley printed *kamiz* over it. Around her shoulders and over her head is draped a white muslin *dupatta*. "Mina, come and meet Zubaida," Mangla says.

Mina holds Zubaida's hand without reservation and pulls the girl towards the door. Zubaida follows her.

Mangla is relieved to not worry about Mina, and tells Zubaida, "Why don't you take her for a walk?" She wants to observe their interaction from the window before she hires.

She likes what she sees. Mina runs and Zubaida runs after her. They are both laughing and giggling and playing. Mangla hasn't seen this carefree side of Mina before. She hires Zubaida without reservations. Anand supports this decision as it frees Mangla to pay more attention to him. They discuss salary and even travel to Allahabad for Mangla's delivery.

"Rehman, I want to take Zubaida with me to help with Mina and the new baby there. Will your family be OK with this?"

"Yes, memsahib. It's part of her job. Besides she's never been on a train, and it will be nice for her to see our big country."

"Hopefully it will be raining and cooler than last time I went," Mangla says.

But to take a Muslim girl into a Hindu home poses a problem with *Mataji*, though the other family members are OK with it.

Anand and Rehman come up with a solution. They'll change Zubaida's name to Radha and teach her Hindu customs. She can do her *namaz* in the privacy of Mangla's room where she'll sleep with Mina.

"Zubaida, just don't "*Hai Allah*" in front of *Mataji* when you're there," Rehman laughs and pats her on the head.

***

Mangla is in her seventh month when travel begins again. It is still beastly hot and dusty on the train, but Zubaida's help and company make it more bearable. Excited and curious, Zubaida runs from window to window and points to the countryside and asks about the birds, animals, and people's clothes she's never seen before.

Everything Zubaida does, Mina copies silently.

"If you go to school, Zubaida, you'll learn a lot about this beautiful country of ours. It's all part of India," Mangla says.

They arrive in Allahabad, and Mina and Zubaida/Radha adjust to the new realities and routines of a larger house and family. This time Mangla is more prepared for what to expect. A couple of Anand's siblings are married or in college, so Mangla gets her own private room where Mina, her Ayah Zubaida, and the new baby will sleep.

A week before the baby is to be born, Mina falls desperately ill, with rasping breath and a high fever. The doctors don't know what's wrong with her. She gets worse, as do Mangla's labor pains.

Vishnu Lal comes in and picks up Mina in his arms and holds her. Mangla lies in her bed nearby as Zubaida/Radha massages her belly and feet. Mangla notices Mina's eyes roll up into her head, and she tries to get up and help her daughter, but pain drives her back down to the bed. Plus, she doesn't want the doctor distracted from Mina to her own labor pains. Mina needs all his attention.

The doctor shakes his head. "Sorry, *bhaisahib*. There's nothing more I can do. She's in God's hands, now." He walks out of the room.

Despondent, Mangla wants to hold Mina, but this is Vishnu Lal's prerogative as the shadow of death descends upon the room.

Soon there is a knock on the door. "Is anyone home?" A woman calls. When no one answers, a very attractive woman walks in to witness their anguished faces. "What's the matter?"

"Sumi, Anand's daughter, Mina, is dying. The doctor just left," Vishnu Lal says. "She was so lively when she came from Lahore. She worked her way into our hearts. Now look at her. We've tried everything." He shakes his head as he hugs and rocks his grandchild tighter.

"*Bhayya*, I'm sorry. I was just driving through this town and thought to pay my respects to you."

"I'm sorry, too, that we can't greet you with more joy."

"Have you tried Brandy?" she asks.

"You know that I'm a teetotaler," is his reply.

"I have some brandy in my car. Would you mind if I give her some? We've nothing to lose, have we? She's almost gone anyway." Mangla lies there praying for god's miracles to save her daughter,

"I guess, Sumi. You're right. God tests our love over our principles," Vishnu Lal says.

Sumi runs out to her car and brings back a bottle of brandy. She pours it in a large tablespoon and puts it to Mina's lips. Everyone watches, as Mina's eyes flutter. Her breath returns hesitatingly in a whimper before she opens her eyes and looks around.

Mangla watches. Her labor pains grow more intense. A sweat breaks out on her face. She doubles over and yells and screams, "Ah--ah—ah. " Primal instinct makes her breathe and push. Everyone's attention turns to her.

"Sumi, can your driver take Mangla to the hospital please?" Vishnu Lal asks.

"Of course."

They carry a writhing Mangla to the car outside.

But the baby's head is almost out. Mangla groans, breathing and pushing. Parvati says, running forward, "It's too late," and catches the emerging baby as an exhausted Mangla spits him out of her cervix.

The infant gives out a hearty bellow. Everyone rushes out to the car.

Parvati yells, "It's a boy. We have a grandson! Someone get Kalyani from the houses in the back to help. Radha, go get hot water from the cook and ask him to put the knife on hot coals before he sends it here. Hurry, girl."

Mangla is grateful for her mother-in-law's experience in home deliveries. She's relieved at having finally given them a son and eager for the umbilical cord to be severed. Exhausted she asks, "How's Mina?"

All eyes turn to Vishnu Lal. He looks down at the little girl in his arms and smiles with the jubilant final words. "Parvati, ask someone to send a telegram to Anand. Mina lives. Son born.

That night the community singers gather and with every drumbeat announce arrival of good tidings to Vishnu Lal's home.

The date of the naming ceremony is set, and the priest is engaged, the guests invited. On the seventh day, the barber comes to perform the boy's *mundan* ceremony. The baby's head is shaved as Mangla holds him in her lap, and the community singers play the drums and sing.

Mataji supervises the process herself. She says, "Collect that hair in a banana leaf. We want no one to cast an evil spell on my great-grandson through tantric *jadu tona,* black magic. I'll take it to the Ganges myself to dispose of it."

Mangla observes with some regret the difference in her attitude from a year ago, for Mina's birth.

Zubaida/Radha and Mina play with the wooden toys on the floor. Vishnu Lal walks in, standing taller with pride. Mangla covers her head, gets up and touches his feet. He hands her the baby boy and says, "Bahu, look after my grandson, he seems hungry. Anand's telegram says that he arrives on tomorrow morning's train. She looks up and smiles, and thinks, of course he now has a son and can't miss the naming ceremony and festivities of being a father to a boy. So different from a year ago.

Later, Mina hears *Mataji*'s walking sticks make a now familiar "tuk tuk" sound. Her walking stick supports her bent aging body as she walks in to view her first great grandson, whose birth guarantees her nirvana once she has her symbolic golden ladder.

Mataji was married at six and widowed at twenty-two, with seven children to feed. She never learned to read and write. But through stitching and selling clothes, community help, and following her orthodox Hindu practices, she brought each of her children up to be successful adults. Mangla thinks of Basanthi and the projects they worked on to ensure uplifting of the social plight of women to bear sons.

"Namaste, *Mataji*. Here he is. Radha, hold him near her so she can touch him." After Mina's birth, Mangla feels cautious around *Mataji*. She touches her feet as she hands over her whimpering baby boy.

The matriarch demands, "Why don't I have my golden ladder? At my age, who knows how long I'll live."

"*Mataji*, it is ordered. The jeweler says it will be here any day."

Curious, Mina runs to touch the "tuk tuk" sound source.

Mataji stiffens and pushes Mina away with her stick.

"*Hai, Hut*! Don't touch me! Get away from here yo*u churail, demon. Don't defile me. All those Muslims touching you! Chhi Chhi*! Who will marry you? No one listens to me. Make sure you wash the golden ladder with Ganges water before you give it to me." With that she gets up and leaves, muttering, "I'm the only one that cares. Vishnu and Parvati corrupted their house the day he joined Gandhi." But here Mangla is succumbing and kowtowing to the pressures with two children in close succession so she can oblige his family and his grandmother's superstition and backward thinking of having a great grandson.

How would she answer Basanthi and other BHU women and live up to her words that seem hollow in the moment? She can't understand her emotions. She loves the two children equally and is proud of the fact she has a son and daughter. *Mataji* disappears into the courtyard yelling to her widowed daughter who lives with her.

"Where's my hookah? Ram- Ram you're the only one of my children I can trust. You didn't join that caste-defiling Gandhi." She sits down on the charpoy and begins puffing furiously with the hookah tip in her mouth.

Mangla shakes her head and mutters as she takes the baby boy back from Zubaida. "She has no problem touching the boy, but she's prejudiced against Mina. Like Muslims aren't human! Oh Mina! I hope in your lifetime this curse will be obliterated!" Mangla holds Mina close.

***

Anand tells Mangla in a letter that Rehman will be his office *chaprasi* when they return to Lahore. It's a promotion for him. He won't be working as a domestic in their home anymore except on special occasions if Mangla needs extra help.

Mangla writes to *Ammaji* of her impending domestic woes. *Ammaji* replies that she is sending her trusted Hindu servant, Roopchand, to travel to Lahore with Mangla. He came to *Ammaji* after Mangla's wedding. Hence, Mangla has never met him, but *Ammaji* has written high praises for him as to the wonderful help he is to her. Mangla's concerns are waved aside by *Ammaji*. She is doing this for her only daughter and grandchildren. Domestic help is easier to get where she is in Benaras, different from the big city like Lahore in Punjab where Mangla is.

She's talked to Roopchand and he is willing to give it a try. Beside he will bring her an understanding of her own culture in Lahore home. *Ammaji* has taught him all their festive and daily cuisine. At Mangla's behest, it is arranged that he arrive before the naming ceremony and the children get used to him before they travel back to Lahore.

Roopchand is a tall man of a slender build. He wears a kurta shirt, an embroidered vest over his kurta and loose pajamas.. On his head, he wears a starched turban that he takes off when inside at home to reveal his curly black hair. Mangla likes him.

"Mina, come here and meet Roopchand. *Nani* sent him to travel with us to Lahore," Mangla says. Mina looks at him with her big eyes. Then she moves closer to hold his hands and pulls to take him outside.

"*Bibiji*, doesn't she talk?" says Roopchand.

Mangla's face clouds as her worries take shape. "I don't know what to do. The doctors say give her time. But people say her silence at this age is unusual."

Zubaida says, "I will ask God in my prayers."

"Roopchand, meet Zubaida. She helps me with Mina. She is Rehman's sister. We call him Ram and her Radha while in Allahabad because of *Mataji,* who believes in caste like my own *Nani*. Please remember to call them that while here," Mangla says with a sigh.

To Mangla's relief, the children, and Zubaida like Roopchand.

***

When Anand arrives, Mangla hears his younger siblings yell, "*Bhaisahib*'s here!" Mangla, although happy, stays in the room with the baby so as not to appear too eager and be teased by her brothers-in-law. Mina runs out and hugs her father's legs. He shakes her off as he enters the room. "Where's my son?" he asks. He gathers him in his arms. Rehman brings in his luggage.

"Call Rehman Ram in front of *Mataji*," Anand repeats. "I've arranged for Zubaida and Rehman to sleep with the servants as Hindu brother and sister. It gives us privacy in the room. We'll still have the baby boy and Mina of course."

"That's a good thought."

His voice rising, he says, "What a charade, all because my father doesn't have the guts to challenge his mother and practice what he preaches to others."

Mangla, tuned to that rise in pitch, changes the subject. "Are we going back to Lahore soon?"

"In a few days, after the naming ceremony. It'll be good to have you and my son home after these two long months."

"And Mina," Mangla says, but Anand says nothing.

That night, Anand approaches Mangla with ardor. She shrinks involuntarily, still not healed from the birth, and she feels her injured groin raw as he forces his way in to reach the climax. Mina wakes up to the unfamiliar rocking motion and starts yelling just at the crucial moment. Knowing how it will aggravate Anand, Mangla pats her back to sleep with one hand and attends to Anand with the rest of her, then curls her body upon itself, away from Anand, and manages to sleep.

***

The day of the naming ceremony arrives, and Anand's sisters are in the verandah humming and busy creating a *mandala* in the space around the bricks on which sits a *havan*. They use different color powders—white flour, yellow turmeric, red sindoor, green henna, black charcoal powder, and brown dirt.

Its irony is not lost on Mangla. That Anand made such a fuss about her *havan* yet acquiesced to his parents' celebratory one. She has learned that by silence she can douse the flames of his fury. Bit by bit she finds her voice silenced.

She invited Basanthi to come to this ceremony but there is no response from her, and she hasn't shown up. Is she still angry? There is sadness within her even at this joyous occasion. With these thoughts, Mangla sits cross-legged with the baby in her lap to feed him. Mina hovers over them in the verandah, and when the boy begins to nurse, Mina pats him hard until he cries.

"Mina stop that," Mangla says. "Radha, please take Mina outside to play." Mina resists, but Zubaida/Radha offers a shiny hand-held red and green wind spinner, and Mina follows her, squealing in delight.

The verandah overlooks the courtyard where the brahmin cooks have set up a temporary catering kitchen for cooking the special naming ceremony celebratory feast. In the outdoor kitchen, professional *halwais* cook syrup in a huge wok, while frying the chickpea flour into little pebble shaped *boondi* in another. They'll soak the *boondi* in the syrup before making the round sweet yellow balls called *laddoos*. These will be placed in *dona* little disposable boxes made of dried *peepal* leaves and stacked to be distributed after the priest has named and blessed the baby.

The cooks next get busy making dinner for invited guests: *kachori*, the stuffed fried bread, and potato and pumpkin curries that will be served on *pattals*, the disposable plates made from large, dried, peepul tree leaves that are put together with small twigs. Everyone will be served tea in the disposable earthenware *kullarhs* that are stacked near the *pattals*. In big vats sit mango and jackfruit pickles to accompany the lavish meal, whose tantalizing aroma pervades the entire neighborhood, announcing the happy tidings of this family.

For the naming ceremony, Mangla has embroidered a special red christening outfit for the boy. *Mataji* makes sure that he has a little black mark inconspicuously placed on the side of his face, so as to ward off the evil eyes of other women who may not have sons or may covet her beautiful *parpotha, great-grandson* and cast a tantric spell. One cannot be cautious enough in this evil intentioned world of envy she tells all.

Mangla and Anand sit on one side of the *havan* and the priest on another. Vishnu Lal and Parvati sit on the third. On the fourth side sit a few of the honored guests from the community. The sacred *havan* fires are lit. Mangla steals a glance at Anand. He chants the prayers with the priest, holding the baby. The priest blesses the boy and his parents. He gives him the name Arun Kumar, an auspicious name that is part of his horoscope—already written ages ago and read by the priest. He will be the charioteer to the sun, riding high and ahead of dawn. In addition, the horoscope predicts the boy's future. This document will stay with the priest on the banks of the Ganges. Should it be necessary, the family can consult it in time of need for the boy's welfare, especially to ensure that he marries a suitable woman at an auspicious time. After the *havan*, professional singers bedecked in silk and gold sing holy chants to bring the blessings of long life to Arun. Children dance with bells on their ankles to the rhythmic beats of *dholak* drums, *manjira*, and ancient cymbals.

Vishnu Lal has spared no expense.

The guests sit on mats on the floor. The cooks serve their tasty food on disposable *pattal* plates with hot tea. On their way out, the guests bless the baby by sprinkling holy Ganges water on the family as they collect their packet of *laddoo*s.

Mangla looks dispassionately at this scene. She feels that as a woman she is only a breeding machine to give birth to the wanted sons. These sons belong to the family and grandparents. Not to her as a mother. What double standards they have—one for girls and one for boys. Even Anand. She's disgusted. Her old rebellion against her brothers resurfaces within her. She silently vows that before her voice is completely silenced, she will work hard to equalize this discrimination in their community, Basanthi or not.

XXXXXXX

Love Partitioned

19 Mina, Arun, and Roopchand

When they reach the Lahore station in the old city, they look for the *tonga* to take them to the Railway Colony.

Mangla tells Roopchand that the Colony is near the cantonment, the British Army base where the British families live. Mina holds onto Zubaida's hand as they climb in the front with Rehman and Roopchand. Mangla and Anand sit in the back with Arun. Their bedding is placed below their feet on the trunk. To balance the *tonga* better, the other trunk is put on the front floor below Mina and Zubaida's feet. The *tongawallah* has a dirty white loose shirt and a plaid *Tehmad* tied to his waist. A beard covers his face. He wears a white muslin *kufi* cap. Around his neck he has a silver *tabiz* with Allah written in Arabic strung on a black thread. With a whip in his right hand, he squats on the tonga frame near his horse.

It is a pleasant day. The driver has the *tonga* canopy folded. Their home is a considerable distance from the station. They travel through small lanes lined with old terraced three-story houses. Roopchand looks around with eyes opened wide. He says that it's a much bigger city than any he has been to.

They first go through a large old Lahori gate past a mosque. Mangla points out to Roopchand men that are dressed like the *tongawallah* or in *salwars* and women in black *burqas* covering them from head to foot. There are more Muslims than Hindus and Sikhs, here, and they are poorer too. They are mostly laborers and blue-collar workers.

Zubaida turns to them and points her fingers down an alley and says, "That's where my house is!"

Anand says, "*Tongawallah*, what's happened in the city during the last week?"

"Not all that much, Sahib. There was a meeting of the Muslim League. Jinnah was here. Lots of people attended. He was talking about creating Pakistan, a holy land, for us Muslims."

"What do you think? Should we have one?" Anand says.

"Sahib, it's not going to do much for us poor Muslims. But the rich people and leaders think it will be good. It'll get the wealth back to Muslims from the Hindu *baniyas*."

"But it'll mean lots of people will lose their homes and friends will be separated, families divided," Anand says.

Mangla tells Roopchand, "Plenty of Hindus live here, too. There is the temple if you need to pray." As they pass it, spice smells waft past their noses. Women are dressed in saris, and most have their heads covered. The men wear loose *kurta* pajamas or traditional white cotton *dhotis* around their waists. *Baniya* shops have sacks of grains and spices stacked on the floor and metal pots hanging off the walls. "Personally, I wish Jinnah would stop this talk of division", Anand says. As Gandhiji says, "we, Hindus and Muslims are brothers. We are connected at the hip. Our food, cultures are so intertwined."

"I agree. Why put mistrust between us now?" The *tongawallah* says.

They approach the area where the Sikhs live. Mangla points out to Roopchand the golden domed *gurudwara*, literally meaning door of the guru.

Anand adds, "Guru Nanak founded the Sikh religion to bring Hindus and Muslims together. Their holy books, Quran and Guru Granth Sahib are kept together in many *gurudwaras*. "They're educated, mostly farmers and police, or in the armed forces."

"But Sikh's are so hot blooded," Rehman says. "They're ready to fight anytime. They make good soldiers."

Soon they come out onto the *maidan*, a parkland beyond which the canal flows. Close by is the Colony where the railway officers live. Anand tells Roopchand that the Christians and Anglo Indians live closer to the Cantonment, where the British live. There are churches for them there.

Soon they hear the flow of the water and smell the familiar decaying vegetation and cow dung coming from the canal that flows nearby. *Kikkar* trees line the wide road. Mina points and holds her nose and giggles as the horse every so often pulls up its tail and drops green lumps of shit.

Finally, Mangla recognizes their home. It appears smaller than she remembers, especially in contrast to her in-laws large mansion. The small garden in front looks neglected. The path with brick trim all around it takes them to a screened front door.

Mina, still silent, jumps up and down eager to get off the *tonga*. Roopchand's quick reflexes hold Mina under her arms. He swings her off, and she squeals in delight.

Zubaida's job now is to help Mangla with both Arun and Mina. Roopchand takes over the kitchen and household chores as Rehman becomes Anand's office peon.

Whenever Mangla feeds Arun, Mina is more obstreperous and throws things around, bops him on the head, or pinches him. Mangla begins calling upon Zubaida to take Mina out for walks so she can feed Arun in peace. Watching Mina skipping in delight, Mangla says to Roopchand, "I wonder if she purposely acts mute so she can go for walks. She seems to feel better when she returns."

When they come back, Zubaida tells Mangla of their adventure by the canal watching the cows and pigs and birds. Some days she brings home tamarinds and guavas. Zubaida sleeps in Mina's room when Arun is sick, or Anand is away. Other nights Zubaida goes home with Rehman.

Since Arun is often sick, Mina gets plenty of Zubaida's company and attention. She sits with her through her five daily *namaz* prayers. But still, she doesn't speak. "I wonder why she's silent?" Mangla ponders.

Zubaida says, "I'll ask Allah for her speech in my prayers. I'll do *tawba* prayers for her starting tomorrow."

"If it works, why not. My prayers haven't," Mangla says as she spins her *charkah*.

"Allah gives us what we want from our heart. It says in Quran," Zubaida says. How would you know? Mangla thinks. You can't read. Out loud she says, "Zubaida, do you want to go to school?"

"No *Bibiji*, my parents say it spoils a girl's mind. I know some Urdu, I have learned housekeeping and cooking, and that's enough to keep a house and bring up children."

"Maybe you can learn to read and write as I teach Mina, then."

Mangla reads picture book stories to them every day. She shows them the alphabet chart. She tells them stories of great Gods like Ram and Sita and the monkey God Hanuman, and the pranks of Krishna. On these occasions she points to the alphabet charts and shows Mina the letters with which the God's names begin. Or she tells tales from the Panchtantra, stories about animals, especially monkeys and crocodiles that talk and teach lessons to each other.

***

One day, as they take a walk—Mangla pushing Arun in a pram, Mina skipping alongside Zubaida—they see two young men riding bicycles. One is Muslim and the other Sikh. Seeing the girls, the two get off their bicycles. "Salaam, *bibiji*. Jasbir, this is my young sister, Zubaida," says the Muslim boy.

"*Namaste, bibiji* and Zubaida. I didn't know you had a sister, Gulam Ali," the Sikh with the red turban says. It's clear he admires Zubaida.

"*Adaab*," Zubaida replies, shyly touching her forehead with her cupped hands. "*Bhaijan*, where're you going?" Zubaida asks her brother.

"We're going to see our English friend. He lives just across the bridge in the officer's barracks. He tells us a lot about England and cricket. He even lets us play cricket with him in the *Maidan*," Gulam says with puffed chest. "Yes, we learn a lot from him. Sometimes he invites us to have tea in the canteen," Jasbir adds. Soon they are by the bridge, and a young man in a khaki uniform comes and meets them. He is an Englishman about the same height as the boys.

"Hello, Ted! This is Mrs. Rai, for whom my sister Zubaida works. This here's Corporal Edward James."

"*Namaste*," Ted says to Mangla and Zubaida.

"*Hai Allah*! *Adaab* Sahib," Zubaida says. Flustered, she puts on her scarf to cover her head, her eyes downcast.

"You have a beautiful sister, Gulam. And who do we have here?" Ted says in understandable Urdu. He sits on his haunches near Mina and touches her shoulder lightly.

"This is Mina, who Zubaida takes care of. She lives in those houses there," Gulam says, pointing.

"No need for formality. Call me Ted."

"We'd better get home. It's children's lunch time soon," Mangla says. Nice meeting you, Ted."

Zubaida says, "*Khuda hafiz*," with cupped hands to her forehead. Silently Mina copies her actions.

"Mina's quite a monkey, isn't she?" Ted ruffles her hair.

As they walk home, Mangla says, "What pleasant men. They seem to get along well. Maybe you would like to take Mina and visit them, sometime."

Daily Zubaida says her *Namaz* and *Tawba* prayer, and Mina sits with her and rocks back and forth. One day Zubaida comes running to Mangla and says, "*Bibiji, Bibiji*. Allah be praised. He's all merciful and powerful. Mina just took Allah's name with me."

Mina says, "*Amma laillaha ill Allah*. I can say it. I said the whole *namaz*." She dances around.

Mangla's jaw drops. "How did you do it? Roopchand!"

Roopchand comes in. "Yes, memsahib."

She picks Mina up. "A miracle just happened. Mina can talk."

"Roopchand, I want a biscuit," Mina says.

Roopchand laughs. "Of course, you can have as many as you want. I'll go to the temple and offer *prasad*."

"Wait till Sahib comes home. He will be surprised," Mangla says. Relief from her worry brings tears of joy as she hugs Mina.

"I'll go wake up Arun," Mina says.

"Oh no you won't. But I'm glad you can speak." All of them laugh and dance together.

"She speaks in sentences. No baby talk for her." Mangla shakes her head and looks to the heavens.

***

In the Hindu calendar, the *Shankranti* festival is on the 14th of January. The Sikhs call it *Lohri*. It marks the end of winter when the sun changes its direction. People celebrate by flying kites, and Mangla tells Mina to go to the maidan and fly her kite with Zubaida.

Mangla puts finishing touches to the pink silk frock she's stitched for Mina to wear for the festival. On its bodice she embroiders pretty birds with little colored glass beads and brightly colored silk and gold threads. The frock has a wide purple sash around its waist that is tied in a big bow in the back. Its flounce will allow Mina to pirouette like a ballerina.

Roopchand cooks a special yellow sweet rice dish with raisins and blanched almonds.

Soon Mina runs in breathless. "We met Jasbir. He asked us all to come for the *Lohri* bonfire in the *maidan* this evening."

"That'll be fun," Mangla says. "Sahib's travelling and won't be home. Let us all go. And you can wear your new frock. I just finished it."

Zubaida combs Mina's hair into pigtails and ties a pink ribbon.

Jasbir comes and meets them with the Sikh *"Sat Sri Akal"* greeting. Zubaida wears her red and gold *salwar-kamiz*. She looks stunning and grown up, with her long hair braided and tied with black and gold beaded *chutila*. All the young men turn to look at her as she and Mina join the dancing around the bonfire.

They see Ted standing in the corner. Mina runs to him and embraces his legs. Zubaida follows. Ted looks down and says, "Looky who we have down here!" With that Ted picks Mina up in his arms.

She says, "I'm Mina."

He smiles. "Hello Mrs. Rai and Zubaida. How're you?"

"OK, sahib. *Adaab.*" Zubaida says, with her covered head bent. She looks around for protection from Gulam.

Ted points towards the wood heap set for the bonfire. "I saw Gulam that-a-way."

All of them move towards the musicians.

"Come and join us, Ted sahib," says Jasbir. "So glad you could come. Oi, Zubaida and Mina, you both look like princesses."

The drummers beat their drums in a fast tempo. Others accompany them with tambourines and bells. Their sonorous voices join and resonate in unison with other singers. Everyone is singing and dancing *Bhangra* together in an ecstatic frenzy—a dancer's high. Sounds of *"Wah Guru"* can be heard all around them. As the music and its beat strum through their bodies, Mangla's heart feels light and bubbly. When has she last felt this way?

Ted says, "I wonder if that's the reason it is called *Bhangra*--maybe they took *bhang.*"

They all laugh.

"Come and join the dancing." Jasbir leads bouncy Mina to the circle and Gulam and Zubaida follow as the air fills with the catchy sounds and beat of "Rabba! Rabba."

The fire is lit, and the momentum increases. People jump with the music, legs swinging, arms flailing all around them, unaware of anyone but themselves and the energy pouring out of their souls. Jasbir, Gulam, Ted, Zubaida, and Mina gambol to form their own dancing frenzy. Mangla sways with Arun in her arms.

Soon, someone passes sweets around and they eat and dance. Mangla feels the raw energy from the fire, music, and dance rejuvenating her soul. Laughter and joy reverberate in her sinews. She hasn't been this happy and carefree since she was in the hostel at BHU, singing with the other students. Reluctantly, her mother's duty kicks in, and she says, "Zubaida it's getting late and past the children's bedtime. We need to go home."

"I have my jeep," Ted says. "I'll take you home. It's on my way."

"That will be nice. Mr. Rai is out on tour and we walked here."

The next day, Zubaida comes to Mangla and says, "Bibiji, I know to read and write some Hindi, but I want to learn to read and write English, too. My friend Fatima can. She works for an English Memsahib. Her father works for Ted sahib. Mangla wonders if Zubaida wants to work for English people, but soon lets go of the thought. Rehman won't allow that transfer.

"That's wonderful! When do you want to start?"

"Today? But please don't tell Rehman *Bhai*. He won't allow it."

"We can do it during the day when Rehman's in the office and Arun's asleep. We can begin with Mina's books."

Mangla is encouraged by Zubaida's interest. She will risk Rehman and Gulam finding out—it furthers her own aspiration of advancing literacy in women.

***

In March, warm weather arrives. The Hindus celebrate with a bonfire in the *maidan*. They meet Yasmeen and her husband who works with Anand at a dinner in their home. Mangla really likes her. They find needlework as a common interest. Soon they spend time: Yasmeen teaches her gold *salma* a hollow springlike tube, beads and silk thread craft used by Muslims to embroider. She has plans to make a dress for Mina for her birthday. Yasmeen and her husband have no children but keep a lot of toys and like to spoil Mina and Arun.

When it comes time for the Hindu festival of Holi, Mangla invites them along with Jasbir, Gulam, and Ted. It will be a chance for the young men to meet Anand. Anand drives his family to the *maidan* in his car. It is his prize possession, his '38 black Ford sedan. He bought it secondhand a few months ago from an English soldier who was recalled to England to fight in the war. They could ill afford the expense, but the mechanic said it was a good buy. Mangla was against the purchase at the time, but she's become grateful for the mobility and comfortable transportation it provides them. Plus, owning a car brings her social status.

Mina gets to sit in Anand's lap as he drives. She feels important and he lets her pretend that she is driving. It is her favorite spot. Arun sits in Mangla's lap in the back sucking his thumb. His favorite spot. This arrangement keeps the warring factions separated.

In the *maidan*, the Holi story is in progress—how Lord Vishnu saved this world from the excessive violence of the demons. Then the pyre is lit to burn the effigy of Holika, sister of the demon Harnyakashyp, signifying the destruction of evil. People dance around. Anand takes Arun in his arms and dances. Mina grabs his legs to join in. Anand gets cross with her and shrugs her off.

"Don't make me fall down, Mina."

She is about to cry. Jasbir sees this and comes over. He takes Mina in his arms and says, "Oi Mina, no one is dancing with me. Let's dance together like we did for *Lohri*. Remember?"

Mina is all smiles as Mangla thanks Jasbir with her smile.

That night, Roopchand helps Mangla prepare many kinds of sweets to share at the Holi community party to be held in the *maidan* next day for lunch.

Everyone wears old clothes and comes to the center of the colony to put colored powder on each other's faces. Big vats of *tesu* flowers are boiling on a wooden fire. They give the water a bright saffron color. Everyone throws colored water on each other using water guns. This is to honor the playful Krishna and his tricks on Radha and her friends the *Gopis*. It is time to put away any differences of class and age and just have community fun. One of the participants brought their flute and starts playing a melodious tune. Others sing and accompany him with a Krishna hymns. Radha Krishna Radha Krishna--   Anand helps Arun to douse Mina, Mangla, Roopchand, and Zubaida.

"Mina, you are a big girl. Go on give me a good soaking," he tells her.

She looks at him as if to say, can I?

With his nod and pointing to the big *pitchkari*, a water bazooka, she yells "*Holi hai*" and laughing she soaks everyone. Then she goes and refills it before finding other targets. With dismay, Mangla looks at Anand and Mina's interaction. Mina's already aware of the power dynamics in their family.

Anand says, "Zubaida, watch Mina like a hawk. and don't let her eat anything before checking with me. It may contain *bhang*. Also, with the drinks."

"Yes, Sahib." She takes Mina for a walk around the ground and joins Gulam and his friends.

"How well do you know Ted?" Anand asks Mangla.

"Sometimes, we meet him on our afternoon walks when he invites Gulam and Jasbir to go with him to play cricket in cricket grounds. Why?"

"I wonder if Gulam and Jasbir know that they need special passes to go over to the cantonment." He tells her that the English have passed an edict to enhance their divide and rule after the Quit India movement. The incarcerated Indian leaders cannot alert youth about the seditious nature of the law that gives police undue power over the trusting Indian youth. He wonders why Ted's putting them in harm's way without telling them the truth.

"Ted seems nice. Maybe he doesn't agree with the English policy? Anyway, I told Zubaida that she could take Mina to Ted's house especially as it will improve their English."

"I just wonder if that is wise if they don't have their passes. He may be jeopardizing their lives, even if he doesn't know it."

Mangla doesn't want to believe him. "You are always trying to over protect us." She reminds him how it was in NWFP when she went to Mrs Desai's and nothing happened, but she omits the incident in the market. "Still, I will be on the watch," she says. "Thanks for telling me."

In a few weeks as May approaches the weather has become very hot. In these hot evenings, Roopchand has the spiced roasted mango water ready for everyone. A small amount of quinine is added to the mango drink to prevent heat stroke and malaria.

Mina scrunches her face.

"Drink it Mina, so you won't get a heat stroke," Mangla says.

"It's bitter. I want more sugar in it."

Roopchand obliges her.

"You're naughty Mina," Mangla says.

They sweat a lot and need a bath in the morning and evening. They take advantage of the cool of the night and sleep outside with a mosquito net canopy over their bed. However, when Jinnah visits, she can see fires burning in the city. She wonders if these portend future trouble. When Anand's away, this frightens her, and she asks Roopchand to put his cot near theirs.

Mangla and the children go for their walks earlier at dawn as soon as Anand leaves for work. This way they can enjoy their exercise in the coolness of the morning before the heat becomes unbearable.

Along the path there are many *harsringar* trees loaded with divinely scented white flowers with bright orange stems. In the early morning they fall like snow and cover the ground.

Mina and Arun run and collect them into their little cane baskets.

"Do you know what *harsringar* means?" Mangla asks. The children stop and look at her. "You know *har* is God right? *Sringar* means adornment, like when I do your hair and make you look pretty. So it means God's adornment. Isn't it a fitting name?"

Mina nods and says to Arun, "See, I have more than you. 'cause I'm older."

He takes some from her basket and points to himself and says, "More." "Amma, look, he cheats." Mina turns to him and makes a face. "You're too little and can't even count. See I can count till one hundred." She begins to count.

Arun punches her. She punches back. In their scuffle the flowers fall out of their baskets.

Mangla sighs. "Come on children, pick up your flowers. We've got to take them home and make garlands for Aunt Yasmeen. Remember she's coming today?"

Mina immediately picks up her flowers and some of Arun's as well and puts them in her own basket.

Arun wails as he snatches his own flowers back.

Their constant competition and fighting makes Mangla feel ragged even this early in the morning. To bring peace she placates him. "Don't worry *beta*, I'll help you pick more." She begins to help him, galling Mina who increases her pace.

"Ok, we have enough. Let's go home or we won't have time to make our garlands for Aunt Yasmeen."

"Will she bring us a toy?" Mina asks before she turns and skips in the direction of home. Arun runs after her. Mangla enjoys her walk as peace descends, however temporarily.

They arrive home and Mina runs to the sewing basket and collects needle and thread. Mangla has been teaching Mina simple threading skills, and she begins to thread the flowers. Mangla helps Arun make his garland. Roopchand brings in tea, with glasses of milk and biscuits for children, which they devour without delay. When they finish their garlands, they wrap them in wet rags to keep them from drying or rotting as the heat of the tropical summer day increases. Mangla helps Mina spray the wrap to keep the flowers fresh until Yasmeen comes. The children take their afternoon nap in anticipation of Aunt Yasmeen's visit and the possible loot of a toy she will bring as she usually does.

XXXXXXX

20 1945 Divide and Rule Foment

"*Bibiji*, the *tonga* you ordered is here," Roopchand hollers from the kitchen.

"Mina, Arun, are you ready?" Mangla shouts. "We need to go to the station."

They arrive at the platform as the train pulls in and Vani alights. The children run to her. They hold their *harsringar* garlands and wave as they yell, "Vani *Mausi*! Vani *Mausi*!"

She sees them and waves back. After the coolie picks up her bags, she comes to them. They run and fight each other as to who hands her their garlands first.

Mangla says, "Arun goes first because he is little. Be patient, Mina."

Mina sticks out her tongue at Arun and takes a step with him. She's been prepped for this visit since the letter arrived.

Vani smells the garlands then reaches up and drapes them around her braids. "Umm-- so nice. Did you make them?"

They both nod.

Mina says, "I helped Arun. He's too little."

"No, I'm not," he protests.

"You are, too."

So, it begins.

Mangla says, "Mina, Arun, go and hug Vani *Mausi*."

Vani picks up Arun and holds Mina's hands as the coolie follows them. "Did you have a comfortable journey, Vani?" Mangla asks.

"Yes, as much as can be expected, given how hot and long it was. Sleeping on the train for three nights and changing trains wasn't fun. But I survived."

"Don't I know it. At least you didn't have any children to worry about." She gestures the coolies towards the waiting tonga.

"I wanted to meet you in Anand's pride possession, his '38 black Ford sedan. But I don't know how to drive. Anand doesn't have time nor patience to teach me." Mangla says. Internally she adds, nor the inclination to risk the car in hands of a woman, or to give up any of his control. But she is not ready to confide in Vani that she is still learning to navigate this minefield called marriage as an independent woman in a world full of social privileges for men. It would feel strange to rat on her spouse. *Ammaji* never did. *Pitaji* was always God to her. She would be appalled if she heard her thoughts.

Mina interrupts, "I love my car and I am learning to drive with *Pitaji*. He takes me for a ride in his lap, not Arun. He's too little." She shakes her head and hands as she puts him in his place.

Mangla and Vani look skywards with a smile.

"How well she speaks now. *Ammaji* worried about her when you wrote that she was silent," Vani says.

"She speaks a lot," Manga says, laughing.

"We'll take the train to Rawalpindi tomorrow to meet Sabiha," Mangla says to the backdrop of the horses' clip-clop. "By the way, congratulations on graduating with your BA from BHU. Quite a feather in your cap."

"Oh thanks, now on to the next chapter."

"That is---"

"That's what I want to talk to you about. My parents want me to marry but I want to go on for my MA. How did you decide?"

"Yes, we have a lot to talk about," Mangla says with a sigh.

Vani's parents wrote that there's a suitable boy, Kishan Chand, in Rawalpindi, one of the railway officers. Anand knows him from work and believes it to be a good match for Vani. The parents have corresponded and decided that as a modern couple it would be good for Vani and Kishan to meet. The plan is that they will have the *dekhao* at Sabiha's house. They will leave Zubaida behind, and Vani will act as the children's governess so she can travel free with Mangla to see her in her new home.

***

Rawalpindi is a big train depot towards the end of a major line. Lots of steam noises, whistles and other train activities keep the children running from one side of the compartment to the other so as not to miss anything. Soon the train stops, and when Mangla opens the compartment door, Sabiha is coming towards them.

She looks beautiful in her aquamarine satin outfit—pants with a sequined skirt that flare out below the knee and a matching sequined shirt and chiffon scarf for her head that drapes across her chest. The sequins catch the morning sun and twinkle like stars. Quite chic. It's hard to believe that she is mother of two children. Mangla feels plump in comparison as she alights the train and waves to her. "Sabiha*jiji*, Sabiha*jiji*. We're here."

"*Salaam alekhun*," Sabiha greets them and embraces the children. "How are my little darlings?"

She turns to Vani whose slender figure is dressed in a slightly rumpled white cotton sari with a blue embroidered border that drapes over her shoulders.

With an adoring look she says, "Vani, how many men have you killed? Mangla, did you put a black dot on her to ward off an evil eye?"

Vani folds her hands and says, "Namaste Sabiha*jiji*. You are such a tease. It's been a long time. I haven't seen you since Mangla*jiji*'s wedding."

"I know. Rawalpindi is not easy to get to. You must have your BA now. Ready for marriage, right?"

Vani's cheeks color a little. She ducks the question and says, "I plan to follow Mangla*jiji's* footsteps and enroll in graduate school."

"Where are Abdul and Aziza?" Mangla changes the subject.

"In school. You'll see them in the afternoon."

"School starts early here."

"Not really. Your train is a few hours late."

"Oh, I forgot, anyway, so good to see you. You look lovely as always, my dear." "Go on, so do you. It seems like ages since I last saw you."

"I know. We seem to be always moving, and life gets so busy with two little ones. I'm glad that Vani provides us an excuse to rectify this."

Arun and Mina follow the chauffer. They drag Vani ahead with them to the car. Mangla and Sabiha trail with the coolies.

Sabiha says, "I met Kishan Chand the other day. I like him. Did you tell Vani about him?"

"Kind of, not really. I just dropped hints. She seems resistant."

"I hear her. She'll come around when she meets him, and the time is right. They'll make a handsome pair. Anyway, I've got the party all set. Now Anand Bhai has to bring the chief guest."

"He will, even though he's very busy and on travel often. He promised." The car stops in front of an old colonial bungalow, a perk that Sabiha's husband, Mahmood, enjoys as a recently appointed district judge. He is the first Muslim judge that the British have ever appointed in this part of the country. It is Mangla's initial visit them since Sabiha moved from Sindh to Rawalpindi.

A guard in a white uniform opens the iron gates for the car to drive through to a portico in front of the house. The driver parks the car and gets out to open the door for Sabiha and the others. Mangla and Vani follow Sabiha to the front verandah. She says, "Don't worry, Mirza will bring the bags in later. Come."

"What a lovely home you have. I love your garden," Vani says.

"It's even more beautiful than I could imagine from your letters, Sabiha*jiji*. I'm so glad I was able to come and see it," Mangla says.

"Allah's blessings. Anyway, all this later—you must be hungry and thirsty. Mirza, *are'- oh* Mirza—please bring in tea for the guests."

Sabiha invites them to sit down on the sofa in the living room. "This is the first time you've come and blessed my house. I am so honored to have you here, my dear sisters," she says in formal Urdu. Mangla thinks being a Muslim judge's wife makes her a woman of importance now, requiring this level of sophistication in her language. It is like hearing someone who comes from an aristocratic family. Her sister is moving up in social echelons, and Mangla feels proud.

An older lady, with an arthritic limp, walks into the room. Her greying temples peek from under the white scarf draped around her head.

Mangla gets up and bows her head in deference to her. "Namaste, *Khalajan*. How are you? I haven't seen you since Sabiha*jiji*'s wedding."

Khalajan says, with her hands on her prayer beads, "*Salaam Alekhun, beti*. Allah is most merciful and compassionate. May you enjoy Allah's blessings every day of your life. Sabiha tells me that you are married and with two children and living in Lahore."

"Yes, *Khalajan*. Vani, do you remember Mahmood *bhai*'s aunt? She lives with them. Mina and Arun, come and say namaste to *Khalajan*. She's Abdul and Aziza's *dadi*aunt."

They all move closer to *Khalajan*. She puts her hand on top of each one's head and says, "May Allah's blessings be with you and may you live to be thousand years, with each year having thousand days. Come sit near me, Vani." She pats Vani's back with affection.

"Vani is my *mamaji* mother's brother's daughter," Mangla says. "She lived with us until she went to college. She just finished her BA."

"It is good that girls are educated these days—not like our time. Your parents must be looking for a husband for you—no?"

Vani flushes and lowers her eyes.

"You are embarrassing her, *Khalajan*," says Mangla. "You know these days girls don't like to talk about these things."

Vani gets up and says, "Sabiha*jiji*, do you mind if I go and look at your garden? The red roses are lovely. And is that a peach tree?"

"Can we go too?" the children ask. Mangla nods and they escape, skipping and dragging Vani with them.

Sabiha walks over to the divan on which Mangla sits next to *Khalajan*. She hands them both their cups of tea and asks, "You didn't bring Zubaida with you, Mangla?"

"No, *Jiji*, we brought Vani as the children's governess. She gets free travel. I hope your Ayah can help us for the few days we are here."

She puts her cup of tea on the table and frowns. "You know, recently Zubaida's been learning English with a friend an Englishman."

"Oh?" Sabiha raises her eyebrows.

"Mina's so fond of her. I don't want to lose her to the English." Mangla sucks her lips.

"Wouldn't she be in *purdah* soon? "Sabiha asks.

"Her brother hasn't mentioned anything about it. There are fourteen or fifteen children, and they probably need her to continue to work to bring in good money. Her brother Gulam now helps with the yard work."

"Mahmood brings from court such tragic stories of beautiful girls impregnated by Englishmen. Families disown them or sell them to *kothas* where they end up in *nauch* houses to please the British men and nabobs. It's terrible. Sometimes the families just kill them." *Khalajan* shakes her head.

"Yes, it's a real problem. I'm not saying it will happen to Zubaida. But just be watchful," Sabiha says.

"Thanks, *Jiji,* for this warning. I'll keep my eyes and ears peeled. It's difficult to keep girls safe. I worry about Mina and her spirit."

They both nod in agreement, continue to sip tea and chat as they exchange information about friends, family, and the difficulty of bringing up girls with independent spirit. They worry about Aziza too.

How's your friend, Basanthi?" Sabiha asks.

"I was just thinking of her," Mangla says. "I think of her often, but I haven't heard from her since I got married."

"You remember Mahmood's cousin, Farida? She and Basanthi came last week to visit us."

"Really?"

"They work and live together in Murree hills where they teach in a girls' school. I believe Basanthi's doing her Ph.D. research there."

Mangla feels her heart drain of life. "You know more about her than I do," she says.

"Well, Basanthi is a Muslim convert now, and is an important member of Jinnah's Muslim league. She is quite an activist. They were here for some political rally for the elections."

"I'm surprised," Mangla says. "She wasn't religious when I knew her, although she was raised Christian, and always wore her mother's cross. I can't believe it! I am the one who introduced her to Farida, to Anis Kidwai, and even *namaz* in college." How far Basanthi has come. How far removed from Mangla's choices she is.

"I'll be sure to give them your address," says Sabiha. "But you move so much. It's hard to keep track."

Sabiha collects the empty cups and puts them on the tray and says, "Before Vani comes in let me tell you that I've arranged the party for Vani and Kishan Chand to meet next week. I hope that's still OK?"

"Yes, and that gives me time to better prepare Vani for that occasion. I'd better go and see that the children take their bath.

"Of course. I guess you'll want your bath too, after that sooty train journey. Leave your dirty clothes in the bathroom. Ayah will make sure they are washed and ironed. Ayah-*are'* oh-Ayah--" she calls out.

Mangla is fascinated by how well Sabiha runs her household despite having a crippled widowed aunt-in-law living with her. She's dutiful. Mangla feels fortunate to have access to her wisdom to bring up her children in this part of the world. She tells Sabiha that over the next week she hopes the two of them can sit down and talk about how to manage the difficult interactions of Mina with Arun. She has trouble negotiating her relationship with Anand who often puts restrictions on her movements. She is conflicted between *Ammaji*'s ways and her way. There is no one else for her to turn.

Sabiha reaches out and gives her shoulder a squeeze. "We'll have plenty of time to talk about such matters," she says. "Now, Mangla, go and take your bath and get ready for lunch before the others come in."

***

The day of the party arrives. Sabiha has been busy supervising her staff to clean, dust and polish the furniture. She has brought out her best Royal Doulton china with pink periwinkles and gold leaf design, an expensive set she got for her wedding. Mangla helps her set them carefully on her best lace tablecloth.

"I really want this party to go well to repay some of what I owe *Ammaji*," Sabiha says.

"The table looks so lovely, Sabiha*jiji*. I love the crystal glasses," Mangla says. "When we went to Ireland, we visited the Waterford factory. Each one is blown individually." Sabiha gives the table a satisfied look. Then puts her hands on her mouth. "Oh, I forgot the center vase. Where did Mirza put those flowers?"

Mangla looks at the corner table. "Here they are." She carefully picks up the vase and hands it to Sabiha. "What else can I help you with?"

"I will go and help *Khalajan* and the cook with the dinner. Why don't you go and check that Vani is dressed properly."

Mangla walks into Vani's room and sees her lying on bed, reading her novel, still in the cotton sari she was wearing earlier. "What are you going to wear to the party tonight, Vani?"

"This. Why?"

"Anand's coming and bringing some people who work for him."

"So, what's so special? Doesn't this look nice on me?"

Mangla thinks, ooh—this is going to be difficult. "Well of course you look beautiful. But your mother--"

Expelling air forcefully from her puffed out cheeks, Vani says, "I'm not stupid. I know she's been trying to marry me off. I've told her so many times, I want to study further, like you did."

"Yes, but I left before finishing my Masters. Between you and me---" Mangla breaks off. She is wondering if she can help Vani avoid that boobytrap she herself fell into. Maybe by meeting and working with her betrothed, she can negotiate where she will do her graduate work, rather than feeling as Mangla has—torn between anger and self-betrayal, cultural and religious pressures for giving up on her own dreams.

"I understand. Your mother asked us to arrange for you to meet Kishan Chand. Didn't she tell you?" Mangla says.

"Oh! She went on and on about what a good family he comes from etc. etc. She wanted me to wear her expensive *zari* sari and jewelry. I told her what I'm telling you--what's wrong with my everyday clothes?"

"Well, it is a way to impress--"

"It's so disingenuous. After all, isn't this how he'll see me every day?"

Mangla doesn't miss Vani's defiant look. She saunters to the window and looks out and says, "You can always say no if you don't like him. I'll support you." She tells her that both she and Anand have met him. He's handsome and forward thinking, and maybe willing to let her study further. Worth a try. But Mangla won't lie. She admits that until one lives with someone, one won't know what they are really like. And even when one lives with someone. Take her friendship with Basanthi. They roomed together for 3 years. Did Mangla really know her? Does she really know Anand, even though they have two children? To herself, she thinks that maybe she can't help Vani. Afterall, she hasn't been able to negotiate her own studies with her husband.

Mangla thinks about her own *dekhao* to which Basanthi came an eternity ago. Could she be putting the same pressure on Vani that *Ammaj*i put on her? The fear of losing a good match? She corresponded with Anand for many years but didn't insist on meeting him and spending time with him and allowing herself time to adjust to his inconsistencies and limitations. "I wonder if it would have made a difference," she wonders aloud for Vani to hear.

Hearing but not hearing Mangla's revelations, Vani continues to read her book. "I know, Vani. Perhaps you can do it for me so I can fulfill my duty to your parents. Hunh? How about we make a pact on that? Afterall, they did let you study beyond 6th grade." She extends her hand.

"Anyway," says Vani, "I left all her finery behind. I don't have anything fancy" Mangla gently takes the book from Vani and puts her hands on the gray silk *kanjivaram* sari with a red gold border on it that has been laid on the bed. Then she holds out a gold chain with a ruby pendant in a dainty paisley setting with matching earrings. Mangla brought them with her for the occasion. "See, aren't they beautiful? They're in vogue with the younger set."

Vani's eyes open wide as she looks at the beauty of the filigree work around the pendant. "This is beautiful. I remember selecting it for you."

"So, wouldn't you like to wear it? Sabiha*jiji* and I are dressed up. She's gone to so much trouble. Can't you just do this little bit for us if not your parents? What's the harm, my beloved sister?" She holds Vani's face in her hands. With that, she gently steers Vani towards the bathroom. Keeping her fingers crossed, she enters the kitchen to the enticing bouquet of simmering chickpea curry.

"It smells so nice. They should be here any minute."

"Dinner is almost ready. *Khalajan*'s here so I don't need any help. Make sure Vani is ready. Wait for your husband to arrive with Kishan Chand. I'll get the appetizers started."

175

Mangla goes to check Vani's appearance. She hasn't put on any lipstick. She goes to her own room and gets red lipstick and returns to Vani. "Vani, how about a little bit hun-h?"

"Yes, Vani *Mausi,* you'll look lovely," Aziza chimes in clapping her hands. The other children join her. Vani relents.

"Doesn't Vani *Mausi* look lovely?"

"Yes," they say in unison dancing around Vani.

"When will they all come?" Mina asks her mother. "I'm hungry."

"Should be soon, a little patience will go a long way. It feels bitter now, but its fruit will be sweet as you can get extra dessert."

Anand's late, Mangla thinks as she returns to the living room. She hopes that the second-hand car made the long arduous drive without mishap.

She hears a car outside. In walks Mahmood *Bhai.* He looks around. "They haven't arrived yet. It smells nice, I'm hungry. Sabiha*jan,* I'm home." He walks towards the kitchen. Mangla's eyes follow his broad figure until he disappears, and she hears Sabiha's voice telling the servant to get Sahib's evening party clothes ready.

Time holds still and so does her heart. What could have happened to Anand? It's a long drive, and he drives so fast and with such abandon. She taps the table and as her tempo increases, she shivers with worry.

Then, after what seems to her like eternity, Mangla hears the familiar purr of her own car. Her fingers relax. It's about time. Anand walks in with Kishan Chand. Looking nonchalant, she greets them with a *namaste* and calls out, "Vani, children, our guest is here."

Mahmood walks in with Sabiha and she says, " Anand *Bhai,* hope all was OK with your journey. We were getting worried. What happened?"

Anand frowns and his fingers comb his hair. "Sorry about the delay. We ran into a big Muslim League procession yelling Pakistan *Zindabad* to drumbeats of excited followers. It was followed by another rally by the Congress Party in their Gandhi caps. They were demanding India's freedom and unity with their own *dholak* drums and frenzied dance. We had to wait them out, too. I'm hoping no trouble starts between them. That delayed my picking up Kishan Chand."

Mangla wonders, with a tight stomach, if Basanthi and Farida were among the demonstrators.

"It mustn't have been planned," Mahmood says. "I didn't hear about it or read about it in the papers. It wasn't mentioned in the news. It stayed peaceful then?"

"Mercifully, yes."

"I read about clashes in Sindh between Hindus, Muslims, and Sikhs, but nothing around here. I hope it stays that way. Praise to Allah."

"You must be hungry and thirsty after all that excitement, and that too, after your long drive." Sabiha signals the servant.

Just then the children enter dragging Vani. Anand introduces them. Kishan Chand turns. He sees Vani. His hands go to his lips, pleasure written all over his face as he taps them.

Vani steals a glance at him. A good sign, Mangla thinks.

Anand talks about politics—the rise of Jinnah's Muslim League with their Pakistan for Muslims movement, and the Indian National Army, and Subhash Chand Bose's defection to help Germans and Japanese against the British.

"Peace unites. Fighting destroys. Hindu, Muslims, and Sikhs are brothers. Our food, culture, and lives--everything's so intertwined," Kishan Chand says as Vani watches him with relaxed sensual eyes.

"The central tenet of Gandhiji's independence movement is unity amongst all castes and creeds," Mahmood says with an edge in his voice. "He has many followers, but the divide and rule platform of the British has divided the Muslim, Hindu, and Sikh communities right down the middle. He has many enemies as well. It's like we're sitting on a tinderbox. In our courts we have seen an increase in conflict cases between religions."

Anand talks about Jinnah's fiery rhetoric that voting for the Muslim League's like voting for Muhammad. Voting for Congress is voting for the evil *Shaitan*. They are promoting Hindus and Sikhs as a danger to Islam. That was behind the bloody riots in Sindh.

"Listen," *Khalajan* interjects. You can talk about this later. The children are hungry."

The dinner is served. The children run to the dining room. Sabiha follows and gets them seated.

Mangla ensures that Vani and Kishan Chand sit side by side, so they have some time to get to know each other. The children sit next to them. Aziza and Abdul give a knowing giggle. Mina sits next to Vani and Aziza next to Kishan Chand.

Kishan Chand asks the children, "Have you heard the story of the monkey and the crocodile?"

"No," they answer in chorus.

He animates the tales from the *Panchtantra* and keeps them mesmerized and entertained. All the while he includes Vani with his eyes and smile. Mangla thinks he's quite an intergenerational charmer. Before they know it, the dinner comes to an end, but the conversations continue as they wait for dessert.

Kishan Chand steers the conversation to movies playing in the theater. He saw that *Zeenat* is in the Regal and *Badi Maa* in the Odeon.

"Come on, Vani, let's hear the song. You sing so well," Sabiha requests. The children jump and clap, "Yes, Vani *Mausi* we want a song," and Arun apes them. She sings the song, and everyone gives an appreciative round of applause, including Kishan Chand.

The servant serves rice pudding and refills their glasses with water.

"We're leaving tomorrow, but Vani's staying over with Sabiha*jiji,* so maybe you and Vani can go to the movies," Mangla says to Kishan Chand. "It will give Vani an outing and Sabiha*jiji* a break!"

"Will that be OK with you? Would you like to go out with me?" Kishan Chand asks Vani.

She nods. "Of course. You decide which movie and surprise me."

"Tomorrow I'll be out of town for couple of days--but maybe we can go to see a movie on Friday evening. Will that be OK Sabiha*jiji?*"

Sabiha and Mangla exchange knowing smiles as she replies, "Of course."

"Can I go with them, *Ammijan*? Please?" Aziza asks.

"If Ayah goes with you," Sabiha says.

"Yes, I can truthfully tell Vani's parents that they didn't go out in public alone," Mangla laughs.

"Can I stay with Aziza*jiji?*" Mina says.

"No," Anand says.

"Zubaida is waiting for you as is Roopchand," says Mangla, though she, too, wishes they could stay. "We'll come again soon. I promise and cross my heart."

The next morning, Mangla and her family leave early to begin the two hundred-plus miles back on the Grand Trunk road. Sabiha has packed them lunch and drinks and snacks for the trip. They need to get home that night as Anand has an important meeting the next day. In an excited clamor, Mina and Arun sit in front with their father. He entertains them with the stories of the animals they see on the road. He teaches them the poem of *Shrawan* that his mother recited to him when he was a boy. Mangla sits in the back and listens to his deep voice. Dark ominous clouds gather above warning her of an impending storm.

XXXXXXX

21 India's Social Fabric Cracks

Zubaida meets them when they arrive home.

Mina jumps for joy and runs to her. "We missed you. It was so much fun. Did you know we saw an elephant on the road? We stopped the car and got to pet the elephant and feed him leaves."

Arun dances trumpeting like an elephant and wags his arms.

"Yes, and the *mahout* put us on the *howdah* and we got an elephant ride." Mina dances around Zubaida.

"*Hai Allah*! So much fun. Maybe I can have an elephant ride as well."

"Can she, *Amma*?" Mina asks Mangla.

"Yes, of course. How are English lessons progressing Zubaida?"

"Good, memsahib."

Mangla notices the pink in her cheeks and her flustered looks.

"Is Gulam Ali learning with you too?"

Zubaida's color deepens to a deeper red. "No memsahib. He works. Sometimes he comes after work, and they go to play cricket with Jasbir. Only Fatima and I learn English."

"Well, you can tell me what you've learned one of these days. Has he given you a book?"

"Yes, memsahib."

"I'll have a look at it. Let's go in now."

On their evening walk to the *maidan* near the canal, Mangla sees the Englishman Ted standing there smoking a cigarette. Mina runs to him and he picks her up. "Hello, Mina. How're you, Zubaida, Mrs. Rai?" He tips his hat to Mangla. "OK, sahib. *Adaab*," Zubaida says with her hands on her forehead.

"Namaste. How are the English lessons coming along?" Mangla asks.

"Super. Aren't they, Zubaida?" Ted says with his attractive smile. Mangla notices the red spots on Zubaida's cheeks again. "Gulam and Jasbir should be here any moment. I'm waiting for them to go and play cricket. Speak of the devils. There they are." Ted waves.

"Oi, Zubaida and Mina, you both look like princesses as always. *Sat Sri Akal Bibiji*." Jasbir greets Mangla with his Sikh charm.

Gulam says, "*Adaab, Bibiji*."

179

"I guess we'd better go before we run out of light. I'll see you with Fatima for a lesson," Ted says as he hands Mina to Zubaida.

She notices that they are headed away from the cantonment, so she doesn't have to care about Anand's misgivings.

Mangla notices that when handing off Mina, Ted's hand touches Zubaida. They also exchange a small, secret glance as Zubaida fans herself with her scarf. Clearly there is a hidden minefield here. *Khalajan*'s cautionary words about impregnated girls come to her mind.

"Let's go home," she says with a frown.

***

Mangla is in a little grocery shop when she hears news on the radio. She stops in her tracks. "Last night, The Regal theater in Rawalpindi was bombed." She must have heard wrong. She was there only a few days ago. Mahmood *Bhai* had said that everything was calm. He's a judge. He should know.

The announcer continues, "The authorities speculate that it was a surprise bombing by Muslim League *goondas* to create fear in the local communities. The Regal was playing *Zeenat*, a Muslim melodrama. People think they picked that movie theater to bomb so that the local Muslims will think that Hindus are behind it. The government has put Hindu communities there on high alert. We will give you an update as we learn more."

They will be going off air soon, Mangla thinks. She'll have to wait.

Sabiha wouldn't be affected because she's Muslim—but she has Vani, a Hindu, staying with her, putting them both at risk.

Mangla thinks, last night would have been Friday night. Where did they say they were going to see the movie? Did they say the Regal or the Odeon? She tries to remember. They hadn't decided. She fervently hopes they went to the Odeon as she hurries home. Maybe by some miraculous means she will learn that they are all safe in Rawalpindi. Maybe Anand, as a railway officer, will make it all right. She grasps at straws.

"Roopchand, please feed the children. I'll wait till sahib comes home." "Mina, Arun, come eat. Wouldn't you like to play with your friends next door? Zubaida can take you there."

Competitive to the core, the children scramble over each other to the table. Before long they are out the door with Zubaida.

Mangla wants to be alone and undisturbed to collect herself. If indeed Sabiha and her family are in danger, she needs to catch the next train to Rawalpindi. With that thought, she packs her bags.

Anand comes home and with sagging shoulders, says, "I heard the news that there are riots in Rawalpindi."

"I know, I heard it on the radio at the shops," Mangla replies.

"I sent a telegram to Kishan Chand from the station but haven't heard anything back. That worries me."

"Weren't they going to the movies last night?" Mangla asks. "Do you know which movie? Do you know which theater?"

"No. But all the trains are stopped. The train tracks were vandalized near Rawalpindi."

"I can't just wait here. I must go to them." Mangla's hands shoot in air and her voice rises a pitch.

"I know Sparkles. Be patient. Let me think."

"It's easy for you to say that—your family isn't affected. Why don't we drive there?"

"You're being irrational. Two hundred odd miles? At this time of the night? The roads may not be safe either."

"I'll risk that. Perhaps our neighbor's driver will drive me there. He's Muslim and I'll make sure I wear a *burqa*."

"Don't be ridiculous, you don't want to put the children at risk. Let's sleep on it. Besides, what can you do? I asked the stationmaster to send me word if they get a reply telegram from Rawalpindi."

As she looks at him her lips curl. He's efficient and officious as always. Doesn't he have a heart? How can he act so calm? She paces up and down like a tiger. If something happened to Vani, what will she tell her aunt? Why did she leave her with Sabiha? As a judge, how could Mahmood *Bhai* not know of this unrest?

Unless--now that she's been immersed in Muslim culture, like Basanthi, what if Sabiha's loyalties have shifted, and she only set this charade up to fool her? Was that why she didn't tell Basanthi where Mangla was? Were Basanthi and Farida involved in the attack? A sharp pang shoots through her chest as wild suspicions chase her tortured mind. How fickle is her filial love? She chides herself for her prejudicial thought. She's now shaking. What will she tell her aunt?

How selfish was she, herself. Did she really need to take Vani to Rawalpindi? She could have arranged the *dekhao* in her own house. Self-doubts and mental agony burn her insides like dry matches ready to explode. The more she 'could-a and what-ifs' her actions, the greater her anguish.

"Mangla. Sit down. Roopchand, bring some hot tea for memsahib."

She hears Anand as if from a thousand miles away as he holds her and lowers her rigid tense body into a chair.

She hears a knock on the door. He restrains her attempt to get up. Roopchand answers the door to let in the assistant stationmaster to hand Anand a note.

He reads, and shakes as his hands comb through his hair. The creases between his already furrowed brows deepen.

"What is it? What is it?" Mangla gets up and claws at his chest. "They were at the Regal, weren't they? Vani wanted to see Zeenat." She starts to pound her own chest her inside already knows the heartbreaking truth. An inner knowing drives her eyes vacant as she looks at his grief-stricken face. She starts to beat her head on his chest. Vani and Kishan Chand are dead aren't they?"

"Yes. I'm afraid they found their bodies in the rubble. But Aziza and her Ayah are missing." She hears through his chest. A loud wail escapes her. Through it she whispers. "Vani is dead. Aziza is missing. I must go to Sabiha*jiji* right away. She'll need me right now." She thinks if something happened to Mina how would she feel. Her wails get louder and, tears flow faster as her nose runs

"You can't. Please be sensible. Let me go to the station and see what I can arrange for you. Ummm-- give me time. Please, Sparkles." Unlike him, he pleads. "I'm coming with you. I'd rather be at the station ready to leave."

"What good will it do? Alas, the world doesn't rotate around us, Sparkles."

It's a long time since he used this loving nickname for her.

"Roopchand and Zubaida can take care of the children here. I'm sure Yasmeen will help."

"Give me time. I promise to be back soon. Besides, the next train is not until tomorrow. Hopefully the trains will be running by then."

Roopchand enters with tea and dinner. He bows as he sets their plates on the table.

"I'm not hungry," Mangla says.

"Well, if you won't eat, I won't either." With that Anand walks towards the front door.

Remorse smites her as her body crumples, and she realizes that he hasn't eaten anything since lunch. "OK, I'll eat if you will, too." She picks up her plate. He walks back and does the same. She picks at her plate while he wolfs his food down. After dinner he's out through the front door. She's unable to lift her legs and follow him.

"Roopchand, can you bring my *charkah* please."

She spins in slow motion. Its rhythm focuses her mind and slowly, ever so slowly, breath by breath she finds her calm returning. She hears the muezzin's final prayer call for the day. She prays. That is the least she can do for Sabiha. In need of compassion, she thinks of Yasmeen.

"Roopchand, can you go to Yasmeen memsahib's house and see if she's still up and can come and sit with me?"

She waits, and drains her tea, refills, and repeats staring into space as Sabiha's anguished face floats before her eyes yet again. How treacherous can God be? Did *Khalajan* have a premonition when she said it is difficult to protect Aziza? Thousands of questions pop up in her grief-stricken mind, but no answers come. How would she let *Ammaji* know of this tragedy? Vani was so dear to her. Would she be still forgiving of her Gods?

Roopchand refills the teapot and brings the children milk and dinner as they return from their friend's house.

Mangla says, "Zubaida, please put the children to bed." She gives them a hug. "Go on, be good for her. I'll come later. She can tell you your favorite Akbar Birbal story. Won't you like that?"

"Will you, Zubaida?" Mina asks, skipping around Zubaida as they go to their bedroom.

Soon Anand returns. "Good news, Sparkles. They've repaired the tracks and the train to Rawalpindi will be running tomorrow. To be safe, they will run slowly and with an army escort. It will be late but hopefully we will reach there without mishap. I am called to supervise this operation."

"Oh, thank God. Maybe I can get there in time for their cremation."

"Given the situation, I think we should let the children stay here. I'll go over and see if Yasmeen*jan* can help us take care of them. Zubaida and Roopchand can help her."

She nods. "Yasmeen should be here soon. I sent Roopchand to see if she can come over. We can ask her."

"Given that the children are so fond of Vani and Aziza it'll be least traumatic for them not to go." Anand moves towards her as if to embrace her. But she is not ready to be comforted by him, and he drops his arms.

***

In Rawalpindi, Mangla finds *Khalajan*, Sabiha, and Mahmood sitting in the living room on the sofa with their heads in their hands. *Khalajan* has one arm around Sabiha's shoulder. They are both sobbing quietly and blowing their noses. Mahmood *Bhai*, with his ashen face, shakes his head, blaming himself as he mutters quietly and repeatedly, "How could I be so blind and stupid?"

"Sabiha*jiji*," Mangla calls. *Khalajan* turns around as she pulls her arms away from Sabiha and slips her *tasbih*, prayer beads from her wrists to her hands and says, "Praise to *Allah*—Mangla, you are able to come." She moves her prayer beads with her fingers.

"Yes, they were able to fix the tracks. Anand is there."

Sabiha looks up with swollen face and tearful eyes. Mangla runs to embrace her as tears flow down her own cheeks. They hold each other, rocking back and forth. Sabiha shakes her head and tries to speak, but silence alone greets Mangla. She pats her back. "Sh sh—it's OK. Your sister's here." Sabiha shakes even more, as the flood of tears intensifies. They hold and rock each other, lost in their own nightmarish thoughts.

Mahmood says, "I feel so bad. I had it all wrong. I wish I could rewrite the last few days. But these are *Allah*'s wishes. He's most compassionate and merciful."

Mangla thinks of the 99 qualities of Allah. God's mercy and compassion is unfathomable to her in this carnage and loss. Her sister is dead, and Mahmood's daughter is missing. How can he have faith in God at this time? Hi lack of anger is incomprehensible.

"Vani and Kishan both were meant for each other and can now live in paradise together forever. These are *Allah*'s wishes," *Khalajan* says.

Their consoling words help Sabiha to compose herself and calm down. She forces a smile for Mangla.

"What a bad sister I am. I didn't even welcome you at the station. You must be tired and hungry after your journey." She calls Mirza to bring in tea and snacks.

"The driver brought me home. Where's Abdul?"

"At his aunt's. I'm so glad you're able to come," *Khalajan* says.

"I'm not a good daughter to *Ammaji*," Sabiha says. "I didn't protect Vani." Tears recommence their trek down her cheeks.

"It was so unexpected, a surprise move. Our intelligence failed us," Mahmood *Bhai* laments. "They almost went to the Odeon--but at the last minute, since Aziza wanted to go and Ayah with them, the extra tickets were only available at the Regal. They had two seats together. That's how Aziza was saved but kidnapped. They know she is my daughter. I'm sure they'll demand a ransom."

"Vani wanted to see *Zeenat* and was happy. Praise to *Allah*. He has mysterious ways. We don't know. He's the most powerful and high. *Bismillah ar Rehman ar Rahim*. Allah the most compassionate and merciful." *Khalajan* repeats her prayers on the beads in her hands.

"They've kept their burnt bodies," Mahmood says. "They were hard to recognize, but Vani's bracelet and Kishan Chand's ring and the proximity to their seats provided the police their clue. The impact threw them some distance. You'll have to be their surrogate Hindu family. The collective cremation will be held tonight. You can take the ashes back to their family to scatter them in the Ganges. Of course, the Muslims will be buried here. "Sabiha continues to look down and every so often gives a dry lurch. In a barely audible whisper she says, "Vani was so young and vibrant. *Allah* must have loved her to want her back so soon."

Mangla squeezes her hands as fresh tears pour down her own face.

"Oh, it's so remiss of me, Mangla. You haven't even had a bath after your travel." She calls "Ayah--," then her hands wring together as her gaunt look returns and her hands go to her open mouth.

Compassion floods Mangla as she gets up. "I don't need anyone to help me, *Jiji*. I'll be right back. It will be nice to freshen up before we go for the cremation."

Khalajan limps after her. "I can help you, *beti*. Sabiha*jan*, you keep sitting. I'll be right back and make sure that Mangla has all she needs."

As they walk out, *Khalajan* says, shaking her head, "It is so distressing. This waiting and not knowing. We can only pray that *Allah* has Ayah and Aziza safe." What can she say? Mangla just listens.

"They couldn't get four seats together, so they split. Aziza and Ayah went upstairs in the balcony, while Vani and Kishan were downstairs where the bomb exploded. That is why they were killed. In the chaos that ensued in the balcony, people there escaped. *Allah* is merciful. Praise to *Allah*.

"But we don't know what happened after that. The police are still putting the story together. Mahmood expects foul play, because recently he gave some difficult decisions in favor of girls and women and against the *goondas* who sell girls and destroy their lives. There are many rich evil men. He's an honest officer. That is why he's worried for their safety."

Mangla looks up at her. "In my haste I forgot my prayer beads to pray with. Could I borrow your nice Chinese jade *tasbih Khalajan* blessed by your *Pir?*

"Of course*, beti* I don't use it. In fact, you can keep it for later to give to Mina if you wish."

When Mangla returns into the living room, Mahmood and Sabiha are still in the same place and position as she left them in, their eyes vacant and sorrowful. Mangla thinks of Aziza. How distressing it must be for a seven-year-old to go through this ordeal. Her heart goes out to her sister. She sits down and holds Sabiha's hand.

There is a knock on the door as Mirza brings in a note and hands it to Mahmood *Bhai*. Mangla sees his breathing change. His face whitens as his hands go to his chest. Sabiha looks at him and asks, "What is it *Janu?*"

He hands her the note. It's in Urdu. She reads it and hands it to Mangla. The ransom note reads: Judge sahib, we have your daughter Aziza. Please send us sixty thousand rupees if you want to see her alive. It's a price you must pay for being a Hindu lover. They give a location and time where the money is to be dropped with a warning to not get the police involved. No mention of Ayah.

"Where will we find the money?" he says.

"We have to. *Allah* will provide. At least she's alive," Sabiha says, reaching for her prayer beads.

Mangla thinks the thugs are treating Aziza like she is a commodity, not a living breathing human being. Who could these callous, heartless fortune hunters be?

The community hears of Judge sahib's predicament. All holy texts teach that no good person should suffer at the hands of those who are evil.

Hindus, Muslims, Christians, agnostics, the political, and apolitical, police, and businessmen all have a townhall meeting and decry the incident at the Regal. They praise the courage and honesty of their judge. They pledge whatever money they can muster. Each donor has written him a personal note with the money they give to the mayor. Every note reads a variation of this theme. In no time his grateful community provides Mahmood *Bhai* the money he needs.

***

The ransom day finally arrives, and Mangla, Sabiha, and Mahmood go to the place specified in the ransom note. They wait with the bag of payment and scan around for their little girl.

Then Mangla sees a shadow. Her mouth opens as her hand goes to it. No, it can't be. But she sees her again, she'd know her anywhere, making agitated hand movements, talking to some men. Beside them is Aziza with her hands tied in a rope and held by one of the men.

Sabiha looks at Mangla and in shock says it first, "Basanthi?"

Then Basanthi unties Aziza and sets her free to run to her parents. Crying, she comes to their outstretched arms and that is it.

Then they are all gone, including Basanthi. Mangla feels a deep wound open within her, as she feels the pain of Basanthi's betrayal once again. She didn't even come and ask about Vani. Is she changed so much as a Muslim fanatic? What about Farida? But no one comes for the money.

Aziza tells them that in the morning Farida *Khala* came with her important friend who got angry with the men who kidnapped Aziza. They were all very angry. But finally, *Khala*'s friend set her free, and here she is. There is no sign of the kidnappers.

Mahmood says, "I'll have to press charges against Farida and Basanthi for being accomplices."

Sabiha says, "*Janu*, but they set her free and demanded no money. You can't do that. There's no crime. We'll donate all this money back to the community. Tell them their love, compassion, charity, *dua*, and *Allah*'s mercy, set Aziza free. The family is grateful."

"Yes, *Abbajan, Khala* and her friend were so angry at the men for being mean," Aziza says.

Mahmood says, "Where's Ayah?"

"I don't know. Two nights we slept in the same room then some mean men came and took her away. They were not nice. They dragged her and beat her. I told them to leave her alone. But I was tied and couldn't help her," Aziza says, and begins to cry.

"Don't cry Aziza*jan*. I'll get the police to look for Ayah. Maybe Basanthi and Farida heard about the ransom and found the *goondas* through their political contacts. I'll be forgiving," Mahmood says.

"*Allah*'s been merciful," Sabiha says. "And we have lost so much already. Maybe one day we'll learn the truth. Now let's go home and let Aziza rest and celebrate our good fortune."

"What would you like in this moment, Aziza?" Mangla asks.

"A big bowl of Mango *kulfi* ice cream," she says with a big smile and her arms stretching wide. They all hug her and laugh as Mahmood picks up his daughter and puts her on his shoulders.

XXXXXXX

22 Mina's Healing by Pir

The hot air, *loos* are gone. The monsoon rains fill the canal. With it the animals, plants, and insects come alive. Fishermen fish on the banks. The children carry umbrellas and wear their galoshes for walks. Mangla practices English with them. Zubaida imitates frogs and they giggle. She playfully splashes with them in the rain puddles and dances with the peacocks who display beautiful plumes. Mina and Arun's mouths open in awe of the splendors all around them. Despite the humidity, it feels good to go out and get the light breeze with fall weather around the corner.

The geckos have taken over the house ceilings. They gorge themselves on the insects and, when full, fall to the ground. Arun chases them. Sometimes they lose their tails. Mina laughs as she points to them hissing and fighting over a moth with their missing tails and Arun, the ape he is, imitates her every move and words.

On their walks, Mangla tells the children stories from the *Upanishads* and the *Panchtantra,* about the fecundity and regrowth of life. She gets Roopchand to put up a swing for them in the backyard. The neighborhood children join them as well, and Zubaida and Roopchand take turns swinging all the children.

Mangla sings *Teej* songs to them as she fondly remembers her carefree BHU days with Basanthi. But now her heart is heavy with treachery. She still can't shake off the feeling of Basanthi's involvement in Vani's death. Suspicions gnaw inside her. Now Vani's gone. Mangla still mourns her.

When Fatima comes, Zubaida goes off with Mina for her English lessons with Ted. Mina is getting quite adventurous in her language and has even developed an English accent. Fatima works in the cantonment for an English lady and her father works for Ted.

There is talk of possible flooding in the city. However, the cantonment and the Railway Colony are far enough away to prevent such a calamity. The bridge is solidly built, wide enough to take care of such eventualities as water swirling around its piers. Access to Ted's house is easy for them.

The monsoon ends, and nice, balmy days follow. *Dussehra,* the defeat of evil, and *Diwali,* the Hindu new year, are just around the corner.

Anand is away on extended travel, and Rehman has gone with him, but they will be back for *Diwali*. For the holiday, Mangla makes new outfits for the children with smocking and embroidery. It helps to keep grief at bay.

***

One morning they wait for Zubaida to arrive and take the children for a walk. But she doesn't come. The next day it is the same. This has never happened before. After a week of no word from her, Mina is inconsolable. Mangla asks Roopchand to find out what happened.

Mangla asks Mina, "Won't you want to go and see the fireworks? Remember they will burn evil *Ravan*'s ten heads with fire sparkle." Mina shakes her head no. She won't go anywhere without Zubaida.

"Mina, standing there won't bring Zubaida back. Maybe I'll take you and Arun for a walk, and we'll see frogs and turtles near the canal."

Mina refuses.

"Mina help me decorate the house and put out the oil lamps to welcome Goddess Lakshmi. You'll like to do that right?"

The girl shakes her head.

"Come help me hang these paper lanterns," Mangla keeps trying, to no avail.

"What will I do with you?" She shakes Mina in exasperation, hoping this will get her out of her doldrums.

Nothing. Then Mina gets sick with dysentery. There is still no word from Zubaida. Mina makes a mess by the door, where she has been waiting for her for over a week.

"*Bibiji*, don't worry I will clean up. She seems to be heartbroken and in shock," Roopchand says.

The allopathic doctor has no cure for it. Mina dehydrates quickly and once again is near death. One morning Mangla finds her collapsed by the door. But when Roopchand tries to pick her up to take her to her room, she holds on to the door harder, crying for Zubaida.

Roopchand says, "My wife has heard of a good Ayurvedic doctor in the old city. He cured another child. Shall I go and get him?" Wringing her hands, Mangla says, "She will die if we don't do anything."

The ayurvedic doctor gives her a concoction made of Himalayan herbs called, '100 year old woman's herbal *ghutti*, elixir.' It works like a charm, and once again Mina's life is saved physically but still shows no signs of mental wellness.

On Yasmeen's next visit, Mangla, with embroidery in one hand shakes her head. "*Begumjan* I don't know what's happened to Mina. It's like her tongue's been cut."

"It looks to me like her heart's broken."

"That's what Roopchand thinks also. Mina has taken Zubaida's absence very hard."

188

"Did Roopchand find out what happened?

"He says that the family's decided to put her in *purdah* and she's not allowed to go out. They're going to marry her off soon."

"That's odd that no one warned you."

She begins, "In all fairness, Rehman is on travel with Anand. It's hard when Mina gets unreasonable like this. The other day Anand got angry with Gulam. You know how he is! He hit him in a fit of temper! Mina ran and bit Anand's arm! He hit her. Their conflict scares me."

"She's not yet three. Be patient Mangla," Yasmeen says.

"But *Begumjan*, other children don't bite whoever's holding them. She bites for little things. Zubaida knew how to calm her. When the other children around here talk to her and she doesn't respond, they tease and shame her by calling her dumb.

"Patience, Mangla. *Allah* is merciful and compassionate. I know it's hard with two children so close together and losing your ayah."

"Both children have been sick, *Begumjan*. I feel tired. I miss Zubaida's help." Mangla begins to cry. Arun reaches and touches her as Yasmeen puts her arms around her.

"It's been a difficult time for you," Yasmeen says. "Next time Anand goes on tour, why don't you go with him? It'll get Mina away from here. *Inshallah*! God willing. She may come around. I'll pray for her."

When the opportunity for travel arises—some problems on the train line, sabotage—Mangla tells Anand she'd like to come with him.

"Are you sure?"

"We'll take Roopchand. Besides we'll have extra help with your other staff!"

She tells Mina "Zubaida has married and gone to another city. Let's pack up and travel with Rehman to see if we can find her new home." Mina perks up and silently volunteers her help.

The *tonga* takes them to the station. As they come closer to the Muslim sector of the city, Mina points to the alley where Zubaida lived. She tries to get down.

"Mina. Bad girl. Stop fidgeting. Sit still. You'll fall off the *tonga*," Anand yells at her trying to restrain her in his grip.

Her eyes blazing, she scratches him with her other hand.

Mangla yells, "Mina, that's not nice! Stop that! Now why did you do that?"

In defiance, Mina hits Arun again, this time harder.

He yells, "*Amma---*"

"Mina, you awful girl. Don't hit your younger brother. You love him," Mangla says.

Anand's hand comes down with a tight slap across Mina's face. Zing! its force brings welts of his hand on her cheeks.

Mangla winces at the escalating violence. "She's a child. She didn't mean to be bad."

"You just spoil her. Give in to all her whims. That's why she's not talking. That's why she doesn't behave like other children. She's got to learn." Anand grabs Mina by her shoulders and shakes her. "You do that once again and I'll hit you even harder. You listen to your mother, do you hear? When she says stop, you stop."

Mina starts to scream and yell and stomp and hit Anand. He hits her harder. Her face is red and her eyes full of hate. Arun starts to cry. Mangla pats him.

Red with rage, Anand yells, "Stop this *tonga*. I'm going to show her who's the boss."

"Let it be. We'll be late for the train. You hold Arun and let me calm her," Mangla says.

"You stay out of it." He pushes Mangla away so forcefully she almost falls off the *tonga*. "*Tongawallah*, I told you to stop. Do it now."

The *tonga* slows and stops. People gather all around to witness the commotion. Anand yanks Mina off the *tonga* and drags her on the road. She's screaming and kicking. He hits her harder. "Stop crying right now. Or I'll leave you here."

Welts rise on her face. Mina's hoarse from crying. Helpless tears roll down Mangla's face.

"Let her be Sahib, she's only a child," says an old Muslim on the street. "None of your business. She's going to learn even if I've to kill her. She can't have her way in this world all the time. We all have to learn to live with others."

"Yes, Sahib."

Roopchand looks away.

Mina suddenly goes limp in Anand's hands. He picks her up and throws her into the *tonga*. Mangla tries to reach her.

"Leave her alone," says Anand. "Don't reward her behavior."

Mangla moves away, sobbing.

"*Tongawallah*, Drive fast. We need to catch our train."

"Yes sahib," he says as he whips the horse in to a gallop with his whip. Anand says, "Roopchand. When we get to the station you take the family and the baggage to the train. I'll go to the station master to be sure that he delays the train until we board."

Mangla has learned to fear his power, and even defiant Mina now shrivels in his presence with her dry sobs of humiliation.

Clearly, he thinks might is right. Mangla doesn't. Zubaida was kind and playful with Mina, and there was a bond between them. No wonder her absence traumatizes her, just like Basanthi when she lost her Ayah.

At the jobsite, Anand is very busy with his work and gives them plenty of space to be by themselves. As he returns tired late in the evening, Mangla realizes how much pressure he is under on these trips. How the safety of rail travelers depends on him. She is glad she came to witness this. She feels more compassion for him. She keeps Mina from harm's way by going for long explorative walks in the lush green countryside. Roopchand designs races for the children that Mina can win. By the time they get to their railway rest house and have dinner, they are yawning and fall asleep just sitting up.

By the time Anand comes home, they are out of his way. It works.

***

As soon as they return to Lahore, they learn that Anand is to be transferred to Sukkur in Sindh.

"Memsahib, I just heard some news of Zubaida," Roopchand tells Mangla, who is combing Mina's hair in a braid.

"Yes? Did Rehman or Gulam finally say something?"

"No, Memsahib. I found out from our neighbor's new servant who lives in the same *muhalla, residential area* as Rehman."

"Oh!"

"Zubaida was found in the cantonment in an *Angrez* sahib's house by Fatima's father. "

"That was probably Ted's house."

"He didn't know. There was a big commotion in the community. The English guard found that Zubaida, Jasbir and Gulam had no papers to be in the cantonment. Zubaida ran away. The guard killed Jasbir and wounded Gulam before the *Angrez* Sahib returned and stopped him."

Mina squirms under Mangla's hand.

"Oh no! I hope Mina didn't see all that. Did you Mina?"

"Oo----- ooaw--- ouch!" Mina screams.

"Uffo Mina! What's into you? Sit still and your hair won't get pulled."

"Memsahib, the policeman found Zubaida"—

Mina pulls loose from Mangla's hold and goes and hits Roopchand hard. "Her community publicly flogged her for putting her family in disgrace."

Mina bites Roopchand's hand. Her sharp teeth draw blood .

"Mina! Stop! Roopchand didn't do anything! You know we don't hit or bite people! Bad girl. See you hurt him. What's the matter with you?"

Ignoring Mina, he continues, "That's why Rehman took a vacation and transfer. They've found an old respectable artisan who'll marry her in a village some distance away. No one there knows about the scandal here. Her family here can save face and other children's lives will be unaffected." He heard that her husband makes aluminum cooking utensils. She'll be a great help to him and bear him children to help with the business. He has two other wives who will train Zubaida into helping with the house and business."

Mangla muses. Girls and women are given no education. They have no rights to make their own life decisions. Without fair play and laws these old-fashioned practices are so inhuman. She is determined to work for providing them choices. Aloud she says, "It's a sad story. I miss Zubaida's help and Mina misses her. It would have been nice to have her help when we move to Sukkur in Sindh next week."

"Maybe we'll find someone there," Roopchand says.

***

Mangla packs all their belongings with Roopchand's help. A week later they move to Sukkur, some 700 miles southwest of Lahore. It is a city in Sindh on the west bank of the mighty Indus River. The train ride takes two days and two nights. It is cold as the train goes over the mountains, and their quilts aren't adequate. They shiver. Anand works on his office files, while Mangla entertains the children by reading stories and letting them play with their toys.

Mangla has packed enough food for a day. In Multan, they change trains and have a long enough layover for her to buy more food and replenish their water. The children, freed from the cramped train, run around on the station platform.

Mangla feels a tug on her arms as Mina points to a cute furry little toy bear for sale in the station window. "No Mina, you're too old and it's too expensive. Besides, you don't need it." As she pulls her away from the toy trolley, she feels Mina's teeth sink into her arm.

"Mina," she cries out in pain and hears the sharp zing of Anand's hand on Mina's cheek.

"Mina, stop. You will learn to behave. This is no way to act. You don't bite your mother."

Mina looks daggers at him and then goes and kicks Arun, who is standing some distance away. He starts to cry.

Anand closes the distance between Mina and him, picks her up and shakes her hard. "Mina, you obey, or we'll give you to that beggar there in that big turban and beard."

Mina takes one look at the man Anand points to and freezes on the spot. She slouches as she goes and sits on their big trunk. Mangla feels sad for Mina's wounded spirit as she looks at men and exhibits fear.

When they arrive in Sukkur, they learn that housing is in short supply due to the European war. Temporary tents are erected for them. Their tent, as a railway officer's tent, has two bedrooms and an attached bathroom with a commode. The bathroom also has a tap with a steel bucket underneath, and a mug with which to pour water over oneself while taking a bath. There is an enamel piss pot nearby that is kept on a stool for the men to use; another table has an enamel basin with a jug of water that they use to wash their hands.

Mangla feels the pain of her childhood when she hears the jeering call of "*Bhangin, Bhangin*," after the untouchable sweeper woman and her little girl come to carry away the soiled pots twice a day. Her ire rises and she yells at these cruel jeering children, "If you don't stop that nonsense, I'll get you to clean our commodes. That is part of her job. She's proud to do it."

192

Mangla then talks to the children about Gandhiji's efforts to remove untouchability. In free, secular India there will be no such discrimination. Mangla's father taught her to clean latrines as a part of social service and Gandhi's movement. She goes and asks the sweeper woman if she can help her. "No, no, memsahib. It's my lot. Thank you for your kind offer. It already makes my job easier. God bless you."

"Why doesn't she talk?" the sweeper woman asks, indicating Mina.

"I don't know," Mangla says

"Memsahib, there is a *Pir* who knows how to help children like her talk. He lives some distance away. There is a Sufi shrine near Rohri railway station. If you would like, I will be happy to help you meet him.

It's the first ray of hope Mangla has been given. She is grateful. She gives her extra money to help her and sets up a time to teach her daughter to read with Mina and Arun. Soon her daughter and the children play together in the central area of the city.

***

It is early January. The temperature at night drops to 40 degrees, and with no heat in the tent it feels very cold. Mangla buys some heavy blankets. They have to really rug up at night. In the mornings Roopchand lights the fire in the coal-burning stove and heats a big kettle of water in the little adjoining tent that is their kitchen. He brings the hot water in a bucket to the bathroom. Anand shaves and takes his bath first by mixing the hot and cold water in the bucket. Mangla calls for the second bucket of hot water with which she washes Mina and Arun before taking her own bath. Roopchand then serves them their usual hot porridge before Anand leaves for the office. On Sundays, he also serves omelets with onions, tomatoes, and green chilies.

During the day, the sun is warm. Roopchand, Mangla, and the children walk to the central bazaar where big Afghan Pathans with camels, trade dates, almonds, raisins, apricots, walnuts, and pine nuts for cotton and silk handloom cloth and garments, cigarettes, lime, cement, leather, sugar, and grains. They sell at reasonable prices and their products are fresh. They love children and give Mina camel rides.

The children love to watch the *Ghanta Ghar*, especially when its clock chimes the loud twelve gongs that Mina and Arun count at the noon hour. The people in the bazaar are Muslims, Sikhs, Hindus, and Sindhis who speak their own Sindhi language. But everyone here also speaks Urdu, so Mangla gets by.

The Indus River is big. One weekend they take the children for a boat ride, and Mangla enjoys listening to the gentle soothing sounds of the oars splashing in the water. The boatman is playful with the children but, keeps them within the boat. He tells them to be careful as dangerous crocodiles are looking for little children to prey upon. A big crocodile took a baby from the riverbank when the parents weren't watching. When the boatman points to a crocodile in the distance both children duck under Mangla's sari. "Clearly the boatman's message got through," Mangla laughs.

The boatman points a little distance away. "See that little animal there? That's the Indus Dolphin. It's only found in this river."

"I've never heard of it," Mangla says.

"They move continuously against the flow of the water and are totally blind due to silt in the river."

Amazing, Mangla thinks. Even blind fish are free to go where they want, while Mangla, who can see, feels tethered and Zubaida is punished for a lot less.

The boatman makes a good guide. He tells them he travelled with the English and learned fishing and rowing a boat. For his good work, when the English left, they gave him this boat.

She asks him why the city is called Sukkar.

"Memsahib, in Arabic, *Saqar* means intense. In the 10th century, when the Arabs invaded Sindh, they found its climate extremely harsh, cold in winter and hot in summer, so they called it *Saqar*, and the English called it Sukkur. Local people also called this city Darya Dino, meaning 'gift of the river,' because without the Indus, it would be like Egypt without the Nile -- a desert."

"How many people live in this area, do you know?" Anand asks.

"Sahib, about 200,000. Most of them are farmers and fishermen. Even in 326 BC when Alexander the great invaded India, Sukkur was important. One can see the ruins of this ancient city in Rohri. It's believed that it holds the hair of the prophet Mohammed, which gives power to the *Pirs* who live in the shrine near the train station. People have seen lots of *Unani* healing miracles performed by them. That is what the sweeper woman was talking about. Curious, Mangla asks, "What is that?"

"Some voodoo medicine," Anand says, his lips curling. The boatman stays respectfully quiet.

Mangla makes a mental note to investigate that for herself. She will visit the shrine when Anand is away. On the way home, she tells him that she will investigate the ruins and check out the boatman's story by visiting Rohri. She asks Anand how far the Rohri train station is from their tent city. He tells her not that far, just a couple of hours easy drive. To see the ruins, she will be better off driving there during the day.

***

When Anand is away on business, Mangla hires a driver. She leaves Arun behind with Roopchand. A girl's future is too important, and Mangla has a good feeling about the *Pir*.

When they arrive at the shrine, there is a big *dhammal* as the dervishes dance to the sound of drums. The audience is also in ecstasy. Mina begins to go round and round like this is something she's done all her life. Mangla wonders if Zubaida took her to some Sufi *dhammals*? She follows Mina and joins in. Soon she feels like she is floating in air. Nothing else matters except the movement, as though she is at one with the universe. She looks at her daughter and deep compassion flows into her. The words come from nowhere 'to have loved and lost. That love is the deepest sorrow of all. There is no grief like it.' Zubaida gave Mina profound love. Like God's messenger, she was there when Mina needed her. But she is there no more. It is like a light from within Mangla touches Mina. She feels a broken connection mend. Mina looks at her and then away. She continues to dance with her arms stretched out.

The head *Pir* approaches in his long white robe and tall headgear, holding his holy prayer beads. He holds his hands over Mina's head then looks at Mangla and says, "My beloved you suffer because your daughter doesn't speak. *Allah* wants her to speak, but she's suffering from shock. Her energy to her tongue is blocked. "He holds out a silver locket on a black cord, just like the one Zubaida wore, and says, "Take this *taweez* and tie it around her neck before she goes to bed. And say *Allah*'s name 50 times. Say *tawba* prayers 50 times and the 99 names of *Allah*. I will say prayers for her tonight, and tomorrow *Inshallah* she'll speak. Now let *Allah* bless her and use his mercy to heal her."

He tells Mangla to sit down and hold Mina in her lap. He asks her to hold the *taweez* over Mina's head. He moves his hands near her temples, and they begin to vibrate. As he says his prayers, *"Bismillah ar Rehman ar Rahim..."* Mangla finds her own lips move to the familiar words. His eyes go heavenwards, and his body radiates light that penetrates Mina's little body. Mangla can feel something move in her own hands and body. Mina closes her eyes and begins to chant *Namaz* prayers in a whisper.

Mangla feels apprehension. Her eyes close. What's happening? She feels like someone is holding her and Mina in their arms. She is unable to control anything. She lets go and just trusts the energy flow. That night, Mangla ties the *taweez* around Mina's neck and says *Allah* 50 times. While Mangla is saying *tawba* and the 99 names of *Allah*, Mina falls asleep.

The next morning, Mina comes running into her room. "*Amma* wake up, it's morning. I am hungry."

Anand stares at Mina. "Mina, you're speaking. What happened?"

"I got Zubaida's blessed *taweez*." She holds out the silver locket so Anand can see it.

He shakes his head and says, "whatever."

Mangla holds her hands together and says her own prayer of gratitude in all the religions she knows of. *Allah* is indeed compassionate and merciful.

XXXXXXX

Manjula Waldron

23 1946 Direct Action Day Violence

The World War is over in Europe. Everything in England is rationed, and the scarcity trickles down to the Indian colony. The government has rationed essential supplies like rice, wheat, dairy, etc.

The good news is that liquor, too, is rationed. That means that the club doesn't have any extra. The large populations of Muslims in this part of the country want this alcohol limit to stay. Mangla approves. It limits Anand's collegial intake after work and leads to more family peace at night.

Everyone now must depend on local produce. In their greed to make quick money, merchants jack up their prices, making poor people suffer. On the radio, Gandhiji implores the rich to take better care of their community's welfare by helping the poor rather than gouging them. It aligns with Mangla's beliefs of how to manage social disparity.

The weather is beastly hot and dry. Without the monsoon rain, it is much hotter than Lahore. The tents become like ovens. Daytime temperatures can be as high as 120 degrees in the shade. With his sola hat donned like a *pukka* sahib, Anand goes out for his inspections of the tracks and ensures they won't buckle. He and his assistants measure the gaps in the rails during the worst of the heat, A tedious dedicated work. "Mad dogs and Englishmen go out in the midday sun, and they make us do the same," he says with a dry, hollow laugh. She smiles but, worries about him becoming dehydrated. She sends tons of water with him. That's the least she can do.

All the servants have left to go to the plains. Roopchand has gone for his sister's wedding and family business. Mangla has no help with the children in this heat.

She cooks all their meals before the sun rises so she doesn't have to face the stove in the kitchen in the heat of the day. When Anand comes home, she has a raw roasted mango and mint drink ready. The children love it, too—it has lots of sugar, and their anticipation of it helps them pass the day. They eat late at night when it is cool enough for them to have an appetite. During the day, they try to rest. There is a vent on the top of the tent, and an outer awning acts like a verandah to keep the tent relatively cool, but it's less effective in the afternoon. Mangla keeps rubbing water on herself and uses a hand fan on her wet skin to keep cool. She teaches the children to do the same. They are not allowed to go out and play in the day. It's too hot. To burn their energy, they run around the tent like caged animals.

They leave the tent flaps open to circulate the air. Hot air outside brings limited relief.

It's a long season. People in the compound complain of theft and pilfering. Soon Arun gets sick, developing a high fever and boils all over his body. He is all skin and bones. The doctor says he has rickets. He needs sunlight. Mangla's is torn about whether to expose him to the sun and heat or let him suffer from rickets. They have no cure for the boils. He squeaks like a mouse when he tries to talk.

A Sindhi neighbor refers her to the *Hakim* who cured her son of this malady the summer before, and the *Hakim* tells Mangla to grind up pure ocean pearls and let Arun lick a little bit every four hours, with a lot of water. It works, and soon Arun is cured of rickets and boils.

***

Neighbors decide to eat their evening meals together, as none of them have servants to help. They start to share their political learning and leanings—about the recent elections and congress and Muslim league leadership.

The All-India Congress leaders are released from jail. A new Labor government headed by Attlee is in power in England. Churchill is out. There is talk once again about India's freedom. The Indian elections to the legislative assemblies are over. The Muslim League has done well in East Bengal and the Northwest and in western Punjab, where the majority of residents are Muslim. They celebrate their 'victory day'. But Congress has ninety percent of the votes overall, and the country is divided along religious lines. The Viceroy asks Congress to form an interim government, but the Muslim league doesn't cooperate and declares a Direct Action Day in August to demand Pakistan become a separate country. Gandhi is opposed to a divided India. He says: "You cannot divide a body into half without destroying the whole." Now, at seventy-five years of age, he has turned his efforts towards helping people to improve their physical and community health with his naturopathic practices.

"He seems to be spending more time advising villagers and untouchables in ways of enema and fasting," Anand chortles after dinner. "He needs to give India an enema!"

Someone says, "That isn't respectful of the Mahatma."

"Respectful? You talk about respect when our country's future is at stake? You know Attlee invited Gandhiji to go to London to talk about the independence, and he spent his time telling Londoners about the virtues of mudpacks and drinking goat's milk. He's too old for the job. He should take *Banprastha* and go to the Himalayas and become a *sadhu* and pray. Let Nehru run this country."

"He did help Sardar Patel regain his health through natural cures!" Mangla says. "It was the doctors that gave the right medicines," Anand says his voice an octave higher.

Mina runs out of the room Arun follows.

"He doesn't ask of others anything he doesn't do himself," says another at the table.

Another Congress supporter says, "He's empowering the poor and untouchables to improve their lives through better sanitation and holistic health, including chanting and prayer. Don't get upset with him because you can't do it." Their tempers and voices are hot like the weather.

Anand thumps the table and yells, "You mark my words. Jinnah will do anything to win power. He eats pork, married a Parsi woman, drinks whiskey, doesn't pray or know the Quran, but he can whip up Muslim passions through his oration."

Mangla shivers at the intensity of Anand's outburst. Feeling loyal to Gandhiji and Sabiha, she says, "Gandhiji stays in the sweeper colony, where Muslims and Hindus are dividing the party as well. It's not all Muslims, you know."

"Shut up!" Anand says. "What do you know about politics?"

Everyone looks down in embarrassed silence at the verbal slashing his wife receives. She colors and says feebly, "I got my degree from BHU and wrote a paper on Indian politics." Realizing how long ago that was, Mangla becomes quiet. When she hears a noise in their bedroom tent, she is glad for the chance to escape and investigate. A stranger stands there with her jewelry box in his hands. When he sees her, he runs out.

"Thief! Thief!" Mangla yells.

Everyone comes running.

Mangla points in the direction of the tent flap door, and everyone runs outside, but the thief has disappeared into the dark of the night.

"We had better report this at the police station tomorrow morning," Anand says. "Hopefully we'll be able to find your jewelry box."

"It's lucky. I didn't put all my real gold in it which is mostly in the bank," Mangla says. "We need to make sure the flaps are secure when we aren't in the tent."

***

"Sparkles, guess what? I need to move back to Lahore in a week."

"That'll be wonderful! This heat here is murderous."

" Mina, Arun, we're moving back to Lahore. Nice right?"

Mina claps and dances. "Oh goody, maybe Zubaida will meet us."

Mangla stays quiet thinking soon she'll forget.

Anand says, "By the way, I asked you to keep expenditure accounts, Mangla. I haven't seen how you've been spending money."

Mangla keeps quiet. She doesn't overspend. Doesn't he trust her financial acumen?

"What do you do all day? It's not much to ask so I can tally our fiscal spending." She seethes inside. Is he trying to pick a fight? What does he mean? Who got the sick children well, without servants who does the cooking and cleaning in this beastly heat? Maybe she should quit, too she thinks. The few times she's shown him her written accounts, he spends the rest of the night criticizing and nickel dimes her spending habits, making her more reluctant to oblige. Her silence infuriates him further but, talk of money does them no good. She doesn't like it and finds his brutish behavior on the topic despicable.

Silence is her best ally. It's easier to lose her voice than to fear its repercussions. She wonders, now, about her own parents. Was that how *Ammaji* became a "yes woman?" Did she realize it was happening or did she just wake up one day, changed? Perhaps Mangla will have a chance to ask her one day.

***

Roopchand returns from his vacation to Lahore and meets them at the familiar Lahore station. Their brief absence ensures that they get their old familiar house back. On their way, they see recognizable neighborhoods. Mina points and talks about who lives where. Nothing is wrong with her memory. When they go past Zubaida's alley, Mina points to it and says calmly, "Zubaida lives there."

"Yes, but not anymore. Remember I told you that she's married now and lives in a village far from here with her husband?"

No tantrums as Mina accepts this and moves on to point, "That's Aunt Yasmeen's house."

A sigh of relief escapes Mangla's lips.

Suddenly lots of men wearing Muslim clothes, playing drums, and carrying banners come marching by. They shout slogans. Muslim League Zindabad Jinnah! *ki Jai*! Death to Gandhi and Nehru! We want Pakistan!" The procession passes by. Mangla looks for Basanthi and Farida but doesn't see them.

"What's this all about?" Anand asks the *tongawallah.*

"I guess they must have got some news from Simla about Wavell's commission. It doesn't take much for the Muslim League leader Jinnah to get the mobs riled."

A few months later they think of visiting Delhi. Mangla's parents now live in old Delhi with Shabbu and his young family. It's been a long time since she has seen them. She asks Mina if she wants to spend her third birthday with her grandparents, her *Nani* and *Nana?* She will love meeting them and Shabbu *Mama* and her baby cousin. She hasn't met them yet. "Everyone has a father," Mangla says. "*Nana* is my *Pitaji*."

Mina agrees. "Will my *Pitaji* be there when I blow my candles?"

"Why not?" Mangla replies. Mina helps to pack for travel.

200

Love Partitioned

It's decided that Roopchand will accompany them. While they visit Shabbu, he will take a train to his village to take care of his family affairs. Then he'll return to accompany them back to Lahore. Anand will be taken care of by his other staff until he comes to Delhi.

***

Shabbu meets them at the Delhi station and hires a *tonga* to take them to his home in *Darya Ganj*. They drive in silence, each in their own thoughts. It appears that Vani's shadow is cast over them, each too afraid to ask how the other feels about her death or how it has affected the family. Since her death, they've only communicated through the medium of letters, and with *Ammaji*'s limited writing ability, it's often been one sided.

They stay on safe subjects, talking of Shabbu, his wife and little baby. They live with *Ammaji* and *Pitaji* in a modest two-bedroom apartment. Surjjo is now married to a farmer in the mountains and lives there.

There is a little storage room on the side that Shabbu and his family move to in order to give their room to Mangla, Anand, and the children.

"Shabbu *Bhayya*, you shouldn't have," Mangla says. He tells her that her visit is perfectly timed as his wife and son will be visiting her parents to help them with their health issues. He will not be too cramped. Nevertheless, their thoughtfulness makes Mangla relax for the first time in a long time, and she looks forward to being pampered by her family.

Mangla walks in and her parents greet her. She touches their feet and asks the children to do the same. *Ammaji* seems to have aged before her eyes. Mangla is too afraid to ask about her suffering, too afraid to add to it by bringing up Vani. She tells *Ammaji* what a boon Roopchand has been. He's gone to his family home so won't need accommodation. When Anand arrives, they will all go back together to Lahore. *Ammaji* blesses her and tells her to take her bath and wash the children. She will make sure their lunch is ready

The apartment is located in the historic part of old Delhi on top of the shops on the main street. After the long, cramped train journey, Mangla takes the children for a walk. She points to the *Khuni* gate.

"Why do they call it a bloody gate?" Mina asks.

Mangla tells them a simple version of complex history that they can understand. Almost a hundred years ago there was a fight between the last Mogul, King Bahadur Shah, and the British led by Major Hudson. When British won, the major offered Bahadur Shah the still bleeding heads of his sons on a platter. It is said that the grief was unbearable for the father, and he collapsed and died in that instant. It is believed that their bleeding heads are buried in that gate, hence, the name *Khuni*.

"Why did he do that? That was mean," Mina says, shivering.

"Like bullies, some people are like that when they win a fight. Cruel."

Mangla points to red and white minarets of Jumma Masjid, the Mosque. That's where Muslims pray on Fridays. It's one of the biggest. "

"Like Zubaida," Mina says.

Mangla points to the right of it. "Yes. That's the Delhi gate. We go through it to the Red Fort *Lal Kila. Shah Jahan* who built the *Taj Mahal* in Agra also built that walled city. We'll visit it. Like in old Lahore, there are lots of things to see here. You'll love it, Mina."

Looking up, Mina says, "Where's Agra? Is Taj Mahal like a Rajah's crown?" Mangla smiles and says, "Agra is some distance from here. The earth there is red. Taj is made of white marble, very smooth and pretty. I first went there when I was a little girl like you. Maybe when your father comes, we'll go on the train after your birthday, Yes?"

Mina claps her hands and skips on the pavement as she sings Happy Birthday to me. Mangla laughs. Arun copies.

The apartment is in an ancient stone building and has a very steep set of old and worn stone steps. Mina must climb on all fours while Mangla helps Arun. When coming down, Mangla warns Mina while she holds Arun's hands, "Slow down Mina and be careful!" A little too late for Mina, as she trips, plunges, and rolls down the steps and cracks open her forehead. Mangla calls for help, and *Shabbu* comes running. He picks her up and says, "My God, she's bleeding heavily. I'm taking her to the dispensary around the corner. Hopefully the doctor's still there." With that he carries her in his arms. Mangla follows holding Arun.

The doctor has one look at Mina and says, "She'll need stitches. Nurse, please get my things ready. You can lay her down on that table there." He beckons Shabbu. Mina screams as the doctor comes near with his sterilized instruments.

Mangla hands Arun to Shabbu and holds Mina's hands to calm her down. "There, there-- you'll be better soon."

"No! I want to go home!" She starts to struggle.

"Keep her still," The doctor tells the nurse and Mangla as he cleans and deftly puts a couple of stitches across the torn gash in the skin. He bandages her forehead and gives her a candy. "Now that wasn't bad was it. You are a Rani with a crown." The nurse holds the mirror for Mina.

Mina gets up and, pain forgotten, dances around with a ditty. "I'm Rani *ki* Jhansi. I'm Bahadur Shah. I'm royalty. Bow now."

The doctor tells Mangla to keep the wound dry and clean and let him look at it in a couple of days.

They pay the doctor for his services, and as they leave, Mangla says to Shabbu, "Well, this is a great beginning to our vacation. I hope the bandage will be off by the time her birthday comes around."

"I don't want my bandage off. I want to look like a *Rani*," Mina says.

"Brave girl," Shabbu and the nurse say.

Mina's stitches come out a week later, and although the scar is visible as an angry jagged reminder of the ordeal, the doctor says if Mangla leaves it uncovered it will heal faster in fresh air. Soap and water will be fine to clean it.

"*Amma*, I want my bandage. I am a *Rani* now." "Yes. I'll stitch you a real fancy crown. We'll go to the shop downstairs, and you can pick shiny diamonds for it," Mangla says.

"I want to be a king too," Arun says.

"I'll make you one also, then one can be a *Rajah* and other the *Rani*. Won't that be fun?"

***

That same day Jinnah gives a gashing wound to the country with his, "We shall have India divided or we shall have India destroyed," speech. He announces that the Muslim League will observe "The Direct Action Day" on August 16th, Mina's birthday. According to him, on this day the Muslims are going to prove to Britain and the Congress that they can take the law into their own hands and begin whatever direct action is necessary to establish Pakistan.

From that day on, the early morning Mullah prayer calls of *Allah O Akbar* take on a particularly fiendish tone. People reciprocate passionately from their rooftops. Drums beat and cries of "*Hare Krishna, Hare Krishna, Ram Ram hare hare,*" ring from Hindu rooftops. In response to which, the Allah cries become louder. It seems they are trying to drown each other out. Everyone feels the ominous tension, and a shiver runs through Mangla.

Ammaji puts her hands to her ears. "*Haramzadeh*! They took our Vani away. She was only a child. Is their *Allah* great? Is He satisfied? Is that how they pay us for our goodness?" Her anger revives her own grief.

They all sit around the radio to listen to the news. In predominantly Muslim areas, Muslim League members are holding meetings and stirring up Muslim fervor and playing on the long cultivated communal distrust. Jinnah's rhetoric of "whatever it takes" makes the family vulnerable in this predominantly Muslim area.

Ammaji says, "It is like *Chauri Chaura* all over again."

She tells Mangla that Shabbu manages his brother-in-law's wholesale spice business in *Chandni Chawk Sadar Bazaar,* not far from their apartment. It is near the slums where these uneducated Muslims and Hindus live. The passions of Muslims are easily excited by a charismatic leader like Jinnah, and the Hindu religious leaders fan the passions of the Hindus with their chants of Hindu supremacy. These two bigoted factions live in close quarters. Often a drain, an alley, or a piece of cloth strewn on bamboo is all that separates them.

"Mangla, we'll need to be more cautious when we shop in the bazaar," *Ammaji* says, taking a deep breath and rubbing her hands over her mouth and eyes. "This doesn't sound good to me.

***

On the morning of August 16, Shabbu leaves home as usual. He rides off on his bike. Before long, Mangla hears him shutting and bolting the front door and running up the stairs as he tears in through the top landing. His hair and eyes look wild. Fear is etched on his face as he pants heavily. His clothes are torn, his knees scraped. He is without his sandals, bike, and lunch pail. Shuddering violently, he describes his ordeal to a frightened family clutching each other. Mangla notices his childhood stuttering has returned.

"It's m-mayhem out there. Before I got to *Jumma Masjid*, I c-can see black smoke and fire blazing towards *Chandni Chowk*. I c-can see that hooligans are on the prowl ahead and unwary people are being butchered. I c-can see the gutters red with blood. Hindu women are lying there naked and mutilated. K-killed! I see a man a little ahead of me manhandled and p-pulled off his bike. I don't need to see more. I turn around and s-started to ride back as f-fast as I can. T-Then I hear their cry 'Muslim *bhai Zindabad*, Hindu dogs *Murdabad*! Pakistan *Zindabad*! Jinnah *ki jai*!' Then they tried to p-pull me off my bike. I-l-let them take my bike and my lunch pail. I p-pull away and start running. I f-fall but pick myself up. My s-sandals slow me down. I take them off and throw them at the m-man chasing me. I y-yell, *"Haramzadeh*, sister f-fucker, take this." Once I get near our street, I know the back alleyways and make it home." He puts his face in his trembling hands shaking his head as if to dispel a nightmare.

"Were the police not stopping them?" *Pitaji* asks.

"I d-didn't see any, m-maybe they ran away. Cowards!"

Everyone sits there in silence. Mangla goes to the front window and looks out. The street is deserted today. All the shops are boarded shut. No one is about. Only a stray dog runs around sniffing at the red gutters. She can smell smoke and sees a black column rise in the distance. Suddenly she hears thunder. Dark clouds roll quickly over the city and the monsoon rain abruptly comes pouring down. The heavens themselves want this carnage to end and want to wash away the sins of human outrage.

Ammaji breaks the ominous silence. "That rain at least should put out the fires and stop the *Goondas."* *Pitaji* turns on the radio to listen to the twelve o'clock news. They hear Nehru's voice entreating Hindus to stay at home and not take revenge. Everyone should stay indoors. There is a 24-hour curfew in the city. They have called army battalions to help.

The newscaster comes on next and says that the situation in Calcutta is grave. The Muslim threat has taken on a grim reality. The weak, helpless and the poor are suffering the most. The leaders there are taken by surprise by the intensity of the hatred present in the community spilling on to the streets. In Bombay, slums are painted red in blood. The streets are littered with cadavers and broken skulls. Mina comes to Mangla and says softly, "*Amma* will the doctors stitch them all up like me?"

A smile comes to everyone's face and the gravity of the news is lightened some. "I hope they will," answers Mangla.

"Will they too have scars like I do?" Mina says pointing to her forehead. Mangla says quietly, "We all will."

Mangla looks around with sadness at all the food that she and *Ammaji* prepared for a party that is not going to be. She cannot bring herself to break this shattering news to Mina. But Mina asks, "Shouldn't we go to the station to get *Pitaji* for my party?"

"I haven't heard from him, Mina. I'm not sure he can come now." Mangla says. Shabbu went to the station, but Anand wasn't on the train. Inwardly, she prays that wherever Anand is he is safe. She tells Mina curfew means that everyone must stay at home as they heard on the radio. No one will be able to come to the party. Mina says, "*Pitaji* will come. He keeps his promises." She runs to her room and puts on her tiara. "*Rani* is here. All of you kneel before me. Put your swords down. I am going to bring my *Pitaji* to my party."

Mangla pats her head and wonders what is happening in Lahore.

Ammaji sings her protection prayer song: *Jai Jagdeesh hare Swami Jai Jagdeesh hare Bhakt jano ke sankat shin me door kare, Swami ----*

Then she follows it with, "Let's say our *namaz*, have *havan,* and spin our *charkahs.*"

Mangla's father gets up and says to Mina, "Come *beti* let's get things for the *havan.*"

With her head held high and tiara proudly perched on her head, Mina cups her hands like Zubaida and says, "I am *Begum Sahiba*. Let's all kneel and pray for my *Pitaji. Bismillah ar Rehman—*"

Even Ammaji and Shabbu join her entreaties to God. Then Mina follows her grandfather to prepare for their *havan.*

XXXXXXX

24 1946-47 India Cracks Wider

When the time comes for Mangla and children to return to Lahore, Anand is not able to get leave because of growing unrest there. Gandhi and Nehru, with the help of the army, have quelled some of the heat from the Direct Action Day mayhem. They are in discussions with the British government as to the terms for possible Indian independence, though Jinnah's "partition sword" is held against their necks. Things have returned, tentatively, to a changed "normal"; it seems safe for Shabbu to go to his spice business.

Mangla is sad to leave her family. But the children are tired of the cramped inner-city existence. Excited, they board the train, eager to return to their own spacious home in Lahore. Anand arranges for their return travel and Roopchand accompanies them as the children's guardian so they can travel together in the same compartment. As they pass stations, they see a few Congress and Muslim League marches, with their signs and drumbeats, but nothing seems violent or threatening.

Mina puts on her tiara and says she is the Muslim League and sings *Allah O Akbar*. Arun puts on his crown and becomes the face of Congress and sings Gandhi *Zindabad*. Roopchand entertains them with patriotic songs and telling them stories. The louder they get, the happier they sound, and they march up and down the train compartment holding the placard Roopchand made for them. Mangla escapes into her Hercule Poirot Agatha Christie mystery novel that Shabbu gave her. Overall, the journey is pleasant for her as she gets to rest. The future and Direct-Action Day is far from her mind now.

***

Anand is now in the head railway office. He and his construction bosses and buddies have all been promoted. Hanfi Bhai and Mr. Desai are there, along with Ashraf Mian. They all live nearby in the colony and share car rides to work. It saves on rationed petrol. But Jay has gone back to Jammu and Kashmir.

"You remember my assistant, Urmila's husband?" Anand says to Mangla. "He has been promoted and is in my office as well. They live in this colony."

Mangla looks at his face and wonders if his old crush on Urmila is still alive. But he gives no outward indication. She likes Urmila; she provided her a lot of help with Mina's pregnancy. Maybe she'd like to become part of a tea klatch, if

Mangla started one. Mangla loves the concept of a tea klatch to bond with community women through sharing their talents and stories, as a way for them to all keep their ears to the ground and learn about community events and the future implications for their families. Mangla makes invitation cards with Mina and Arun's help and sends the kids with Roopchand to invite the women over for gossip and crafts. Then she prepares to go to the Anarkali market to get what she needs for her tea klatch party.

"Bibiji, we shouldn't go to the Anarkali market today," Roopchand says. "People say there is a big riot outside Anarkali bazaar."

"Why, what happened?"

"There are revenge killings, they think. Revenge for what happened to Muslims in Delhi and Amritsar. The Muslim League *goondas* are on the loose in the city. They looted some Hindu shops, set fire to them, and killed their owners."

Jinnah has increased his offensive to pressure Britain to create a separate Pakistan. It is to be in the west of Punjab and in the Bengal delta where there is a Muslim majority, and his party has representation.

Mangla feels dismay. She really needs to go shopping. She wants to invite her friends' children to Arun's birthday party too, so that they can reestablish connections with their friends. She needs jackfruit, carrots, cauliflower, oil and spices to make pickles for winter. These will be available there. The local markets only sell local limited produce.

She says, "I suppose we'll just have to wait a few days. It'll probably settle down. It always does. Next time, we'll buy extra so in the future we don't have to worry if there are problems in the city."

The weather is cooler, and the days are shorter. Urmila drops by; she now has two children about Mina and Arun's age. The children delight in each other's company. Also, Urmila has put on a lot of weight. Her singing voice is still delightful, though, and she gladly sings at her dinner parties. But to her surprise, Mangla no longer feels threatened by her.

Mangla goes forward with planning the tea party, and on the appointed day, she welcomes Yasmeen and Kamala, her old neighbors.

The women talk about Captain Khalsa, a brawny, handsome Punjabi Sikh from Amritsar whose wedding is coming up. He is in the army. Mangla's family friend Hari *bhai* is related to him, and he and Anand play tennis on weekend mornings at the Gymkhana club. Mangla is very fond of Khalsa sahib and promises to invite him to her next dinner so the women of the tea klatch can meet him.

Each time the tea klatch meets, the women bring whatever craft project they are working on. Yasmeen's gold and bead embroidery on velvet is craft extraordinaire. Urmila knits well, and Kamala does great crochet work. Mangla always has embroidery and sewing projects and supervises the klatch repast so that teacups are filled, and the snack trays replenished. During one meeting, Kamala tells the group about the young man who jumped over her fence and hit her with a bat as she sat sipping her tea on the back porch. Luckily her servant came out with another fresh pot of hot tea and threw it at the intruder, who ran away.

As a result, the women decided to move their tea Klatch indoors. And they make sure that one of the servants is always with the children to ensure their safety. "I was going to go to the bazaar to buy my groceries and fruit and vegetables, like I usually do," Mangla tells them, "But, Roopchand said it wasn't safe and persuaded me to not go." Shopping at Anarkali bazaar pleases Anand, since she can boast that she saved money. She's become a husband-pleaser, she comments ruefully to the klatch. No more of her bravado as an educated feminist from BHU. "No matter what our education, we seem to be relegated to being just mothers and housewives by society," Urmila adds.

Yasmeen says, "Hopefully all this unrest will settle down soon. Are the local shopkeepers promoting it to sell their products at steeper prices, or is it for real? Who does one trust?"

"That's the greatest casualty of Jinnah's Direct-Action Day. When trust goes, so do communities," Mangla says, as her face clouds. The memory of Vani's death still haunts her psyche, and she shares the story of the Rawalpindi bombing with the group. Then she shakes her head and changes the subject to a more pleasant one like the upcoming wedding of Khalsa sahib.

He is engaged to marry a Muslim girl who now lives in Lahore with her parents. The two have known each other since childhood when they were neighbors in Amritsar and went to the same school. He decided then he was going to marry her. She went to BHU and he joined the army before their parents finally agreed to let them marry. He's kept her name a secret from everyone. He doesn't want the army to know as they may not give him permission to marry a Muslim, violating their divide and rule policies that take away ordinary freedoms of Indians. He has invited them all to his Sikh *lavaan* and Muslim *nikah* wedding ceremonies a month away. It is going to be a lavish affair, she is told, but is asked to keep it a secret until closer to the date. She asks her friends to respect his wishes. Mangla is looking forward to the wedding, but there is disquiet that she feels within. She can't seem to shake off the suddenness of Vani's death, the Muslim goonda's taunts about Mahmood *bhai* being a Hindu lover, and the kidnapping of Aziza. Then there's Basanthi's involvement and betrayal in the whole sordid affair. However, she keeps these details to herself.

Over the regular meetings of the tea klatch, Mangla has made a beautiful new red velvet dress for Mina to wear to the wedding. On its bodice, she has embroidered monkeys on a tree covered with petunia flowers and with mirrors and golden *salma* string. She has also sewn on colorful beads, a craft she learned from Yasmeen. For Arun, she has stitched navy pants, a sailor collar shirt, and a new pair of suspenders.

"These are exquisite, Mangla," Urmila says. "You're such a wizard with your hands. Mina is fortunate to have a mother as talented as you."

***

At nights, Mangla hears ominous sounds and smells fire smoke coming from the city. Anand being away so much is unaware and no patience with negative news. Children want to know but she doesn't want to alarm them after the Direct-Action Day.

"I need to go up North tomorrow," Anand says to Mangla one night as they are going to bed. "There have been reports of contractors cheating. I need to investigate these charges. I may be gone for a while."

"You've been promoted. Can't someone else go in your place?"

"No. I am the only one qualified. The enquiry has to be discreet."

"Then perhaps postpone by a day and we could drive with you and shop in Anarkali market for Diwali, before you leave," Mangla says. "People talk about increased violence in the city. I feel afraid."

"That I can't. I am to travel with Hanfi *bhai* as a witness. Mangla, don't listen to gossip. I've told you a thousand times, gossip's destructive."

"Make light of it if you will," Mangla says, her voice rising. "You don't care about us, do you? Roopchand was saying—"

"Roopchand! Roopchand! Like he's God. For heaven's sake, Mangla, go to the market on your own, in the car. Let the neighbor's driver drive you." "But you don't like that. Besides I worry about you without the car."

"I'm OK now that we share car rides. Try it tomorrow. I will be away."

"Don't you see the fires in the distance? And hear the screams or the bullets?" "No, I don't! Let's go out and see!" He goes to the window.

"You wouldn't see an elephant even if it stepped on you!" Mangla says. In anger, Anand throws his pillow across the room. It hits the table, and a bottle comes crashing down.

Mangla is terrified when he gets like this but, is reluctant to admit it. Her quiet, disgusted look only infuriates him further. His voice rises as he snatches the book, she's reading from her and hurls it across the room. It hits the wall of the children's room with a loud thud. He bangs the table with his shoes. Her eyes get wider.

"You'll wake the children," she says.

Mina yells from the other room, "My stomach hurts."

There, you did it, Mangla thinks.

The next morning, Anand leaves for his trip and Mangla discovers that Mina has wet the bed. The child is mortified as Roopchand changes her sheets. At least Anand has given her permission to go to the market, which is so different from when she first came to live with him. She must look for the positives.

***

The next night, while Anand is away on travel, Mina and Arun are in Mangla's bed jumping on her.

"I'm tired. If you want to be here you've got to shut eyes and go to sleep," Mangla says.

They both instantly lie on either side of her and squeeze their eyes shut and giggle.

"Stop giggling, you two. If you are quiet and lie still, I'll tell you your favorite story." Soon the children fall asleep to her sing-song story voice, and she is able to doze.

She wakes up to a cool breeze blowing on her face. Groggy with sleep, Mangla thinks it's strange she did not close the window. Perhaps she's dreaming. Her arm goes out to feel for Mina's sleeping next to her. Arun is on one side, but the other is empty. She hears Mina's voice in the next room She sits up and calls, "Mina."

Mina says, "Look *Amma*, Gulam's here. He came through the window. "Mangla's eyes dilate and her muscles tense as she adjusts to the dim streetlight that comes through the open window and recognizes his familiar figure. She relaxes and says, "Gulam, what're you doing here?"

"Where's Zubaida?" Mina asks.

"She's married with her husband in another village."

"Oh, and Jasbir?" Mina continues.

"He was helping us get Pakistan. He died for us. He's no more," Gulam says.

"Gulam, why are you here at this time of the night?" Mangla says. She tries to make her voice friendly, but she gathers Mina to her.

"We heard that the policeman who killed Jasbir lives here. He kills my friend, I kill him. That's God's law. Clearly, memsahib, our information was wrong."

"Yes, at the last minute we were able to get our old home back," Mangla says. "Perhaps the man was living here before?"

"Did Jasbir turn into a ghost?" Mina asks

Gulam Ali pats her head. "Maybe. *Bismillah*."

"His ghost will protect me," Mina says, nodding.

"Who told you about ghosts?" Mangla says.

"My friends. They talk about it when we play. They say if we've been good, the ghost of a dead person protects us, but if we've been bad, they haunt us. I've been good, haven't I, *Amma*?"

"Yes, Mina," Mangla says, and thinks that if such a fantasy has healing powers during times like these, then where's the harm. She stays quiet and puts her hand on Mina's small shoulders.

"I'm sure he will protect you," Gulam says. "Just be good, Mina." To Mangla, he says, "Don't you worry, Memsahib. I'll take care of your family *Inshallah*, God willing. I'm sorry to frighten you. Your house will be safe. I'll tell them. You don't worry. We'll protect you."

With that, he climbs out of the window. It is then Mangla sees the streetlight reflect off the steel in Gulam's hand.

She feels God's grace gave them protection that night.

They go to the window and wave to Gulam as he meets with couple of other men and leaves under the bushes in the dark of the night.

Mangla gently shuts her window and locks it. She climbs back in bed with Mina and says, "Mina let's do the prayers like Zubaida. *Bismillah ar Rehman*--"

The next morning Mina, with new confidence, points to her heart and says, "*Amma*, Gulam and *Pitaji* said we're safe. I feel *Allah* and Jasbir are protecting us." Mangla smiles at the innocent faith of her child.

January of 1947 brings peace within the community. Jinnah is busy negotiating a country for himself with the British. The tea klatch is once more comfortable sitting in the sun, supervising children as they play hopscotch, ball, and hide and seek.

Mangla sees something dangling from Mina's hands. She yells, "Mina drop that thing. Roopchand, Mina has a snake. Come quickly, bring a stick." Mina drops it. The other children run away screaming. Roopchand comes running and puts the stick in front of the snake. It climbs on to it.

"I got it. It's a garden snake, *Bibiji*. Quite harmless. Children, it's a good snake. It's bad luck to kill a good snake. Because the dead snake has a picture of its killers and the snake's family hunts them down. I'll take it to the field."

Mina follows him.

Mangla is petrified of snakes. She's glad to see the last of that snake, harmless or not. She shivers at the ominous event as the community is being bitten by a bigger, more venomous threat.

***

Mangla often talks to Kamala, who is her neighbor, over the fence.

"I need to go to Anarkali Bazaar," she tells her. "Could we go with your Muslim driver? I feel that it may be safer if we go with him."

"Sure, Mangla *di*. No problema. I went there only a few days ago."

"How was it?" Mangla asks.

"Seemed pretty peaceful to me."

"Still, I have trouble trusting this peace. How long will it last in the city? I hear it is like a tinderbox there. Do you hear the bullets in the quiet of the night?"

"I've noticed that you frighten easily since you returned from Delhi," Kamala observes. Mangla ignores it.

They drive to the crowded Anarkali bazaar. Roopchand holds onto Mina and the driver holds onto Arun. Mangla is happy to see that the fruit and vegetable carts have fresh and varied produce. She tells the children the names of the things she buys, and Roopchand lets them feel and smell the supplies as he puts them in the shopping bags.

In the shops, Mina points and says, "I want that ball."

Mangla says, "You have so many balls. You don't need any more."

Mina points at the stuffed monkey that the shopkeeper is holding.

"No Mina, we don't have money for a monkey. It's too expensive."

"*Bibiji*, its only 5 rupees. Buy it for the little girl. She'll enjoy it."

"No. I told you, it's too much money."

The shopkeeper sees Mina looking at the doll. "Here, Bibiji every girl should have a doll. This one just came from England. I'll give it to you for three rupees." "*Amma*, please."

"You have so many dolls, Mina. You never play with them."

"None like this. Look it even opens and closes its eyes. It came from England only yesterday," the shopkeeper says.

Mangla wards him off and says to Mina, "I got you a top last time. Because you wanted it."

"Yes, and Arun and I play with it. Now he won't give it back to me. You favor him."

Mangla says, "Let me finish grocery shopping then I'll buy you a kaleidoscope. OK? This shop doesn't have it. I think we'll need to go to the other toy shop."

Mina gives the doll back to the shopkeeper, and Mangla sighs with relief. Tantrum avoided.

When she finishes her shopping, the driver and Roopchand carry the bags to the car, and they drive to the other toy shop. Suddenly they hear the beating of loud drums and see a crowd of men with fists in the air and holding big banners. The crowd is moving towards their car, chanting, "Give us Pakistan now!" "Pakistan is ours!" "Death to Nehru!" "Death to Gandhi!" Death to Mountbatten!" "Pakistan *Zindabad*!" Someone bangs on the car door.

Mina says, "Who's Gandhi?"

Mangla puts her finger on her mouth and shushes her.

The driver says, "*Allah* be praised. What're they up to? Muslim Leaguers! Memsahib, please put your heads down so no one can see you. Without a burqa they'll attack you." He puts his Muslim cap on his head and drives the car backwards into a side street and asks them all to get out and go into the nearby store where the owner is shutting down the shop doors.

Roopchand and Mangla, shaking, hold on to the children and enter the shop. She hears the storeowner pull out stools and say, "*Bahinji*, you and your children are safe here. Please sit and have some tea until they go away. Those sister-fucker *Goondas* have nothing better to do than disrupt the peace of our community. The police should jail them all."

Soon the big procession is gone, and their shouting fades into the distance. The driver comes to escort them back to the car. "I think we should go straight home," he says. "It's not safe for you to be here today. These people may come back any minute."

Mangla looks out of the back window and sees buildings burning in the distance. Mina looks backwards, too, and says to the driver, "Driver, the toy store is back there."

Driver looks ahead and ignores her.

"*Amma,* you promised to buy me a kaleidoscope," Mina cries.

"I know. I'm sorry that the stores closed early. Next time, Mina."

"It's going to get worse before it gets better," says the driver. "The Muslim League has fired up the *goondas* and they are creating chaos in the old city. They are told that partition will make them rich if they kill Hindus before they leave and take their properties."

Mina says, "See, *Amma*, Jasbir's ghost saved us because I was good."

***

Anand is constantly traveling due to increased sabotage on train lines. Mangla and Kamala ride together to the Khalsa wedding in Anand's car, with Kamala's Muslim driver. Attending the Sikh *lavaan* and Muslim *nikah wedding* would make the day too long for Mina and Arun. Instead, they decide to go to the reception that evening where the children can play and dance with their friends in the *shamiana*. The wedding reception is spectacular in every way. The *shamiana* is open on all four sides to accommodate the large number of guests and their families. The bridal family has spared no expense. Every so often the turbaned waiters come and spray *kewra* water with its beautiful and cooling scent.

The reedy *shehnai* music is melodious and the dancing is elaborate with professional dancers as well as the *dholak* for *Bhangra* that energizes the whole crowd as they join in.

Mangla relays to her friends up about her experience in Anarkali market. "If it wasn't for Kamala's Muslim driver, the car would have definitely been destroyed, and we'd probably have been attacked."

"That's awful." Hanfi *begum* says. She tells them about skirmishes that happened in Amritsar. "It's like it doesn't take much for the *goondas* to take the law into their own hands."

***

As the reception progresses and their friends begin to depart. Mangla says, "Come let's go home too. Your friends are gone."

"No, I want to watch and dance some more," Mina says.

Mangla picks up Arun, wondering how to persuade Mina. Usually, Anand picks her up and controls her when she throws a tantrum. But she can see that Mina's going to test her authority tonight.

Kamala appeals to Mina's vanity. "I agree the night is young and you are older. Little Arun can't keep up. He's half asleep. Let's go home. I will give you hot Horlick milk and the Bournvita biscuits you love. We'll put your favorite song *Awara Hoon* on the gramophone and you and I will dance more. Won't you like that? She moves to take her hand.

It is then that Mangla looks at the bride. Now married, she has taken her veil off. Mangla's jaw drops. Its Shamla from BHU who came to Sabiha's wedding with Basanthi. She has just seen Mangla, too, and is moving towards her when there's the sudden neighing of a horse and the thundering sounds of its galloping hooves.

Mangla hears a scream. On the bridegroom's decorated horse, a masked man is charging into the open *shamiana*. He scoops the bride in his muscular arms, yelling, *Allah o Akbar*, and as fast as he enters, he leaves. Behind him, Mangla sees a woman who looks to be Basanthi on another thoroughbred. What's she doing here, she wonders. Is Shamla with her and has planned this attack or something else is afoot. Her tortured mind asks. Since Vani's death she has no compassion for any traitors.

"I want to go home." A terrified Mina runs and whimpers in Mangla's sari.

Someone yells, "Call the police."

"The police are Muslims."

"Call the white police then," a voice yells.

"They won't come for Indians," another voice offers. In the meantime, the groom and the Sikh guests draw out their *kripan* from their waist and lash out at the men on the ground, who follow in the wake of the horseman, wielding their swords as they yell *Allah o Akbar*.

Steel clashes on steel. Gun shots are heard.

Mangla sees some of the intruders bludgeon the young Sikh girls who were dancing earlier. Then they pick them up and drag them out of the tent. A few more men enter on horses; they, too, pick up and carry out the shocked girls.

The guests stand frozen in shock. Masked men with torches set the *shamiana* ablaze. The fire moves towards the guests as they scatter.

Kamala and Mangla drag the now compliant children and run towards where the cars are parked, hoping to leave before complete chaos descends. Fear and motherly protection for her brood gives Mangla wings. She keeps running hard until she spots the driver who is running towards them. He grabs the children in his arms and says, "Hurry, *memsahib*, come this way." He opens the car doors and pushes them in. She feels the engine of the car running as she closes the door. The driver puts the car in gear and begins to drive away from the blazing *shamiana* with screaming, fleeing guests.

"Kamala, do you know when I finally saw the bride's face, I realized that she is an old friend from BHU? I haven't seen her since I got married. I wonder if that is why she didn't want anyone to know who she was. Was she double crossing Khalsa Sahib to get army information?

"Oh! Mangla why torture your mind with these useless speculations? God has given us all life to live another day. Let's be grateful."

On the radio, the announcer says that Lord Louis Mountbatten is the new Viceroy of India. He and his wife Edwina met in India in 1921, when he was visiting this country with King Edward VIII. King George the VI and Mister Attlee have given Mountbatten the needed political power to give India its freedom in 1948.

"But that's a year away. Finally, but at what cost? Mangla turns to Kamala. Her heart is still beating fast. "I'm glad we escaped tonight. I hate to think what if we were taken?" Mangla puts her shivering arms on Mina's shoulder, glad to feel her body under her hands. She wonders if Basanthi was able to save Shamla? They are safe by *Allah*'s mercy and compassion, but what about the other guests, the bride and the girls? Was Jasbir's ghost indeed protecting them as Mina believes?

The next day in her tea-klatch, they talk about how Captain Khalsa was wounded in the crossfire. It appears that the bride was spared by one of the Muslim League women. No one knows the whereabouts of the abducted girls, or who the attackers were, other than 'clearly they were Muslim Leaguers.'

XXXXXXX

25 1947 Desperate Dangerous Departure

Holi has come and gone. The weather is quite warm. Hot winds are around the corner. It's a couple of months since the Khalsa wedding, and Mangla hears in her klatch that the army is investigating the whole attack. However, it is still top secret—no one knows the outcome.

One morning late in May, Mangla and Anand sit down to breakfast. Anand has his head buried in the newspaper when he suddenly starts an animated tirade against the ineffectiveness of the elected political leaders for acceding to Partition demands of Jinnah to geographical division of India. "India without Indus is like the US without Mississippi."

"I heard that in the Northwest frontier, when Mountbatten visited, Hindus and Sikhs were massacred by Muslims to demand Pakistan," Mangla says.

"We know the Pathan's are uneducated," Anand says. "It won't happen in Lahore where people are educated and civilized."

She hasn't told him about the Khalsa wedding. He won't believe her, anyway. He'll probably attribute it to some personal vendetta by Muslims against an interreligious marriage.

How to tell him about her increasing distress? He downplays all her concerns. "Don't believe anything unless you get it from a reliable source," is his mantra. It is hopeless. Who is reliable and trustworthy today, she wants to know? She gets up and leaves the room. It takes her all her courage to defy him with her action. The children follow her in her wake like ducklings to get away from his increasing angst. So different from when they first married, and she was in NWFP.

Roopchand returns from the grocery shop and says to Mangla, "*Bibiji*, I just heard that they have decided to create Pakistan and India on August 15 of this year. It will happen. The astrologers say that is not an auspicious date. The stars are not in the right position."

"But that is a year earlier than when Mountbatten announced," she says.

It's already June 3rd. They haven't even selected where the lines will be drawn. Mangla's body tenses. Lahore could be in the part that will become Pakistan. Or it could stay in India. They don't know. What should they do? She wonders.

That evening, Anand tells her that the railway has begun planning meetings for the mass migration. He was asked whether he and his family wanted to be in Pakistan or in India. He opted for India to be closer to their families.

"For an orderly migration, we need to fix a date in July, so that all the government employees are already transported before the rest of the civilian population is moved. Before August 15."

He tells her that since the partition lines are not decided, they'll be moved to Delhi. At least that's the plan. They estimate over 250,000 people will choose to move across the border in the Punjab and equal numbers in East Bengal.

"We could do worse. Why don't we move on July 15, that'll give us about a month to put our affairs in order and book our luggage to go on the freight train," Mangla says.

Mina with a confused look asks "Where is India? I thought we live in it."

"Yes, we do, but soon it will be divided into two separate countries, India and Pakistan. Like I divide a toast for you and Arun when you fight," Mangla tells Mina.

"You'd better think about what you really want to take," Anand says. "I'm sure they'll give us some restrictions. If every Hindu in the Railways decides to move to India, there are not enough goods trains to carry their every possession."

"Is there anything you think we should definitely take?"

"Whatever you think is fine with me," Anand says. "I have no preferences. What we own is mostly yours anyway."

"Go on! That's what you say, but then when something happens to anything we own, why do you throw a fit?"

The next day, Anand comes home and tells her, "Mangla, I was able to book tickets for us to leave on the 24th. There's an important talk on bridge construction that the Institution of Engineers wants me to give at the railway officers club on the 23rd. I'll be paid 300 Rupees, money that will come in handy in India."

Mangla starts in earnest to look at what she owns. In the five years of their marriage their several moves have been unrestricted. But this is a new game. She will take everything she's able to. She decides to prioritize and label the piles. The lighter things that she needs have higher priority. Heavy furniture probably will not fit in the allotted square feet. She doesn't know, and neither can Anand guide her. They are flying blind with no guidance from the railways on the move. It is unsettling. How to decide?

What does she really want to take? She knows she wants to take the china that she bought from a departing English family. She loves it. She paid for it from her precious house allowance. What a fight she had with Anand when he found out! But it was a lot less than he paid for his car.

She uses this fine china for all her dinners and hand washes them afterwards. Her guests always comment on how lucky she is to have it. It has more than paid itself back. Even Anand has come to like it.

Mangla takes a deep breath and begins to pack each piece carefully in newspaper and then in clothes so that the dishes will not break in the rough transit of an Indian steam freight train.

Her saris, jewelry, and her handiwork are also a must to take. She calls out, "Mina! Look into your things and see what you want to take with you to India. I'll take care of Arun's things."

"I want to take everything, *Amma*."

"We can't do that. We can only take important things. That brick and big stone you have we won't be taking."

"But that's my precious brick and the stone I found with Zubaida."

"I know, but I'm sure there'll be lots of bricks and stones in India."

"But not these ones! I want to take them!" Mina starts to whimper and stomp her feet.

"Be reasonable, Mina. You are a big girl now. What about the toys you bought in the bazaar? Bring them and I will wrap them up for you. Bring your books, too.

"Mangla packs her embroidered cushions, tablecloths, and pillows. She next tackles all the pots and pans that she will need in her home in Delhi. She'll probably need to leave most of the big and heavy furniture even though she loves it and bought it at great expense. However, the lighter sofa and tables she will be able to move, she is sure.

She goes out to the yard and finds Mina busy digging and burying her bricks and big stones.

"What are you doing that for, Mina?"

"So, when we come back, I can play with them since you won't let me take them. They are precious. My friends did this with their things before they left," she continues in earnest.

***

By July, there is increased bloodshed in Lahore, where the Muslim men are looting Hindu shops, defacing their temples, violating, and raping women, and forcing them to eat beef. In retaliation, Hindu men are dishonoring Muslim women, forcing them to eat pork, and defacing their mosques.

"They still don't have details of the dividing line," a worried Anand tells Mangla. It makes planning impossible. His temper is even more volatile than usual and makes for increased father-daughter blowups.

Yasmeen comes to see Mangla, her face ashen. As they sip their tea, tears pour down her face. She shakes her head and says, "I just heard that my pregnant cousin was taken from her home in Amritsar by some Sikh men. She was-----" She chokes over her words.

Mangla puts her arms around her and pats her. "Sh--sh. It's OK."

"I have to speak to someone, or I'll go mad. How can men be so evil?" Slowly and haltingly, Yasmeen tells her the sordid story. How they disrobed and paraded her cousin naked through town with other captured Muslim women. Her breasts were cut off in front of everyone and then several men raped her and killed her in mass rituals by slashing her womb and killing her fetus. The Sikhs were protesting the partition and the Northwest frontier massacres of Sikhs and Hindus by Pathans. The women were not responsible for those atrocities, but still paid for it.

"I'm so sorry to hear this, sister," Mangla says. When the country is free it will be a safer place for women. A better and more equitable place for Mina to grow up in. And how many women will suffer before that happens? "Together we will achieve it," Mangla reassures Yasmeen.

Amritsar is only 25 miles away from Lahore. In Amritsar, Muslims are a minority although there is a large population of them. The converse is true in Lahore. Hindus and Sikhs are a minority though present in large numbers. What if Muslims retaliate in Lahore? A shiver goes up Mangla's spine.

"Do the British think we're without feelings? How can we uproot a lifetime of memories at a moment's notice? Why don't they announce the dividing line? Anxious people make bad decisions." Yasmeen shakes her head. Her eyes are swollen. "They've brought this man Radcliff from England to draw the lines. This is the first time he's set foot in India! He doesn't understand India's people or its culture. How can he do a decent job? He's holed up in a hotel and has consulted no one. No wonder people are getting antsy."

"May your family find peace in your loss, Yasmeen*jan*. Have you decided to move to India or stay here?"

"My husband's family is mostly here, even though I grew up in Amritsar. It's a tough decision, but because we're Muslims, we've decided to stay in Pakistan. After this incident, I'm sure that my family will want to move to Pakistan from India."

"We've opted to go to India." Mangla tells Yasmeen about her departure plans. This partition was going to separate lifelong friends into strangers overnight. So much heartache in store for everyone. The two women's tears pour unchecked.

"Why're you crying?" Mina says, waving her fist at an unknown enemy. "Who hurt you? I'll go and give them a big punch in their stomach." Yasmeen smiles through her tears and runs her hand over Mina's head. "*Allah* be praised, you're so precious. I'll miss you, my beloved daughter."

"After partition I'm sure we'll be able to visit each other." Mangla says. "*Inshallah*. I hope so. I'd better be going. Thank you for being here to comfort me. *Khuda Hafiz*."

"Please wait."

Mangla returns with a green cutwork tablecloth she hand-embroidered. It took her almost a year to make it. She hands it to Yasmeen. "This is for you, sister; to remember me by."

"How beautiful. Thank you. May *Allah* protect you and your beloved family. *Khuda Hafiz*." She puts her cupped hands to her forehead.

"*Khuda Hafiz*," Mangla and Mina say.

By the middle of July, even though the India Independence Act has been signed into law, there is still no dividing line. Anand tells Mangla that for now, railway planning decided to adopt the Wavell line and then iterate if the Radcliffe line is different. "This uncertainty is so hard for everyone. Tempers are shot everywhere," he says in an uncharacteristic admission.

She nods.

"It's only a week away. The logistics for smooth operations is in place. There's nothing like a well laid plan. But it's no use talking to you. You won't understand," Anand says, finding his official voice of power. It always sounds hollow to her. She doesn't confront him with "I am an educated woman, remember?" He seems to have forgotten these facts.

***

It's only a couple days before they leave, and Mangla is already looking forward to being closer to her parents in Delhi. Her *charkah* is packed away. She needs a walk to clear her head.

Roopchand tells her that he is going to the corner store to get milk, vegetables, and bread. She says, "Wait. We'll come too." Mina and Arun skip along her side.

The storeowner, a Hindu, has a sign up saying that he is closing his store next day. "Why so suddenly, brother?" Roopchand asks him.

He tells them that the train that arrived from Amritsar contained the corpses of Muslim men, women and children. The killers wrote on the side of the train that it was in revenge for killings of Hindu and Sikh women in Amritsar. He expects Muslim retaliation in Lahore and is not waiting around for Radcliffe to decide whether Lahore will be in India or Pakistan. He's taking his belongings and is going to get on the next train."

"Did you get a ticket?" Mangla asks.

He says that he isn't waiting for it. He'll find a way even if he must ride on the roof. He isn't going to let his girls be subjected to the atrocities of Muslim men. His wife is only packing essentials in a cloth bag so they will not need much space on the train. He'll start fresh in India. He has a brother in Amritsar. He'll go to his place first.

"In Amritsar, Hindus and Muslims are killing each other," Roopchand says.

"Maybe we'll go to Delhi then. Thanks for the warning. Now I know I'm doing the right thing," the shopkeeper says.

"We're leaving the day after," Mangla says as they walk back.

Roopchand says, "I don't know what to think, *Bibiji*. I'm sensing danger. Please forgive me. I must go home and get my wife to pack up for us to leave right away for Delhi. I can't wait." He wrings his hands in apology.

"Roopchand, don't be silly, we're all booked to leave the day after. You may not get a ticket."

"We'll go on the roof, if we have to, like the shopkeeper. Amritsar's not far. We'll make it or continue to Delhi to be safe."

"OK, Roopchand. I understand. You can go if you must."

"I've already finished cooking dinner. When we get home, I'll boil the milk and then if you'll excuse me, I'll hurry home to make sure we can leave on tomorrow's train."

Mangla has never seen Roopchand so rattled. He's usually Mr. Calm. Is he just influenced by the craziness of the shopkeeper, or are they both right and she wrong? She sits there twiddling her thumbs and drumming her fingers on the table in front of her. The images from the past and those painted by Yasmeen*jan* come afresh in her mind. Then with a determined thrust at the table she gets up and calls out, "Children, we're leaving on the next train tomorrow for Amritsar to make our way to Delhi. We'll go with Roopchand."

"Hooray!" Mina does a joyful dance and claps. "Arun, we'll go to Delhi with Roopchand on the train's roof." She runs out of the room skipping and yelling. "Then we can play our King and Queen games like last time." She runs out to bring their tiaras.

Mangla sees Roopchand leaving and calls after him, "Roopchand, on your way can you please order a *tonga* for us to catch the Amritsar train tomorrow morning with you?"

With a surprised look on his face, he says, "Yes of course, *Bibiji*." With that he's gone, and the backdoor closes with a thump. With no guarantee of a compartment at this late a date, they'll all need to wing a place for themselves on the train, she thinks.

She looks around the kitchen. Roopchand has cleaned everything and put the dinner on the counter for her to heat later. He's cooked fried bread for their breakfast. He's made sandwiches that they can take for the train journey along with the extra buttered bread with jam for the children. She puts them in a little tiffin carrier. That should do for the few hours train ride to Amritsar. Roopchand has already boiled the milk.

That night when Anand comes home, Mangla says, "We must leave on tomorrow's train."

"Are you crazy? Don't be silly. We're booked on the train the day after. Nothing awful is going to happen in a day."

"Indiscriminate killings are happening in the city and on the trains," Mangla reiterates.

Anand thumps the dining room table with his fist. "Damn it! I've to give this talk tomorrow night. We'll get a lot of money for it."

"Well, you stay back then. I'm taking the children and leaving on tomorrow's train with Roopchand." She walks to the kitchen with the plates. "Don't be foolish! What if you can't get a seat on the train?"

"We'll ride on the roof if we have to!" She repeats the shopkeeper's line.

"You're totally insane!"

"You can say what you like. I'm leaving," she yells from the kitchen as she drops the plates in the sink.

"What about all our stuff?"

She looks around her at all the packed boxes and suddenly doesn't care for them. "If it comes, fine. If not, we'll make do somehow and start fresh from scratch. I'm sure my family will help the children and me."

"It's only one more day. What's wrong with you?" he says, following Mangla to the kitchen. She has a knife in her hand.

"I'm not staying here to be butchered," Mangla says. "You can live with your money if that's important to you."

"Who says that'll happen?" He leans against the sink.

"My *atman*, that's who, that small voice inside of me that guides me, and I trust it. I've already ordered a *tonga* for us to catch the Amritsar train in the morning." With a satisfied feeling of empowerment her eyes grow wide. She can't believe it. Did she really stand up to him just now? There that was not so hard. He didn't kill her. She glares at him waving the bread knife high as she moves towards the sink. "What are you doing with that knife? Are you mad?" He yells at her.

She ignores him as she walks around him to throw the knife in the sink. With her eyes blazing, she pushes past him and goes to the children's room to repack things into a smaller box. Mina follows her, whimpering and holding on to the end of her sari. Anand follows her to the children's room, where Arun is playing in the corner with his toy jeep, just as Mangla is about to throw a top into the box.

"OK, if you must insist! I'll tell them that I'm leaving and won't be available for the talk. Are you happy now?"

She ignores him and continues repacking.

With an aggrieved thunder, he says, "I said I'll come. Damn it. What more do you want? You're never satisfied with anything I do, are you?"

Mangla doesn't let his anger deter or ensnare her into engaging with him. "You know, I am determined to leave with you or without you. I will leave tomorrow even if I never see you again." There, she articulated her ultimatum. He shakes his head and stares at this new Mangla.

The next morning, Roopchand's already gone to the station. The families put their meager repackaged belongings in the *tonga*. Mina, Mangla and Arun sit in the back seat of the *tonga* with their box. Anand sits in the front with the Muslim *tonga* driver who releases the leather reins and gives the horse a little tap on his rump as he makes the familiar "tut- chut- tut" sound, clicking his tongue in his mouth.

The drooping, bobbing, dispirited head of the horse mirrors Mangla's own sagging spirits as they make their way to the train station through the busy streets of Lahore. This feels like a familiar journey, although possibly they're making it for the last time. Her heart feels heavy, and a lump rises in her throat. There is an uneasy silence among the passengers, occasionally broken by Mina and Arun's discord. "*Amma*, she hit me." "He hit me first." Mangla lets them carry on. She has no energy to make peace between them. Isn't it what all the discord around her is? Grown up siblings fighting over trivia?

Mercifully, Mangla notices that for once Anand doesn't talk about politics to the driver. As they drive past Yasmeen's house, Mina says, "Look *Amma*, aunty Yasmeen's house. Will she be coming with us? Can we see her?"

"I don't think so. We don't have time. We have to hurry to catch the train." Then Mangla loses it, and tears start to pour down her cheeks. Deep sorrow engulfs her as she realizes she may never see Yasmeen again. The finality of this journey is like a brick on her heart, an abyss that she has never looked into before.

She feels Mina's gaze on her face as she hears her say, "*Amma* why are you crying?" She reaches to her face and wipes the tears with her hand.

 Mangla tries hard to swallow her tears and smile, but she gives up and just puts her arms around Mina, grateful that they are all together for the moment no matter what the future holds. She notices Mina's eyes are moist as well.

She looks back at the house receding in the distance. There is an inner knowing that this is the last time she will ever see Lahore. Her stomach flutters and a renewed burst of tears pour down her cheeks. She wipes them with the end of her *pallu*. Anand turns around as if to say something, but there is only a deep furrow in his forehead and moisture in his own eyes.

They arrive at the station. The scene is chaotic. There are people everywhere, pushing and shoving to get on the train. Already the roof is packed with people sitting with their families and their belongings. Others are climbing on, trying to find any small bit of real estate.

Anand hurries and says, "We don't have a reservation. Let me talk to the stationmaster and try to get a private compartment. It will be safer."

Mangla hires a coolie to pick up their luggage and follows with Mina, Arun, and the coolie. They walk towards the platform where the train is standing. She calls out to Mina while carrying Arun in her arms, "Come on Mina please don't dawdle. We need to hurry!"

Mina stops to look at a family with small children climbing the sides of the train as they try to get on the roof. "I want to be on the roof with Roopchand," Mina says.

"We want to get a place on the train, not on the roof. We need to catch up with your father. Move please."

Before long, walking at breakneck speed, Anand returns. With urgency he says, "Lucky for us, the stationmaster is Abdul Rafi. I helped once in settling a wrongful case against him. He is bending the rules and doing us a favor. He said if we hurry, we can claim one of the first-class coupe compartments, but we need to claim it fast before someone else gets it. C'mon children. Make a move."

"It is good we came early," Anand says in a grim voice. He holds Mina in an iron grip "We are lucky he remembered."

At the train, Anand moves to the carriage marked with "I" and gets in a coupe. It has two beds, one on top and the other on which all four of them sit. Anand goes out to ensure that Roopchand has a place a couple of carriages down the train. The coolie brings in their luggage and Mangla opens her purse and pays way more than the usual rate. She is grateful he hurried and got them to the coupe. He had to dodge people and their baggage, not to mention stray cattle foraging on peels and other trash thrown by the travelers.

Anand returns soon and puts a card in the slot on the door.

"What's that?" Mangla asks. He locks all the doors and windows with shutters down.

"Our new name. We are Mr. and Mrs. Asif Hussain for now. The stationmaster said so for our safety. My fluency in Urdu will serve us well. Hopefully they didn't see us in our Hindu attire."

"I want to look out," Mina says.

"Well, you can't until the train moves out of the station. The stationmaster was very clear that the fewer people see us in here the better. He gave me a *burqa* for you for safety's sake. Put it on." He hands it to Mangla.

"Why? What did he say?" Mangla asks.

"He's afraid that Hindus may be in some danger because of the Amritsar murders and the dead Muslims that arrived on the train yesterday. It's good Roopchand put on a Muslim cap and his wife dressed in *burqa*. Once we get into Amritsar, we can change back to being Hindus. The stationmaster gave me another nametag for outside our door when we get past Amritsar. I can't believe this," Anand says shaking his head

"That was decent of him to help us," Mangla says.

"I'm not sure it's necessary," Anand says, to save face.

"How can you say that? Well, I think it is necessary. I'm glad you came with us and found us this compartment, and I'm grateful to Abdul Rafi."

Soon there is a knock on the door. Anand asks them to be quiet. "Mr. Hussain are you there?" a voice asks.

"Yes, what do you want?" Anand replies in Urdu.

"Open the door."

"My wife's feeding the baby," Anand bluffs.

"We need to see your ticket."

"The station master's already seen it. Please talk to him."

"OK." They move on.

There comes a loud sound of shattering glass and piercing screams from down the corridor as the train starts to move. Mina holds on to Anand. "What happened?"

"Sh-sh-sh Be quiet," Anand whispers.

Love Partitioned

XXXXXXX

26 July Travel to India Begins

Frightened, Mangla slips the *burqa* over her head. That was a close call. What if Anand had not locked the door and windows? She didn't even want to think about what might have happened if they had captured her. What was the screaming about? Her legs suddenly buckle, and she sits heavily down on the seat.

The train begins to move ever so slowly and doesn't pick up speed as she expects. With a shallow breath she whispers, "Shouldn't the train be moving faster by now?"

Suddenly it stops. "Maybe someone pulled the chain by mistake," Anand says. She looks at him with her eyebrows lifted.

He points to the chain above their heads, where she reads, "Passengers pull this in case of emergency for train to stop."

Anand continues to have his hands over Mina's mouth and whispers to Mangla, "I don't know what's happening. I'll keep her quiet, and you make sure that Arun stays quiet. We all need to speak in Urdu. We don't know who may be listening. It's good Zubaida taught Mina and Arun Urdu."

Mina tries to talk, squirming to get free of her father, but Anand's grip is firm. "Even though its quiet outside now we still need to be cautious," he whispers. "The quieter we stay, the better. Hopefully whoever was threatening people got off the train."

"Can't we open the window a little?" Mangla says. "I need some air. I'm suffocating." She fans herself with the little hand-held raffia fan she carries in her bag and holds another out to him. Mina grabs its loose bamboo casing on the handle and rotates it round and round to generate faster airflow.

He looks at the dim light and the ceiling fan that is hardly moving. After he fiddles with controls he says, "OK, maybe for a little bit. But I'm worried someone may be lurking outside our window."

The train chugs forward in fits and starts, with big clanging and banging of the steel buffers at the end of the carriages. The carriage wheels grate and screech on the steel rails below them. They are jolted backwards and forwards. "At least the train is sort of moving," Anand says as his hands drum on his thighs. His eyebrows are furrowed, and his lips pursed. Mangla thinks he looks worried, which scares her.

Then the train comes to a screeching halt. Both Mangla and Anand look at each other with raised eyebrows.

"I'm hungry," Arun says.

"Me too," Mina seconds. Mangla realizes they haven't eaten since well before they left home.

She reaches in the box and brings out some of what she packed and pours a little milk for each from the flask. "This should be adequate until we get to Amritsar. It shouldn't take us more than three hours. Oh, how my head aches. I dream of some hot chai."

"Well, at this speed we won't be at any station for a long time," Anand says. "It might be much longer than three hours."

Mangla puts some toys out for the children and takes her sewing out of the box. She begins working by the faint light of the ceiling fixture reinforced by the sunlight from the crack of the open window. It calms her mind.

Anand brings out a magazine from his briefcase and begins to read. Soon their faces are dripping with perspiration. Mina whispers to Arun, "You fan *Amma*, and I'll fan *Pitaji*. We'll see whose sweat dries faster, OK?" and Anand's eyes slowly close.

Mangla watches the children burn some of their pent-up energy chasing each other. She puts her index finger on her mouth and shushes them. "We must be very quiet—we don't want to wake up your father."

They stop for a moment and then begin again. As Arun trips, Mina catches him. He yells. Anand suddenly wakes and reaches out and whacks Mina.

She stops in her tracks. "I am just playing with him like you asked me to."

"Yes, but not in here. We've got to be quiet. Don't we have cards?" Anand asks. Mangla brings them out. "I will lay cards out and you put them in sequence. Whoever can do it fastest and without a sound will get a biscuit." "I feel rested," Anand says. "Why don't you get your forty winks?" She lies down and closes her eyes, glad for the respite.

When she wakes, Anand tells her he will check things out and slips out of the compartment. It isn't long after that Mangla hears a knock. She puts her ears to the door and Anand whispers through the crack in Urdu. "It's me, *begum*, open the door."

She heaves a sigh and unlatches the door and lets him in. "Well, that didn't take long."

"I used the toilet. All is quiet out there. This is a good time to go and get comfortable. But don't tarry. The train is crawling slowly as a goat on a rickety bridge. Things may change at any moment."

"Why don't you hide under my *burqa*, Mina, and I'll carry Arun on my hips. Just be very quiet, OK?"

"OK. *Amma*," Mina says with a gravitas much beyond her three years. There is no one else about. All the other compartment doors are closed, and their windows are shuttered. Mangla lets Mina and Arun walk back. She is peering out the corridor windows at the passing landscape when two bodies fall from the roof. It happens fast, but Mangla still registers that neither body had its head. She tries to pull Mina under her *burqa* but it's not soon enough. The girl's eyes are enormous. Mangla drags Mina behind her, shaking, she runs to their own compartment. Once inside, she throws the *burqa* off her like it is a traitor.

"What's wrong?" says Anand.

Before Mangla can say anything, Mina pipes up, "It's raining headless people outside."

He puts his hand over her mouth.

"Sh-sh softly, Mina. Is this true?" Anand asks.

In a shaking voice Mangla replies, "I think the killer *goondas* must still be on the train. The people we saw had Hindu clothes on. One of them looked like the shopkeeper. Oh, thank goodness the stationmaster was kind to Roopchand and us to find room inside."

The train continues its slow crawl. Mangla can only imagine what is going on above them.

"Hurry up, hurry up-- come on!" Anand says. "This isn't right. Where's the military escort that was promised for every train?" He shuffles and mutters as his hands move back and forth, hitting his forehead.

Soon the train comes to a complete stop. They hear running feet and banging on the carriage from the outside, as well and banging on the doors from the corridor. They freeze and hold onto each other. Mangla reaches for her *burqa* and puts it on. She covers the children with it.

They hear gunshots and the clash of steel accompanied by the cries of, "*Allah O Akbar*," and "*Sat Sri Akal*."

Then the screams and the thuds of bodies falling reach them.

"I want to go home," Mina says from under the *burqa*.

"Maybe I should go and see what's happening," Anand says.

"N--No! What will you do? It's too dangerous," Mangla says. "I don't want to be the widow of a curious Railway officer."

***

It feels like the clock has stopped. Anand looks at his wristwatch and says, "The way the train is moving concerns me. It's too slow. The movement's all wrong. The train driver is facing some problems, maybe trying to make sure it doesn't derail. I wish I could talk to the engineer."

"That would help," Mangla says. Afterall, Anand is the one who trains drivers/engineers about safety procedures. "The shopkeeper said that the train that came in that morning was full of the dismembered bodies of Muslim men women and children. He feared that there would be reprisals against Hindus. That's why he decided to leave on this train," Mangla says. She thinks about the headless bodies and their fall. "I don't think he fared well."

Anand is bringing out a set of Muslim attire—*shalwar kameez* and a fez cap—and Mangla points to a red spot on the bag, "What is that, blood?"

"Abdul Rafi was saving the clothes of Muslims killed on the train to give to charity. I miscalculated the gravity of the situation. I hate to admit it, but I am grateful to you for making us leave early on this train." Anand reaches out and touches her arm, then dons the *shalwar kameez*. "So, what do you think, will I pass as a clean shaven Muslim Asif Hussain *bibijan*?"

Mangla shakes her head and with a tense frown, "With that handsome face? Sure. But why are you acting so strange?" she whispers.

"This bag was a gift for us from the grateful stationmaster to ensure our safety." They hear a knock on the door. "Mr. Hussain, open the door." The knocker tries to turn the door lock.

Anand's eyes grow big as he quietly closes the window and asks, "Who is it?"

"I'm Abdul Rafi, the station master from Lahore. Please let me in. I need to see your ticket, Mr. Hussain. "

"How do I know you are who you say you are," Anand asks.

"You helped me with my case 3 years ago and I gave you a bag of clothes today," comes the reply.

Anand lets Abdul Rafi in and locks the door behind him.

"What's the matter with the train, Abdul?"

"The Muslims are retaliating on tracks by loosening the fishplates between Lahore and Amritsar. You'll probably be safer joining a *kafilla* of refugees going to Amritsar. I've arranged for a car with a trusted Railway driver at the next station. He has already left Lahore and should be waiting for you. I'll ride with the train and ensure your safety until you join the *kafilla*."

"Is Roopchand OK?" Mina interjects.

"I'm sure they locked their compartment like we've done," Anand says. "We'll know when we get to Amritsar. Let me go out with Abdul and talk to the engineer. Maybe I can help him."

Mangla frowns at him.

"My Urdu, this outfit, and Abdul's escort will shield me in case there is trouble," Anand says, and Abdul nods in agreement.

"You all go to the toilet and get comfortable before I leave you. I'll accompany you there for your safety," Abdul says. Then he lays down a package on the table. "Here's some food and milk I picked up for you."

"Mangla, lock the door behind me until I return. Don't open it for anyone else," Anand says.

"I want to go too!" Mina yells and tries to run past Anand. He gives her a whack across her face, then picks her up and shakes her. He throws her on the seat and whispers through clenched teeth, "Please be good if you don't want to be jailed." Arun smirks at Mina. She pokes her tongue at him.

Mangla says, "Thank you for your caring for us, Abdul *bhai*."

"It's the least I can do to repay Mr. Rai. I owe him my freedom."

Anand turns to Abdul and says in a humble voice, "It was the right thing to do Abdul. Mina is finding this travel difficult. We all feel anxious."

"*Allah* be praised. It is understandable," Abdul replies.

Mangla looks at Anand. Instead of his usual braggartly bravado. She sees a new modesty. A glimmer of hope and love rises in her heart as he leaves, and she locks the door.

In no time she hears a knock on the door. Anand says, "*Bibijan* it's me." She opens the door. He is shaking his head as he enters.

Abdul says, "I'll see you at the station," and leaves as the train begins again to move slowly in fits and starts.

Anand tells Mangla, "These *goondas* are killing machines. They kill. They put up track blocks and force the driver's hands. If he doesn't stop, the train will derail and everyone dies, but if he stops, then the *goondas* get in. That's why the military and police were supposed to accompany the trains. They talked about it in our meetings. Abdul Rafi will stay with the driver until the next station, then I will talk to him and decide the best course of action." In his anger he thumps the table.

Mina looks at him. With her index finger on her lips, she says, "Sh-sh, *Pitaji*." He looks at her with a sardonic smile, and for once he is without words. Mangla picks up the fan and begins to fan herself as if warding off the evil spirit that surrounds them. Mina copies her with the other fan.

The fan has dark brown and beige woven Mandala patterns with red edges, and as it moves back and forth, it creates a hypnotic trance. Mangla begins to sag in her seat as sleep overtakes her.

The train comes to a screeching halt and jolts Mangla out of her fitful sleep. She hears horses galloping past; then running feet, and steel clanging against the body of the train. There are gunshots, again, outside their window. Mina climbs onto Anand. He shoves her aside and rushes to the window, pushes it down, and locks it shut. He sits down and heaves a big sigh of relief. Sweat pours down his face.

"Wh-- what happened?" Mangla asks as she stares at him.

"There must be a *goonda* attack again. It appears they are on horses as well this time," he whispers. "We should be very quiet just in case there are any cracks in the windows and doors. They'd be high enough on horses to see in." The beastly humid heat bears down upon them. On the floor below the door, Mangla notices what looks like a poisonous copperhead snake making its way inside in the dim light. She puts her hand on her mouth to stop the scream that is about to escape. It can't be. She moves closer and sees that it is blood seeped in from outside, now drying and glinting in the dim light. She lets out her breath and scrunches up her nose, not wanting to go near it, trying to find a way so Mina won't see it and ask her interminable questions for which she can't think of suitable answers.

She puts on her *burqa*, taking no chances. She wraps her sari *pallu* around the children's ears, trying to suppress the sounds of danger coming from outside. In an orchestral suite her heartbeats join the loud thumping of the hoof beats of the horses galloping outside. She clasps the children to her bosom and feels the wetness of their sweat. For once, mercifully, Mina utters no words.

Anand moves their boxes against the door and turns off the light. They sit in the dark in the claustrophobic heat. He puts his fingers on his mouth and signals them to lie low on the floor.

Soon from the trackside she hears shots fired at the steel shutters of their window. Right where she was sitting a moment before. But for now, the shutters' thick steel forms an adequate shield to keep the bullets out. Mangla looks at the door handle. If those outside have guns, they can easily blow it open. Her heart leaps to her mouth as she hears an earsplitting banging of steel on the door. Instinctively she tightens her grip around the children. The *goondas* turn the door handle, but the lock is solid. It appears that these people don't have guns like those on horseback outside.

"*Allah* be praised," she whispers to the children, and recites silent prayers in every religion she knows.

Outside, jeep engines roar closer and then stop. The intensity of the crossfire increases and Mangla hears bodies fall, horses neigh, and people cry and moan in distress. She hears running footsteps outside their door, then more gunshots. Outside, bodies fall with a series of thumps. Then there is sinister silence.

The train begins to move again, slowly. Soon it comes to a halt, and she hears familiar small station sounds. Abdul Rafi knocks, and Anand opens the door.

"Good you are in a *burqa*, Mrs. Rai. Please hide the children under it. With all the blood and decapitated bodies, it is horrific outside. We haven't had time to clean up."

"Sahib, Ahmad, the driver, is here to take you to the *kafilla* in the car "The Muslim driver steps forward and says, "Which bags, memsahib?"

"Mangla, take the children in the car and join the *kaffila*. It will be safer for you. I will stay with the driver until the promised military and police escort arrives," Anand orders her.

"What if the *goondas* kill you? I don't want to leave you and be a widow," Mangla articulates her fears.

"Abdul will keep me safe," Anand says with confidence.

"Yes, *Inshallah*. *Allah* be praised," Abdul says.

Mangla looks back at Anand who is following her with Abdul framing the train and shivers. She turns around and follows Ahmad to the car.

XXXXXXX

Manjula Waldron

27 *Kafilla* to Delhi

Ahmad takes Mangla and her bags to a waiting black 1939 Ford outside the small station. He has brought an earthenware *surahi* pitcher full of water with three cups stacked on its neck. He places a box of food on the floor and says, "The station master sahib sent this to make sure we have food and water even if we are delayed."

"I picked this station because there are very few people to see you aboard the car," Abdul says.

"It's good you wear a *burqa*--that makes you safer. We aren't that far away from Lahore."

"Oh goodie, Amma, look, this car is like our car in Lahore. I miss riding in it." Arun claps his hands as he runs to the car yelling, "I beat you to it."

Mina retorts, "I didn't declare so it wasn't a race."

"How far is the *kafilla* they'll join?" Anand asks.

Abdul says, "I hear there's a *kafilla* coming from Rawalpindi that will pass a few miles from here to avoid Lahore turmoil. Ahmad knows where." "Sahib, I'm not sure if they're going to Delhi or Amritsar only," says Ahmad "We'll see."

"Ahmad, please let Abdul know when you can where we can meet you," Anand says. "Ok, Abdul, let's get back to the train and figure out a safe strategy for the train to get to Amritsar and ensure as few lives are lost as possible."

With big eyes Mina says, "I want *Pitaji* to come with us."

"He has work to do," says Mangla. "We'll pray for him and us. He should join us as soon as possible."

"Now Mina and Arun, be good for *Amma*." Anand pats their shoulders and waves to them as he recedes towards the waiting train.

***

Ahmad opens the windows and closes the door. Mina sits in front, and Mangla and Arun in the back.

He says, "*Allah* be praised--that should bring us a cool breeze." He puts the car in neutral and starts it with the crank mounted on its side. He gets in, changes gear, and begins to drive.

Mina looks out and points to a racing camel beside them. She sways as she rocks, "Arun *OONT*."

Mangla points. "It's carrying the owner, a big *mashak* of water, and a bale of hay on its back."

Arun looks out of the window and points to the elephant, He sways his body, "*Hathi*."

Mangla says, "Yes, Arun, it is swaying its trunk with the *mahout* sitting on the *howdah* on its back. Look at the big branch with leaves in its mouth." They fall in behind a bullock cart that slows them down. Ahmad is trying to get past it, but the villagers herding their goats block the other direction.

Mangla looks out of the window. By the road she sees dried up bodies of three women. Their abdomens have been slashed open, and their fetuses lie beside them in neat arrangement. She distracts the children. "Mina, Arun, I wonder if we'll see a tiger. Look far into the jungle and keep your ears open to hear a roar."

Ahmad looks in the rearview mirror and says, "We hear stories of *goondas* abducting women from *kafillas* to commit atrocities."

Mangla says, "Then how is the *kafilla* safer?"

"Well, there's safety in numbers, as well as police escorts, and the ability to hide. That is not possible on trains when *goondas* get on board. Ultimately, it's *Allah*'s will."

They stop for lunch and a potty break near some shrubs.

When they get out of the car, Mina and Arun begin to run.

Ahmad yells after them, "Please run near the car, we need to be able to drive away fast in case of trouble."

Mangla sends the children one at a time to relieve themselves as she spreads a blanket on the ground, pours milk for them in cups, and arranges lunch on the plates Abdul provided. Ahmad watches as the children eat, and Mangla goes into the bushes herself.

From the shrubs, she hears Ahmad's worried voice. "Memsahib, please hurry, I see trouble coming from ahead. I'm putting the children and things in the car. We need to leave right away."

She returns to the car and pulls her *burqa* over her head. Ahmad has put both children in the back, where Mangla joins them. He rolls up the windows and says, "Memsahib, it will be good to put the children under your *burqa*.

Mina squirms. "It's too hot," she says.

"Yes, it is. But you'd rather be hot than headless, wouldn't you?" She hates to scare Mina, but it's important that she stays quiet under the *burqa*. Who knows what trouble they might run into?

As they creep forward, Muslim *goondas* suddenly emerge from the scrub alongside the road and appear in front of their car, chanting *Allah, Allah* to a drumbeat as they dance. There are four naked Hindu women tied together behind them. They stop in the middle of the road to chop off the head of one and slash her abdomen. When they find a fetus, they kill it; cut her off from the group and let her drop to the ground. Then each one takes turn to kick and abuse the writhing body of the victim. Mangla keeps the children under her *burqa* to protect their innocence and to hide from them her own horrified face. She puts her sari *pallu* over her mouth and her nose under her *burqa*.

Ahmad swears under his breath, "*Allah ki kasam*. These *haramzadeh* are up to no good." He reverses the car, turns around, and puts more distance between themselves and the *goondas*. With pursed lips he says, "I will need to join the *kafilla* nearer Lahore."

Mangla hears a muffled sound from under her *burqa*. "I can't see, *Amma*."

"Yes I know, *beti*" Mangla rubs Mina's head under the *burqa* and reassures her that soon Ahmad will find a nice place for a break and children can run around. "A little more patience, Mina."

Ahmad stops and asks about the *kafilla* to Amritsar and finds out that there is one that is coming from Rawalpindi. But it is a little west of where they are and may take them a bit longer. Still, it may be safer for them. Mangla is excited and wonders if they will meet up with Sabiha and Mahmood in case they have opted to go to India. She tells Ahmad to go ahead and join that *kafilla*.

They finally arrive at the Rawalpindi *kafilla* camp. The sun is setting, and there is not much twilight. Ahmad says he will go and see if he can find a place for them, but when he comes back, he says it's too late. The offices are closed. They decide to sleep in the car and wait till the morning to find a tent. Ahmad sleeps outside near the car as the sentry walks around with his *savdhan* and his rifle in his hands, pounding the ground as he turns around. Mangla and children fall asleep in their locked car.

They wake up to the hum of the *kafilla* camp as refugee travelers begin their day activities of bathing, dressing, and cooking. The smell of food wafts up from the community *tandoors*.

Ahmad finds a tent for them and rations from the store. He will cook. It may take a few days before it is safe for them to move forward. People talk to each other to find out migration stories of friends and relatives.

Mangla wakes Mina and Arun and takes them to pray at the community *namaz* and *havan*.

Ahmad brings milk and *jalebis* for children. He brings Mangla fresh tea in a *kullarh*, cooked Naan, Dal, and vegetables. Mangla holds out her hands to take "*kullarh ki chai*," the steaming hot, milky white sweet tea in an earthenware cup. The wonderful scent of liquid on the dry clay comes wafting through the air and engulfs her nostrils. The smell fills her with a sense of hope—she associates it with the first monsoon raindrops as they fall on the scorched land during a hot, dry summer, quenching the thirst of all the parched creatures.

She tries to pay Ahmad, but he says, "Memsahib, Abdul sahib arranged for it." She borrows a community *charkah* and spins with the children. It calms them all. In talking around with people, Mangla discovers that the campers are Hindus, Muslims, Christians, and Sikhs—all from different parts of what will soon be

Pakistan. They are migrating to soon-to-be-declared India as their new home because of family and the secular freedom promised by Indian leaders. They are united in the horrors they've witnessed due to a monolithic religion and Jinnah's dictatorship. Most of them are going as far as Amritsar, but some will go on to Delhi by joining other *kafillas*.

People keep coming. They come on foot. They come on carts, by cars, trains, and buses, despite threats of ambush. They bring whatever they can carry with them. More than five million have migrated, and many have lost their lives in the attempt. She hears that every so often, the *kafillas* get ambushed despite sentries guarding them as best as they can. The *goondas* then attack women. Older and pregnant women are taken as family slaves or second and third wives. Virgins, for new grooms, are captured for prize money.

Every day, for various reasons, people move in and move out. The *kafilla* migrants wait until it is safe to move to the next *kafilla* stop, and then the next, and the next, until they reach their destination. Everyone is fearful. Those who want power to manipulate ordinary people. especially young, to commit barbarities against those who not so long ago were their friends and neighbors.

Mangla thinks that people in the camp may know about Sabiha and Mahmood and whether they decided to migrate to India or stay in Pakistan. Maybe she can find someone who knows of them.

She walks around the *kafilla* and finally finds a family from Sabiha's neighborhood. But when she asks them if they know Judge Mahmood, they avert their eyes.

"Why, what's the matter?" Mangla asks.

Everyone looks at each other but they all stay quiet.

Finally, one compassionate-eyed woman speaks up. "It's really tragic. He was such a fine and principled official. So much loved by everybody in the community."

Why is she using past tense for him? Her heart sinking, Mangla asks, "What happened?"

"We don't know all the details just what we heard," says the woman. "When we left, the police were still investigating."

It appears that Judge Mahmood passed judgment in favor of a Hindu and against a Muslim. He always applied the law fairly, regardless of the possible cost to him personally. They painted his house with "Hindu Lover" signs and then some spineless Muslim League *goondas* came to the house at night while everyone slept. They beheaded all members of the household, including their children and servants. The woman shakes her head. "The family did so much good and were beloved in Rawalpindi. It was heart-rending for us. Everyone participated in the funeral with a heavy heart."

"We decided to migrate to Amritsar. We have family there." Mangla stands with her mouth open. She is still looking at the group as she collapses and falls. A hand comes and steadies her. Another brings her water.

As she comes to, she says, "Sabiha*jiji* was my sister." After a moment, she manages, "Do they know who did it?"

"The rumor has it that they were Muslim league fanatics. We also heard that the judge's sister, Farida, who was visiting them for Eid from Murree, was defiled and beheaded."

Mangla thinks of Basanthi. She could not have been involved if Farida was killed. But then Vani was killed, wasn't she? What if Shamla herself did the awful deed and Basanthi didn't know? Where are they? she wonders. She slowly walks back to her tent. Her heart is tortured and filled with misgivings. Her trust in humanity feels eroded. How will she tell *Ammaji* about Sabiha and her family How could she ever have wondered if Sabiha was responsible for Vani's death? She remembers how distressed *Ammaji* was last year on Direct Action Day.

From the *kafilla*, Mangla is unable to send any messages to *Ammaji*. She finds it hard to sleep at night. Safe or not, she wants to get away from this place and its horrible news. She wants to be held by *Ammaji*. Feel her compassion in her heart.

***

It is now over four days and Mangla has not received any word from Anand. A thousand questions in her mind make her anxious. Is he OK? Have they made it to Amritsar or not? In the morning, when Ahmad brings them their breakfast, she asks him if he's heard anything.

"No, Memsahib."

She thinks they can meet Anand in Delhi, the sooner they get to Delhi the safer they will be. Things seem to be deteriorating quickly on the migration trail to Amritsar. "How long do you think it will take? She asks.

"I don't know, Memsahib. We have to go back some before we go forward. But we will avoid the rush of Amritsar. It depends on the bridge over the river Ravi. We'll only know when we join the *kafilla*."

"Can we leave tomorrow? Please check at the office."

She brings the clean laundry in from the clothesline and begins to put their things in the box.

They leave early next morning to find the Multan *kafilla* on their way to Delhi. Ahmad makes sure that there is food and water in the car for their journey.

They make good time for about ten miles. Being on the move is easier for Mangla than hanging around in limbo with her silent grief. The mental torture it brings her. Sabiha's face keeps appearing before her. Tears pour from her eyes. Fortunately, Mina and Arun are in front with Ahmad and Mangla's *burqa* gives her the privacy to be with her thoughts.

Soon they come to a procession of people walking on the path next to the road. Ahmad asks where they are coming from. They tell him from Multan, and that they will be settling in their camp by late afternoon on the banks of river Ravi. They want to get on the bridge to cross the river. They're diverting a bit to the north to avoid Amritsar city center. Beyond that, it should be smooth sailing to Delhi.

They reach the camp by the river and register to get a tent for the night. Soon a bus load of people arrives. As they disembark, Mina points and gives a loud squeal and a clap as she yells, "There's Roopchand."

Indeed, there he is with his family. Provides Mangla hope that he might have news about Anand.

"Ahmad, let's go and meet him." The children are near the bus. They return with Mina dancing around Roopchand and Arun following him like a cat's tail.

"Roopchand what happened? Why are you on the bus to join the *kafilla* to Delhi?"

"*Bibiji*, there was another attack on the train. Around 2:30 in the morning."

He tells her that he heard the glass window break outside his compartment. There was banging on their door, and all the passengers rushed to put their belongings against it. They locked all the windows and turned out the light. Another bullet lodged in the door, and the latch rattled. His wife held his daughter as they waited. Other children shook with fear. Crying, they clung to their mothers. There were more gunshots outside, and groans and successive thuds on the ground. Then there was an ominous silence. A voice of authority broke it to tell them that they were police and had everything under control. They said that the *harami*, Muslim League *goondas,* had made life hell for the passengers. It was not safe for them to continue on the train. They were finding buses to take them to join a *kafilla*. They were removing the bodies; cleaning the station; had posted a policeman outside; and locked the compartments, to keep them safe until the buses arrive.

"Was Rai sahib on the bus?"

"Not on our bus. And I didn't see him at the station. Sorry, *bibiji*, we weren't allowed to wander at the station when I tried to look for him. I hope he was in front with the engineer."

Mangla's heart sinks and she says, "*Inshallah* that you are right." A silent prayer rises from her heart for his safety.

"Do you have a tent to stay here?" Mangla asks.

"Yes, my wife and daughter are in our allotted tent. She's pregnant and tired. We are all together. The railway is providing us dinner tonight."

Mina says, "Roopchand, please take us for a walk to the river. I want to see if there are turtles, fish, and crocodiles. Maybe there will be a *khilonawala* and we can buy a toy and candy."

Roopchand looks at Mangla, and she says, "Why don't I come. I can use a walk before dinner." She puts on her *burqua.*

"Ahmad, we are going for a walk to the river." She calls out to Ahmad who is preparing their dinner.

"Be careful, Mina and Arun, of *ghariyals.* Stay with Roopchand," he cautions the children as they skip ahead holding Roopchand's hand. Mangla follows. The golden sun is getting low on the horizon.

"Look, children, there is a ball of fire in the sky," says Mangla. "If you look hard enough sideways, you can see that it is the Sun God's crown, and he is riding his chariot to the right to watch the earth during the night. So we can all be safe." Mangla holds her hands in prayer to the Sun God.

Soon they are at the banks of the beautiful Ravi River. Roopchand sees them first, and an expression comes over his face that Mangla doesn't understand until she sees them, too, the decapitated bodies lying in the river.

Quickly, Roopchand turns around and says to the children, "I can smell Ahmad's dinner. Let's see who gets to the tent first!"

"I want to see the toy seller," Mina repeats.

Roopchand says, "It's getting dark. The toy sellers will have gone home to eat their dinner. Maybe we will return in the morning when sun is up. Now let's get back to the tent and eat our dinner so we can go to bed soon and get up early morning to walk to the river. OK?"

Mina is not sure. She hesitates. Roopchand says, "Ready, steady, G—" Both children take off ahead in the direction of the camp outracing each other.

As they follow the children, Mangla says, "Thank you for distracting them. I saw some beady eyes of crocodiles too. Mina's having a hard time with these brutal killings."

"We all are, *Bibiji.* And no child should have to witness this. Least of all a girl." "I'm having a difficult time too. Looks like the refugees were hacked and thrown from the Ravi bridge. They were fresh bodies."

"Yes, *bibiji.* The police seem to be building a funeral pyre for mass cremations. Some of the bodies were already on the scaffold. They probably do it at night when everyone is asleep so as not to perturb them. That way, if anyone is alive, they can bring them to the camp and provide them the medical help they need."

He will pray and look for any news he can find about Anand from those who were not on the bus. With that, he says goodnight and leaves to check on his own family.

In the morning when Mangla wakes up, she finds Mina missing. Arun is still sound asleep. Worried, she runs to Ahmad who is in the kitchen getting their breakfast ready.

"Ahmad, Mina baby is missing. I have a feeling she's gone to the river. She was upset last night that she didn't get to look for toy vendors. She thinks that the riverbank is for festivals."

Ahmad looks up.

"Hurry, Ahmad. I can cook breakfast." She shoos him off. He runs.

He returns with a barefoot, screaming Mina pinned on his shoulders saying, "Mina baby that *ghariyal* looked hungry. It's good I came in time to rescue you from his jaws."

"Come eat your toast with jam and drink your milk." Mangla pats on the seat next to Arun, who is devouring his breakfast.

"I don't feel good. My stomach hurts. The smell was bad," Mina whines holding her stomach and nose.

Mangla feels her forehead it is cool. "Good. No fever."

She goes to her special first aid box and brings out her herbal candy medicine for stomachache. She mixes it with *ajwain* and salt in a spoon and gives it to Mina to drink with warm sweet tea. "See, Mina, I made *chai* with lots of sugar." She adds more sugar for show and stirs it."

Mina is happy to take the medicine with tea and asks for toast.

"After that, before it gets hot, go and rest, Mina. It is best for stomachaches and nausea from bad smells." She pats her on the head. Mina lies down. Her eyes close and she's asleep. Ahmad goes to the kitchen to make breakfast for Mangla. She follows. "What's the bad smell about?"

"When I got there, I saw her standing in water only inches from a big crocodile, watching bodies burn. The singeing smell of flesh was stringently strong, like the grilled steak English sahibs eat."

"Praise to *Allah* you got there in time, Ahmad."

"Yes, I rushed in the water and dragged her out before the *ghariyal* turned its head and snout to smell us."

"*Bismillah*-----" she says, and he joins her in the prayer.

Roopchand comes a little later. "A railway officer's car just arrived. They are stopping for rest and vittles before being escorted across the Ravi bridge towards Amritsar."

"Was sahib with them?"

"No. They said Rai and Abdul Sahib were sent towards the Delhi trains because there were more attacks on those trains now. They said that Rai sahib averted a derailment by his keen knowledge of track safety and guided the engineer to bring the train to a safe stop. Thus saving many lives still on the train

"Maybe we should go with them," Mangla says.

"I asked. They told him that their car is full and there is no place for transit refugees to Delhi to stop in Amritsar. Going to Delhi, Amritsar should be avoided. There are no refugee camps there. All the inns and rest houses have become emergency hospitals for the injured from previous trains. Conflict between Hindus, Muslims, and Sikhs in Amritsar is very bad. They advised us to take the *kafilla* route together. The government can provide army escorts and catch *goondas* before they get to camps. There is safety in numbers, and information is more accurate as the groups move from camp to camp.

"God's blessings. *Inshallah,*" Mangla says.

XXXXXXX

28 August 1947: Indian Independence

Mangla asks Roopchand if his family would like to travel with them to Delhi in the car. He and his wife, Sushila, have a two-year-old, and Sushila is pregnant with their second. He agrees. Sushila and her baby sit in the back, Roopchand, Mina, and Arun in the front. They pack enough food and water so if they are stranded it won't matter.

Roopchand becomes the travel guide to the children. He points to the birds, naming each one. He tells them stories about his farm life, tilling soil with bullock carts. With the stories he makes sound effects, and soon the children are laughing, happily entertained.

Ahmad avoids the trouble in the big cities by following the refugees' *kafillas* to Delhi. From their car, Mangla watches many travelers walking. Sons carry their aged and frail mothers on their backs, or two young sons share a bamboo pole on their shoulders with their mothers sitting in a makeshift hammock made with sheets. Men balance baskets tied by sheets to their poles like makeshift paniers— inside, babies lie, or young ones sit on comfortable quilts. Every so often, she sees families who have laid the paniers on the ground under sparsely shaded *kikka*r trees, stopping for the lunch they packed at the last *kafilla* camp. Once satiated, they hoist the paniers and begin their journey again.

Mina questions. "Are they snake charmers with serpents in their baskets? Where are their *beens*? She begins to sway like a snake charmer and makes the *been music* instrument sound. Can we ask them to show us their snake dance?

"No, Mina," Mangla says. "These look like the snake charmer's paniers but they really are carrying their belongings across the borders as they don't have a car." She tells her that they are very lucky—because of her father's job, their belongings will come on the goods train. They are grateful to Abdul to get them the car and to have Ahmad as their driver. *Inshallah*, they will be in Delhi soon and their things will be waiting for them.

Still no word from Anand or Abdul. Mangla thinks Abdul probably went back to Lahore, but what about Anand? The last word she had, was that he was inspecting the troubled Multan and Jammu to Delhi lines. How much danger does that put him in? Her mind can't help but imagine the worst. She wipes her brow to put these anxious thoughts out of her mind. It doesn't help. She imagines him dismembered in some makeshift hospital without being recognized. Even though she has prepared herself to be a widow—is she really prepared? To honestly look in her heart at this moment, she realizes that these words were full of false audacity. It's been a long and desperate journey full of losses. Can she really bear another? At least Mangla has *Ammaji's* place to stay in case Anand is not back to get them accommodation. Ahmad and Sushila both have family in old Delhi where they can stay.

After three days, they reach Delhi and *Ammaji's* house. Mangla gets Ahmad and Roopchand to bring their meager possessions in. She climbs the stairs, and Mina feels and rubs the scar on her forehead. She puts on her tiara. At least in this house she will be a queen.

Ammaji opens the door, and her mouth drops like she's seeing a ghost. When she recovers, she claps her hands happily and pats the children's heads. "Mangla I didn't know when to expect you." Her letter had given them a train time. But when Shabbu went to meet that train, they wouldn't let him into the station. The station master told him to go home. That there was no one alive on that train. They had all feared the worst. She sees Mangla's pained suffering expression, then changes the subject.

"Let me look at you. Mina and Arun, how grown you look. Are you real?" *Ammaji* pinches them, then looks around. "Where's Anand?"

Mangla says, "We don't know. It's a long story, Let's talk another time. Roopchand is here also, *Ammaji*. He'll help you during the day in the kitchen and with children. But now he can cook food for us. We are all hungry and thirsty. He knows this place. Right, Roopchand?"

Roopchand nods as he bends and touches *Ammaji's* feet in a revered greeting.*Ammaji* looks at worried, tired, and exhausted Mangla and says with compassion, "You are right *beti*. How selfish and unthoughtful of me." She walks towards the kitchen and calls her husband. "Look who's here. The children want a drink. Could you please take them downstairs to the *panwari* shop and get them ice cold lemonade?"

Pitaji walks in and with a happy smile takes Mina and Arun's hands.

"Roopchand will stay with Sushila's relatives at night. They don't live far from here," Mangla says.

"Shabbu's wife is away to help her ailing mother. Anyway, come and make yourself comfortable. I will see to dinner in the meantime. Will the driver stay here?"

"No. He has relatives also near Jumma Masjid. He will take Roopchand to his relatives and then spend the night with his own family. Then he will bring Roopchand back in the morning to help us. They'll leave right after Roopchand makes dinner. Everyone's tired and needs to get rest. It was a long drive."

She tells *Ammaji* that they are moving to Delhi to be closer to the family. When Anand arrives, they will know about their accommodation. Until then, Mangla and the children will stay with her.

That night after the children are in bed, Mangla finally gets to talk with her parents about her journey.

"I'm worried," Mangla tells *Ammaji*. "We tried to get out on an earlier train and had to transfer to a car, for safety. But you know Anand how dedicated he is to his work. He is still on the train lines, inspecting them. He's supposed to join us when he's finished, but I haven't heard a word from him."

"Yes, definitely ask at the station. Surely the station master can address your concerns.

"I do plan to go to the station every day and check for news of Anand."

***

Life falls into a pattern *Pitaji* resumes teaching the children *havan* and spinning *charkah*. When they hear Muezzin call Adhan from Jumma Masjid, they say their *namaz* with Ahmad.

Then he takes Mangla to the station. She waits until the end of the day and returns home when she finds nothing. A few days later as Mangla arrives at the station, there is total chaos. The train from Sindh arrives full of dead and decapitated bodies, and blood runs everywhere. Hopeful families sift through the corpses, just in case one of their loved one is alive. But, alas, no one is. Soon The station fills with soot, smoke, and the stench of singed burnt flesh. It is sickening. Mangla puts her sari *Pallu* around her nose as bile rises to her throat and gut heaves. She remembers this smell from the *Kafilla* near Ravi. Mangla walks over to investigate and finds the Railway police bring out the bodies from the Sindh train, and the sweepers go about washing the blood from the station. They take all the dead passengers' boxes to be given to the destitute refugees who lost or left behind everything they owned.

They wash the Hindu bodies and drape the collective dead with white sheets monogrammed "Indian Railways." They load the bodies in a cart to take to a makeshift mass crematorium, which is presided over by the chants of a brahmin priest.

Next, they hose down the Muslim bodies, pile them into another cart and shroud them with large sheets. They are buried in a mass grave dug on the side of the station for their *janaaza,* with a brief funeral prayer presided over by a mullah facing Mecca. Whether they are Hindus or Muslims, they all need comfort in their time of transition.

***

Mangla waits daily at the station for news from Anand. A few days later, another train arrives from Karachi. Cries from injured passengers arise from among the dead. The families waiting run to see if, by chance, their loved ones are among the living.

In the crowd, Mangla recognizes Mrs. Kidwai from her BHU days, approaching the train. She introduces herself, and Mrs. Kidwai remembers her. She introduces the woman with her as Mrs. Sarabhai. They are working with refugees, meeting the trains to watch for orphan girls to find them homes and educate them so they will not be sold as sex slaves. She remembers Mangla and Basanthi's dreams of advancing women's education and invites her to come and work with them in the refugee camps if she is interested. Is Basanthi here with her, Mrs. Kidwai asks.

Alas, they drifted apart after her marriage, Mangla tells her. She describes her own escape from Lahore and the atrocities she saw on the way. She is looking for her husband who hasn't come yet. Mrs Kidwai suggests talking to the station master, and Mangla realizes that after the unfortunate incident with the evil man on her way to NWFP she has avoided station masters' offices.

She makes her way to the office and asks the station master, who is a Muslim, about Anand. He tells her that Officer Anand Rai is on a train from Multan, and that it is believed Anand has saved the train from derailment. It was supposed to have arrived with an army escort, but trains are still under attack, and there are many delays. Most likely, both Abdul and Anand are with the engineers, helping to keep the train safe. If they manage it, they will surely be honored with a medal for bravery on Independence Day. Mangla says a prayer of thanks as she waits in his office. Eventually, with no news forthcoming that afternoon, she returns home and updates the family. A few mornings later, the Multan train arrives on platform 7. Mangla runs to meet it, and when Anand steps off, she hardly recognizes his gaunt and tired countenance. He seems to have aged in the intervening days. There is gray at his temples that wasn't there when they boarded their train in Lahore. She wants to sing and dance for him, embrace him and thank him for making it home to her. Alas! this is neither the time nor place to show such jubilation. When they get home will be soon enough. But, wanting to feel each other they, briefly and discreetly hold hands. Then he goes to inquire about whether they have been allocated accommodation. When they get to Shabbu's home, Mina and Arun are jubilant to see their father and dance around him, telling him all the excitement of riding with Roopchand and listening to his stories. They keep repeating them.

"Your father is tired," Mangla tells them. "Let him rest a bit and eat."

When *Ammaji* asks if she has heard from Sabiha and Mahmood, if they too will be moving to Delhi, Mangla stalls her. She doesn't know for sure. Once Anand gets some rest and time and they settle in, he will inquire about them from the Rawalpindi authorities.

One day when the children are out on their walks, Anand confirms the *kaffilla* stories about Sabiha and her family. Mangla's last hope for them is lost. She is unable to hide her pain from *Ammaji*. She unburdens her heart as she repeats what she heard from the travelers. Tears roll down *Ammaji's* face. Sobs rack her body. *Pitaji* hears it and in a very uncharacteristic, repressed rage, with swear words Mangla had never heard from his mouth before, blames the Muslim league for the partition and their *goondas* for the carnage.

Ammaji is the first to recover and says that they must say a *janaaza* prayer for Sabiha and her family soon. She regrets she never met her grandchildren, and now it is too late. May their souls rest in peace.

Knowing how fond the children were of Sabiha and her family, they keep all this death news from them. Children don't need to know now, to them, the reality is that Sabiha and her family live far away in Rawalpindi, and Mangla lets them live with this.

***

Due to the influx of refugees to Delhi, Mangla finds herself once again in a temporarily erected tent city. It feels strange to be known as a "refugee" in her own country. But at least this tent colony is commuting distance to Shabbu's home. Some days after Ahmad drives Anand to his office, he is able to take the children to Shabbu's house to spend the day with their grandparents and Mangla can have much needed quiet day to herself.

The British government is still in power. Independence Day is less than a week away, and Radcliffe still hasn't announced where the partition lines will be drawn. The boundary commission is still diddling around. The air is escaping from the British Government balloon faster than their ability to fly it. They are floating to the finish line with no plan for the people they will leave behind in this chaos and violence.

Mangla feels chased by an unnamed predator. Her nerves are taut. Her headaches have increased; her muscles are tight, like a *sitar* string being tuned by a distant, inaccessible musician. She increases her intake of aspirin to get relief. Life feels like a yo-yo.

Along the planned border, they don't know if Lahore will be in the new India or Pakistan. What nationality will people along the border be? Will they have to move? Will all the refugees have to flee the borders to a safe location like Delhi? The *goondas* are still on the lookout to capture whatever was left behind. They stalk the fleeing migrants like vultures.

It appears that captive travelers on the trains are *goondas'* easy prey. New *kaffila* arrivals tell Mangla of the increased tensions on the border. Anand is once again away a lot, ensuring the safety of trains and train tracks especially between Amritsar, Lahore. and Jammu. Mangla agonizes over this. But what can she do? She married her railway officer. However, nothing about married life was as she thought it would be—all lovey-dovey and peaceful between Anand and her. She is too afraid to talk to *Ammaji* about the mixed feelings she has for Anand. Besides, she already knows that *Ammaji* believes that husbands are gods to their wives, well above reproach. With this increased tension between mother and daughter and husband and wife, Mangla is happy to be in her own home small as it is far from the prying eyes of *Ammaji*. The last month has shattered much of her naivete. It has forced her to grow up and question her assumptions of the married world. Mangla tries to keep herself distracted by getting things ready for the fast-approaching independence. Their tent is one room with a roof and canvas flaps that they can tie down at night for privacy. But the humid monsoon air is oppressive and turns the tent into a steam bath. There are shallow channels dug around their tent, and when it rains, the water overflows and creates a river below their feet. They have one large charpoy that Mangla and the children share, and a twin bed where tired Anand can sleep in peace when he is home.

They share the bathroom tent with five other families in their cluster. Mina refuses to go there, especially when it rains; instead, she wets her bed at night. When Anand is home, he yells at her. He slaps her and picks her up and drags her to the bathroom tent, adding to her shame. But Mangla remains quiet. It will only add to the cacophony of loud fights that emanate from the adjoining tents. These discordant sounds amplify the sounds of security guards stomping their sticks and yelling '*Savdhan:* Beware.' How would they achieve anything against the knives, guns, and bombs of intruders? She swishes her raffia fan over the family trying to cool off the heat emanating from their tense bodies.

During the day, when monsoon rain pours around them and water flows into their tent, the children build a bridge between the beds using wooden planks.

"Look at our Ravi bridge," Mina shouts to Mangla, who is embroidering a frock for her with the tricolor Indian flag to be raised on Independence Day.

"Arun, here is the dividing line. You must stay on that side. You are Pakistan. I am on this side I am India. OK?

"No, I 'm in India you're in Pakistan," Arun says.

"No, you're smaller than me and a boy, you're Pakistan. You are bad. I'm bigger and a girl. I'm good. I'm India," Mina says.

"I don't want to play. Not fair," Arun says. They begin to wrestle.

"Don't fight, children. Play something else," Mangla says.

Mina tells Arun, "OK. I'm the Lahore express going to Lahore from Delhi. I go fast. You're the passenger train going to Delhi. You're slow. You have to stop for me." Then as they run in opposite direction they collide and fall into the water below. "Oh, an accident. We have to tell *Pitaji* when he comes home."

"Mina, I've told you often, don't get wet. With this rain it's hard to get clothes dry, and we've so few," Mangla says.

Their things still haven't arrived from Lahore. They may never have left the city, or they may have been looted by the Muslim League *goondas*. For the time, they make do with what they brought with them. She misses the feel of her fine silk clothes and Royal Doulton china, but then there is no food to entertain with. She sighs.

Aloud she says, "Come on and change. Let's hang up wet clothes and walk to Connaught Place." Connaught Place has upscale British shops. The children love to run freely and chase each other under dry covered arcades. Mangla likes to window shop, dreaming of things she will one day buy. It also distracts her from the gnawing stress pains in her stomach.

The impending partition and war rations make the food supply short, and they never have quite enough to eat. In addition, Anand hasn't been paid because of undeclared partition lines. The treasury money is not yet divided between the budding nations.

The Brits are already absentee landlords and doing nothing to help the citizens they control. Mountbatten is too busy with meetings and royal pomp and show. They may be in charge, but with no practical outward tangible plans and results. People are angry and hurting in a country that is in utter disarray. Do the colonial rulers even care about common Indian people?

Why are Indian leaders silent? Can't they decide and share their plans, or won't the Brits let them? It is hard to make out what's going on, and Mangla's mind is in constant turmoil.

She is able to pawn her jewelry to the local jewelers to make ends meet. Her own family has loaned them some furniture and kitchen utensils, but they, too, are hurting for food. She tries to avoid being a burden on them. The ethnic tensions are still high in Darya Gunj since Direct Action Day. Despite that, *Ammaji* scrimps and saves to make special dishes for Mangla and her family and sends them with Ahmad when he comes.

Mangla wants to spin, but she can't buy a *charkah* in the market in *Pahargunj*, the local Indian shopping *gali,* lane. Hers is still in transit. The shop venders say that carpenters who make *charkahs* are Muslims and have left for Pakistan or are in refugee camps. For this reason, most things are in short supply as Muslims— according to the Hindu caste system—are untouchables and *karigar*s. They do all the craft and cleaning work in communities.

***

Abdul and Ahmad share a small tent as they wait for the partition lines to be declared so they know where to return. People in the tent city are an amicable group of both Muslims and Hindu railway officers and their families and staff who have chosen to be in India.

As a railway servant, Roopchand shares his tent with many other servants and their families. Each has a cot, dormitory-style, in a large shamiana. There is a community kitchen where the servants cook for the families they work for. Their own families cook on fires near where they sleep. Every family has their own ration card. Sushila continues to stay with her relatives. Roopchand, on the days when Ahmad goes to his family, goes with him to visit Sushila and her family.

Roopchand brings tea and milk in the morning with some bread. For lunch he supplements the rationed staples with whatever he finds in nearby *Sadar bazaar,* the vegetable market. It is meager compared to what they are used to, but times are not what they were. Mangla finds herself longing for those days. Maybe once they are free and independent things will be available aplenty.

In the cool of the evening over dinner they exchange news and common experiences of hardships and losses sustained by refugees. Hearing the stories of migrants in this makeshift community lessens Mangla's pain of her perilous migratory journey. In Connaught Place one day, Mangla finds a cloth with the Indian flag imprinted on it. She buys it for making clothes for Mina and Arun to wear on Independence Day. Her machine is still in transit but, undeterred, she takes her sewing over to Shabbu's house and uses her sister in-law's machine and finishes hand-stitching them in the tent city. Over dinner, she shows these to other refugees. Soon she is inundated with requests from others to make clothes for their children. They pay her in advance. The money comes in handy, and she gets her jewelry out of hock.

***

On August 15, 1947, India is made independent from Britain. New Delhi will be its capital. Ahmad brings *Ammaji*, *Pitaji* and Shabbu in the car for them to ride together to the Independence Day celebrations at Red Fort.

Ammaji spoils the children by buying them every tricolor toy she sees. She gets them one stringed *ektara* made of round *diva* and played expertly by the seller with a bow; kites; drums, horns, whistles, flying saucers; you name it, she gets it, despite Mangla's protest. *Ammaji* has been saving her money for a while for this extravaganza. After all, finally India is getting the freedom that her family has fought for so long. *Pitaji* and *Ammaji* are smiling from cheek to cheek. Happier than Mangla has seen them in a long time.

The family is invited to a separate railway ceremony that will be held in *divane khaas in the red fort* to recognize Anand's bravery. He will be given a *vir-chakra*, a medal of honor for saving so many lives and trains. *Ammaji* is proud and Mangla feels thrilled. Even though the ceremony is short, the elated feelings stay with them for the rest of the day. At the Independence Day ceremony, the Union Jack is lowered and the Indian tricolor flag of green, white, and orange, with its blue wheel of life in the center, is raised for the first time. Mangla and her family join others by waving paper flags and singing together patriotic chants, "*Bharat mata ki Jai. Hindustan zindabad. Nehru, Gandhi ki jai.*" Children dance around in their new clothes and join in the shared national pride of being independent.

The adults hear Nehru give his "Tryst with Destiny" speech and wave their flags. The speech is repeated over and over on the radio. They repeat its words---"At the stroke of the midnight hour, when the world sleeps, India will awaken to life and freedom—"

On their return to the refugee city, the children are still singing in discordant tones. They make up songs as they go: "We are the leaders of tomorrow in a free India," accompanied by the instruments their grandparents showered on them. They pound on their tricolor toy drums. The parents revel in their exuberance.

The adults sit around for a potluck in the dinner *shamiana*. They all share their hopes and dreams of a free India after freedom struggles that have lasted so many years. British rule is finally over. They are the architects of their own destiny. With it comes the personal responsibilities of education, and of creating a world they want to see in their new constitution. Nehru and Gandhi are helping to craft it. They say that women and untouchables will have equal rights to privileged brahmins. The refugee dining tent is full of revolutionary zeal, reminding Mangla of how she felt in college, when everything seemed possible. They will 'step out from the old into the new.' Hope is rampant in their hearts.

They make a ditty out of Nehru's speech and sing and dance together as someone keeps time banging on the tables with silverware. Even Anand seems relaxed, as he picks up the children and dances and sings, displaying his medal for Arun and Mina to touch. Mangla feels high spirited. She hasn't felt this free and energized in a long time.

***

Finally, two days after Partition, Radcliffe's boundary line is announced. Lahore goes to Pakistan and Amritsar to India. It passes through the middle of houses. One family's cattle go to Pakistan but their house goes to India. Their parents go to Pakistan whereas they go to India. It only reinforces people's feeling that British are uncaring. People now need permission from the police to cross the boundary that is being enforced by the Muslim league leaders. They will collectively need to fix this divide and rule through democratic principles.

The partition lines increase the violence in Punjab and it finally reaches the capital in all its vengeful fury.

The refugee city is vulnerable. Despite the security forces around them, the ethnic violence has increased. Every evening someone reports being robbed and beaten in the night. If they resist, they are killed. The guards nod their heads but don't seem to try to find the perpetrators. There may be too many. It alarms Mangla. Her sense of safety and trust in authority is threatened once again.

The next day, Anand comes home and tells her that they have been allotted a house not far from the refugee city. They can move there anytime. "Let's move tomorrow, she says. "You're here now. Let's do it," she says. She wants to be somewhere she can lock the doors and feel safe when she's asleep by herself at night. The sooner the better.

XXXXXXX

Love Partitioned

29   Curfews and Hate Crimes

One enters their new housing complex by a large driveway shared by the adjoining houses. They also share a large front yard where children play in the evenings. The wooden front door to their own terrace house opens into a courtyard with high walls all around it—but not high enough to stop an intruder from climbing over. Maybe Mangla will ask Anand to put glass shards or barbed wire on top of the wall. A back door opens onto a path that leads to the servant quarters. Roopchand and other servants live there with their families. She likes being able to bolt and lock the doors at night after Roopchand leaves.

The three-room apartment has been kluged like an afterthought to accommodate multiple families. On one side of the courtyard there are three rooms with high masonry ceilings. A small, barred window sits high on the wall. Through it you can see the staircase of the neighboring house. The bars provide safety but no privacy. Mangla will make curtains when her machine arrives.

On the other side of the courtyard is the kitchen and dining room. The floors are concrete and painted in different earth toned colors. The outhouse is near the back door. The toilets have big steel pans underneath them that the sweeper can easily access through a hatch from outside. The door on the toilet has a latch that can be bolted from the courtyard. In her current state of paranoia, Mangla bolts these at night, as well, to make sure no intruder will enter over the soil collecting pans. Next to the toilet is the bathhouse with a tap, metal bucket and a *lotah* cup. The open drain goes to the outside so that the sweeper can clean it twice a day.

Nearby is a papaya tree. Guava, mango, tamarind, and neem trees also shade the courtyard. Previous residents planted a vegetable garden that needs watering. Mangla calls Mina and Arun to fill the watering cans left behind to water the garden so they will have nice tomatoes, squash, and herbs. Soon they will plant winter vegetables.

She sees a few monkey mothers feeding their babies in the trees grooming and enjoying the cool shade. They treat it like their day home. In the early evening, they decamp to the *Hanuman* temple next door to eat and sleep. There, the priests treat them like monkey gods, feeding them sumptuous dinner and breakfast of fruits nuts.

In the heat of the day, mynahs, crows, little bulbuls, and occasional kingfishers come to rest in the trees. Mangla hears the melodious song of *koel* during the day. In the evenings, parrots descend, with their green feathers shining in the setting sun. They roost for the night, sharing the day's adventures with loud chatter. Watching them, hopes of flying free rekindle in her heart. She sings the freedom song *Mai azad hun*, I am free. She learned it from her father when she was young, and she teaches it to her children.

Mina and Arun love to climb the trees and chase monkeys. They jump from the trees and shout, "OOK OOK," scratching their armpits.

Mangla cautions, "Be careful, don't tease them. They can scratch you and it will hurt."

They buy a cow with a calf that they tie in the courtyard and allow to feed on the grass in the front yard. The cow provides free milk for family and friends. After their horrific journey and tent life, living here feels like a luxury. In the daytime, Mangla loves to listen to the birds and watch the children freely run around in the safety of the courtyard. Her activities, and safe feeling, keep her from fretting about Anand's frequent absence. Truly, she doesn't mind a respite from his mercurial temper under stress. She just wishes her *charkah,* clothes, and furniture had arrived from Lahore so she could decorate her house. Now it still feels like a campsite. Everything is in shortage and prices are high due to post-war England and the bare treasury they left behind. The flight of craftsmen to Pakistan has left them with no available goods that they can afford. Now that they live in a free country, Mangla hopes all will be restored soon.

At nights, especially when she's alone, Mangla is fearful. In the middle of the night she gets up and checks and rechecks the locks. She misses the sentry's *Savdhan* night calls. She takes the flashlight and checks the trees to ensure that no one is lurking above. She double-locks the bedroom door and keeps the children sleeping next to her. Her disturbed sleep increases her daily headaches. She feels tired all the time and increases her aspirin intake, which takes its toll on her gut.

***

One day Anand brings home a sleek black, almost new, 1939 Buick Roadmaster car he bought from an English colleague returning to England. "It must have cost a fortune," Mangla protests. "We don't have much money ourselves. Our stuff hasn't arrived from Lahore. We need other things!"

"I know," says Anand. "But the guy selling it reduced the price for quick sale. One of my rich Roorkee buddies, hearing about my medal gave me a low interest loan. It's such a steal for what I paid."

"But I don't even drive. We don't have a garage. You're gone so much the car will sit in the driveway. Vandals will get to it."

"Once again we lucked out. Our neighbor has a garage but no car. He said I can use it until I get more permanent housing."

Mangla walks around the car and feels its silky, unscratched paint. Mina and Arun run around it. Excited they climb its step and jump off it like they did on their car in Lahore.

"I can teach you how to drive," Anand says, almost gently. "Instead of being stuck at home you can go out. Let's start the lessons tomorrow."

Mangla thinks that she can then visit Mrs. Kidwai in the refugee camps to begin working towards her dream. Basanthi or no Basanthi.

The first lesson begins inauspiciously. He yells and screams and points out her faults.

She comes home sobbing and locks herself in her bedroom. Subdued children stand and watch. She yells, "You clearly think I am an idiot. You have no respect for my abilities." Resentments past and present spew forth. She should know better than to let him teach her anything.

"Sparks, open the door. I promise it won't happen again. Shall we give it another try tomorrow?"

They do. Nothing changes. After several repetitions of this she refuses to learn to drive. She would rather forego this freedom than suffer humiliation at his hands. After almost five years of a troubled marriage, she wonders even if they even have compatible outlooks and personalities. But where would she go with two children as a single mother in these troubled times? At least Anand has a good solid job and provides a roof over their heads. She feels the loss of her material things, like her sewing machine, with which she could supplement their salary.

Mangla has all day to muse on the quirks of her fate. The news on the radio is full of a new spate of widespread looting and ethnic killings, producing increased number of orphans. Arson destroys many neighborhoods. Food is scarce and heavily rationed. It is dangerous to stand too long in line for bread and milk. The cow's milk pays them for its weight in gold. Anyone may be attacked and killed for a ration card.

Is this chaos what freedom is about? She ponders.

Gandhiji has moved into the *Bhangi* colony, where many lower caste untouchables and poor Muslims live. It underscores his belief that one needs to obliterate caste and untouchability from free India. *Ammaji* and *Pitaji* join him there and are kept busy practicing what they have worked towards all their lives. Mangla mass distributes Gandhi's *Harijan Hatao, remove* untouchability newsletter in her neighborhood. The conservative Hindus, such as members of the rightwing orthodox Hindu extremist RSS party, have increased their offensive against the liberal, caste tolerant Hindus. This results in more atrocities against Muslims, who subsequently flee to Pakistan. It's a vicious cycle denounced by both Nehru and Gandhi. The continued violence between Hindus and Muslims leads Gandhiji to declare fast unto death, until the killings stop. The rage against those perceived as the enemies of Hindu religion escalates. Women are the real victims. They are disfigured, gang-raped, maimed, and then killed. News of this enrages Mangla. She is ready to rehabilitate and save them from such atrocities, but how to get to these refugee camps? She feels like a caged tiger. She decides she needs more education. But from where?

Mangla finds that there is a parents' training program to teach them about Montessori methods of letting their children learn through their endowed strengths. Annie Besant was a proponent of this type of learning and opened many schools for girls and women. The school is within walking distance of Mangla's house, and she decides to seize the opportunity.

Soon after her training finishes, and she's made her teaching materials for math, science, and arts. The school closes because of increased ethnic violence. Eventually she is afraid to let the children out of the house, even to go with Roopchand to the corner shop, lest they be abducted, maimed, and then sold into slavery. Newspapers caution parents not to let their children out of sight. Mangla and Anand forbid the children to go out of the house alone with a threat of reprisal, but one morning Mangla hears Roopchand call out to her. He comes running in, carrying Mina.

"*Bibiji*, come quick. Mina baby is hurt."

"Why, what happened?" Mangla joggles herself out of her shock.

"Apparently, Mina ran out of the house to play with her friend across the street and a bicycle hit her," Roopchand says.

Mangla looks at Mina's bleeding forehead. "I told you to watch her. How could you let her run away?"

"Sorry *Bibiji*, I was cutting vegetables for lunch, and someone must have left the front door unlatched. You know how quick she is."

"We told you not to go out of the compound alone, Mina. Why didn't you ask Roopchand?" Mangla examines the wound. "We should take her to the railway hospital next door and let a doctor make sure she is OK."

"He was busy, he just told you," Mina says. "Besides, we're now free. You said so."

What does it mean to be free? Will one ever be free to do as one pleases? Mangla ponders this as she goes to the medicine chest. "Mina, we may be free, but we're not safe right now. You're lucky your father isn't here, or he would thrash you for your defiance of his order."

"Will I be headless or put in jail?" Mina says with a frown, as Mangla bandages her head.

Later, at the doctor's office, Mina proudly shows him the little scar she has on her forehead from Direct Action Day and declares that now her forehead looks balanced.

Mangla takes the opportunity to consult the doctor on her own headaches, paranoia, and sleep problems. He listens to her with compassion and says she is not alone. These are difficult times for everyone. "Mrs. Rai, reduce your aspirin intake and take this pill at bedtime every night. It will help you be more confident and sleep better."

***

Ten days or so later when Anand returns, Mangla doesn't tell him. Mina's wound is hardly noticeable, and Anand is oblivious to the catastrophe that took place in his absence. Mangla's mood is much improved with the new medicine.

Anand and other men are away a lot to keep the railways safe. A curfew is imposed in the city and keeps everyone behind their gates. Mangla calls in the children playing soccer in the yard for their lunch. She stops by the adults gossiping, sitting on a cot in the front yard watching the distant fires burning. They're airing their concerns about Gandhiji's deteriorating health.

Suddenly, all talk stops, and the children stop playing as their eyes rivet to the scene unfolding on the road out front. RSS-flag-waving men emerge from the shadows and stop a *tonga,* defying the curfew the *tongawallah* probably didn't know about. They kill the driver in front of the appalled spectators. The Muslim cap of the *tongawallah* waves in the air as his head is disconnected from his torso. Then they set the *tonga* on fire and stab the horse to death. Mangla stands there and shivers, vitriol rising to her throat when she realizes that the children can see it too. She runs with the other parents to hide the children's eyes from the scene but it's too late. Mina puts on her imaginary tiara chasing the Hindu RSS *goondas* who run to the side alley to find their next victim. She runs to the side of the house yelling "I am *Jhansi ki Rani.* Come you cowards," Mangla afraid of her running to the road asks the neighbor to mind Arun as she runs after Mina.

Mangla and Mina both freeze as they come to the side wall. There are dead, decapitated, half-decomposed, and part-eaten bodies of men, women, and children strewn down the alley beside her house. It was hard to fathom of what religion the victims are. All faiths appear to have met the same fate at the hands of the others. But as it was near the *Hanuman* temple, there seem to be more Muslims than Hindus in the pile. She looks above. The sky is black with the hordes of hovering vultures waiting to swoop in for their turn at the feast after the jackals are finished. With police patrols on the main road, they are lucky that no one has broken into their own compound.

She instinctively covers her nostrils. All time stops, before she realizes that Mina is viewing the horrific sight, too. holds her daughter close as tears of helplessness flow down her own cheeks. Is that what the freedom they fought for so long looks like? Death, destruction, and massacre from the ethnic violence of hate. It's been a long, relentless nightmare that doesn't want to end.

Mina asks, "Why are you crying, *Amma*? Who hurt you? I will make them headless," and she swipes her imaginary sword in front of her, copying the RSS men she saw. It makes Mangla's sobs even louder. Mina wields her sword more fiercely to defend her mother.

After that day Mangla hears Mina moan and walk in her sleep She must make sure that the doors are latched and bolted all the time. She watches Mina to make sure she doesn't run away. When she leaves for her card games with Anand in the evenings, she tells Roopchand to do the same.

***

Mangla feels more and more ill every day. She is nauseous at the sight of food and has no interest in life. She's lost weight and finds the sleeping pills enticing. She increasingly takes more than is prescribed. Even Mina notices. "*Amma*, what are these for? Are you sick?"

"Oh no, remember the doctor gave me these so I can sleep better."

"I want one. I can't sleep. My pee comes at night in sleep. When Roopchand hangs the sheets, Arun laughs and calls me a baby."

It jolts Mangla as she appreciates the shame Mina feels about her night accidents. Life is hard for all of them, right now. Perhaps it isn't worth living if they will be killed anyway. What's the point? She wonders as despair envelopes her exhausted psyche. She gives Mina a lozenge and says, "My medicine is for grownups. I'll ask the doctor what is right for you."

Mangla is lonely, and her uneasy mind sees no future for herself and her children. She's failed them as a mother and thinks of ending her life and theirs. Maybe their next life will be a better one. She has taken out a handful of pills, and is looking at them, when she notices that Mina is rummaging in her jewelry box.

Mina brings her the Chinese jade pendant that *Khalajan* gave her when Aziza was abducted, and Vani killed. *Khalajan* told Mangla that the two Chinese characters together mean crisis. One character meant danger and the other opportunity. In a crisis, one always has a choice whether to cave in and be destroyed or to see it as an opportunity to grow and transform. In Sufi Islam, there is only one life, and it is not up to a human to take it away. Life is given so that one may love *Allah*; only *Allah* can take it away. It is a gift. Whenever Mangla was despondent, growing up, Sabiha told her to have faith and do good in *Allah*'s name.

In killing herself and the children, Mangla, too, would join the *Shaitan* and act like the *goondas* she has come to despise. What would be the difference between her and them? She remembers Sabiha's wisdom guiding her. "Praise to *Allah*," she says.

Mina says, "Look, Amma you dropped all your pills."

Mangla glances at them on the floor. She takes the pendant from Mina and puts it around the girl's neck and tells her what *Khalajan* said.

"This *taweez* is very special. Blessed by *Khalajan*'s *Pir*. Before going to bed, say *Allah*'s name until sleep comes. I will wear mine also. And maybe by *Allah*'s *dua* we will not need any pills. She gets her pendent out as well. Mina strokes the cool jade with its black inscription smiles and says, "like Zubaida taught me."

Mangla picks up the pills and walks to the outhouse and throws them down the hole to join the human excreta.

She kneels with Mina, and together they say their *namaz*. Mangla is grateful that they were saved from her destructive suicidal thoughts. She misses her *havan* and next time she sees *Pitaji* she'll join his.

By early September, the violence in the city has not diminished. The schools are still closed. Mangla home-schools the children with her learned Montessori techniques so that they keep up academically. She sits on the verandah, reading a book to Arun and Mina, when she hears Anand return from his travel to Jammu and Kashmir. The children rush to meet him. Mangla looks up and sees he has a visitor with him.

Anand says, "Do you remember Jay from NWFP? He was my trainee assistant in the construction project."

Mangla looks up. Like Anand, Jay shows signs of partition fatigue and seems to have aged. Mangla closes the book and says, "Yes, of course. Namaste. Mina, Arun I'll read the book later. Please say namaste to Uncle Jay."

"Jay will be in training with us in Delhi for the next four months, and then he is assigned to be my assistant on a new construction project I will be working on in Punjab," Anand says. He goes on to tell Mangla that housing is still scarce in Delhi. He's asked Jay if he will want to rent their little attic room, with its own separate entrance, as well as a small adjacent room that can serve as a private bathroom. He can eat with them, and his peon can help Roopchand with kitchen chores as the children are getting older and demand more attention. They can use the extra money to pay for the car and for the children's education. With that, they take Jay to look at the room.

"It's perfect for a bachelor like me," Jay says.

"Great, and if we can find a fourth in the neighborhood, we can have evening card games here," Anand says.

Mangla nods.

"You were so good at bridge, *bhabiji*. You used to beat the pants off us men." Mangla laughs.

"Maybe you can teach her how to drive. I tried. It didn't work."

"A husband teaching his wife never works," Jay says.

Mangla smiles.

"Close your eyes," Jay tells the children as he reaches in his pockets and brings out two little cream colored Kashmiri paper mache pencil boxes, beautifully painted with red and blue flowers and maple leaves. "OK, left or right," he says.

Mina and Arun both say, "Left," and as they begin to fight Jay says, "OK, the older one gets the first choice."

Mina picks the hand she wants, and the way she smiles at Jay and pokes her tongue out at Arun tells Mangla that Jay has won her over.

"These are from Kashmir for your pencils," Jay says as he bends down and lifts both children like feathers.

"Children, go tell Roopchand to bring in some tea and biscuits for *Pitaji* and Uncle Jay," says Mangla. "Then go and put your pencils in your new box."

They run to the kitchen to show off their loot.

"So, it's settled," Anand says. "I leave again tomorrow to make sure the line to Hoshiarpur's safe. Will we ever feel completely safe again?"

He looks tired, Mangla thinks. She has come to care for him despite her disappointments in their relationship.

Why does Jay have this effect on her? It's been since the first time she saw him, since even before she met Anand. Does he know that she is Basanthi's friend? Would he have any news of her? She wonders and wonders how to bring it up with him.

"How are things in Jammu and Kashmir?" Mangla asks over their cup of tea.

Jay tells her that when he left last week, the Indian army had halted Azaad Kashmir's advancement to a Pakistan controlled border territory. "Our Hindu family in Srinagar suffered a great deal. One of my cousins is still missing. We fear the worst," Jay says. "I am surprised that they haven't been able to stop the RSS cruelty here. The hatred of the other is so unfathomable to me."

Mangla ponders if he knows that Basanthi is a Muslim and in Azad Kashmir. But is she alive? Is she a traitor to her father? Would Jay know? How did your family treat Basanthi? Mangla thinks. She wonders if Jay even knows anything about it. She wants to say, I knew your cousin Basanthi when I was in college at BHU. I visited her in Jammu during the summer at the end our first year. Her face clouds over as she remembers Sabiha's whole family is killed by hate. "Yes," she says, "it's hard to understand such hatred of others."

Jay tells her that in Jammu food is in short supply. Christians, Muslims, and Hindus are killing each other as the English leave. Then he tells her—as if reading her mind—that he never knew he had a cousin, Bhumi George Raina, who is Anglo-Indian, until he accidently met him through his stepdaughters at a dance." I was so ashamed when he told me how my family treated them."

Mangla wants to ask him of the whereabouts of Basanthi, but something in the sadness on his face tells her that now is not that time.

He tells her that he became engaged to Alice, Bhumi's older stepdaughter. They were to be married in church when he finished his training here. Jay didn't care about his family's Brahmin orthodoxy that opposed his liaison. They were wrong about Bhumi's parents and Bhumi, and they were wrong about his daughter, Basanthi.

"I believe in Gandhi's secular thinking: that we are all human beings born to love and we have the power to create the world we want to see. I learned about theosophy from Bhumi and am a great fan of Annie Bessant's thinking," Jay continues. He puts his head in his hands and is quiet before continuing to tell her that before he left, Bhumi and his family were all killed in cold blood in their home by extremist Hindu RSS *goondas*—all because the family had defied the Hindu caste system by being Anglo Indians. He looks up through tears of deep anguish. He shakes his head. "I haven't told this to anyone. I don't know how it came out. Please forgive me for unburdening myself to you in this way, *Bhabiji*."

Mangla's heart goes out to him. She wants to know if Basanthi knows that her father is slain. She remembers how devastated Basanthi was when Bhumi had his first heart attack all those years ago in Murree. Was Basanthi visiting him? Is she dead, too? But Mangla holds onto her questions for another time.

"I know," she says. "These are times of grief. My sister, Sabiha, and her family were similarly murdered in Rawalpindi by the *Muslim League goondas*. Because they thought the family were Hindu lovers." Her voice breaks and tears flow unchecked. Finally, she whispers, "Perhaps we can go to church and mosque and say prayers for them."

Jay soon becomes part of the family. He eats dinners with them. The children love their Uncle Jay. He regales them with stories about Jammu and Kashmir. About how he tamed wild animals, giant monkeys, and black-faced langurs that chase children. He tells the children, like Basanthi told Vani that, when fall arrives, the beautiful poplar trees that line the roads turn from bright green to gold. On the peeling bark of *Bhojpatra* trees, the ancient scholars wrote stories and love letters. He'll make a great father, Mangla thinks.

A couple of weeks after he moves in, when Anand is away, Jay asks, "Shall we give the driving lesson a try? If you drive, it will lessen Anand *Bhai's* anxiety when I finish training and leave, and you are once again all alone. We'll surprise him."

Mangla says, "OK, I'm ready if you want to take on the challenge." She gets behind the driver's wheel. Jay gives her basic instructions on gears, clutch, brakes, and the engine. Then he starts the car and gets in beside her. He puts one of his hands between hers to guide the steering wheel and the other on the hand brake should it be necessary. His proximity arouses her, but she understands at a deeper level that his touch is platonic. In larger scheme of things the complexity of love in a relationship is more than carnal passion. She has learned this living with Anand and bringing up children. Love is not simple. It grows slowly and surely over time. Basanthi used to say her Ayah told her that in bible it says love is kind and patient It has its sweet and stressful bonding moments. The more she reflects the more she can let go of her anger. Her love for *Ammaji*, Basanthi, Anand, children, and Jay feel different. Like they inhabit different parts of her body, mind, and soul. She's experienced all dimensions of love. It feels wholesome.

Jay has her practice taking the car to the gate and reversing back. A few times, the car hiccups, and stalls. But he is patient until she gets the hang of the coordination of clutch and accelerator. Mina watches her mother in awe. Why can't Anand be as understanding with her Mangla wonders.

"At this rate you'll have your license in no time, *Bhabiji*," Jay says. He turns to the children. "You know, your mother's already a wonderful driver. She's such a quick learner. You must get smarts from both your parents."

They practice together each night after he returns from work. Even Anand acknowledges that Mangla's becoming a good driver. "You're a miracle worker," he says to Jay.

"No, I'm just not her husband. That's all. Your wife is smart, and a patient teacher to the children," Jay says.

"Even though I don't want to admit it, I suppose you are right," says Anand, with a sheepish grin on his face.

Mangla knows better than anyone what that humility costs him.

Within the month, Mangla has her license. They all pile together into the car and Mangla drives them to the ice cream store, where Jay treats them all. "We're celebrating a very historic occasion," he says to the children. "*Amma*'s wonderful driving."

"Yes, better than *Pitaji*," Mina says.

Both Arun and Mina clap while licking their ice cream on a bumpy road. Arun's is all over his face. They laugh at him, and he gets cross.

"*Amma* drove well and there was no fighting. She's even better than you, Uncle Jay," Mina says with an impish grin.

The thorn in Mangla's side is still that their belongings from Lahore have not arrived. When she asks Anand, he only gets cross with her. He stalls her by saying he doesn't have time to find out. They will arrive one day, he is sure, and endless fights ensue, with their frustrations about the last few months coming to an emotional eruption.

One day Mangla asks Jay if he can find out what happened to their belongings. When he comes home, he is shaking his head. Regretfully, he tells her that the goods train was looted by the Muslim League, and no trace remains of its contents from when it left Lahore. Mangla will have to begin afresh. She begins to cry at yet another loss. It feels like the last straw. She wonders if Anand has been just shielding her from this out of kindness.

"I am sorry, *Bhabiji*, I don't have better news for you," Jay says as he picks at his dinner.

She looks at his sad face. Compared to his loss, and to her loss of Sabiha and Vani, the loss of the things feels trivial. It is hard to love oneself if you love things, someone once told her.

At nights, Mina and Mangla smell Jay's cigarette smoke. When Mina follows it, she finds him in the courtyard, deep in thought. Mangla watches from her bedroom as Mina runs to him and he picks her up and rocks her like an infant until she's asleep. He carries her back and puts Mina in her bed.

She whispers, "You are so good with her. You'll make a great father one day." Jay murmurs, "There's plenty of time for that. Like me, she just needs love right now. Life is hard these days with all the losses we have sustained." His face still showing his grief, he extinguishes his cigarette against the wall and walks out.

Mangla stays with Mina and ponders whether Basanthi knows of Bhumi's murder. Have her prejudices and losses over a lifetime made her turn against even her loved ones? Some answers Mangla will never know. She and Basanthi now inhabit different countries, each inaccessible to the other. Life has a strange way of twisting one *around*. Who is running this show?

XXXXXXX

30 1948 Cost of Freedom

The increased violence, curfews, and civil unrest prevents Mangla from visiting her family in Darya Gunj or the *bhangi* colony. She has more time to devote to the children's home education and drive to nearby shops for essentials. The first thing she does is to find a secondhand sewing machine and a *charkah*. She also acquires paints and brushes to begin the arts and handicrafts she learned during Montessori training. She continues to teach Mina and Arun to spin cotton. She takes their spun cotton to the local Gandhi shop to exchange the skeins of yarn for cloth as she did when she was young. Spinning with the *charkah* helps the children to settle down and concentrate better on the lessons afterwards. Mina, especially, seems much calmer now, with her jade *taweez* around her neck and spinning her *charkah*. She's good at it.

In the Illustrated Weekly, Mangla reads an inspiring article about Anis Kidwai and her life after her husband, a prominent Muslim, was brutally murdered by the RSS. They justified his killing as all Muslims are untouchables and low-life and deserve to die.

Bitter with grief and distress, Mrs. Kidwai visited Gandhiji in the *bhangi* colony. He counseled her to practice her religion from her heart. Islam doesn't allow anger and bitterness against anyone who has sinned. They are all God's children. She must free herself from the corrosion of bitterness. She can do *tawbah* prayers of repentance and forgiveness for those who are without remorse in their sins like the RSS *goondas*. When her heart is free of these sinful thoughts, *Allah* will guide her to salvation. As a result, Mrs. Kidwai now feels drawn in love and selfless service to both Hindu and Muslim refugee women and their children in *Purana Quila*. Putting this in practice brought untold peace and transformed her relationship to *Allah* and those around her, the author reported.

She shares this article with Jay and works on her own grief by working on her alienation through her faith, her inner voice, her holy spirit like Ayah used to tell Basanthi when they practiced in their meditation and raj yoga. What would Jay do she asks him? He stays quiet. His loss is still too recent he tells her. He needs time and she patience.

Inspired, Mangla goes to the nearby refugee camp to set up for those in transition and teach children there. It takes her mind off the troubles that surround her. She buys teaching materials and secondhand *charkahs* for the refugee children and keeps them in the back of the car.

***

Nehru blames the orthodox RSS Hindu political party for the escalating violence of Hindus that is driving Muslims to Pakistan. It is having deleterious effects on the economy. Muslims perform most of the skilled labor and infrastructure jobs, like working with gold and silver; black smithy; crafting leather goods; food processing; clothing manufacturing; car mechanics; plumbing; and working aluminum foundries etc. If they all leave enmass the country will come to a standstill.

Many Muslims have abandoned their homes and dwellings in fear and are in the refugee camps until they can get to Pakistan. However, because the police and authorities at these camps are Hindus, they face more and more reprisals in the form of delayed or cancelled departures. More cruelties are unleashed on them. There is more denouncement of Gandhi and demonstrations against the Government by extremists Hindus and RSS-backed groups.

Nehru allocates treasury funds to entice the Muslim refugees to return to their homes in India and provides them safe housing, food, employment, and education. He provides police escort to the communities where these Muslims have lived for generations, since Mogul times. This overt flouting of the Hindu caste system by congress further enrages the RSS Hindu extremists.

Riots in Delhi show little sign of abating. The RSS-backed media funded by some of the big conservative Hindu industrialists is behind the escalating violence. They accuse Gandhi of destroying Hindu social order and giving up too many resources and land to Muslims, untouchables, and Pakistan. Muslims were invaders, they say. To them, if Pakistan is a Muslim nation, then India should be a Hindu nation and not a secular one as envisaged by Gandhi and the Congress Party. They feel that Gandhi has betrayed them. Their ire translates into creating more orphans. Everyday over the radio, Mangla hears more stories of terrible things that are happening to Muslim women and children at the hands of RSS Hindus.

Gandhi's fast continues as the conflict persists. He is dying in the *bhangi* colony. Nehru persuades Gandhiji to move to Birla house and take care of himself as he entreats people to stop the violence. One day it happens. There is no violence in Delhi. Nehru runs and tells him, jubilant. Gandhi stops his fast and takes juice from Miraben, who tends him. Gandhi makes clear, though, that if the violence restarts, he will again fast.

Nehru is frustrated. What good will his death do?

But Gandhiji is steadfast in his resolve. *Ammaji* and *Pitaji* and others go door to door to bring Gandhi*jis* message of peace.

***

In the beginning of 1948, Jay is pleased that Jammu and Kashmir, J&K, will be part of India until UN-mandated plebiscite allows its citizens to vote which country they wish to belong to. For now, with his limited troops, the Hindu Maharajah of J&K is happy to be part of India and be under its protection.

Their long evening dinners allow Mangla to tell Jay, finally, about her friendship with Basanthi before she married Anand. She even tells him how she went with Basanthi to Jay's house in Jammu, and how he totally ignored them.

"Back then, I joined my family in upholding their culture of segregation and apartheid thinking, as Kipling's poem so elucidates. He begins reciting words of Kipling's "we they" poem.

--"All good people agree,
And all good people say,
All nice people, like Us, are We
And everyone else is They:"--

"I'm ashamed of my behavior now."

"Basanthi and I studied theosophy together at BHU. Annie Bessant was our role model. We wrote papers about her." But that was then and now is now. What a difference a decade can make. Mangla has changed and Basanthi has changed. She would love to know more about her whereabouts.

He tells her that once she went to Azad Kashmir, Bhumi lost touch with her. After independence the mail cannot go between the two countries. And they were unable to let her know about Bhumi's murder. I'm hoping things will change as the UN intervenes, "but for now these two countries are sworn enemies with severe travel restrictions even on families. It is tragic."

Mangla and Jay spend time sharing their understanding of theosophy. She tells him that Basanthi is quite a scholar on this subject, having learned from Bhumi and her grandfather.

"Bhumi, Jill, and I also had long discussions on this topic before they were slaughtered," says Jay. A dark shadow crosses his face.

After independence Basanthi couldn't leave Azad Kashmir, a Pakistan army-controlled Kashmir. She became the principal of a women's college that she and Farida founded in Murree.

"I introduced her to Islam and Farida at my sister Sabiha's wedding," Mangla says. "Farida was Sabiha's husband's niece. It's all so tragic. I wonder what contributed to her radicalism."

Mangla reflects on the complexities of love relationships. Its fickleness, if one can weather its turbulence, an equanimous transformation it brings to those involved. She reflects on her evolving marital relationship to Anand. If she lets go of her moments of passion of regrets and disappointment felt from the past she feels compassion for him in the present. It's a wisdom that is slowly percolating to the higher echelons of her mind. She takes a deep sigh.

Jay tells her that since independence, Basanthi has been unable to cross the border to visit Bhumi. Kin separated from loved ones. It is so sad.

Mangla tells him of Basanthi's distress over Bhumi's heart problems. It all seems a lifetime ago now. The despair of lives lost bring them suffering. What a chess game God is playing with their lives, as Munshi Premchand wrote in *Shatranj ke khilari*—a book she and Basanthi debated. Mangla is happy to share these memories with Jay, if nothing else but to hold Basanthi in a place of forgiveness for Vani's death. Mangla will never know of Basanthi's involvement, but at least in this moment she feels love in her heart.

Once the travel restrictions are lifted between India and Pakistan, Jay hopes to visit Basanthi and formally apologize for his family's behavior and their segregationist attitudes.

Mangla shares with him the possibility of one day reconnecting with Basanthi. "I'd love to see her school," she says. It seems impossible that Basanthi has gone through with their plans without her. It is difficult to comprehend the different paths their lives have taken. But perhaps not its destiny.

***

Mangla drives to the evening prayer meetings of Mahatma Gandhi in Birla House with Roopchand, Mina, and Arun. People gawk at a woman driver. She lets them. She loves driving. Even when Anand is with them, she insists on driving so bystanders, even as they heckle, get used to women drivers. If Mina and Arun have been good and quiet during the meeting, she buys them little toys, or ice cream, or charcoal broiled corn from the vendors outside Birla house.

During his meetings, the Mahatma delivers meaningful talks on the value of unity and peace in nondenominational prayers of love. Mangla is impressed by how deep his knowledge is of this subject and how firm his commitment is to the idea that all people are created equal in the eyes of God. Usually, he ends his prayer meetings with inspirational freedom songs of unity and one God. *Allah tero nam, Ishwar tero nam. Sabko sammati dey Bhagvan.*" Literal meaning, Allah is your name and Ishwar is your name, give everyone wisdom, oh God. Children sway, clap and join the audience in these hymns.

On the way home, Mangla leads them in singing patriotic songs honoring the freedom they now enjoy—fragile as it is. They sing *Vande Matram, Sare jahan se accha ye Hindustan hamara*, Our country is better than the whole world, vaishnav *jan to taine kahiya* ,A compassionate person knows empathy for those suffering.

266

When getting close to home, they end with Tagore's *Ekla chalo re*, If no one else walks, walk alone that she sang at BHU. It lifts her spirit and adds meaning to her life.

They are in the audience that fateful evening on January 30, 1948, waiting for the Mahatma to begin his prayer meeting. He is late. Then they see him walking towards the podium. Suddenly they hear three shots, and his voice, *"Hey Ram, Oh God, Hey Ram, Hey Ram,"* as his body falls. Like Gandhiji's three monkeys, Mangla doesn't want to see, hear, or speak about the evil unfolding in front of her. She stands frozen as Roopchand holds the children in his arms, crying, "Oh my God, Gandhiji's been shot." The crowd captures the man who fired the shots.

They learn from the authorities over the loudspeakers that in the morning the Mahatma's body will be placed in the big *maidan* before it will be taken to the *ghat* the following afternoon for cremation.

"What's cremation, *Amma?*"

Mangla's energy is sapped. She cannot attend to Mina. Roopchand answers her. Mangla heaves a sigh of relief when she learns that the man who shot Gandhiji is a Hindu RSS member—Nathu Ram Godse. Apparently, the police had been tracking him for days. They were just too late to prevent this tragedy. "Thank God it's a Hindu and not a Muslim," Mangla says. "All hell would've broken loose. No Muslim would have been spared if that was the case."

Over the radio, they hear that Gandhiji's sacrifice is not in vain. It has brought peace between the Hindus and the Muslims all over the country. People are surrendering their arms to the authorities and joining in prayer vigils to put an end to the ethnic violence. The peace that eluded Gandhiji in his life, he achieved in one moment through his death.

Hearing the news, Jay and Anand return early from their tour in the middle of the night. The next morning, when Roopchand arrives, they walk together to the big memorial gathering in the *Maidan* in Connaught Place. Loudspeakers blare Gandhiji's favorite hymns, and his followers join in, clapping and swaying to the beat.

The mourners come from all walks of life: rich, poor, Hindus, Muslims, Sikhs, and Christians. They march past Gandhiji's garland-covered body with folded hands and bent heads. They touch his feet with their foreheads as a sign of profound respect.

The body is placed on the flower-decorated open truck that starts its slow journey to the banks of the Jamuna river. Mourners follow this makeshift hearse, crying and chanting, Gandhiji *ki Jai. Hindustan zindabad. Om Shanti Shanti Shanti.* Jay and Anand follow the truck to the cremation grounds. Mangla chooses to return home. It is too far for the children to walk, and today she doesn't want to leave them alone.

There is a breeze blowing. It is an ideal day for kite flying. The sky is full of children's kites in the open maidan. Ahead, Mangla sees Roopchand teaching

Mina and Arun to fly the kite he bought from a vendor nearby. The string on the spool is coated with fine sharded glass paste. It is used to cut the competing kite nearby and capture it as a loot of their combat. Roopchand warns the children to not get their hands on the string. He guides Arun as he runs behind them holding the spool. And directs Mina to release the string so her kite soars high like a *cheel* kite chasing its prey.

Mangla is in no hurry to get to an empty home today. She finds a bench nearby and holds her aching head in her hands as the floodgates of grief engulfs her and tears finally pour out from the depth of her heart. She remembers Mrs. Kidwai's transformational story. Victory lies in repentance and the eternal love for all.

Mangla's heart calls out. Mina, learn to cut the other kite lest yours be cut. May you fly free, unfettered, my young one, to where your providence wants to take you. Don't let your wings be clipped like mine. I will dedicate my life to educate girls. So, help me God. *Jai Hai,* victory be. "

Mangla looks up and sees a kingfisher on a nearby *neem* tree and hears her "*chee- chee*" sound. The bird seems to communicate that life's freedom unfolds bit by bit with every decision and action. Just like an eagle swoops low to soar high.

The kingfisher spreads its wings. As if on cue, the bird takes off and flies right by Mina's kite, its iridescent blue green feathers shining in the sun.

XXXXXXX

GLOSSARY A-Z

Should the reader need translation of foreign words

Aarta: arrangement of oil lamps on thali dish
Abba, Abbajan: father
Achkan: a long buttoned coat
Adaab: Muslim gesture of greeting
Adivasis: native tribes
Ajwain: ajowan caraway herb
Allah o Akbar: God is merciful
 Allah tero nam, Ishwar tero nam. Allah and Ishwar is your name
Alpana: motifs and sacred art
Amma, Ammaji, Ammijan: Mother
Anarkali: a dress like garment
Apna Desh Hai Apna Ghar: my country is my home.
Are: hey
Arya Samaji: non denominational social Hindu sect
Atta: whole meal wheat flour
Aum Bhur Bhuva Swaha: Sanskrit chant
Ayah: a governess
Babul mora Naihar --Hi Jaye: father, I am leaving to meet my lover
Bahinji: respectful name for sister
Bahu: Daughter in law
Baniyas: merchants
Banprastha: retiring to the forest
Baraat: the groom's wedding procession
Been: snake charmer's pipe
Begum: Muslim married woman
Beti: daughter
Bhabi, Bhabiji: sister-in-law
Bhai, bhaijan: brother
Bhajan: Hymn
Bhang: cannabis
Bhangi, Bhangin: cleaning person, a dalit (untouchable) caste
Bhangra: Punjabi folk dance
Bharat mata ki Jai.: Long live India,
Bhaat: a wedding engagement ceremony
Bhayya: brother
Bhojpatra: birch tree
Bibi: miss or madam
Bindi: a colored dot worn on the forehead by Hindus,
Bismillah-ar-Rehman-ar-Rahim: part of Muslim prayer in namaz

269

Boondi: snack made from fried chickpea flour
Bua: aunt father's sister
Burqa: the veiled gown worn by a woman in purdah
Chacha: uncle; younger brother of father
Chai: Indian spicy tea
Chandni Chawk: market district in Delhi
Chapati: flat roasted bread
Chappals, open sandals
Chaprasi: valet
Charkah: spinning wheel
Charpoi: jute woven bed
Chauki: small table
Chauri Chaura: a town near Gorakhpur 1922
Chawkidar: watchman
Cheel: kite bird
Chikkan: Embroidered muslin clothes
Chundri: fancy wedding bridal shawl
Chunnis: a long scarf
Churail: female demon
Churis: colorful bangles
Churidar: tightly fitting trousers
Chutila: braid decoration
Dadi: paternal grandmother
Dal: lentils
Darya Ganj: a district in Delhi
Dawat-e-walima: the wedding reception
Dekhao: young man sees a girl as a possible life partner
Desis: local people
Dhaba: roadside restaurant
Dhammal: Dervish dance
Dharti mata: Mother earth
Dholak: a two-headed hand drum
Dhoti: traditional homespun male dress
Divane khaas: hall of private audiences in the Red Fort
Diwa: earthenware Diwali light
Diwali: Hindu festival of lights ; end of Rama's Exile
Dua: blessings
Dukanwallah: shop owner
Duniya rang rangeeli Baba: the world is colorful?
Dupatta: shawl
Dussehra: festival to celebrate slaying of evil Ravana
Ek Bangla Banai Nyara: Build a Wonderful House
Ekla chalo re: If no one else walks, walk alone
Ektara: a stringed musical instrument
Farishta: someone from another world and time
Gali: alley?

Garara: woman's flared pants
Ghagra: woman's long skirt
Ghariyals: crocodiles
Ghat: a flight of stairs leading into a river
Ghutti: herbal mixture for intestinal problems
Gooler: Gooler tree berry?
Goondas: troublemakers, hoodlums
Gurudwara: Sikh temple
Gwala: a milkman
Hai: Oh! an exclamation
Halwai: chef, Confectioner
Hakim: A country Doctor
Hanuman: the Hindu monkey god
Harami: evil doer
Haramzadeh, Haramzadi: a son/daughter of a whore
Harijans: members of an untouchable caste
Harsringar: night jasmine tree
Hatao: remove
Hathi: elephant
Havan: Hindu prayer ceremony
Havan kund: fire bucket used for Havan ceremonies
Hazrat Isa: Jesus Christ
Hazrat Miriam: Mother Mary
Hindustan zindabad: long live India
Howdah: seating carriage on the back of an elephant
Hua kya qusoor—Tell me my crime that makes you distant?
Hukkah hukka: hookah to smoke
Hut: Move
Inshallah: God willing
Izzat: respect
Janaaza: Muslim funeral
Jai Jagdeesh--Bhakt jano--: Hindu song of blessings for devotees
Jalebi: a sweet made from fried batter and syrup
Jao: go
Jadu tona: Tantric black magic
Janvasa: Grooms family hotel
Jab dil hi toot gaya-: when my heart is broken; friends leave
Jan, Janu: beloved terms of endearment
Jhansi ki Rani: the queen of Jhansi
-ji, -jiji: an expression of respect, sister
Jutti: closed toe shoes
Kafilla: group. Caravan, camp
Kajal: eye liner
Kali: black, Godess
Kalma: Muslim prayer
Kamiz: a shirt

Kanjivaram: silk sari from Tamil Nadu?
Kansi: bronze brass copper amalgam
Kasam: oath
Katoris: small metal plates
Kabbul hai, I accept
Kadam chale aage--: my steps go forward
Karigars: craftsmen
Kathak: a type of dance?
Kewra a scented reed
Khadi: homespun cloth
Khala, Khalajan: aunt in Urdu
Khes: bedcover
Khilonawala: toy seller
Khuda Hafiz: May God be your Guardian
Khudai Khidmatgar KK Gafar Khan's Pathan nonviolent group
Khuni: bloody
Khuskhus punkah: a manual fan made of fragrant grass
Ki Jai: victory to
Kikkar: acacia tree
Kismet: fate
Koel: cuckoo
Kothas: of singers and dancers to please men
Kripan: short knife carried by every Sikh
Kufi: cap
Kulfi: traditional Indian ice cream
Kullarhs: disposable earthenware cups
Kurta: a jacket
Kya se Kya: radio program called what from what
Laavaan: part of Sikh wedding ceremony
Laddoos: spherical balls of edible sweets
Lal Kila: Red fort
Layhe layhe ilaha ilallah ilallah: there is no God but God
Lohri: Sikh's festival at time of *Shankranti*
Loo: Hot dry winds can cause heat stroke
Lotah: a round water vessel
Mahout: elephant driver
Mai azad hun: I am free
Mai man ki baat bataun: l will tell you my mind-talk
Maidan: open park
Mama, Mamaji: mother's brother
Mandap: A canopy for wedding ceremony
Manjira: small hand cymbals
Manusmiriti: ancient Indian bible how to live life
Mashak: goatskin water bag
Mataji: mother?
Maulavi: Muslim clergyman

Mausi: aunty, mother's sister
Moti: fatso
Mian: mister in Urdu
Mundan: the baby's first head shave
Namaste: Hindu greeting *I bow to your light*
Namaz: Muslim prayer
Naan: a baked bread
Nani: mother's mother
Neem ki nimboli: yellow bitter fruit of neem tree.
Nikka: Muslim wedding ceremony
Nimboli: yellow neem fruit
Nauch: Indian raunchy dance for men
Om or *Aum*: Holy sound of the universe
Oont: camel
Paan: betel nut leaf
Paijebs: anklets
Pakora: vegetable fritter
Pallu: the free draped over the shoulder end of a sari
Panchtantra: ancient Indian collection of animal fables
Paneer: fresh acid-set cheese
Pankah: a fan
Papis: sinners
Parai: a stranger
Paratha: pan fried bread
Parmatma: Almighty God
Parpotha: great grand son
Parvati: a Hindu goddess, name
Pashto: Pathan, Afghan language
Pattals: disposable plates made from peepal tree leaves
Peepal: sacred fig tree with heart shaped leaves
Piaow: water dispenser station
Piddhas: low stools
Pir: Sufi holy men and religious masters
Pita, Pitaji Abba Abbajan: Father
Pitchkari: water gun
Potha: son's son
Prasad: sweet sacred prayer reward
Pucca: Pukka, proper
Purana Quila: Old Fort (district in Delhi)
Purdah: Covering of women in public wear burqa
Puris: deep-fried bread
Quawali: Urdu songs
Ramleela: theater depicting life of Lord Rama
Sabzi: vegetables
Sadar bazaar: general market
Sadhu: a Hindu ascetic who has renounced worldly life

Salma: gold and silver tubular embroidery thread
Salaam alekhun, Salam: Urdu greeting peace be with you
Sala ullu ka pattha: swear and curse *someone*
Sat Sri Akal: Sikh greetings
Savdhan: be alert
Shalwar: pants, usually worn with *kamiz*
Shanti: peace
Samagri: a herbal mix that is burned to purify air for Havan
Sanskar: life rituals
Sawan ki bahar: monsoon blessing teej song
Sehra: groom's head dress
Seva: volunteer service
Sevaiin: thin vermicelli cooked in sweet milk and dried fruits
Shalwar: Afghan pants
Shairi: a form of Urdu poetry
Shaitan: Satan
Shamiana: ceremonial tent
Shankranti: festival of end of winter 14th of January
Shatranj ke khilari: The Chess Players
Shehnai: an Indian wind reeded musical instrument
Sherwani: a man's formal long jacket suit
Shikara: a Kashmiri small boat
Shrawan: a dutiful son
Sindoor: red powder
Sitar: a stringed Indian musical instrument
Soniye: beautiful
Suhagan: blessed married woman
Surahi: earthenware jug
Swaraj: self rule campaign
Tabla: Indian drum
Tahri: yellow rice dish
Taiji: aunt father's older brother's wife
Tandoor: Clay oven
Tanjore: a district in Tamil Nadu State
Tasbih: Islamic prayer beads and talisman
Tauji: uncle; older brother of father
Tawba: Muslim prayer of repentance
Tawiz:, Taweez: sacred blessed amulet
Teej: a festival to celebrate monsoon
Tehmad: lower half wrap worn by a Muslim man
Tesu: flower used to color water for Holi festival
Thali: a flat metal dish with raised edges
Tonga: a small horse cart
Tongawallah: tonga driver
Tulsi: holy basil
Unani: Muslim traditional medicine

Upanishads: ancient texts of Hindu philosophy
Ustad: master
Vaid: Unani doctor
Vaishnav jan to taine--: An empathic person knows suffering
Sare jahan se accha ye Hindustan--: Our country is the best
Vida: the bride's departure from her home
Vir-chakra: medal of bravery and honor
Wakil: attorney, deputy
Wallahs: merchants
Zanana: women's quarters?
Zari: brocade cloth with gold or silver thread interwoven.
Zindabad: long live

Acknowledgements

My Writing Journey

Any writing effort and journey that has an impact cannot happen without the support of many who are living or who have passed on. My writing journey is complex. Paraphrasing Carl Sagan, from Darwin's time, science has always been inspired by spirituality; there is no conflict. I began exploring science and spirituality in late 1990s obtaining my holistic coaching certificate and began teaching for Stanford Continuing studies in 2001. That year I was a chaplain resident for those with no religious preference at Stanford hospitals. My science of theology is freedom of thought and belief and help find compassion for each other; to build our resilient being and accommodate individual beliefs. I wish to thank Dr. avid Spiegel for introducing me t the value of collective supporti women's group in bringing better integrative health. In 2003, I was fortunate to be part of Stanford's Interdisciplinary research conversation conference: Becoming Human: Evolutionary Origins of Religious, Spiritual and Moral Awareness, funded by the Templeton Foundation. I owe thanks to Bill Durham, Bill Newsome, and Bill Hurlbut for that learning.

As for those who have passed on:

I want to honor my beloved mother, Shreemati Swarna Lata, whose stalwart support, encouragement, and creativity helped me to discover my own abilities. She was an accomplished writer and crafts person. She quilted and repaired lace at the lace museum. Before she passed away in 2002, Santa Clara County in CA recognized her leadership in volunteer teaching other seniors: needlecraft, writing, and the sharing of stories.

I want to honor my father, Shree Arya Bhushan, who joined Palo Alto senior writing groups and established Chachhju ka chaubara, where Indian senior citizens could share their life stories. His own memoir *World Under One Roof* is about embracing the other. This ability gave him life force and he continued to write well into his 90's, and be part of Avenidas writing program in Palo Alto. Thus, encouraging me to have courage to continue to write well into my retirement.

My grandfathers in support of Gandhian values, taught me the importance of diverse communities and be a tireless and dedicated activist across gender, race, and beliefs.

Through the partition years, both my parent's journeys kept me alive and ultimately allowed me to study and work at Stanford.

As for the living:

Love Partitioned

My 95-year-old uncle, *mamaji* P.S. Mittal, who, despite his vison and hearing difficulties, mastered technology enough to read my draft and fact-check my writing about Indian railways, theosophy society in India, religion, history .and partition which he lived through. After his retirement he learned about Annie Besant and theosophy; he rose to be the president of the Indian theosophy society. His son, Professor Ashok, and daughter-in-law, Professor Poonam Mittal, both researchers at the Allahabad University, help *mamaji* to communicate with me through hearing and smart phone technology to provide me his valuable weekly feedback on my manuscript to keep my narrative historically and geographically reliable. Many thanks to my brothers and aunt Madhu for their encouragement and for holding me accountable to finish my final edit.

To my husband Ken, for believing in my ability to tell my story and for supporting me through the trying health problems I've suffered in the last four years; Should the readers need it Ken created an exhaustive glossary list of foreign words to help readers through these italicized words in the text; His patient reading and editing of this manuscript is appreciated.

Thanks are due to my children Andrew, Lalitha, and Ravi for teaching me about living in a segregated society and discovering social empowerment despite disabilities.

Thanks to all the members of my extended family and friends, in USA, India, and Australia, my long-time friends Gwyn Dukes, Bob Spears, and Anne Galli from the Bechtel International Center at Stanford who checked on my health and welfare as well tracked my novel revision progress.

In 2013, the first 2 year online novel writing course was announced by Stanford Continuing Studies. It was expensive, but Ken and decided to give each other a 45th wedding anniversary present. We completed our application were accepted and able to participate from both Sydney, Australia and Stanford CA, where we were professors.

In novel writing I learned the skills of fiction writing. In 2016 it helped me complete the first draft of Love Partitioned. I owe the online novel writing instructors especially Malena Watrous, and Angela Pneuman (author lay it on my heart), my deep thanks.

However, my writing adventures continued with the med writer's group where I met Dr Stafford, an internist. He and I incorporated science and spirituality in our healthy aging classes to include meditation and relaxation and created our REWARD training program. We used knowledge from Theosophy, Compassionate care, Healing touch, Sufi Healing, Enneagrams, Ayurvedic, Yoga, Somatic experiencing, Tapping, EMDR, and other holistic healing techniques, that complemented my biomedical science and engineering training.

I was fortunate to have Angela Pneuman, Stegner Fellow and acclaimed fiction writer, as my one-on-one reader at the end of the novel-writing training program. Her comments helped me learn the craft of novel writing, including how to revise my first draft into its current form. But then life intervened and the revision has taken much longer. I am fortunate that she returned to the task and help me edit and complete this version of *Love Partitioned*.

Thanks, are also due to other writing giants like Professor Nancy Packer, who provided me valuable feedback on my writing and recommended me to the on-line novel writing program; and Alyssa O'Brien, who invited me to join her weekly women writers' group in Palo Alto. The creative and memoir writing teachers like Carol Goodwin, in Stanford continuing studies helped me to explore my memories of the Indian Partition. Thanks are due to my fellow novel writing cohort who read various segments and provided honest and valuable feedback.

Sharon Bray (author *writing through cancer)* and Professor Audrey Schaffer MD, part of the Stanford Med-writing group, met regularly for writing workshops and helped me to learn how writing helps healing. In these workshops I was fortunate to meet Professor Randall Stafford MD, and our writing and healthy aging collaboration began and continues. Dean Scotty McLennan and George Fitzgerald, director of Chaplaincy, through case studies taught me much about writing about healing. Mudge Schink brought the healing touch and Sufi healing workshops to Palo Alto. Sheri Espar and her art-expressive workshops taught me the power of expression. I am indebted to all these people who advanced my understanding of spiritualty and science healing writing. Sharon Bray for her workshop about writing through grief. Doctor Ed Crangle Professor of Buddhist studies at the University of Sydney and James Doty MD director Stanford CCARE helped me to learn the power of compassion. Stanford CCARE compassion training program taught by Dr. Kelly McGonigal further refined my meditation practice. Ellen Dinucci, and Fred Luskin's (author forgive for good) 2000 SAGE (Successful Aging and Growth Education) program, impressed upon me the power of an integrated daily practice. Fed Luskin's training on healing through forgiveness using Heart Math taught me the benefits of forgiveness. Finally, I would like to thank Tommy Woon, retired associate Dean for diversity and First Gen at Stanford. He taught me about reevaluation counseling and Somatic healing. He continues to mentor me and inform, my understanding of being "the other" and evils of colonial oppression and its sources.

Where regionally and culturally appropriate, some of these healing techniques are included in *Love Partitioned.*

The revision took more than four years and extensive research of facts, but the work is much stronger for it. I hope the readers will enjoy reading *Love Partitioned* as much as I enjoyed writing it.

XXXXXXX

About the Author:

Manjula Waldron is US and Australian citizen. She grew up in India and earned her PhD in engineering from Stanford University in CA and has over 100 technical papers and books. She retired twenty years ago as a professor of Bioengineering in US. to explore science and spirituality. She taught these courses in Stanford Continuing Studies. She co-taught REWARDS and AIMING Higher program for designing healthy aging in the second half of one's life with Dr. Randall Stafford MD in Stanford Medical School.

She learned creative and novel writing at Stanford Continuing Studies. Love Partitioned is her first novel based on her harrowing escape and transformation of women as chronicled by the protagonist Mangla's journey. In the largest mass migration of 20 million refugees, about a million were massacred and hundreds of thousands of women were abducted or killed when Pakistan was created in 1947.

***

2022 marks the 75th anniversary of this gruesome period in India that ended in creation of Pakistan and a redefined India. It will make an enjoyable read for both young and old.

Made in the USA
Las Vegas, NV
22 February 2022

44375763R00164